PRAISE FOR GARRETT LEIGH

"Emotional and brilliant..."

— ALL ABOUT ROMANCE

"Tastefully erotic ... more smart than smutty..."

— PUBLISHERS WEEKLY

"Powerful and compelling..."

— FOREWORD REVIEWS

DELIVERANCE

A DARKEST SKIES NOVEL

GARRETT LEIGH

FOREWORD

Welcome back to the Darkest Skies world. As with Redemption, Deliverance is set in modern-day South-East England and uses street slang that international readers may not be familiar with.

"Road man" and "on the road" refer to gang life. Similarly, when you see the police being referred to as "feds," it simply means the regular police, not the American FBI. "Ends" means the neighbourhood where you're from. Like, if you were from Queens or Brooklyn or Lambeth, that would be your ends.

Like *Redemption*, it goes without saying that street talk is fluid. If you're reading this beyond 2021, it's likely that language has, as it always does, moved on.

Also, a note on the use of "poppers" in this book: At present, they're legally sold in the UK under various and ever-changing guidelines to what they can be called. They are widely used in the queer community as a safe enhancement to a healthy sex life. I haven't written them into many books, but it would be an inaccurate representation to pretend they don't exist at all, so you will find the occasional sprinkle of them in this book.

1

———

It was a zombie knife. Curved and spiny, as the blade pierced Benito's skin.

Blood oozed, thick and red, and the sight of it shocked him, though it shouldn't have. He'd been running from the knife his whole life.

Metaphorically.

Literally.

At this point, who the fuck cared?

Not him. Only the anger coursing through his juddering heart exposed him as a liar.

You killed the wrong king. Figuratively speaking . . . that was the right adverb, right? If Dante Pope wasn't dead?

Stop thinking about Dante Pope. It ain't him that just shanked you.

Benito forced his eyes open, and a gasp rattled through him. Blood dripped down his torso, soaking into the grimy floor of the abandoned warehouse. Dizziness set in, unnerving him more than the searing pain radiating from his left side, and panic hit him, sharp, cruel, and more painful than any blade. His cool head was his best weapon, and it was slipping away.

Everything was slipping away.

I just want to sleep.

Cold laughter kept him awake.

Grinning, Asa Gerrard crouched in front of him, still clutching the zombie knife. "I like this version of you. It's better than not knowing your plays before they happen, even when you tell me all about them."

Benito swallowed a groan and spat on the floor. "It's not my fault you're too slow to keep up."

"Wasn't tonight, though, was I? Kept up with you just fine. And here we are."

Asa's smirk grew.

Benito shivered. "What do you want?"

"I haven't decided yet. Whacking you would be the easiest option. Then I'd never have to think about you again."

"Do it then." More blood poured from Benito's mouth, choking him. "I don't care."

"You see, that's the problem, though, ain't it?" Asa twirled the knife in his hands. "You *do* care. About someone. You *love* them. And that makes you too useful to kill."

Benito's heart jolted against his throbbing ribs. He searched for the emptiness he carried on the street. The echoing chamber his heart had become when he wasn't around the *only* soul on earth he cared about. "Whatever, mate. I'm a selfish motherfucker. When have you ever seen me be anything else?"

"Last week."

Asa's tone was casual.

Too casual.

A growl built in Benito's chest. "You're full of shit, Gerrard, unless you're talking about me boning your girl every Friday night."

"I don't have a girl," Asa retorted. "So whatever bitch you've been drilling is nothing to me. Nah. I'm talking about the pretty brunette who takes the bus to St. Marc's High School every day from Barnfield Court flats in Bletchley. And her mum who walks the red ways to Santander five days a week. You care about them, right? Your mama and your baby sister?"

Benito closed his eyes, unable to watch as it dawned on Asa that he'd hit gold. The jackpot of Benito's heart that he couldn't give up.

Asa said more words, but Benito couldn't hear them over his stampeding pulse.

Rough hands lifted him from the ground and dragged him outside. They threw him in the back of a van and drove through the night. It was dawn when Benito woke up.

Fresh muscle ripped the van doors open. New faces Benito didn't know.

He sat up, wrapping an arm around his injured torso. There were two of them, an easy win on a good day—but this wasn't a good day. It was the worst day of his life.

The biggest goon seized Benito's arms and yanked him forward. "I got a message for you," he gritted out, "in case you don't remember what the boss said."

Boss. Benito almost laughed. *Asa, man. How long have you wanted this?*

Long enough to find Benito's weakest link.

Benito leaned heavily against the van door. "Get it over with. I got places to be."

"Right, Martell. Like you're going anywhere but a surgeon's table to sew your guts back in." The man pointed over his shoulder. Milton Keynes General loomed in the distance, and any hope Benito had that Asa had been bluffing died a thousand times.

They brought me home.

"Oi. Wake up." The man slapped Benito's face. "And *listen*. Stay out of London and off the road. Asa says you can live round here so he knows where to find you if he needs you. But stay out of business or you're a dead man."

Benito did laugh this time. "Why not kill me now then? Asa doesn't need me. Isn't that what this bullshit is all about?"

Another slap hit his face, harder this time. "This ain't no bullshit, Martell. You're on retainer. If you want out for good, you gotta pay. A hundred Gs. That's the price, in cash, product, or fucking blood, else you rot here and spend the rest of your miserable life looking over your shoulder."

"And if I don't?"

"Don't what?"

"Look over my shoulder. What if I come for your *boss* in his bed at night and slit his fucking throat?"

The new muscle grinned, showing his missing teeth. "Then your pretty little sister dies. Remember that when you're dreaming of me."

2

Tower blocks never changed. Cityscapes could paint a picture of culture and fortune and the ambitions of a hotshot architect, but the bleak concrete towers on working-class housing estates were always the same. London. Birmingham. Milton Keynes. Every place Benito Martell had ever lived. Nothing. Ever. Changed.

The forbidding block in front of him was no exception. Grimy inside and out until people opened their doors and invited you in, it was pretty much the last place on earth Benito wanted to be.

Fucking Bletchley. How did I end up back here?

He knew the answer to that better than he wanted to. He'd fucked up. Shown weakness. And now he was holed up in his car outside Barndale Court flats, watching over two of the only souls he'd ever cared about, guilt eating his heart that the life he'd led on a shitty housing estate elsewhere had put them at risk. *You're a road man. What did you expect? That Asa would treat you better than you treated anyone else?*

A bitter laugh escaped Benito. He lit a cigarette and blew

acrid smoke out of the cracked-open car window. His noisy brain craved the quieting hit of a joint, but cranking out weed at the side of the road was a sure-fire way to attract the wrong kind of attention—the blue kind—and Benito had spent his entire life dodging the feds.

On cue for poetic irony, a panda car rolled onto the estate, circling the precinct—the betting shop, the pawnshop, and the fried chicken takeaway. It came to a stop where Benito was loitering in his car. The passenger window descended, and a stern-faced copper gestured for Benito to do the same.

Irritation spiked Benito's blood, but years of flying under the radar had taught him to play nice. To be forgettable. Not the arsehole who wouldn't open his window.

He complied, plastering his face with the blandest expression he could find. "Yeah?"

"What are you doing?" The officer peered into his car. "You've been parked here for two hours. Are you waiting for something?"

Yeah. For the end of the fucking world. "My sister." Benito pointed at the bus stop and then at the Barndale block. "I'm waiting for her to come home from school."

"Why can't you wait inside?"

"I don't live there."

"And you couldn't pick her up? Which school does she go to?"

"St. Marc's."

"How old is she?"

"Twelve."

The police officer said something to the copper behind the wheel. The panda car eased forward and pulled into the space behind Benito.

Both officers got out. Benito rolled his eyes and braced himself for an interrogation he hadn't deserved since he'd abandoned road life in London and run all the way home. He slid out of his seat, keeping his hands clearly visible, and slouched against his car.

Waiting.

Still.

Forgettable.

The coppers crowded him, one squinting inside Benito's black SUV while the other confiscated his smoke. "This is an expensive car," the officer said. "Is it yours?"

"Nope. I leased it."

"From where?"

"Motorama, like every other fucker fronting a ride they can't afford."

"Do you have paperwork?"

"In the glovebox. You want to see my licence too?"

"Yes."

Sighing, Benito pointed into the car at his wallet on the console. The officer reached for it and passed Benito's licence to the copper who was already calling his numberplate in for a vehicle check. Chatter blared back over the radio, but Benito tuned it out, already bored.

The other officer circled the car, opening the passenger door and the glovebox under the guise of retrieving the lease paperwork, but his glance under the seat was unsubtle. Benito rolled his eyes again. "You can search the car if you want; I don't care."

"Is there a reason we should?"

Benito shrugged. "Can't think of one."

"Don't try to be funny, mate," the first officer said. "The more cooperative you are, the easier this is."

This. As if Benito had any idea what the charade was supposed to achieve.

The second officer came back with the lease paperwork and Benito's Uber ID. "You're a taxi driver?"

"Sometimes."

"When?"

"Evenings and weekends."

"What do you do during the day?"

"Sleep. Make sure my sister's okay."

"Why don't you pick her up from school?"

Rinse and repeat. Benito folded his arms, caging the impatience that bubbled in his chest. "Because she likes to take the bus with her friends. I wait here to make sure she gets inside safely."

"For two hours?"

"I was early and had nowhere better to be."

It was the truth. Benito had woken at lunchtime with a restless energy that pacing his flat couldn't contain. He'd hit the gym and then run loops around Willen Lake, but his legs had given out long before the monster dancing in his soul ever would.

The questions kept coming. Benito answered them, keeping a sharp eye on the bus stop until the officer so interested in the contents of his car came back and blocked his view.

He emptied Benito's pockets, finding only his phone, a lighter, and a parking pass for the gym, and with Benito's car clean too, the bullshit well ran dry.

"We're going to let you go this time," the officer said. "But in future, if you're genuinely waiting for your sister to come home from school, don't park here until she's due back. We've had complaints about dealers harassing residents coming in and out of the block."

Mental fatigue caught up with Benito. His fierce grip on his patience slipped. A sneer escaped before he could catch it. "I'm not a dealer. I don't have shit on me. And if you've been watching me for two hours, you know I haven't got out of my car and fucking harassed anyone."

"Watch your language," the officer snapped. "We've asked you reasonable questions and you haven't given us plausible answers."

"I don't need to give you plausible answers. It's a public street with no parking restrictions. I could stay here all day."

"What for?"

The officer stepped closer, looming into Benito's personal space.

Benito squared up, muscles bunching, ready to fight despite every age-old instinct he possessed screaming at him to stand down. What did it matter anymore? He had no hustle to protect. He'd left it in flames at the side of the road and he had the scar to prove it. Now he was just a sad sack of anxious shit until he could raise the money to buy his freedom for good.

And wasn't *that* irony fucking beautiful?

Unbidden, Luis Pope flashed into Benito's thoughts. A man Benito had held to ransom the same way some other bastard was holding him now. Benito hadn't cared at the time. His icy heart had stopped beating, and he'd set Pope free in the end because it had suited him, not because he gave a shit that the dude had served his time and fallen in love and just wanted to be left alone.

Was this Benito's punishment?

Karma?

Asa seemed to think so, but Asa was harder than Benito had ever been. Shame it had taken this for Benito to see it.

The cinderblock in his belly solidified. Still smouldering with smoky tendrils.

Rage. Grief. Revenge.

It kept him standing, but so did what remained of his pride.

Your ego, you mean. Ain't nothing to be proud of here.

Whatever. The present returned to him with a cold snap. Barndale. Bletchley. The coppers still up in his face. Anger rippled through him. *Fuck* letting these clowns put him down right now. He let his fists curl and snatched a breath. "Go fuck your—"

"What are you doing to my brother?"

Benito froze, the snarled insult dying on his lips. He knew that voice. It was the one that made his heart clench as if it might break. The *only* one that made him feel things that hurt. Somehow, Benito had missed the bus rolling in. *Some watchman you are.*

Wasteman, more like.

The officer crowding Benito stepped back, putting enough space between them for a slight, willowy figure to slip into the void. The girl wrapped her arms around Benito's waist, pressing her bony shoulder into his ribs as she turned her head to glare at the police. "Leave him alone."

"Gianna." Benito held her close, shielding her from view

as much as he could. "It's fine. They were just asking about my car."

"Why?"

"Because they like it."

Gianna wriggled in his grip and turned her fiery brown eyes on him, glowering, the way only she could. "No, they don't. They think you're too poor to drive it."

"Well, they're not wrong right now. I signed the lease agreement before I lost my job in London. You know that."

Gianna's scowl deepened. "It's a Qashqai, not an Escalade. They're picking on you because no one around here is supposed to be happy."

Pain lanced Benito's chest again, throbbing the raised flesh that ran the length of his ribs. Gianna was twelve—a decade too young to be so astutely *un*happy. "It's not like that, G. We were just talking, honest."

The quieter policeman had seen enough. He spoke into his radio and signalled to Benito's brand new nemesis that it was time to go.

They got back in their car and drove away. Relief flooded Benito, and his body craved the sensation of sagging against the car door, but not with Gianna in his arms. *Never* with Gianna in his arms.

He grasped her shoulders and spun her to face him. "You shouldn't speak to the feds like that. One day you might need their help."

"*You* might need their help too, Beni. But they're too busy harassing people for no reason to care."

"It's not for no reason. I've got flash threads and a flash car. If I was a copper, I'd be all over that shit too."

"You couldn't be a fed."

"Why not?"

"You hate being told what to do. The only way you could do it was if you were chief-superintendent whatsit or whatever they call it."

Benito grinned. "Chief Whatsit? I'll take that."

"You know what I mean."

"I really don't. But it doesn't matter. I have no intention of becoming a fed or bailing you out when you've pissed them off enough to arrest you, so stop with the fighting talk, okay? It doesn't change anything."

Gianna's glare remained. "It's not okay for them to stop and search you for no reason. They told us that at school."

"It wasn't for no reason. They just wanted to know why I was hanging outside Nuggets for bare time when you should've been home twenty minutes ago. Where've you been? Was the bus late?"

"Um . . ." Gianna's gaze flitted away, suddenly fixed on the matte black paintwork of the car that had brought Benito nothing but trouble. "I walked."

"You *what*?"

"I walked, okay? None of my friends take the bus anymore and I wanted to go to the shop."

"What shop? There's one right here."

"Yeah, but you told me not to hang around there without you, so what am I supposed to do if I need girl things?"

"Ask Mum. She can pick up what you need on the way home from work. Or you can just ask me. I'm not a caveman, G. I'm aware you have periods."

Gianna scrunched her face enough to make herself seem like the five-year-old Benito had been too busy slinging to truly know. "Don't ever say those words again."

"Why not? You think you need to be shy about shit like that?"

"No, but I think *you* should be. Ew."

Benito laughed, and it felt good. The brief moments he spent with Gianna were always like this. She was fire and fury. Light and dark. All rolled up with an attitude he could only dream of. He pitied the fool who ever laid claim to her heart. "Don't *ew* me. You shouldn't have walked home without telling me. What if something had happened and I was sitting here waiting for the bus the whole time?"

"Nothing happened, Beni. I was literally with my entire school. Everyone walks home this way. Why do you worry so much?"

Because I've hurt enough people to deserve it. "I don't worry. I just want you to be safe. Especially now it's winter and it gets dark so early. I know I don't get to tell you what to do, but call me next time, okay?"

"Okay." Gianna pulled her coat tighter.

Benito tugged the zip higher as fresh sadness settled into the pit of his stomach. She was going to go inside soon, and he already knew today wasn't gonna be the kind of day when he could face going with her. He was claustrophobic just thinking about it, choking on the herb-scented air of Rosetta's stuffy eleventh-floor flat. A place he wanted to be even less than his own mother wanted him to be there. "Do you have homework?"

Gianna's face scrunched again. "Yeah. Science, and some maths I need to download an app for. Do you think . . . ?"

"What?"

"Nothing. It doesn't matter."

Benito wedged two fingers under Gianna's dainty chin and tipped her face up until she met his gaze again. "*What*?"

She shrugged. "I need an iPad. Or a tablet, or something. All my homework gets uploaded onto apps these days and my phone is too ancient to handle it."

Benito swallowed a sigh. He'd give Gianna the moon if he could cut it down from the sky, but a new iPad was a leap he couldn't make on the trickle of cash he brought in from his Uber shifts. After rent, car payments, and all the bills he'd never worried about until now, he was barely eating. He could only afford the gym because he'd got six months half price when he'd signed up.

Happy, Asa? You wanted me on my knees, didn't you?

Bitterness scorched an oath from his gut to his throat. He pictured the blank face of the man who'd sealed his fate— and Gianna's—and fury burned so hot he couldn't breathe. His hands tightened to fists again, clenching Gianna's coat.

"Beni?"

"What?"

She blinked at him. "You're being weird again."

Benito stared, searching for an anchor in her wide brown gaze. It didn't have to be tangible, only enough to tie him down to the world. "Sorry," he said. "I was thinking about work tonight. I have to drive a long way."

"Where are you going?"

"Uh, to the airport . . . in London. Gatwick, I think."

It was a lie. Benito hadn't been that far south in months, since the barrel of a gun to his temple had warned him what would happen to him and Gianna if he did. But Gianna believed him.

She had no reason not to.

"Listen," Benito said when she didn't speak. "Let me think about the iPad, okay? I don't think I can do it this month, but I'll get you one as soon as I can afford it, I promise."

"You don't need to promise. I know you'd get me one if you could."

"And I will. I just need some time."

"I could ask my dad—"

"No. You don't ask that wanker for anything except to light himself on fire and die."

Gianna bit her lip, laughter warring with the graveness no twelve-year-old should have. "All right. Keep your hair on. I don't think his number works anymore anyway. I haven't tried it since last Christmas."

You weren't here. She didn't say it, but she didn't have to. Benito hadn't been home for Christmas since he was sixteen. But he was here now, and he'd drive every night until the end of time if it kept Gianna away from her arsehole father.

He gave her a hug, burying his face briefly in the soft, dark curls that were so like his own when he let his hair grow out. "I'll sort it. Just give me some time, okay? Don't ask that bastard for anything."

"I won't. It was just a thought."

"Well, stop thinking it. *I'm* here, G. For whatever you need."

A hollow promise, but he meant it. Gianna deserved the world, and he'd happily die trying to give it to her.

"It's getting late," she said. "I should go inside. Are you coming up? Just to the front door?"

Benito glanced at the block he'd spent most of the after-noon glaring at. "Not today. I have to work, and you have homework."

"What about dinner? When are you going to eat?"

"Later," he promised. "There's a hot dog place at the airport I really like. I'll get something there."

"But—"

"No. I'll come up another day, when I've got more time."

"You always say that."

"Because it's the truth. Tomorrow, I'll come up tomorrow."

"Promise?"

"On Sullivan's life, I swear." Benito held out his finger for a pinkie swear on the life of a cat who'd clawed a hole in Gianna's bedroom carpet a week after Benito had got on his hands and knees and laid it himself.

Then it was time to go. Benito hugged Gianna one last time and walked her to the entrance of the block, giving the loitering slingers side-eyed warnings to stay out of his way. His street rep was years old and out of date, but badass enough that no fucker looked at him twice.

Gianna unlocked the door. She hesitated, but Benito pushed her gently inside. "Go," he said. "I'll be back in the morning."

"Breakfast?"

"I'll meet you at the bus stop."

"With croissants?"

"If that's what you want."

Gianna kissed his cheek and left his side. Benito watched her climb the stairs until she was out of sight, then made his escape, jogging away from the concrete prison as if the lies he'd told Gianna were a demon chasing him down.

There was no airport run tonight. Only an itch Benito had to scratch. A soul-deep desire to be somewhere else, somewhere no one knew his name or his face or needed anything from him that he couldn't give.

He got back in his car as darkness fell, and it seemed symbolic. Benito spent most evenings driving to and from the theatre district, ferrying drunk idiots home from rowdy nights out in the city, but tonight he had other plans.

Road life had sucked him dry. This was all he had left.

3

———

The club was dark leather and sultry electronica. Shadowed booths and alcoves. The perfect locations for semi-public hook-ups or a staging ground for something more secluded. Mickey Larwood bypassed the tangled bodies and threaded his way to the bar. He'd already dodged two propositions from men hot enough to warrant a second look, but neither had been what he was looking for. That rare thing that made Mickey's blood sing loud enough to coax him to a booth or a private room upstairs.

It didn't help that he had no clear picture in his own mind. He never knew what he wanted until he saw it. Felt it. *Craved* it. Most nights he came to Freefall, he was content to sip his spiced rum in peace, casting a lazy eye over the heady show before him, imagining what he'd do to the man of his dirtiest fantasies. It was a fun way to spend an evening, but Mickey hadn't given up hoping he'd have more than his imagination for company tonight.

There was something in the air, he could taste it, and it

excited him far more than the poison he'd worked hard to leave behind.

He found a stool at the bar and sank onto it, ordering a large Kraken with ice and lime. Jaiden, the barman, tipped him a wink, as always, the unspoken invitation clear.

Mickey shook his head. "No, thanks, man. I'm just drinking tonight."

"Can't blame me for trying." Jaiden rested his elbows on the bar. "You'll change your mind one day."

"That right?"

"Nope. Not in a million years, but I like making you squirm."

"You're a true friend."

"I'm your only friend."

"Not true," Mickey refuted. "And we're not friends. I've never seen you outside of these walls."

"If walls could talk."

Jaiden winked again, then sauntered away to serve someone else.

Mickey watched him go, rolling his eyes. On paper, they were a good fit. Jaiden was tall and strong, but in bed—or at least on it—he was too easy. Too pliant. Too willing to give Mickey what he wanted without the roughness Mickey craved. A good fuck was a good fuck, but Mickey could find that anywhere. He came to Freefall for something else. Something better than the hit of coke to his veins.

Something fucking magical.

Don't think about coke.

Mickey drank his rum, watching men come and go from the bar. A few acknowledged him, but he ignored them all as the night closed in. He ordered his last drink and turned back to the club. The music was louder now, and the density of bodies tangled together was deeper. In some corners, he couldn't tell where one ended and another began. Skin and limbs. Pants and moans.

It was hot, but not enough to hold Mickey's attention indefinitely. *Call it a night. Go home.* But going home meant being alone, and he was too twitchy for that. A difficult day had left him wired for a long night. Fuck it. Maybe he would hook up with Jaiden. It wasn't like the one time they'd done it had been bad. Far from it. Where was the harm? Whatever happened, it was better than letting his darkest cravings suck him dry.

As the thought crossed Mickey's mind, his gaze fell on a lone figure at the other end of the bar. The man was tall, dark, and broad-shouldered, with a jaw that hadn't seen a razor in weeks. He wore black jeans and a smart white shirt rolled up at the sleeves to reveal tattooed forearms and an expensive watch.

Mickey couldn't see his face, but his body already called to him. He downed his rum and pushed the empty glass across the bar.

Jaiden caught it and shook his head. "You're wasting your time with that one. He's even pickier than you are."

"How so?"

"He doesn't even watch what goes on down here, and I've only seen him go upstairs, like, twice."

"Yeah, well. You don't work every night."

"Whatever." Jaiden rolled his eyes.

Mickey ignored him and slid off his stool. It was late enough for it to be possible the man had already got what he'd come for and was having a drink before he went home, but as Mickey drew closer, the man didn't look like he'd rolled out of a recent hook-up. No messy hair or flushed skin. No hooded eyes or wrinkled clothes.

Yet.

Mickey eyed the vacant stool next to him, but as it happened, the man saw him coming and nodded. Another rum appeared on the bar. Mickey sent Jaiden a silent thanks and claimed his place next to the dark-haired stranger.

In fact, everything about the man was dark: his hair, his gaze, the ink on his arms. Even the shadows beneath his eyes. He had high cheekbones, too, and a full mouth that would look good stretched wide in a smile, but he didn't seem the type. Or, actually, the type to give Mickey what he wanted either, but he'd reached the point where a man's simple company was enough.

The rest was a distant dream.

A *dirty* dream.

Mickey reached for his topped-up drink and took a slow sip, measuring his first words. They were in a sex club, but assumption was still dangerous. "I haven't seen you here before. What's your name?"

"Benito." The man held out his hand and shook Mickey's with a firm grip, his palm warm and dry. "I haven't seen you either, but I don't usually come on Thursdays."

"What's special about today?"

Benito shrugged. "I don't know yet. Am I about to find out?"

Heat pooled in Mickey's groin, but he dampened it down. If this dude was asking to fuck him, he was in for a disappointment, and so was Mickey. He was too intrigued to let him go just yet, though. "Maybe," he hedged. "Or maybe we'll just talk. Doesn't matter to me, no pressure."

Benito lifted his glass and swallowed the last of whatever clear alcohol he'd been drinking. His throat worked, and he licked his lips, his tongue darting out, chasing stray drops. "I don't mind pressure. I didn't come here to talk."

"Then you're missing out. I'm excellent company."

"Yeah? What else are you excellent at?"

"Probably all the things you're not interested in."

"Like what?"

"How about we have another drink?"

Benito smirked, but it was laced with something else. Impatience? Nerves? Mickey couldn't tell.

He drained his glass and signalled to Jaiden for another before meeting Benito's gaze again. "What are you having?"

"I'm good, thanks. I gotta drive after this."

This. Mickey smiled into his fresh drink—ginger ale this time, he was driving too—mind already lit up with all the things he could do to Benito if they turned out to be compatible. Or even if they didn't. Maybe it didn't matter if they didn't have the same endgame in mind. *We could just blow each other.* Benito's mouth was inviting enough for Mickey to be tempted.

"So . . . ," Benito said when Mickey didn't speak. "Do you come here a lot?"

"Enough to know you don't."

"Vague."

"Okay, probably once a month. I only know your habits because Jaiden told me."

Benito's gaze flickered to the end of the bar, then his eyes narrowed, irritation darkening his handsome face. "He don't know shit about me."

"He never said he did. Just that you're not here much. What's so bad about that?"

Benito said nothing. He reached for his empty glass and twirled it, spinning the melting ice that remained. Tension flooded the tenuous connection they'd struck up, but not the kind that warned Mickey off. If anything, Benito's set jaw and hardened gaze excited him, driving any lingering itch for his worst vices away.

He let his attention drift to Benito's corded forearms. The ink on his skin was intricate and expensive, not the kind done in a backstreet scratcher like the mess of bad decisions Mickey had on his own chest. His fingers itched to trace it. To unbutton Benito's shirt and push it away so he could follow where the dark etchings led.

Maybe they could do that instead of fucking. It had been a long time since Mickey had last enjoyed the journey as much as the pot of gold at the end.

"Sorry," Benito blurted suddenly.

Mickey relaxed further onto his stool. "What for?"

"Biting your head off."

"You didn't. And even if you did, you're not the first dude I've met who's jumpy in here."

"You're not jumpy," Benito countered, face blank again, giving nothing away. "You've done this a lot."

"Have I?"

Benito stopped fiddling with his empty glass and leaned closer. The movement eased his legs wider, his knee brushing Mickey's. "I don't know," he whispered. "I can't figure you out."

"Do you need to?"

"That fucking depends, doesn't it?"

Mickey soaked in the way Benito's deep voice wrapped around his rough words. *London, maybe?* He couldn't tell. Down south, accents were harder to place. Either way, it was sexy as hell. Mickey's fingers itched again, and this time, he set them free.

He claimed Benito's exposed wrist with his palm, rubbing his thumb over the warm skin he found there. The contact sent shivers down his spine. He covered it with a sip of ginger ale, trying not to track the subtle cues in Benito's shuttered face—the tick in his jaw, the tightness around his dark eyes. It was hard to tell if he wanted Mickey's hand on him, though he made no move to recover his arm.

"What does it depend on?" Mickey said. "Figuring me out, I mean."

Benito's gaze swept where they were connected. "On where this is going. No offence, mate, but I didn't come here for a chat."

"You mentioned that, and neither did I, but I already told you I don't think you'd want to hook up with me."

"That's not what you said."

"It's what I meant."

"Based on . . . ?" Benito rotated his arm, granting Mickey access to the underside of his wrist. His skin was softer there, smoother.

Mickey slid his hand to Benito's elbow, enjoying the ride. "Based on assumption. You stand like a power top."

"I'm not standing."

"Figure of speech."

"Fuck your figure of speech." Benito spoke low, aggression

simmering behind every ground out syllable. "*You* don't know shit about me either."

"Then tell me." Mickey stilled his hand, sensing the subtle shift. The one that either tore them apart or drew them together to stoke the wildfire that had started to smoulder between them. "Tell me what you want from me."

"Who says I want anything from you?"

Mickey snorted and let his gaze flit lazily from where their knees were pressed together to where they'd somehow leaned close enough to be inches apart. "I'm not saying anything. It's your turn."

"You want me to tell you what I want so you can walk on by? No thanks."

"Who says I'd walk on by?"

"You did. Three minutes ago."

"Maybe I changed my mind."

"That's not how it works."

"Says who?"

Benito swallowed and dug his teeth briefly into his full bottom lip. Mickey took a chance and swiped it with his thumb, a lingering touch that seemed to surprise Benito. He snapped a hand to Mickey's wrist, closing strong fingers around it in a bruising grip. But he didn't pull Mickey away. He held him there, against his face, while his dark eyes blazed an emotion Mickey couldn't decipher.

A stalemate stretched out between them. The club faded, taking with it the heady soundtrack others had found to keep them company. Mickey's heart thumped. He zeroed in on Benito's lips, his own tingling. *I want to kiss him.*

No. I want to fuck him.

But his lips hadn't got the memo, nor had his chest, which *ached* with the need to claim Benito's mouth.

That's new. Mickey was no stranger to strong desires—he was in a sex club on a Thursday night—but he'd never felt so consumed within minutes of meeting someone.

Tunnel vision descended. He found Benito's unyielding thigh with his one hand and gripped his chin with the other, reckless honesty that was equal parts his greatest strength and weakness sweeping over him. "Forget the rules. I'm gonna tell you what I want. What happens next, if anything, is up to you."

Benito wrenched free of Mickey's grip. A flush darkened his cheeks. "You seem so sure we won't want the same thing."

"I'm not sure of anything except that I want to take you upstairs and fuck your brains out."

"What makes you think I don't want that too?"

"Because I'm not that lucky."

"The fuck does that mean?"

Mickey let his hand slide from Benito's thigh, his brain belatedly catching up with the rest of him. "It means aesthetically you're a fucking fantasy, but I need something different up here."

Mickey tapped his temple. Benito's dark brow ticked. "Are you calling me stupid?"

"Not even close. I'm talking about preference, not intelligence."

"Preference? You mean sexuality?"

"No. I mean *sexually*. When I hook up like this—" Mickey gestured around the club. "I like to be in control. I'm not looking for a power top."

Amusement threatened the burgeoning scowl on Benito's handsome face. "And not a power bottom either, huh?"

"Is that what you are?"

Benito shrugged. "I'm a lot of things, just not all the time."

"What are you today?"

"Intrigued. It sounds like you can't decide if you want to fight or fuck."

Mickey chuckled. "Maybe it's both. But I can tell you one thing that never changes."

"What's that?"

Mickey finished his drink and slid off his stool. "I always win."

4

I always win.

Benito couldn't say what excited him so much about those words, but as Mickey stepped away, his hand shot out of its own accord to stop him. "Wait."

Mickey turned to face him again, sandy eyebrows raised. He didn't speak, though. Apparently, he thought he'd said enough, but even if they did nothing but talk, despite proclaiming he hadn't come here for that, Benito hadn't had anywhere near his fill of conversation.

"Um." Benito pulled his hand back, regretting the loss of physical contact the moment it was gone. "I don't think you'd beat me in a fight."

Amusement danced in Mickey's slate grey eyes. "You'd be surprised, but I'm not talking about a street fight. I'm talking about dominance. About resisting the inevitable."

"And the inevitable is that you fuck me?"

"If that's what we both wanted, yes. You could change your mind at any moment and I'd stop."

Somewhere behind the heated thump of his pulse, Benito

struggled to map a trail to how his day had wound up here, in a sex club, negotiating the dub-con encounter of his filthiest dreams with the hottest bloke he'd seen since he'd last set eyes on Luis Pope. If that's what they were doing. Mickey still seemed set to walk away. "What if I changed my mind about dominance and tried to push it back on you?"

Mickey shrugged. "Don't know, mate. It's never happened like that for me. Can you go both ways?"

"I go most ways in most things," Benito said. "Top, bottom, dudes, women. I like everything, but . . ."

"What?" Mickey stepped back into Benito's personal space, crowding him with his strong build and masculine scent. "Are you saying that you want to try this for real? Because I haven't got time for games. I'd rather go home and spend the night with my hand."

"What would you think about?"

"When?"

"When you were home alone." Benito let his legs fall slack, silently inviting Mickey to step between them. "If you left here without taking a chance on me?"

Mickey took another step forward and licked his lips. "Oh, I'd definitely think of you, if that's what you're asking. I already told you you're a fucking fantasy. I'm just wondering if you're too alpha to give it up."

"And you already know you're too alpha to take that risk, right?"

"Maybe." Mickey gripped Benito's chin again, ramping up the pressure with every thud of Benito's pulse, as though testing his resistance. "Some days I think I could like it, but I'm definitely not in that place today. I came here to fucking own someone, and I'd rather go home than be disappointed."

"Harsh."

"I know. But I know myself and what I want and what I need. It's been a long day, you feel me?"

"I do," Benito blurted with little conscious thought, especially in the literal sense of the question. His game of chicken with the police seemed a lifetime ago, and he'd stepped into a different skin the moment he'd entered the dimly lit club, but he needed something too. Perhaps the very thing Mickey was offering. "Listen, I can't promise I'll go down easy, but if you want a ruck to get there, I'm here for it."

Mickey's gaze intensified, unreadable, and for the first time since he'd dropped onto the stool beside Benito, he seemed unsure. He brought his face so close to Benito's that his breath warmed his cheek. "I'm probably making myself sound like an arsehole."

"Doesn't bother me."

"That I'm an arsehole?"

Benito leered. "I didn't come here for marriage."

"Did you come here to get thrown down and fucked?"

"That's what's gonna happen?" Benito's pulse kicked up another notch. His blood rushed south, leaving fire in its wake. He'd told the truth when he'd said he could go either way, but everything about this conversation was hitting the deep chasms inside him that craved exactly what Mickey was offering. Fighting, fucking, thieving. For years it had been all he'd ever known. Ever since his mum left him on the steps of the long-ago burned-down MMA gym on the estate, and grappling with boys—and the effect it had on him—had been his first clue that it wasn't just girls who made his body burn. By the time he'd turned sixteen, it had been clear pretty much anyone could if they caught his attention.

Fighting, fucking, thieving.

He wasn't good for much else.

Mickey drew his wallet from his back pocket. He was still holding Benito's face.

He let go and slid a card from his wallet. "I'm gonna get a room. You want anything from the bar before we—"

"I'm good."

Mickey nodded and turned to the bar, beckoning the server who'd run his mouth about Benito's cruising habits. Ten minutes ago, Benito had wanted to punch his pretty face. Now he couldn't find the headspace to care. He could only watch, breath jammed, as Mickey leaned over the bar and swiped the keycard from the bartender's hand, then stood when Mickey turned to him with an open smirk. "After you."

Benito rolled his eyes and strode across the club, ignoring the mess of people spilling out of the alcoves and booths. He liked the heady sounds of a fuck pit, but he'd learned a while back that he wasn't much of a voyeur. *"You're shy,"* one hook-up had told him. *"You have no idea how hot that is."*

Still didn't. Benito had banged that dude seven ways from Sunday. How the fuck did that make him shy?

They left the club behind and climbed the stairs to the handful of rooms on the second floor. Benito's nerves jangled with every step. He'd made the trip before, but it had been a while, and Mickey wasn't like anyone he'd ever fucked before. For starters, he was light years hotter. But there was something else. His gaze, perhaps, the way it seemed to drill holes in Benito's brain and give voice to a fantasy he'd never known existed.

Mickey stopped at the third door in the dimly lit corridor.

He unlocked the room and stepped back to wave Benito inside.

More nerves dug jagged claws into Benito's chest.

He swallowed them down and slipped into a room that was set up like the hotel rooms he'd hidden out in when his old life had first come crashing down. A double bed and a tiny bathroom. Pink-bulbed lamps and a stack of towels. There was an industrial style cabinet at the side of the bed. Mickey went to it and crouched down, rummaging through the shelves before he came up with condoms, lube, and a small metal bottle.

Benito leaned against the door, tracking his every move, soaking up Mickey's muscled back and strong shoulders. His elegant neck, and the light brown hair that was slightly shorter at the sides and longer on top. He was wearing dark jeans like Benito, and a black shirt. On his feet, battered Vans softened the look, but Benito was hooked on his big hands and how they'd feel on his heated skin. He'd already had a taste—he wanted more.

Mickey set the metal bottle on the bedside table and tossed the rest of the supplies on the bed. He turned to face Benito and arched an eyebrow. He didn't speak, but the challenge in his gaze was clear. *You ready?*

Benito stepped forward. *Yes.*

A heartbeat passed.

A snatched breath.

Then everything changed. Mickey closed the distance between them and shoved Benito back, propelling him into the door. The impact was loud, and jarring, and sent heat rocketing through Benito's body from his scalp to his groin, to the tips of his toes. For a moment, instinct told him to stay still. To wait for Mickey and take whatever he brought to the table.

But Mickey didn't come. He stood, arms spread, a tiny snarl curling his lips.

He *waited*.

For Benito to bite back.

And oh *man*. It was *on*.

Heart in his throat, Benito pushed off the door and tackled Mickey, hard bodies coming together with a brutal thump. Mickey staggered, and Benito thought he might fall and it would be over before it began, but Mickey caught himself at the last second, a low sound rumbling from his chest. "Yeah. This is what I like."

Benito liked it too. Long months of rage-laced frustration bubbled to the surface, tempered only by the growing desire in his veins. Mickey went for a leg sweep. Benito blocked and threw him back, separating them for a split second before he lunged again, unable to keep his hands to himself.

Clothes disappeared, wrenched free and tossed aside. Chest bare, Mickey was every bit as strong as he'd first appeared, his cut torso covered in tattoos that made no sense, his arms corded with sinewy muscle. Without his smart clothes, danger seeped from him, the kind Benito recognised, but his brain was too clouded with heat to think clearly.

He took a breath and found himself against the door again, Mickey crowding him, jeans undone, the bulge beneath a hard mass against Benito's leg.

Mickey braced his forearms on the door, either side of Benito's head. "You're good." He shifted and ground his arousal into Benito's. "Better than I imagined."

"Yeah?" Benito could've escaped or fought back, but he didn't, just for a moment. "When did you imagine it?"

"The second I saw you."

"Liar. You were so sure I wouldn't want this."

"Didn't stop me pretending you might."

"It's not pretending if it's true." Benito pressed his hands to Mickey's chest. *Push him off. Keep going.* But Mickey's dick felt too good against his. He couldn't give it up.

Mickey smirked, perhaps sensing victory.

Benito dug his fingers into flexed muscle and then slid his hands lower, curving around Mickey's ripped torso, urging him closer.

Mickey hummed out a low, gravelly moan and dropped his mouth low enough that Benito thought he might kiss him.

He didn't. He dug his teeth into Benito's shoulder, fast and sharp, then moved like a snake, snatching Benito from the door, spinning him around, shoving his face against the cheap wood.

Benito laughed. In his right mind, no fucker could ever have pulled that move on him, but Mickey's bulk behind him felt so good he couldn't bring himself to feel bad about it. He pushed back, claiming the sensation of Mickey's entire frame against his—thighs, hips, Mickey's chest to his back. "You said you'd fuck me."

"I'm going to."

"Yeah? Feels like you just wanna play."

Mickey grabbed the back of Benito's neck, his hot hand tightening in a bruising grip. "I'm not playing."

"Prove it."

"I'm gonna." Mickey strengthened his hold. His other

hand swooped lower, unbuckling Benito's belt and ripping the buttons from his fly so fast Benito gasped.

Mickey tugged the jeans down Benito's thighs, taking his underwear along for the ride. Cool air hit Benito's weeping dick. He was so hard his stomach hurt, every nerve alight, anticipation and longing so sharp it could've cut glass. *I need him inside me.*

Benito shivered. He'd bottomed before, submitted even, but not like this. Not with so much *want* and soul-deep desire for a man he'd just met.

Mickey kicked Benito's jeans aside and wrestled with his own. He seemed to disappear, then he was back, and his sheathed dick pulsed against the heat of Benito's bare skin.

Benito shuddered again and fought Mickey's hold until he could shift freely. He braced himself on the door and let his head drop, stealing himself for the pain of Mickey pressing inside him, but it didn't come. Not yet. Mickey rubbed soothing hands over Benito's back, paying special attention to the tender flesh he'd already manhandled, a fleeting kindness that gifted Benito a moment to catch his breath. But Mickey's cock remained hot and hard, and his hands eventually drifted to where Benito wanted him most, one to his aching dick, the other to his crease, spreading his cheeks.

Cool lube dripped onto Benito's hole, then probing fingers worked him open.

"I want to slam inside you," Mickey whispered. "But as much as I like throwing you around, I won't hurt you."

Benito hunched his back, a ragged groan escaping him as Mickey's fingers grazed the sweet spot that made his eyes roll. "You wouldn't hurt me. I can take it."

"You don't need to. I'm gonna save it for when it matters most."

"Yeah? When's that?"

"Now."

Mickey withdrew his fingers, replacing them with the blunt head of his condom-sheathed cock before Benito could blink. He eased inside, inch by inch, filling Benito so entirely his jaw unhinged.

On the door, Benito's hands curled into fists, short nails digging into his palms. Burning pain spread through him, blooming deep, but he welcomed it, chased it, and pushed back against Mickey with a silent plea for more.

Hearing him, Mickey grunted and pushed in further, burying himself to the hilt. His thighs hit Benito's, and they fit together like a fucking wet dream.

Another moment of peace passed between them. Benito relaxed and widened his stance while Mickey sucked a bruising bite between his shoulder blades. The twin sensation was mind-blowing, but he still craved *more*.

He pushed back again. "Fuck me."

Mickey laughed, breathless and dirty. "Who says you get to tell me what to do?"

"I'm not telling you what to do. I'm telling you what you want."

"Valid." Mickey drew back, taking his cock with him, then thrust, quickly finding the rhythm he'd promised from the start.

He fucked hard, roaming Benito's back with rough hands as Benito scrabbled for purchase on the door, absorbing every slam of Mickey inside him with a strangled groan. Pressure and pleasure built, fighting for dominance, and the heat coiling Benito's gut was unreal. His vision darkened and his veins burned. More heat unfurled and exploded out of his fist as he punched the door.

The outer panel splintered, wood shards digging into Benito's knuckles.

He welcomed that pain too, but Mickey eased off and pulled out. "Whoa, mate. Let's not get a massive bill for damages, eh?"

Breathing hard, Benito stood tall and turned around, getting his first look at Mickey in all his naked glory. His thighs were perfection, and his cock was every bit as thick and long as it had felt. *I want to suck him dry.*

Mickey smirked, as if he'd heard every thought that passed through Benito's galloping mind. "Get on the bed."

"Make me."

"Yeah? Still on that?"

"Aren't you?"

Mickey moved fast again, but Benito was ready for him, and they spun around and around until they hit the bed and tumbled down, rolling and rolling until Benito gave into the desperate need to have Mickey inside him.

He let Mickey force him onto his belly and then up to his hands and knees. Mickey knelt behind him, smoothed more lube on his dick, and tossed the metal bottle from the cabinet onto the bed within Benito's reach. "I'll tell you when you need them."

Benito eyed the bottle. *Poppers.* He hadn't used them in ages, not since the last time he'd bottomed more than a year ago, and his head spun thinking of the heady rush they'd bring with Mickey driving into him.

This is a fucking trip.

A train he didn't want to get off.

Trembling, he swiped the bottle and clenched his hand around it, tracking Mickey's movements behind him, sensing him drawing closer before he slid his electric palms over Benito's hips with another soothing sweep. The calm before the barrelling storm.

Mickey's thick cock breached Benito again, rougher this time, faster.

"*Fuck.*" Benito rocked forward with the impact, falling to his chest.

Mickey covered him with his body and slammed inside him, a jackhammer of pleasure that drove every coherent thought from Benito's brain, over and over and over.

His body burned.

His cock throbbed.

Benito fisted himself and squeezed, but the double-edged pressure scared him. *Too much. Too much. Too much.*

He let go and hid his face in the unfamiliar sheets, muffling the crazed sounds that fell from him.

Mickey slowed his pace and found Benito's hands. He pulled them behind Benito's back and held them firm at the base of his spine as he tugged Benito upright, gripping his face to look at him. "You need to come. I can feel it, man."

Benito choked out a laugh. "Psychic, are you?"

"Nah, I just know how it feels to be all pent-up and shit. You wanna go hard?"

Pent-up. Benito filed the analysis away for later. With Mickey's cock buried deep inside him, he couldn't think straight enough to ponder it now.

He pushed back against Mickey, absorbing Mickey's murmured groan like it was his own, and his gaze fell on

Mickey's mouth. He was smirking, like he seemed to have been since they'd met, but there was still something else—a hunger that mirrored the desperate, clawing need that smothered Benito. *I want to—*

Mickey's lips crashed to Benito's before the thought completed, his kiss as consuming as every other thing about him. He swept his tongue into Benito's mouth, plundering, exploring, stealing breath, all the while still driving his cock home.

So fucking good.

Entranced, Benito moaned and kissed Mickey back, barely registering the fact that he'd just broken the one rule he had about rando hook-ups—*no kissing*. In fact, he rarely kissed *anyone* anyway, never cared enough to bother, but Mickey was doing something to his brain. His kiss was bruising, biting, and yet somehow hypnotic. Benito couldn't stop. He fused his lips to Mickey's, groaning into the smash of lips, tongues, and teeth, only breaking away when he ran out of breath.

He still clutched the poppers tight in his fist. Mickey nodded. "Now."

Panting, Benito dropped forward again and unscrewed the bottle. The dizzying chemical scent of nitrates hit him, and his brain swam, already bracing for the giddying haze.

He brought the bottle to his nose and inhaled, sucking the fumes deep into his lungs.

For a long moment nothing changed. Then the rush came like a crashing wave. His pulse snowballed, nought to a hundred miles an hour in a split second, pounding in his ears, clattering his ribcage. A fresh layer of sweat burst free over every inch of his skin, and Mickey's cock pulsed inside him, surging and igniting an unbearable pleasure that swept every facet of Benito's body, searing every nerve in its path.

Crying out, Benito buried his face in his forearms, beautiful tension taking hold, priming him ready to snap. Agony battled ecstasy, dismantling his last defences, and he came with a shout that rattled his bones, only distantly aware of Mickey's ragged groan behind him.

"Fuck fuck *fuck*." Mickey collapsed over Benito, milking his climax, his solid build smothering for the few seconds it took for him to collect himself.

Then he said something, eased out of Benito, and rolled away.

Benito was too far gone to make sense of actions or words. He stayed where he was, breathing hard, face still hidden in his arms, dazed and dizzy. Reality seemed far off until warm hands rubbed his back again.

"Roll over, man. Let me check I haven't killed you."

A weak laugh bubbled in Benito's chest. He raised his head and then, slowly, the rest of him, sitting up onto his knees.

Mickey was sprawled out on the rumpled sheets, the perfect image of sex-tousled relaxation, but his grey eyes were narrowed as he scrutinised Benito. "All right?"

Benito nodded, then regretted it as his head swam. "I'm good."

"Lie down, mate."

"What?"

Mickey patted the bed next to him. "Just for a minute. It'll help."

Benito didn't need help, but he obeyed all the same and stretched out beside Mickey, soaking in a moment where he'd usually be sweeping the room for his discarded clothes. He closed his eyes but, sensing Mickey's piercing gaze on him, opened them again with a sigh. "What?"

Mickey shrugged, shifting onto his side. "Nothing. Except you should know you've pretty much blown my mind."

"I didn't blow you at all."

"Fucking hilarious. You know what I mean."

"Do I?"

"I think so. You seem as spaced out as I feel."

The poppers. Fuck. Benito sat up, searching for the open bottle. That shit wasn't safe left to its own devices.

"Easy." Mickey caught his shoulder and eased him back down. "I got them. Put 'em away already."

Benito wondered how he'd missed that. Then decided he didn't care. He'd come here to catch a break from his noisy brain and fucked-up thoughts, not germinate new ones. He focused on his sore body and tingling lips. Revelled in it. He was as battered as the wrecked room around them, but *damn*, it felt good.

I wanna smoke.

As if he'd spoken the words aloud, Mickey reached somewhere and came back with a cigarette and a lighter. He lit up, inhaled deeply, then passed the smoke to Benito. "We ain't supposed to smoke in here, but I reckon it's the least of our worries considering the knuckle print you've left in that door."

Benito took a long drag on the cigarette. "Fuck me."

"Already done, mate."

"Where are you from?"

Mickey reclaimed the smoke. "Up north. You?"

"Down south."

"London?"

"Sometimes."

Mickey nodded, as if Benito's vague answer made sense. Or maybe it was more that he didn't care. This wasn't a fucking date. "I was serious about you blowing my mind," he said. "This shit is like hook-up nirvana for me."

"Nirvana?"

"Yeah. Like, the ultimate. You know those hook-ups that are kinda mechanical? Yeah, I don't like those. I don't want to go through the motions for an orgasm I could easily give myself. I want to *feel* it." Mickey flopped onto his back again.

Benito propped himself up on his elbow to look at him. "I felt it."

"I know."

"And you did too?"

"You're taking the fucking piss, right?"

Benito had no idea. He plucked the cigarette from Mickey's fingers, finished it off, and rose to flick it from the window. When he turned back to the bed, Mickey was sitting up too, scanning the floor for his clothes, and Benito felt the shift like a boot to his chest.

Or maybe it was his stuttering pulse returning to earth from the pounding orgasm he could still feel in his toes. Either way, it was time to go.

Benito snagged his jeans and underwear from the floor and yanked them up his legs. He straightened to find Mickey right in front of him, fully dressed, clutching his phone. "It's dead." He held it up. "Or I'd take your number."

"You don't want to give me yours?"

"Would you call it?"

Benito shrugged. "Probably not."

"Thought so."

"Why?"

"Because I'm a judgemental arsehole and I'm not always wrong like I was earlier."

"When you thought I'd be a shit fuck?"

Mickey snorted out a laugh that briefly changed his whole face. Then his gaze heated again, pinning Benito in place. "I never thought that. Just that maybe I couldn't give *you* what you needed."

Benito slipped his shirt over his shoulders, and Mickey watched as he did the buttons up, tracking Benito's bare skin as it disappeared.

Fresh arousal flared in Benito's groin, but he dampened it down. They were done. It was over.

"So . . . ," Mickey said.

Benito blinked. "What?"

Mickey stared a moment, then shook his head. "Fuck it. I'm gonna write your digits on my arm."

He opened a drawer in the nearby dressing table, fished a pen from inside, and handed it to Benito. "You can fake number me if you want. I won't haunt you."

Shame. But Mickey's word choice brought him back to earth with a shiver. He took the pen and scrawled on the underside of Mickey's forearm, grounding himself in the warmth of the smooth skin he found there. For a moment, it worked. There was nothing but the lingering crackle of what they'd shared and the overwhelming desire to kiss Mickey one more time.

One *last* time. Because hook-ups never called. At least, Benito never did.

He capped the pen and dropped it to the floor.

Then he gripped Mickey's shirt and tugged him closer. "Bye, then."

Mickey grinned. He opened his mouth to speak, but Benito cut him off, kissing him with enough force to make them both stumble. Rough. Hot. Hard. Just like they'd fucked.

Then Mickey pulled away, still grinning, and walked out the door.

His departure felt like tectonic plates shifting in Benito's brain. His fading footsteps dragged Benito from his sex-hazed trance, one by one, until they were gone. Somewhere, a door closed.

Benito found his shoes and stepped into them. In his back pocket, his phone rang.

Unknown number. His heart skipped a beat, and an image of Mickey connecting his phone to a charging point bulldozed his brain. But reality caught up before he could blink, and the thrill died a fiery death. *Wrong phone, dickhead.*

Shadows descended as if they'd never been gone, obliterating Benito's blissed out state of mind. He swept the room for anything he'd dropped, then answered the call as he left. "Yeah?"

A low, humourless chuckle greeted him. "You don't sound pleased to hear from me."

Benito reached the stairs and glanced around, but he was alone. "I'm not, unless you have something useful to tell me. It's been a week since you went dark."

"With good fucking reason. It ain't easy to spy on a king. You should know that."

Benito scowled and jogged down the stairs but came to a stop by the door that would take him back into the club. He found a place where he could see every possible approach and propped his shoulder against the wall. "Don't talk about fucking kings. You know what I need. If you don't have it, this conversation is over."

"I have it."

Benito waited, darkness swallowing every ounce of relief Mickey had gifted him. "Go on," he snapped when silence reigned.

"Watford. The drop is next week. It's not a big one, but I'm driving."

"Where to?"

"Coventry. Same crew as last time, different meet point."

Benito closed his eyes. *Fucking Coventry. I hate that place.* Of course he did. It was where his life had seemed to come together all those months ago, only to fall apart a few days later. "Will you be alone?"

"No. One other dude. But he's not a fighter. You can put him down with your hands behind your back."

Benito pictured himself naked, his hands secure in Mickey's firm grip, his thick cock drilling him. Heat flooded his veins, but with one foot in each camp, it wasn't the good kind. He felt sick. "Text me the details. Then dump your phone. And don't fuck me over or I'll burn your fucking house down."

A sharp inhale was the only reply.

5

Mickey rapped his knuckles on the shiny front door. It was brand new, like the door to every other flat he'd knocked at that morning. Only difference was, he knew this door was never going to open for him. After his sixth visit in ten days, he'd accepted it.

Didn't stop him trying, though. He knocked one more time, then backed up to take a seat at the top of the stairs, ignoring the protest of the fading bruise on his hip. He pulled out his phone and placed a call. It rang and rang and rang before an automated voicemail kicked in.

Mickey sighed, waiting for the beep. "Good morning, Mrs De Luca, it's Mickey Larwood from DOSHA Housing. I'm still trying to reach you about your rent arrears. I'm in the area all day if you'd like a face-to-face to talk about it, or you can call me back on this number anytime. Please contact me as soon as you can. I know it's a difficult situation, but I can't help you if there's no communication between us. Cheers, bye."

He ended the call, cringing slightly. Two years on the job and he still hadn't figured out how to end formal phone calls without sounding like a moron. It had been less of a problem in his old job—*that's what you're calling it? A fucking job? Where's the pension then, mate? The fuel allowance and the friendly boss on the other end of the phone?*

An internal sneer raked Mickey's soul. He bit back a shiver and made another call.

Isha Hussain answered on the second ring. "You must be psychic. I was going to touch base with you this afternoon. Everything okay?"

"Yeah. I just wanted to update you on the De Luca case."

"De Luca?" The tap of a keyboard filtered down the line. Mickey waited, knowing his boss had a hundred households on his books, not just the ones Mickey cared about. "Yup. I see it. Those arrears are pretty substantial now. They haven't made a full payment since last year."

"I know. I set up a payment plan for them six months ago, but they haven't paid anything at all since July."

"Why?"

"I'm not sure. I can't get in there to have that conversation, and every call goes to voicemail." Mickey glanced over his shoulder. The closed door seemed to taunt him, and frustration rippled through him. "I don't know what to do next."

"Yes, you do. Non-adherence to a payment plan coupled with no communication means we have to pass the account to the collections team at the council. It's the agreement we made when we took over the flats in that block."

"But—"

"I know," Isha said, not unkindly. "You don't want to potentially put someone out of their home, but there's a limit to what we can do if we can't get a clearer picture of what's going on. Don't forget that we have a three-year waiting list for properties in that area—families who *want* to pay their rent."

"So, it's about money?"

"No, it's about giving people a hand-up, not a hand*out*. You knew this when you came to us."

Mickey let out another long breath and remembered why he had Isha's number for calls like this and not his other boss's. Dominic Ramos was a softer touch, and Isha had banned him from taking the lead on hard luck cases. If that was even what this was. For all Mickey knew, the unpaid rent could've funded a week in the Maldives.

"What about UC?" Isha said when Mickey didn't speak. "It says here that the tenancy holder was working at Santander. Has that changed? Is there a Universal Credit claim now?"

"I don't know."

"Okay, well, finding out is imperative if we don't want this to escalate. What's your gut telling you? Do these people need help, or are they taking the fucking piss?"

That was more like it. Sometimes, Mickey felt as if he'd woken up in the wrong body, but when Isha cut the formalities and handed out real talk, Mickey's life made a lot more sense. "I don't think they're taking the piss. Something's changed for them, and they don't trust us enough to help. They're avoiding me because they think I'll evict them."

"You might have to if this goes south. It would be a first for you. You haven't terminated a tenancy the whole time you've worked for us."

"That's the point, though, isn't it? To keep families with unstable incomes in secure housing? It's why your company exists."

Isha hummed. "Yes, but we have to be realistic here. We can't be soft on non-compliance at the expense of other families. Somewhere there's a line, and it's your job to find it."

"How long will you give me?"

"On top of the time you've already spent? Two weeks, and that's only if I can reschedule the council meeting on Friday."

Mickey had lost track of his days. He counted them up. It was Wednesday. If Isha couldn't push back the meeting, he had forty-eight hours to find some fucking movement. "*Can you reschedule the meeting?*"

"I'll try. The main issue at my end will be finding time to have it next month. I'm jammed as it is."

"I'm sorry."

"Don't be. We employ you because you give a shit. It's everyone else we need to worry about."

They talked a little longer about other tenants, then Isha had to go. He ended the call, leaving Mickey alone outside the De Luca flat, highly aware of every minute ticking by. He stood, pocketing his phone, and considered the closed front door. *They have to come out eventually.* But he didn't have time to wait. A block on a different estate needed him as much as the De Lucas did, and he walked away with a heavy heart.

He spent the rest of the day negotiating payment plans, calling in maintenance work, and explaining to his favourite tenant ever that he couldn't house any more iguanas in his airing cupboard. It was six o'clock when he climbed into his car. He cracked the window and sparked his first smoke of the day. In fact, it was the first since last Thursday—he was trying to quit, *honest*—but some days took more out of him than he cared to admit, and he lived for the quiet solace of a solitary smoke. *Even more than the post-fuck smoke? You weren't alone then.*

Mickey smirked, then exhaled a deep lungful of nicotine. He was still sore from his encounter with Benito at the club, battered and bruised, and he enjoyed the faint flashes of pain almost as much as the memories of the night itself. Short, sweet, *rough*. Did it get any better? Mickey didn't think so, and he had enough notches on his bedpost to compare.

I've never fucked anyone like him, though. Six days later and long after he'd scrubbed Benito's phone number from his skin, he still couldn't quite believe his luck. *So text him. Set up a meet.*

Mickey jammed his smoke in his mouth and unlocked his phone. He'd saved Benito's number with an aubergine emoji next to his name, then changed his mind and deleted it. Then he'd altered Benito's name to simply the letter B, before changing it back to his actual name. He'd yet to figure out why.

And he'd yet to do anything constructive with the digits. *Because you're scared he fake numbered you.*

True story. But what if he hadn't? What if Benito, his glorious skin, body, and beautiful cock were waiting on Mickey's call for a repeat performance? Worse, what if Benito got bored waiting and hooked up with someone else?

Logic told Mickey it didn't matter if Benito was hooking up with other people. No one went to Freefall for monogamy. But the notion of missing out because he lost a game of chicken with his phone was ridiculous.

Mickey opened WhatsApp and started a new message thread. Then he drummed his fingers on the steering wheel, itching for another smoke—or worse—while he considered his first words.

The truth seemed a good place to start.

Mickey: *want to fuck you again*

He fired it off, then wondered if he should've opened with something more benign. Small talk. Pleasantries. Benito didn't seem the type for either, but it was hard to gauge a man's personality when all you had to go on were the blood-pumping sounds he made when he came.

Sounds Mickey heard every time he closed his eyes.

The message delivered to Benito's phone. Mickey tapped out of the messaging app without waiting to see if he read it and opened his email. There was one from Isha, and it wasn't good news. The council had refused the rescheduled date DOSHA had offered them, and the planned meeting would go ahead on Friday. By then, Mickey needed a workable plan for the De Lucas or their days in the subsidised flat they called home were numbered.

Shit shit shit.

Mickey tossed his phone on the passenger seat and reached for his keys. It was too late to pay Mrs De Luca another fruitless visit, but if he could get home and compose a letter that didn't make him sound like an illiterate idiot, he could come back first thing and slip it through her door.

You're not an idiot. Or illiterate. You're dyslexic.

Another true story, and the prospect of sweating over his laptop all evening made him want to throat punch the reasonable devil on his shoulder, but Mickey would do it a thousand times over if it stopped a family losing their home. *"You haven't terminated a tenancy."* A third truth, but if there was one thing life had taught Mickey, it was he never ran out of time to fuck everything up. There was always enough rope for a—

His phone buzzed, startling him with an incoming WhatsApp message. Heart jumping, he reached for it, expecting Isha, Dom, or a robot asking him if he'd been in a car accident. Anyone except the last person he'd contacted.

Anyone except Benito.

Benito: *can relate. soon?*

Mickey's eyes widened, and his pulse kicked up a gear, blood rushing to his ears. *Soon.* Yeah. He could get on board with that.

Mickey: *how soon?*

Benito: *depends*

Mickey: *on?*

Benito: *how bad u really want it*

Mickey: *want u. is that bad enough?*

Benito: *i think we're both pretty bad at dirty texts, but u get the sentiment, right?*

Mickey sniggered out loud, and it surprised him. The Benito he'd met at the club hadn't struck him as a dude who'd make him laugh, and he hadn't cared. He'd been too busy trying not to come in the first ten seconds, and even then, he'd broken one of the few rules he kept in place for hook-ups like that: condom or not, Mickey didn't come inside random fucks. He pulled out and shot on their back or in their face. Wherever felt good at the time. *Never* inside.

But something about Benito had spun his head enough to forget the rules, and it was all he'd thought about since that night.

Liar. You've thought about everything, not just blowing your load.

Guilty as charged, Mickey let his mind wander, hoping it would help him find the words to text Benito something coherent. He lit another smoke, mind swimming with fragmented memories of their charged encounter—clashing limbs, wild hands, and then . . . another broken rule. Mickey had kissed Benito. A moment of fucking madness that had put the final nail in the coffin of his self-control. He could barely recall what had happened next, at least, not the details. Only the blinding heat. The unreal pleasure that he was still struggling to quite believe.

Mickey: *i'm not sentimenal. just hot for u*

He sent the message before he realised he'd spelt sentimental wrong.

Fucking hell.

His thumb hovered over the delete option, but Benito was already typing back.

B: *that works. i'm free tonight*

Mickey blinked, but whatever reply he may have made was cut off by a tap on the car window. Dazed, he swung his gaze. A teenage girl scowled back at him.

What the?

Mickey opened the car door and stood, pocketing his phone and scanning the vicinity for any little shits who wanted to come at him, road boys in training, too green to realise Mickey was the last person they wanted to fuck with. It wasn't that late, but it was dark already, and he'd parked by an underpass—a prime spot for a mugging.

The girl, however, was alone. And unarmed, unless she had a shank up her sleeve. Mickey shut the car door and leaned against it, keeping space between them. "What are you banging on my car for? Do you need something?"

"Are you the man from the housing association?"

"I'm from DOSHA. We manage some of the properties around here, but not all of them. Why? Are you a tenant?"

The girl nodded. "You're looking for my mum."

"Who's that?"

"Rosetta De Luca. She owes you money."

Mickey frowned, taking in the girl's raven curls and fierce gaze. "She doesn't owe me money. It's her rent. You're the daughter that lives with her?"

"Yeah."

"You've always been at school when I've been there." Mickey took another glance around. If the girl was who she said she was, she was on the wrong estate. Her block was visible on the horizon, but it was a half a mile away. "Do you think you could ask your mum to call me so we can set up a meeting? It's really important that I speak with her."

"Why? Are you kicking us out?"

"I really need to speak with her."

The girl bit her lip, anxiety flaring in her dark eyes. "She won't let you in. She can't."

"Why not?"

"She's scared."

"She doesn't need to be. If I can just talk to her, we can set up—"

"You don't understand!" the girl shouted. "It's not the money, she just *can't*."

"Hey, hey." Mickey held up his hands. "I want to help, okay? But I can't do that if your mum won't talk to me. Do you think she'd answer an email if I sent it to her?"

The girl shook her head. "No. She doesn't do technology. It gives her migraines."

"What about a phone call? I don't have to come in the flat if she's more comfortable talking over the phone?"

"*No.*"

"Why not? What is she afraid of?"

"Everything. Mostly my brother finding out what she did."

"What did she do?"

The girl opened her mouth, then reality seemed to catch up with her and she snapped it shut, more panic clouding her gaze. "Nothing. It doesn't matter. I shouldn't have said anything."

She stepped back and whipped around, ten feet away before Mickey could blink.

Fuck. He could've reached her in two strides, but he knew better than to chase a young girl down and force her to speak to him. "Hey!" he called. "Wait up."

The girl stopped but didn't turn round.

Mickey pushed off his car and caught up with her, rounding her slender frame to stand in front of her, though he kept well back, leaving her space to flee if she wanted to. "Listen," he said. "I *need* to speak to your mum. I can't do anything for you unless that happens. I'm going to write her a letter and put it through your door, okay? It's going to say everything she needs to do to put the brakes on the arrears and how to do it, but she *has* to contact me, even if it's a just a text message. She can do that, right? I have her number, so I'll know it's her."

"She might not have yours. She deletes your calls so my brother doesn't see them."

"He goes through her phone?"

"No. Never. But she's convinced herself he does, even though he doesn't come in the flat anymore."

"Why doesn't he come inside?"

The girl shrugged. "I don't know. They kind of hate each other. It's complicated."

"Families usually are." Mickey pointed behind the girl. "I'm going to get my card from the car. Take it home and give it to your mum, and tell her I'm dropping off a letter in the morning. But she hasn't got much time to respond; I need you to understand that. Between us, we need to figure something out by the end of the week, or we're all in trouble."

He spoke lightly but held the girl's gaze. He didn't want to scare her, but bullshitting wasn't going to help.

She nodded.

Mickey fetched his card from the car and took it back to her. She shoved it in her pocket. Then she stepped around him and disappeared into the night.

Anxiety scraped Mickey's conscience as she vanished into the shadows. He couldn't remember how old Rosetta De Luca's daughter was, and it wasn't as if he could put her in his car and give her a lift, but letting her walk home alone felt wrong enough to leave a bad taste in his mouth.

He returned to his car and slid into the seat, starting the engine and glowering at his empty cigarette packet. His chest already hurt from the two he'd sucked down in quick succession, but the need to dampen his nervous energy trumped his health. Always did, and he had the scars on his soul to prove it. Still, there were better ways of tying his feet to the ground than giving himself lung cancer. *There are worse ways too. Like—*

Shaking his head, Mickey dug his phone from his pocket

and opened WhatsApp again. Benito had gone offline a while ago, perhaps reading into the fact Mickey had read his last message and not replied. *Fuck that.* Mickey's fingers flew over the screen, typing and deleting until he was almost sure what he'd written made sense.

Mickey: *can do tonight but not till late and not at the club. too far. can accom. it's safe*

He hit Send, then dropped his phone on the passenger seat. Every selfish instinct he possessed screamed at him to wait on Benito's reply, but he'd worked hard not to be a selfish motherfucker anymore.

Before he got his dick wet again, he had a letter to write.

————

The knock on Mickey's door came at ten at night. By then, he'd dictated a letter into his laptop, run it through a dyslexia app, and sent it to the office for a final check before he would print and deliver it the next morning.

He'd showered too but missed dinner, and the only clean clothes he had were the black drawstring pyjama bottoms he answered the door in.

No shirt.

Benito lounged on Mickey's porch, shoulder propped against the brick, dressed in designer sweatpants and a long-sleeve tee that clung to his muscles. Casual and cool. Only his eyes gave him away as something more, glinting in the darkness and sweeping over Mickey with such intensity, Mickey shivered. "Hey."

"Hey." Benito didn't move.

Caught in his stare for a thudding heartbeat, Mickey

didn't either. Then a cold breeze rattled him, and he stepped aside, waving Benito forward into his small terraced house.

Benito slipped inside, closing the door behind him. He leant against it like he had at the club, still watching Mickey, dissecting him.

Mickey didn't mind. He'd done the same on the rare occasions he'd hooked up outside of the club. He pointed at the kitchen. "Back door is through there. It's unlocked."

"Why are you telling me that?"

"So you know where the exits are."

"In case we crash?"

Mickey grinned. "If you like. Just letting you know you're safe."

"You don't need to do that."

"No?"

Benito straightened, though he didn't step forward. "I wouldn't have come if I thought you were a weirdo."

You're gonna come.

Smirking, Mickey swallowed the crude joke and considered his options. Throwing Benito back against the door was one. Taking him straight upstairs was another, but Benito's set jaw gave him pause. *He's nervous.* "You want a drink, mate?"

"Hmm?" Despite his sharp gaze, Benito startled.

It was endearing as fuck. Mickey took a chance and held out his hand. "Come on. Let's get a beer."

Benito stared hard at Mickey's outstretched hand, as if he didn't believe it was real. Then he took it, and his cool, dry fingers wrapped around Mickey's palm.

Mickey brought his other hand to the game and rubbed warmth into Benito's fingers. "Cold out?"

"Yeah."

"I've got the cure for that."

"Have you?"

"I reckon so. Let's get that drink first." Mickey let go of Benito's hand and padded barefoot to the kitchen, trusting that Benito would follow. He opened the fridge and retrieved two beer bottles with twist caps as Benito filled the space behind him. "Here. You can open it yourself."

So you know it's safe.

Benito took the bottle. He uncapped it and took a long swig, throat working and leaving his lips wet when he was done.

Captivated, Mickey took it all in, pondering if they'd kiss again. If he could even handle it. Fucking Benito was one thing. His kiss had been something else. In the *frequent* moments he'd thought of it since that night, his lips had tingled, and he'd shivered, a craving he didn't recognise igniting inside, one that distracted him from even his darkest thoughts.

Like now. Mickey opened his own bottle with undue care but abandoned it on the counter without drinking. He didn't need the ice breaker, just for Benito to feel comfortable enough to relax. "Did you have to come far?"

Benito raised an inky brow. "You wanna talk about the weather too?"

"We already did that." Mickey suppressed a grin. "Just making conversation. Let me know when you're ready for something else."

"I was ready when I got here."

"Were you?"

Benito drank more beer. "You think I drove all this way to

have a chat?"

"I don't know how far you drove. You never answered my question."

Benito's lips twitched, and fleeting humour danced in his brown eyes. "I don't remember you being so chatty."

"No? What do you remember?"

"That you wanted to fight me before you fucked me. You want to do that again?"

Fuck yeah. But there was one problem: this wasn't the club. Mickey had neighbours who'd call the police if they heard two men brawling through the walls. "We can do it, but we'll have to be quiet about it. Like, proper silent."

"Roommate?"

"Nah, the old bird next door."

Benito nodded slowly. "I like the idea of silence. It's . . . hot."

Now they were getting somewhere. Mickey pointed to the ceiling. "We can fuck on my bed or down here if you're more comfortable."

"Stop trying to make me comfortable."

"Why?"

Benito drained his beer and set the bottle down by the sink. Then he narrowed the distance between them in one stride, abruptly so close Mickey smelled the faint scent of cigarettes and *man*. His jaw was still thick with dark scruff. Mickey wanted it against his skin. Wanted to grab Benito and shove him against the counter.

He settled for a light trail of his fingertip down Benito's neck, caressing his Adam's apple until he came to the hollow of his throat.

Save a soft inhale, Benito didn't react.

Mickey smirked and pressed his lips to exposed, tender skin, lightly at first, then with a suction that brought Benito's strong hands to Mickey's hips, slamming their bodies together.

Mickey almost groaned, but a challenge hung in the air between them. Could they do this without making a sound? Could *Mickey*? And did it matter if they failed?

Probably not, but Mickey loved a challenge. In and out of bed, it kept him alive.

First, though . . .

He pulled his lips from Benito's throat and fixed him with a hard stare. "It's important to me that you're comfortable. It might not matter to you, but it matters to me. Always."

"You're sweet," Benito said, low, almost a whisper. "No other hook-up ever gave a shit."

"I'm not other hook-ups."

"*That*, I know." Benito gripped Mickey's chin. "I've been thinking about you fucking me ever since that night. I've never come like that."

"What? Hard?"

"No. I mean . . . fuck." Benito let go and rubbed the back of his neck. No flush heated his skin, but Mickey sensed it all the same. "It was intense, you know? Like, I can still feel it."

Warmth flooded Mickey's chest. Despite the mind-fucking orgasms they'd shared, he'd pegged Benito for the aloof type, not a man who gave up that information easily. "We can add to it," he said. "Here and now. Then see how you feel tomorrow. How much you can stand."

"Stand before what?"

"Well, two things can happen. Either you'll get used to it and the buzz will wear off, or . . ."

"Yeah?"

Mickey shrugged. "It's like anything that gives you a rush. You'll struggle to give it up."

Ask me how I know.

Benito didn't. He absorbed Mickey's words with another nod, then flicked his gaze to the stairs in the hallway.

Mickey took the hint. He pushed off the counter Benito had crowded him into and left the kitchen, leaving his beer behind. He climbed the narrow stairs, sensing Benito's presence at his back. They were the same size, evenly matched in build, but like this, filling the space with his broad shoulders, Benito seemed bigger. Mickey liked it more than he cared to admit.

Low lights lit the way to Mickey's bedroom. He pushed the door open, revealing more lamps and his barely made bed, sheets rumpled but clean. He turned to speak, but rough hands caught him before he could take a breath, and he stumbled, colliding with the foot end of his wooden bed.

Sharp pain bloomed in his kneecap. Mickey winced, a growl building in his chest, merging with the arousal he'd carried since Benito had replied to his first message, a heady mix of volatile pressure.

He spun around, tackling Benito before he could lunge again, and they grappled, silent and fierce, the only sound in the dim room that of their impacting bodies.

Benito was as strong as Mickey remembered. His carved biceps popping, chest made of stone. But Mickey was strong too. He battled Benito's hold on him and wrestled him to the bed, revelling in Benito's struggle. A stray elbow hit his ribs, impacting a bruise that hadn't quite healed from last time. The pain made his head spin and his senses come alive in brand new ways. Thunder and lightning. Different, but wild enough to coexist in a mess of breath and limbs.

Mickey was flying. He thought he'd remembered what Benito was like, but whatever recollection he had was a poor imitation of the sharp-edged masculinity oozing from every jarring blow and stifled groan. *Yes.* Mickey pooled his strength and shoved Benito onto the bed, covering him with his body before he could roll away, pinning him down.

Benito vibrated beneath him, his bunched muscles letting Mickey know he could throw him off at any moment, but for now he stayed put, dark gaze searching.

Mickey stared down at him, transfixed, lungs heaving. And very very naked, his pyjama bottoms puddled on the floor with Benito's clothes. "Damn. Is that a scar?" He traced the jagged white line that traversed Benito's left side, marking his ribs. "I didn't see it last time."

Benito flinched. Subtle, but his gaze flashed too. "It is what it is."

He doesn't want to talk about it.

Mickey could live with that. He wanted to make Benito come, not hear his life story.

He let his finger trail from the scar and tried not to stare at it, a feat made easier by the fact that only Benito's underwear remained on his body, a cotton barrier between his straining cock and Mickey's.

Mickey thrust, testing the friction. A low sound rumbled from Benito's chest, fresh sweat beading his skin. Mickey licked his tingling lips, then bit down. They hadn't kissed yet. Maybe they wouldn't. But, *fuck*, Mickey wanted to, perhaps more than anything.

The realisation should've shocked him, but he was too

turned on for deep thoughts. He thrust again and again, teasing them both, until Benito grabbed the back of his neck, forcing him down, their faces inches apart. "Do it. Whatever you want. Just fucking do it."

He means get on with it. Fuck him already.

Mickey kissed him instead, and the heat between them boiled over, incinerating any coherent thought in its path. They rolled over and over, landing back where they started. Mickey tore his lips away and manhandled Benito onto his belly. Then he gripped his chin and turned his face back, kissing him again as he yanked his underwear down. "I'm gonna fuck you just as hard as last time. Tell me if you want to stop. I'll hear you."

Benito glowered, moody and hot. He spread his legs and braced his forearms on the bed, tense and ready, his muscular back a fucking wet dream.

Mickey rolled off him and retrieved lube and condoms from his bedside table. "You want poppers?"

"Nah. I'm good."

Mickey shut the drawer, leaving the party bottle behind. He crawled on the bed, straddling Benito's thighs. The frenzied air had lessened while he'd been gone, but as he dripped lube onto his fingers and trailed them down Benito's crease, Benito reached back and caught his wrist.

"Just fuck me, man. Don't make me wait."

"You don't want me to prep you?"

"No."

Mickey swept his fingers over Benito's hole, leaving a trail of lube behind. "Sure? It might hurt—"

"Just do it."

Mickey didn't need telling twice. He rolled a condom on

with one hand and slicked himself with the other. Blood shaking, he split Benito's legs wider and pushed inside him, pausing only a moment at the resistance from Benito's body.

Beneath him, Benito tensed, limbs taut, face hidden, like last time, in his forearms.

His struggle was beautiful. Mickey's dick pulsed, and he snatched a breath, guilt catching up with him. He liked it rough, but he had no desire to hurt Benito like this, where the discomfort was a one-way street.

He rubbed Benito's back, a slow brush of his palm at the base of his spine.

Benito made a soft sound that wasn't all pleasure.

Mickey repeated the action once, twice, three times, easing tension from Benito's strained muscles with every slow, patient breath. Mickey would take anything and every-thing Benito was prepared to give, but he'd wait all night if he had to.

He didn't have to wait *that* long, though.

Stroke by stroke, Benito relaxed, and the intense *pressure* of his body clamped around Mickey's cock grew unbearable. Mickey's thighs trembled, his control at its limit. He lowered his chest, welding it to Benito's back, and started to move, caging a ragged moan in his throat.

The answering, blistering heat was instant and blinding. Mickey dug his fingers into Benito's flesh, watching as Beni-to's hands balled into fists, and rhythm overcame him, sharp and hypnotic. His noisy brain shut down, carried away, leaving his body behind, and he bucked harder. Deeper. Grinding his teeth, jaw clenched, pleasure firing through his red-hot veins as Benito raised up from the bed, fighting him thrust for thrust.

Benito's hand flew back, clutching Mickey's thigh.

Fuck yes.

This was what Mickey craved more than *anything*—a man who steered him all the way to the edge, then relented enough for Mickey to make the final push for both of them.

Fuck fuck fuck yes.

Caution abandoned him. He reared back, wedging the heel of his hand between Benito's shoulder blades, holding him down. A sizzling coil unravelled in his belly, but he couldn't come yet, not before Benito. Desperate, he pistoned his hips faster, still swallowing every sound that burned his chest. Sensation overwhelmed him. *I can't—*

As if he knew, Benito raised his head, twisting his neck to look over his shoulder. He met Mickey's gaze with a hot stare, jaw set, eyes hooded with pleasure. "Harder."

"Shh."

"*Harder.*"

Leering, Mickey dug in and rammed into Benito, brutal and deep. His vision darkened and he pushed Benito down again, bearing his weight on top of him, one arm around Benito's neck, sealing his mouth shut with his palm. Relentless. Ruthless. No mercy this time.

He bore down, fucking Benito as hard as he could, choking on pleasure, too far gone to stop the incoming train hurtling through him. His bed jumped along the floor, slamming into the bedside table over and over. Mickey gasped, and his eyes rolled back so far he saw fucking stars. *I can't—*

Benito stiffened, a strangled noise catching in his throat. His spine arched and he pressed his face into the bed, clenching around Mickey's cock, his entire body rigid.

Fuck fuck fuck.

It was too much.

Mickey came, friction and pressure coalescing in a nerve-searing wave, and the guttural groan he'd held all this time finally escaped, rattling the walls.

He collapsed on top of Benito. "Fuck."

His chest burned, laboured and tight, and his hand fell away from Benito's slack mouth. He had no breath. It was long seconds before he collected himself enough to remember Benito crushed beneath him. "*Fuck*," he cursed again.

He withdrew, taking the condom with him, and rolled away fast, giving Benito room to move. To *breathe*. "Shit. I'm sorry. Are you okay?"

Benito said nothing. He shifted onto his back, then flopped down, panting as hard as Mickey. His eyes were hazed. Mickey rubbed his arm, then left the bed to clean up.

He chucked the condom and found a flannel in the bathroom. In the bedroom, he lay back down and wiped the warm, wet washcloth over Benito's trembling abdomen. "I love this."

Benito cracked an eye open. "What?"

"The mess we make. You kicked the shit out of me last week. I felt it every day."

A ghostlike smirk lit Benito's face. "Me too."

"Yeah?"

"Yeah." Benito sat up slightly, bringing himself closer. He licked his lips and stilled Mickey's hand on his belly.

Then he kissed Mickey again with none of the fire of before but all of the heat. Slow. Sweet. Sweeping his tongue through Mickey's mouth before he pulled back.

It was as mind-shaking as any climax. Mickey blinked,

counting heartbeats as they thudded against his ribcage. His path solidified, and it was his turn to lean forward and capture just one more kiss. A longer one that went on and on until they were stretched out side by side, kissing and kissing and kissing.

Mickey couldn't begin to make sense of it. And he couldn't stop. Only the desperate need for more oxygen drove them apart.

Panting, Mickey sprawled onto his back. Benito stayed where he was, propped on his elbow, eyes still heavy. He looked like he needed a nap, and Mickey wasn't averse to the idea, especially if it meant fucking again when they woke up. The fact that it was a school night and he had an early start seemed to have deserted him.

He didn't fucking care.

Benito didn't seem in a hurry to move either. He was quiet, though, gaze drifting from Mickey to the big bay window. "It's nice here. Just a street with six houses. It's like a fucking toy town or something."

"I know, right? One shop and a Chinese takeaway. Keeps me out of trouble. I can't handle the big estates."

"Too posh?"

A sharp laugh bubbled from Mickey's chest. "Do I sound fucking posh?"

"Dunno. You're northern. Could be a billionaire for all I know."

"In this house? Your perception of wealth is fucked up."

Something flickered in Benito's dark gaze, something familiar, though Mickey couldn't say why.

Benito sat up, scanning the room for his clothes. Mickey

itched to tug him back down but stayed where he was, watching as Benito got up and dressed.

The scar disappeared beneath Benito's T-shirt. Without the distractions of bare skin and wild sex, curiosity bloomed in Mickey's gut. He opened his mouth to speak, but Benito spun to face him first.

"I know you're not rich. You don't have that vibe."

Mickey raised a brow. "What vibe? Content and successful?"

"You're not a wanker," Benito clarified. "Even though this house could be a front. You could have a wife in a three-bed semi somewhere."

Mickey snorted, amusement cutting through a sudden wrench of guilt. "I don't have a wife. Or a second house."

Benito tilted his head, gaze shrewd. "What is it, then? Girlfriend?"

"What? No. What makes you think it's anything?"

"Dunno. You suddenly look like you're gonna throw up. It's not a good look on you."

Mickey shrugged. "Regrets are a funny thing. How you move past something, then it comes back years later and punches you in the face again."

Benito came back to the bed. "How many years later?"

"A few."

"What? Like, five? Ten?"

"More like two."

"What did you do that was so bad?"

Mickey stopped himself shrugging again and forced himself to meet Benito's gaze. "I never had a wife or a secret house, but I had a girlfriend . . . for a long time. She never knew this about me. No one did."

Benito sat on the edge of the bed, close enough that Mickey could've dragged him on top of him, but the fire between them had simmered down. "Does anyone who matters know now?"

Mickey laughed softly. "Define who fucking matters? Turns out it's not a lot."

Benito's dark eyes swam with something too deep for a conversation between casual hook-ups. He took a breath, then shook his head. "Never is. You have to dig hard to find out, though, or it fucking flays you alive, man."

"Or it keeps you alive. Took me a while to see that."

Affinity flowed between them, undefined but shiny. And fleeting. Benito ripped his gaze away and bent over, searching for his socks. "Sorry," he said. "I didn't mean to go deep. Tell me to go fuck myself if I do it again."

"I don't want you to fuck yourself, mate. I'm here for that."

Benito smirked and retrieved his socks from the floor. He sat on the edge of the bed to pull them on, close to Mickey's legs. "Sweet. I'm going to take you up on it as long as the offer's still open."

"Yeah?"

"Yeah." Benito finished dressing and laid a scorching palm on Mickey's bare ankle. "Might not be around for a while, though. I've got some shit to do."

"Work?"

"Yeah."

"What do you do?"

Benito squeezed Mickey's ankle, then pulled his hand back, leaving Mickey reeling from the simple touch. "This and that. You know how it is."

Not anymore. The words bubbled in Mickey's throat, but

he swallowed them down. *Idiot. He's probably a personal trainer. Or a bodyguard. Or a—*

Benito stood before Mickey's brain could generate any other occupations Benito's ridiculous body would come in useful for. His immaculate Yeezy trainers were abandoned on the landing. He padded to the doorway and stamped into them.

Mickey forced himself upright and grabbed his drawstring trousers from the floor, but Benito shook his head. "Don't get up. I'll see myself out unless you're worried about me rinsing your yard on my way out."

"I'm not, but you should know I don't have jack shit, so you'd be disappointed."

"Hasn't happened yet."

Benito turned away, the low light casting his face in shadow. He moved across the landing towards the stairs.

Mickey watched him go, still clutching his trousers. It made sense to stay where he was. The front door would lock behind Benito. There was no need to follow him, dressed or otherwise. But his nerves jangled. It felt wrong.

Unfinished.

Mickey scrambled off the bed and yanked his pyjamas on as Benito's footsteps faded on the stairs. He dashed after him, skidding to a stop on the ancient floorboards in the hallway.

Benito turned, thick brows raised. "You really did think I was gonna nick something?"

"Fuck no. Why have you decided I think you're scum? You have *way* better clothes than me. And—" Mickey pushed past Benito and opened the front door. A black SUV was parked on the kerb next to Mickey's Ford Focus. "Yup. Better car too. Trust me, mate. It's me that's scum."

Benito blinked as the humour in Mickey's rant expired before he was done.

Mickey shook his head, clearing the fog that remained from the firepit they'd left upstairs. "That came out wrong."

Benito stepped towards him until he was close enough to pry the door from Mickey's hand and push it shut, trapping them both inside. He backed Mickey against it, caging him like Mickey had done to him more than once. "You're intense," he said. "I like that."

"Why?"

"Because it's real. We don't have to know everything about each other to get off on that."

Mickey's heart hammered as much as it had when he'd had his dick buried deep inside Benito. "You think we know enough to justify that I want to kiss the fuck out of you, then push you to your knees and shove my dick in your mouth?"

Benito pressed closer, his rough lips an inch from Mickey's. "I wanted all that the moment I saw you. We don't have to know shit to make it a reality."

"No?"

"No." Benito punctuated the single syllable with the hard kisses they'd perfected already. But with their clothes on, it felt different.

The desperation was harsher.

Sharper.

Mickey let it skewer him, surrendering to it as Benito took what he wanted. Maybe he'd suck Mickey's dick; maybe he wouldn't.

Right now, his kiss was enough.

6
———

Benito: *thanks for last night. sorry if it got heavy.*

Mickey: *if it gt hvy it was my fault*

Mickey: *im sorry*

Benito: *don't be. next week, yea?*

Mickey went offline. Benito waited a moment to see if he'd come back, but he didn't.

Eight hours later, he was still waiting. Sighing, he stuffed the phone in his pocket and scowled at his surroundings. Toddington Services were a shithole. He sank low in the car he'd bought for £200 from a scrapyard, tracking the lorries and caravans as they came and went, gaze sharp as he watched for the nondescript Vauxhall to make its scheduled fuel stop. It was already an hour late, but Benito wasn't worried . . . yet. He knew how this shit went down, and it wasn't fucking black ops. It was two idiots in a car with a kilo of coke under the seat—idiots who were stupid enough to make the drive at night, when the feds were watching the motorways the most.

Shoulda gone for rush hour, boys. Blend into the chaos. But

Benito wasn't calling the shots anymore, and for the first time, it had gifted him an advantage. Stupid people did stupid things. They left themselves open. Vulnerable. They were blood in the water, and Benito was the motherfucking shark.

At least, he would be if the marked car ever showed up.

He lit another smoke, staving off the hunger pains in his belly. Grocery shopping had fallen by the wayside after he'd emptied his bank account to buy Gianna her iPad, and he still hadn't managed to give it to her. It was sitting on his kitchen counter where he usually kept the eggs, reminding him that living off baked beans for a week was worth being too fucking hungry to lift weights at the gym.

The hours ticked by. Benito clutched the burner phone to his chest, waiting for a signal from the deep, while his other phone lay dormant in his pocket, silent and still, like it had been all day. Not that Benito had been waiting on a text. No. Definitely not. And he hadn't been obsessing over his latest encounter with a six-foot sandy-haired northerner either.

Much.

The kiss went on and on, as rough as the first they'd shared, but this felt different. As if every clash of lips and teeth sunk them deeper into something Benito didn't understand. Mickey fucking him was a trip. An out-of-body experience. But it wasn't meant to be like this. It was supposed to ground him, not leave him so dizzy he didn't know which way was up.

Mickey kissed Benito harder, fighting Benito's hold on him.

Benito kept him pressed against the door, just for a moment, before he relented and let Mickey spin them around. As tempting as it was to push their physicality to its limits, instinct told him this wasn't the time. Not yet.

But fuck, Benito wanted to. Almost as much as he wanted Mickey to fuck him again.

Right here.

Right now.

Against the front door—

The phone buzzed.

Benito's eyes flew open. He bolted upright and grabbed it as it slid off his chest. *Shit.* Had he fallen asleep? It wouldn't be the first time he'd drifted off to dirty memories of Mickey.

He rubbed his face and opened the text.

Unknown number: *5 mins out. Fuel then KFC. Follow us.*

Benito rolled his eyes. What kind of idiot stopped for dinner on a muling run? But again, it suited him. Their stupidity was his gain. *Snap to.*

It was late. And thanks to the extra half hour it had taken Benito to leave Mickey's house the night before, he hadn't slept. Not because he'd lost the time, more that he'd been too keyed up by the second drilling Mickey had gifted him in the hallway. Hard. Fast. Frantic. It hadn't hurt, but it had been as close to the edge as Benito could bear.

If he closed his eyes, he could still feel Mickey's thick—

Damn it. Snap the fuck to.

Benito jerked back to alertness, cold muscles protesting as he stretched his arms and legs. A blue Astra cruised into the service station, easing past the dark parking bay Benito had taken up residence in and onto the forecourt. So close to London, the fuel pumps were busy, even at this time of night. It took a while for the car's occupants to fill up and pay.

The Astra joined the queue at the fried chicken drive-through. Benito watched as it crawled past each window and accepted a big bag of food, and flicked the ignition on the ancient SEAT Ibiza. The old engine spluttered to life. *Don't fucking die on me.* Benito pumped the accelerator a few times, warming the engine, then slipped into the exit lane to follow the Astra out of the services.

Toddington was a strange place, both efficiently connected to the capital and surrounding towns and yet remote enough that deserted country roads weren't hard to find. The Astra passed the M1 junction and headed away from civilisation. It wasn't the quickest route to where they were going, but so far, the most sensible thing the muling crew had done.

Shame, for them at least, it was also going to be their biggest mistake.

Benito nursed the SEAT along the unlit road, tracking the rear lights of the Astra. The road was littered with tight bends. Three miles in, it narrowed to a single lane, serviced by shallow bays for passing vehicles.

Counting them, Benito covered his face with the camouflage scarf around his neck and pulled his hood up. The fourth bay was tucked under a copse of trees, half hidden by overgrown hedgerows.

The Astra pulled in. Killed the engine and lights.

Benito gripped the SEAT's steering wheel. Took a breath. Then he stomped on the accelerator and motored around the bend, roaring into view of the Astra's occupants and blocking them into the bay.

Engine running, he seized the metal pipe stashed in the passenger footwell and leapt out of the car. His combat boots hit wet ground. He sprinted around the bonnet and straight into the path of the driver climbing out of the Astra.

Benito raised the pipe and hit the tall man in the gut,

driving him to his knees before hitting him again in just the right place to knock him out without causing serious damage.

The man crumpled. Another took his place. Benito put him down, then faced off with the last man standing, a stocky dude Benito knew could punch like an incoming freight train.

They circled each other, bracing for impact, then the stocky dude stood down, dropping his fists.

He backtracked to the Astra and reached inside.

Benito waited, still armed and dangerous, though if the dude came back with a piece, it was over. Scaffold pole versus a fucking Glock? Yeah. *Goodnight, Benito.*

Fuck. He couldn't let that happen. Who would take care of Gianna? *The same people who'll take care of her if the feds pick you up. Prison or death. Same fucking thing.* Benito had seen road boys make it out of prison and turn their lives around, but they were better men than him.

The Astra's passenger door slammed shut, the dull sound unnaturally loud with no traffic noise to drown it out.

Stocky Dude stepped closer to Benito, holding out a package. "It's all there," he said. "Find me in a few weeks with my cut?"

Benito nodded, stuffing the package into his front pocket without checking the contents. He pointed the bar at the ground. "On your knees."

"All right, all right. Make it look good, but mind my teeth, yeah?"

Benito rolled his eyes, then advanced on the kneeling man without stopping to try and make sense of how his life had come to this. He swung with pinpoint precision, catching sensitive skin that would bleed a lot but leave the man conscious.

Stocky Dude slumped forwards, clutching his hands to the wound, smearing blood as it pulsed from the broken skin.

He nodded.

Benito nodded back and made his escape.

He dashed to the SEAT and slid behind the wheel, slamming the door as he gunned the engine and sped away, tyres squealing, dirt clouds misting the night air.

The Astra faded into the distance. Adrenaline coursing, Benito floored it to the main road, then slowed down to drive like a sensible old man in the opposite direction to anywhere he wanted to be.

The quiet stretch of the A5 had no traffic cameras. Benito followed it for an hour, then headed east to the coast, driving and driving and driving until he saw signs for the arse-crack town that could turn his financial fortunes around.

He parked by the beach. A dark van was already waiting for him. Two men got out. Benito steeled himself for the riskiest moment yet and left the sanctuary of his car behind.

The package changed hands. Then an envelope of rolled notes. No words. But Benito didn't need validation. Just enough cash to—

To what? You want to be king again? For this shit to be your whole fucking life?

Nah. Fuck that. Benito wanted to be free, and the money in his pocket was just a fraction of what he needed to make that happen.

"A hundred Gs. That's the price, in cash, product, or fucking blood. Else you rot here and spend the rest of your miserable life looking over your shoulder."

Self-loathing boiled in Benito's gut. He melted away from the meet and retrieved his car, pointing it back inland in a blind haze.

He was a half a world away before he took a breath. At least it felt that way. Ten miles from home, he skidded the SEAT to a stop in another country lane and killed the engine. With tired legs, he jumped from the car and moved to the boot. Inside, he found the jerry can of petrol stashed there and quickly doused the car interior.

Backing up, he lit a rag on fire. It burned fast, red-hot tendrils snaking up his arm. Benito cursed and tossed it to the open car door, then took off running without stopping to see if he'd set himself on fire.

Farmland surrounded the narrow road. Fields and fields of arable crops and sheep. Benito raced through the mud, jumping fences and climbing stiles, ears peeled for sirens, but none came. The car fire was far enough from any homes that it would burn itself out before it was seen.

He ran for miles until he reached where he'd left his SUV. In the pitch-black lay-by, he stripped his muddy, petrol-scented clothes and stuffed them into a bag with the scaffold pipe. He threw on clean clothes, stamped into his trainers, and dropped the stolen package on the passenger seat.

Despite being abandoned for hours, his car was warm and dry. He cranked the heat and pulled quietly out of the lay-by and made for the main road. Again. *I'm so fucking tired.* And he still had another stop to make—the woods, to bury twenty grand under a burnt sycamore tree.

It was three hours before he made it to his front door. Benito's flat was in the anonymous hub of Milton Keynes. From his bedroom window, he could see the theatre district, the shopping centre, and the old Point cinema. The sight was nostalgic and depressing. He shut the curtains on it and stripped his clothes *again*. More mud. He stared at his hands, flexing his sore fingers. His stomach still hurt, craving a hot meal, but sleep would come first. Then Gianna. As adrenaline faded, he tried to recall what she'd requested for breakfast, but his brain had slowed. It was cloudy now, fogged with fatigue.

Even the *ping* of an incoming message seemed distant enough that he almost forgot to find his phone.

Almost.

It fell out of his pocket as he loaded his clothes into the washing machine. A WhatsApp message lit up the screen.

Mickey.

Benito's heavy heart skipped a beat. He opened the message. Random abbreviations greeted him, more so than Mickey's usual messages, and his heart sank as fast as it had lifted.

Mickey: *hopefly. mbe the weak after if woRk stays crezy*

Another week? *Fuck. I can't wait that long.*

The realisation shocked him. Scared him even. Since when had his sanity rested on a hook-up he'd met twice?

It doesn't. You're tired and acting fucked up.

It made sense. But the more Benito thought about it, the less he believed it, and a new ache formed deep in his chest.

Naked, he went to the bathroom, still clutching his phone. Nausea bloomed sudden and harsh in his belly. He stumbled and upchucked into the sink, heaving until he could barely breathe.

He turned the taps on and stared at himself in the mirror.

I look dead.

Some days, he wished he was.

He turned the shower on and stepped under the spray. The water warmed at the same pace as his chilled blood. Benito pressed his back to the tiles and slid down the wall. He buried his face in his bent knees and wrapped his arms around his head.

Only then did he start to shake.

7
───────

"You brought raisin whirls?" Gianna snatched the paper bag from Benito's outstretched hand. "Yes! You're the best, Beni."

Benito smiled and leaned against the car, tired. He'd only managed a half hour nap before it had been time to meet Gianna by the bus stop, but moments like these made life worthwhile. And he hadn't even given her the iPad yet. *After school*. Perhaps by then he'd have caught up on his sleep enough that she wouldn't keep offering to walk to McDonalds and get him a coffee. "What lessons do you have today?"

Gianna stilled her excited dance and stuck her hand in the bakery bag. "I don't know. The usual. Why are you asking me that?"

"Because I'm your big brother and I want to make sure you don't end up a bum like me."

"You're not a bum. It's not your fault you lost your job."

"I know." The lie choked Benito. He took the pastry Gianna held out and bit into it. "But it was a shit job anyway. And now I drive a fucking taxi. You can do better than that, G. Better than *me*."

Gianna scowled over the bottle of orange juice Benito had brought her. "You always say that, but do you know how many of my friends have big brothers who bring them breakfast and meet them from school every day? Fucking zero."

"Don't swear."

"Why not? You do."

"Yeah, and I just told you to be a better human."

"It's just a word."

"Nothing is just a word. It's about respect and understanding context. If you say that to a teacher, you'll get in trouble."

Gianna twisted the cap back on her bottle and shoved it in the pocket of the Superdry coat Benito had bought her last month. "I wouldn't say it to a teacher. I'm not stupid."

"That's what we all think. Then you normalise shit and it bleeds out of you before you can stop it."

"Don't swear."

"Very funny. Look, I'm trying to be responsible. Don't give me a hard time."

Gianna's expression softened. Her gaze drifted to the block and the windows of the flat she shared with their mother.

Benito didn't follow. He'd given up wondering if their mum had eyes on him. If she watched the daily exchanges between her children and gave a flying fuck that thanks to her, it was all they had. *I hate her.*

He didn't. But some days he wanted to.

"Beni."

"Hmm?" Benito returned to earth with a dull thud. Despite his best efforts, his gaze had drifted to the block. He brought it back to Gianna and braced himself for her sharp tongue. "Sorry. I was thinking about something else."

Gianna bit her lip and turned her head, hiding half her face in the long dark hair she'd straightened since Benito had laid eyes on her the night before, a classic tell that she was nervous.

Benito frowned and gripped her chin with gentle fingers. "What is it?"

"Nothing."

"Liar. Tell me. Are you in trouble at school?"

"You're obsessed with school."

"G."

"Okay, okay." Gianna shrugged free of Benito's hand. "I was just wondering if you were going to go and see Mum today, that's all. It's been ages and I hate that you two never talk."

"We talk," Benito lied. Again. "She knows how to reach me if you need anything."

"That's not the same as talking. You haven't been inside the flat since you moved back from London. How can you know—"

Gianna snapped her lips shut.

Benito raised a brow. "Know what?"

"*Nothing.*"

"It's not nothing if you're bringing it up now, and not every day in the last six months. What's changed?"

Gianna shook her head.

Frustration rippled through Benito, and he hated himself for it. It wasn't Gianna's fault he couldn't be in the same room as their mum without wanting to Hulk smash the furniture she'd bought with her new husband—Gianna's dad—at the expense of everything Benito had ever cared about. Everything his own father had worked for before his dead-end job had killed him. "What aren't you telling me?" he tried again. "Is Roberto back?"

"No."

"Sure about that? It's the only thing I can think of that you'd be afraid to tell me."

Gianna lifted her chin. "I'm not afraid."

"You can be, you know. You'd still be the strongest little fucker I've ever known."

"Don't swear." Gianna tried for a smile, but it was weak and wet.

Benito sighed and drew her into a tight hug. He hated a lot of things, but *nothing* more than seeing her upset. "Look, if it's that important to you, I'll go and see Mum soon, okay? And I'll do it when you're at school so you don't have to watch us fight."

Gianna shook her head. "Not soon. You have to go today. Promise me you will."

"I can't—"

"*Promise* me." Gianna gazed up at him. "Please. It has to be today."

Benito stared at her for a long moment, losing himself to the trust she'd placed in him since the day she'd been born. No one had ever owned his heart the way she did. There was nothing he wouldn't do for her. Not even this. "Okay. I'll go as soon as you get on the bus."

"You promise?"

"I swear down, G. On Sullivan's life, I'll go."

"Don't kill my cat."

"I won't. I love you."

Gianna nodded. "I love you too."

———

Benito pressed his forehead to the cold wood of the closed front door, drowning in silence. Still. After an hour of knocking and pleading. But he knew she was there, watching him through the peephole like she always did. "*Mum.* If you don't speak to me, I'll get Gianna to tell me everything. Don't put that on her. It's not fucking fair."

More silence. Benito exhaled with a loud whoosh and backed up, taking a seat on the top stair of the grotty landing. His eyes hurt, and his head pounded with stress and fatigue as if he'd been hit with a baseball bat. *I don't have time for this shit.*

But he did. He had to, or every moment of his life was for nothing.

He pulled out his phone. A message from Mickey lit up the screen. He forced himself to ignore it and called the same number he'd been calling all morning, but it didn't ring. Automated voicemail kicked in.

"Seriously?" Benito scrambled to his feet and banged on the door again. "You turned your phone off? What if Gianna's school needs to get hold of you? For fuck's sake."

Benito kicked the door hard enough to rattle the hinges. Regretted it and backed up again, but before he could reclaim his seat, the letterbox opened.

A brown envelope dropped to the floor, landing by his feet.

He scooped it up, noting the housing association logo, the same as the letterhead inside.

Jesus fuck. Benito unfolded the letter. It was dated two days ago and already wrinkled and stained with coffee rings and olive oil—a sure sign of defiance from the most house-proud woman he'd ever known. Half of it was illegible, but the first paragraph was unmarred.

I am writing to discuss your current rent arrears of £8787.43. As stated in previous communication, in person, over the phone, and by letter, it has been many months since you last made a payment on your account. No full payment has been made for more than a year.

DOSHA policy has always been to work closely with our residents to support them through any financial difficulties they may experience. However, we can only do this with open lines of communication. Considerable time has passed since I last managed to speak with you. My colleagues have also made multiple attempts to contact you.

It is with regret that I must inform you that if contact and a partial payment plan cannot be agreed by week ending—

The letter was too smudged to read the date, but the next line was bold and underlined.

*. . . **your account will be referred back to the council to begin eviction proceedings.***

Benito's heart thudded, a drumbeat that grew louder with every punch to his ribcage. *Eviction. Fuck.* It was a threat he'd lived under his entire childhood, but it wasn't supposed to be like that for Gianna. Benito had clawed his way out of this damn block to make sure of it. *He'd* paid the rent. For *years*. Odd jobs. Child benefit. Then street money. Every month until Gianna's father had moved in. And out. And in. Too many times to count.

Rage burned Benito's gut. He punched the door. Hard.

"Fuck it, Mum. Open the door or I'll break it down, I swear to god. Then the whole fucking world is coming in."

Blood split Benito's knuckles, seeping through broken skin, but the pain didn't calm him. Not even close. He pulled his hand back, but the door cracked open before he could deck it again. One inch, then two. Benito jammed his foot inside and shoved it the rest of the way.

Rosetta De Luca was already gone, vanished into the depths of the two-bed flat Benito had grown up in.

Benito kicked the door shut and strode through the living space to the kitchen. Rosetta was at the stove, messing with a vat of meat sauce that should've welcomed him home.

It didn't. The scent of it made him want to puke. "You haven't paid your fucking rent. They're going to evict you."

Rosetta inhaled a shaky breath and added chopped herbs to her pan. "That's not what it says. I have until the end of the week."

"It's Friday."

"Friday *morning*. There's still time."

"Time to do what? If you had the money, you'd have paid it already."

"I don't need to pay it all. Just some."

"So why haven't you? Have you cut your hours at work?"

More silence. Rosetta's back was as impenetrable as the shiny front door. Benito stepped closer, then reached around and pried the wooden spoon from her hand. "Turn around and face me."

"No."

"*Mum.* I can't help you if you won't talk to me."

"You don't want to help me!" Rosetta exploded. "You just don't want to worry about us anymore."

Benito rocked back. "What the hell? Of course I don't want to worry about you. I want you to be okay. Because I care. About Gianna, and you."

"You don't care about me."

"That's not true."

"Then where have you been for the last five years? You don't get to show up after all this time and tell me how to live my life, Benito. Not when you spent all those years telling me how badly I was doing it wrong."

Fresh anger surged in Benito's veins. He ground his teeth and took a breath. "I wasn't gone for five years. I was in London. It's not the fucking moon. And before that, what the fuck did you expect when you kept taking that arsehole back? You think I was going to stick around to get my head kicked in and keep my mouth shut?"

"You've never kept your mouth shut. That's your problem."

"My problem is you risking Gianna's home because you've given all your money to that dickstain to spunk down the bookies. Cos that's what's happened, isn't it?"

"*No.* I haven't seen Roberto in months. Gianna can tell you that."

"She's twelve. What the fuck does she know about what you get up to when she's at school? Like now. You're supposed to be at work, Ma. What gives?"

"Gianna knows I'm not at work anymore—I mean, she knows I'm not at work today."

Benito caught the slip as if Rosetta had punched him in the face. "Anymore? What does that mean? You lost your job?"

"I *left*."

"Why?"

"Because I couldn't do it!" Rosetta shouted again. "You don't understand."

Benito drove his fist into the fridge door. Another punch that went nowhere. "Then tell me! Don't act like I don't give a fuck. That's not fair."

Rosetta flinched. Benito hated himself and backed up, crashing into the kitchen table. The wood scraped the tiled floor with an obnoxious screech. A warning siren. *Calm the fuck down or you're no better than fucking Roberto.*

Benito sucked in a breath. "Look, I'm sorry, okay? I didn't mean to shout at you. I just—*fuck*. Why is it so damn hard to talk to you?"

"Because you hate me."

"I don't hate you."

"Yes, you do. You've hated me ever since I chose Roberto over you, and there's nothing I can do to change that."

It was the most honest thing Rosetta had said to him in years. Benito's head swam, but he knew her too well to fall for it. Deflection was her middle name. A trip down memory lane meant a pass on the present. *Fuck that.* "How long?" Benito ground out. "How long have you been out of work?"

"Since December."

"Last year?"

"Yes. I used the money you sent for Gianna for a while, but then you stopped paying it into my account."

A flash of guilt stabbed Benito's heart. "I had to stop putting money into your account. The feds were all over where I was at. I couldn't even bring cash around, but Gianna said you didn't need it. She never said you'd stopped working."

Rosetta sighed. "You should never have used that dirty drug money to pay our rent anyway. It could've got us evicted as much as this could."

"I know that now. But I was a fucking kid when I started and there was no way out."

"There's always a way."

"Oh yeah? So why are we here?" Benito held up the ruined letter from the housing association. "How have you been out of work for eleven months and not paying your rent if you have all the fucking answers?"

"I never said that." Rosetta snatched the letter with shaking hands and tore it to shreds. "Just that you didn't need to waste your life being a—a *criminal* when I raised you better than that."

"You didn't raise me at all," Benito refuted. "You—"

"Stop fighting."

Benito whirled around. Gianna stood in the kitchen doorway behind him, school bag in hand, tie loose around her neck as she clutched her precious orange cat to her chest. Her cheeks were flushed, as if she'd run all the way home. "The hell are you doing here?"

"I live here," she snapped.

Benito advanced on her, two long strides that brought him close enough to see the shivers wracking her slender frame. "You don't live here between eight and four on weekdays. Did something happen at school? Did they try and call Mum?"

"I wasn't sick." Gianna set Sullivan down and he scampered away. "I told them I had a dentist appointment and she didn't answer when they called to check."

Fresh fury corroded Benito's gut. He threw a dark glare at

Rosetta. "See? This is what your bullshit does. If Gianna was a different fucking kid, she could be on a county-lines run right now and you'd have no idea."

Rosetta shook her head. "Perhaps you should explain to Gianna why you know how that works. And don't lie. Roberto told me what you were doing in London, so don't pretend you have the moral high ground here. We *all* fail her, ometto."

Little man. Benito's glower reached nuclear levels. "Don't call me that. I'm not ten years old anymore and you stopped giving a shit about me way before that."

"*Stop it,*" Gianna wailed. "We don't have time for you two to do this. We need money, Beni. By five o'clock, or the housing association are going to tell the council to evict us."

Benito sucked in a hot breath. It seared his lungs and synapses, focusing him, but barely. He reached for Gianna and pulled her close, keeping his gaze on Rosetta. "How much will it take to calm this shit down?"

Rosetta shrugged. "I don't know."

"Because you haven't spoken to them." It wasn't a question.

And Rosetta didn't answer. She turned the stove off and left the kitchen, and with Gianna in his arms, Benito lacked the will to chase her.

He looked down. Gianna stared up at him, eyes wide with worry she was too young to know. "They need two thousand pounds," she whispered. "And this month's rent, *and* a payment plan for the rest of the arrears. The housing man told Mum through the letterbox."

"Two thousand?" Benito's stomach sank. He had ten times that buried in the fucking woods, but he couldn't touch it. Not for this. Rosetta was right: if it hadn't been laundered within an inch of its life, it was no help to anyone. "How much is the rent these days?"

"Four fifty."

Shit. Benito ran a hand through his hair. "I don't have it." The lie made him sick. "I can get some, but not that much, and I don't know how Ma can commit to a payment plan if she's not working anymore. Why didn't you tell me that, G?"

Gianna squeezed her arms around Benito's waist. "She said she was going back. Then she didn't and they sacked her, but she doesn't know I read the letter before she burned it in the sink."

More fury heated Benito's blood.

Gianna leaned back to fix him with a deeper stare. "Please don't be angry with her."

"I'm not."

"You are. I can feel your belly shaking."

Benito snorted. "No you can't."

"I can."

"No you can't. That's not a thing."

"It is with you, because you keep everything inside, like Mum does. That's why she doesn't go to work or let people in the flat, because she shakes all the time . . . because she's scared."

"Of what?"

"Of everything. She's agoraphobic."

"Says who?"

Gianna pushed away from Benito and wiped her eyes. "I don't know. Me? Why else would she be trapped inside like this? Beni, she hasn't been to the shops in months. We get everything delivered."

"How is she paying for it if she's not working?"

"Child benefit. And my dad's money when he remembers to pay it."

"He doesn't forget—" Benito stopped and rubbed his mouth. Did any of it even matter anymore? *Fix this. You promised her.* He took a slow breath and considered his options. Small amounts of cash were explainable as savings if the feds ever came knocking. He could get a bank loan for the rest. Maybe. But even as he thought it, the realist digging a grave on his soul shouted him down. *On what collateral? You're a taxi driver, fam. No one's gonna lend you shit.*

Benito pictured the mountain of money buried in the woods and felt sick to his stomach. What was the point in any of it if he couldn't do the one thing that mattered? If he couldn't take care of Gianna?

You bought her the iPad with clean money.

But an iPad didn't keep a roof over her head.

Or Rosetta's.

I don't hate her.

"Okay," Benito said. "I need to go to the bank. How much time do we have?"

"Until five o'clock. The housing man said we need to call him before then and make a payment over the phone."

"I can't do that, G. Anything I get is going to be cash."

"Maybe he'll come and get it then."

Benito doubted it. He'd never met any fat cat from the social who'd go out of their way like that. "Do you have his number? Mum tore up the letter."

"I have his card."

Gianna flitted from the room, leaving Benito alone with his thoughts. His brain thundered, emotions clattering into him from every angle. Rage. Fear. Sadness. Embarrassment that he was going to have to call this prick and beg for more time. He pulled his phone from his pocket and swiped the screen.

Nothing. "Dammit."

"What's wrong?" Gianna returned, clutching a crumpled business card.

Benito shook his head. "Phone's flat."

"Use your other one."

"I can't. It's for work."

"So? Why—"

"G. I can charge this one in the car while I get the cash. Can you call this dude and ask him to come over? He might say yes to you."

Gianna flattened the business card, already tapping the number into her phone. "He'd come if you asked him too. He's nice, I swear."

"Yeah, yeah." Benito made tracks to the front door. "I don't care if he's nice. Just that he shows up and takes this money from us without fucking us over for the rest of it."

"He won't fuck us over. He already told Mum he doesn't want us to leave."

"Good for him. Don't swear."

Benito backed up and kissed the top of Gianna's head, then he dashed from the flat and down to his car. Behind the wheel, he plugged his phone into the charger. It flashed to life as he started the engine, and he tapped into his banking app.

The online personal loan application took four minutes. The response came back in twenty-nine seconds.

Your credit application has been refused.

Fuck. A heavy weight settled in Benito's chest. He put the car in gear and gunned the engine.

He had a hole to dig, and somehow it felt symbolic.

Literal.

As if the only direction he'd ever go was down to the fucking bottom.

"You have to come. Please. My brother went out to get the money, but he can only get cash."

Mickey suppressed a sigh, eyeing the clock on the car dashboard. He was halfway to London for a meeting with Dom Ramos, his other boss at DOSHA Housing, heading in the opposite direction to Barnfield Court and Mrs De Luca's pleading daughter. "I'm not available for a home visit today. I can come on Monday if—"

"But you said it has to be today. Or our account would go back to the council."

Mickey didn't have the heart to tell her it probably already had. Isha was in that meeting *right now*, and Mickey had already told him the De Lucas had failed to make a payment. The five o'clock deadline was a formality. "Even if I can get there," he said gently, "there isn't much I can do with a handful of cash. You have to make the payment on your account. Is there a way you can do it online?"

"I don't know. It's my brother's money."

"What's your brother's name—"

The call ended, signal cut off in a black spot on the M1. Cursing, Mickey banged his fist on the steering wheel. He'd been hanging on for a sign from the De Lucas all damn day, and now it was too late. Isha hadn't wanted to hand their account over any more than Mickey, but his hands had been tied. *I'm sorry, Mickey. I can't compromise our relationship with the council when we have so many other families to worry about.*

Mickey had understood. He still did. But the guilt in his heart was heavy. His eyes burned and his chest hurt. *Fuck this.*

He pulled off the motorway into Toddington Services and called Dom Ramos. "I need to reach Isha," he said before Dom could speak. "The account he's passing back to the council has come through."

Paper rustled at the other end. Dom was less technologically inclined than Isha and worked out of a leather-bound notebook, a much-sharpened pencil tucked behind his ear. "Which account?"

"The De Lucas."

"At Barnfield Court?"

"Yeah. They had until five o'clock to make a payment, but I jumped the gun and told Isha they hadn't."

"Why?"

"Because they haven't reached out since this started and I let that cloud my judgement. It's my fault. I should've waited."

"But Isha knows they have until five?"

"I think so, unless he's forgotten."

"He won't forget," Dom said. "If they have until five, he won't give them up until Monday morning. It's why we schedule these meetings on a Friday. It gives us more time for shit like this. How much did they pay?"

"I don't know yet. They want me to go over and collect cash."

"So I can stop freaking out that I'm never going to make our meeting in time?"

"I'd say so. I'm about to turn my car round and burn in the opposite direction."

Dom's dry laugh filtered through the car speakers. "Of course you are. Okay, I'll ring Isha and let him know. He'll take my call in the meeting."

"That's what I thought, or I'd have called him myself. Sorry to bother you."

"You didn't. It's me that should be sorry you're facing the wrong direction for no good reason. But listen, Mickey?"

"Yeah?"

"I know it's hard," Dom said. "But you need to be clear headed about this. If you rock up there and they hand you fifty quid, it's not enough. They need to make a substantial payment *and* commit to a repayment plan on top of keeping up with the rent going forward. If they can't do that before Monday or give us a plausible reason why not, it's over for us."

Mickey breathed through his nose, long and slow. "Isha said two thousand. Can we budge on that if they don't have it all?"

"That's up to you."

"Since when?"

"Since now," Dom said. "I trust you to make a good decision. Just keep me posted, okay? So I can simmer Isha down if it goes tits up."

Another sigh escaped Mickey. Though Dom couldn't see him, he nodded. "I will. Thank you."

"No sweat. Drive safe."

Dom hung up. For a moment, Mickey was frozen in place, then his gaze fell on the time: Three o'clock. *Fuck.* If he had any chance of hitting the bank with the De Luca cash before closing time, he had to *go*.

He tapped in a call to the number Mrs De Luca's daughter had called him from. It rang and rang as he drove out of the service station and around the roundabout to the north-bound junction until it eventually clicked into voicemail, and Mickey considered the possibility that he was wasting his time. That he'd get back to Bletchley to face a closed front door and the fact that nothing had changed. But he had to try. He'd be lying if he said he hadn't lost sleep over the De Luca case. Only fantasising about Benito had kept him from climbing the walls.

Unbidden, heat rippled through Mickey as he rejoined the motorway traffic. *Stop it. You don't have time to think about that right now.* But as committed as he was to helping the De Luca family keep their home, pushing Benito out of his mind was impossible. His dark eyes. His soft hair.

His addictive inked skin and cut body.

Even his rough voice made Mickey shiver. *I wanna see him.*

And maybe not just to fuck. Benito's company was . . . intriguing. Mickey had replayed every moment they'd spent together more times than he cared to admit, but was nowhere near close to cataloguing it all. Each time, something else gave him pause.

Each time, he was left wanting more. *Craving* it harder than the devil in his veins craved blood.

And he'd articulated it in the worst text message in the history of text messages. He'd wanted to die when he'd read it back the next morning. *hopefly. mbe the wek after if wrk stays crezy*. Damn. He might as well have sent hieroglyphics. Maybe Benito thought so too. Either way, he hadn't replied.

Mickey's Ford Focus ate up the miles. He ditched the motorway at junction thirteen and drove into Bletchley.

Barnfield Court loomed in the distance. The sight of it made his stomach clench. Always did. As tower blocks went, it was far from the worst Mickey had known in this life and the one he tried to forget, but there was something about this one, an ominous fog he couldn't shake.

He parked outside and jogged up the grimy stairs to the De Luca flat.

The daughter was sitting on the landing, her back to the shiny front door, face drawn and tear-streaked. "You came."

"I did." Mickey crouched to her level, keeping his distance. "If someone had answered the phone when I called back, I'd have told them."

"That was my phone. I'm not allowed to answer private numbers."

"Fair enough. That's a good rule. Is your brother here?"

"He went to get the money."

"Where from?"

"I don't know."

"What about your mum? Will she talk to me? Even if your brother makes a payment today, she still needs to agree to a recovery plan."

The girl's eyes reddened. "She's in her bedroom. She won't come out. You have to speak to my brother."

"I can do that. Do you know how long he's going to be?"

"No."

"Okay." Mickey sat back on his heels, considering his

options. The landing was cold and draughty and no place for a kid to be hanging out with him—an adult she barely knew. "Look, I said you could have until five, so I'm going to wait until then for your brother to come back, but you need to go inside and wait with your mum, all right? Where it's safe and warm."

"It's safe out here."

"I'd feel better if you went inside."

"I don't want to."

Mickey sighed. "Okay. Well, at least tell me your name—"

"It's Gianna."

"All right, *Gianna*. Go tell your mum I'm here, so she can decide if she wants you hanging out on the landing with me."

"She won't care."

"Tell her anyway."

Rolling her eyes, Gianna stood and unlocked the front door. She pushed it open, giving Mickey his first glimpse of the De Luca flat in months. The narrow gap gifted him the perfect view of clean white walls and spotless floors, and he breathed a subtle sigh of relief. Inspecting the property was next on his list after securing the rent, but he'd put off forcing the issue for months, trusting his gut that Mrs De Luca was as house-proud as she'd always been, even if she allowed no one to see her home. If he was wrong about everything else, at least he'd called that right.

Stifling a sigh, Mickey scooted to the top step of the landing and leant against the metal banister. Truth be told, he wasn't that sad about dodging a trip to London and back before his work week could end, but he was tired, his brain more than his body, and his monthly sit-downs with Dom always set him straight again. Dom was softer than Isha, and it made Mickey feel better about his own bleeding heart. *Am I fucking this up?*

"I brought you coffee."

Mickey blinked. Gianna had returned with a steaming mug of black coffee. He cupped his hands around it and took a deep sniff. "Wow. Thanks. You didn't have to do that. Did you tell your mum I was here?"

"She's asleep. I think she took some of her tablets."

"Some?"

"Two. That's the dose."

"What tablets are they?"

"I don't know. She says they're for her nerves, but she hasn't been to the doctor since last year. I googled the name, but I can't remember what it said."

Mickey absorbed that, filing it away for investigation later. The council would be easier to negotiate with if he could plead a mental health issue, but he could only do that with Mrs De Luca's permission. Which meant talking to her, something he'd failed spectacularly at for so long it had come to camping out on the landing with a young child. "Is there anything else?" he pressed carefully. "Anything that would help your mum for me to know? If she's unwell, perhaps her GP could write her a letter?"

"I already told you she won't go to the doctor." Gianna flashed him a scowl that could make grown men cry. "You need to talk to my brother."

"Could you maybe call him? Ask him how long he'll be?"

"I did. He didn't answer. Maybe he's driving."

Mickey let it go and sat back against the banister again, sipping the rocket-fuel coffee Gianna had brought him. The caffeine bulldozed the fog from his brain, leaving jittery fingers in its place. He scrolled through his phone to keep them busy, scanning the news and Spotify playlists. Trying to build his own gave him a different kind of headache, but it was something to do.

Gianna sat by her front door, guarding and glaring. She was fierce, a lioness. In different circumstances, Mickey might've smiled, but there was no humour here. Not until her mythical brother made an appearance with enough cash to send Mickey away.

How much is enough?

Thirty minutes later, when footsteps finally sounded on the stairs below, he still had no idea.

Gianna scrambled to her feet and dashed to the banister, leaning so far over Mickey was scared she'd fall.

"Whoa." Mickey stood too. "Don't do that. We'll see soon enough if it's him."

Gianna ignored him and ducked under his outstretched arm to pelt down the stairs. Bemused, Mickey followed, keeping tabs on her dark hair as she flew to the next landing.

He heard the impact of her body hitting another before he saw the tall figure she'd collided with.

Gianna locked her slender arms around the man's neck. He was wearing Yeezy trainers and Nike sweatpants. He had strong arms, tattooed skin, and dark hair, just like his sister. And the familiarity was more than that. More than the disbelief and incredulity. More than the leaden, painful scrape of Mickey's heart as Gianna's brother set her on her feet and raised his gaze.

No. It can't be. But as molten eyes found Mickey's, hooded with the flat kind of despair that came with whatever mountain he'd climbed to get here, there was no mistaking the chiselled, unshaven jaw Mickey had committed to memory. The high cheekbones and killer shoulders. The bewildered scowl that cut Mickey to the bone.

Fuck. Mickey marbleised, frozen in place, gaze flitting between Benito's stricken confusion and the muddy envelope clutched in his hand. *Did he get that from a fucking swamp?* It made as much sense as Benito's sudden presence in the stairwell.

A thudding beat of silence drowned them, closing in the grimy walls. Benito's free hand curled slowly into a fist. Chaos reached his dark stare, matching the riot in Mickey's brain. He drew back from Gianna and pulled her behind him, lips curling into a sneer. "Gonna ask you this once, then it's fucking *on*. The *fuck* are you doing here, man?"

Mickey blinked, his sparkling eyes darting between Benito and where Gianna had stood a split second ago. "Me? I'm at work, *man*. What are *you* doing here?"

Work. Benito zeroed in on the ID hanging around Mickey's neck, nestled against his chest.

His *cut* chest, with the pale skin and messy scrawled ink.

Two worlds collided.

Benito shook his head, blood roaring in his ears. Emotions—too many to count—battering every sense. *This isn't real.* It couldn't be. For as much as he'd spent the last few days wishing Mickey would magically appear in front of him, that kind of shit didn't fucking happen. There was no logical reason for Mickey to be on the stairs of Barnfield Court flats. No reason at all.

I've imagined him. Jesus fuck. *I'm losing my mind.*

As the seconds ticked by, it was the most rational explanation Benito could think of.

The alternative was Mickey had been fucking with his family the whole time he'd been tapping Benito for sex. The club. At his house. Rosetta had been in debt for months. *How did he find me? Did Asa send him?*

"Beni?" Gianna struggled against Benito's death grip on her. "Let me go."

No. But if he was having a psychotic breakdown, Gianna needed to be as far from him as possible.

He let her go.

Gianna darted in front of him. She ran towards the figment of Benito's imagination and jumped up and down in front of him. "See? I told you he'd come. He's got the money. Tell him, Beni. Tell him you've got the money."

Mickey blinked and seemed to reanimate. His sandy brows raised, disbelief colouring his handsome features. "You're her brother?"

"I am," Benito ground out. "And I already fucking asked you who the fuck you are, so you'd better start talking."

"You asked me what I was doing here," Mickey retorted. "Not who I was."

Benito felt like he was underwater. His hands and arms ached from digging, and the hour of sleep he'd snatched was nowhere near enough to keep his head from spinning off his shoulders. He was frozen, body and mind.

Couldn't think.

Couldn't speak.

Gianna came back to him and pried the mud-stained envelope from his hand. She opened it and her eyes bugged out at the thick stack of notes stuffed inside. "How much is here?"

Benito shook his head. The smell of the wet earth was still lodged in his nose, but somehow, he couldn't remember.

Gianna handed the envelope to Mickey. "Take it. Tell them we paid."

Mickey said nothing. Gianna glanced back at Benito and seemed to notice for the first time the tension straining the air. Tension that had nothing to do with the money changing hands and everything to do with the words she'd missed while fixated on the envelope. "Wait. Do you two know each other? How?"

Mickey opened his mouth.

"From the gym," Benito blurted before Mickey could speak. "He's a prick who hogs the weight benches. Fucking figures now."

Mickey's gaze flickered, stormy. He schooled his features and inclined his head to Gianna. "Whatever I am, your little sister is better off inside, don't you think?"

Benito's brain engaged. He gripped Gianna's shoulders again and guided her upstairs, feeling the heat of Mickey behind him, following.

He's got my money.

More unnamed emotions spun Benito's head. More fury too. At himself. At Rosetta. At Mickey for slamming together two parts of his life he'd never imagined entwining. He could count their encounters on one hand. Half a fucking hand. But somehow he'd spent the last few weeks relying on them—and the promise of more—to keep him grounded. To keep him fucking *breathing*. Now it was gone. All of it. And he couldn't comprehend why.

They reached the landing. Gianna slipped inside. Benito shut the door behind her and turned to face Mickey, blocking him from the flat. "You can't come in."

"I know." Mickey's brows cinched. "We can do this out here."

"Do what?"

Mickey waved the envelope. "What we both came here for. How much is in here?"

"Two grand, give or take."

"Where did you get it?"

"What's that got to do with anything?"

"Everything." Mickey gave Benito an unsubtle once-over. "Especially as you have two phones stuffed in your pockets and this cash doesn't look like it came from a bank."

A breeze block took up residence in Benito's throat. *You're a fucking idiot. You brought too much.* But as Mickey's flinty gaze pierced holes in him, it dawned on him that it wouldn't have mattered. *He sees me.* Benito didn't know what that meant or why it mattered, but the realisation winded him all the same. "Who are you?"

"I'm your mum's housing officer at DOSHA, Benito. What part of that aren't you getting?"

"For how long?"

"A year. Maybe more. I haven't talked to her in a while, though. And I only met your sister a few days ago."

Mickey's stare remained fixed on Benito's pockets before he seemed to shake himself. He folded his arms, still clutching Benito's envelope, and leaned against the banister railing.

Benito took in his clothes, not that different from the shirt and jeans he'd worn to Freefall and yet a world away from the low slung pjs he'd answered the door in two days ago. *Two days.* Damn. It felt like a lifetime. Or a fucking fever dream. "I didn't know. About any of it. I'd have fixed it if I had."

"Which still begs the question, how? Not being funny, mate, but they've never mentioned you. Like, at all. I didn't know you existed until your sister carjacked me."

"She did what?"

"Came up on me on the Lakes Estate and banged on my car window. Scared the shit out of me, but I can't fault her initiative."

A reluctant smirk twisted Benito's lips. "Sorry about that."

"Don't be. Just tell her not to do it to anyone else. It's a snake pit out there."

"You think I don't know that?"

"I don't know what to think. My brain's in bits right now." Mickey's voice roughened on the last few words. He let his arms drop and shook his head. "This is fucking mad."

Benito sucked in a shaky breath. "True that. I'm having a hard time believing it's a coincidence."

"You think I came onto you in a sex club with the purpose of rinsing your savings to pay your mum's rent arrears?" Disbelief coloured Mickey's face again. "That's more ridiculous than what's actually happened here."

"And what's that?"

"Exactly what you said. A coincidence. And believe me, it's as fucked up for me as it is for you. There's a reason I party at a club two hours from where I work."

Benito's mind raced, grasping at fragmented threads, trying to piece them together. But he was *tired*, running on empty. He couldn't keep up. "This needs to end," he said. "Whatever it is, it needs to stop."

"Which part?"

"All of it."

Mickey nodded. "Forget about you and me." He held up the envelope. "Wherever *this* came from, it's not enough on its own. I can negotiate down from the two thousand we asked for, but without a payment plan for the rest and a commitment to make full rent from this point on, it doesn't mean anything."

"I can pay all that."

"With what? Loan shark money? Cash from the road?"

"What?"

Mickey turned his gaze briefly to the ceiling and huffed out a breath. "Can we cut the shit? I'm not an idiot. And I've lived that motherfucking life. I know what dirty money looks like and what you've done to get it, and I'm telling you right now that you can't use it to dig your mum out of this. It can't happen that way."

I've lived that motherfucking life. The coarse words stood out more than the rest, hooking claws into Benito's heart that he couldn't comprehend. "I don't know what you're talking about. I'm a taxi driver. Check my car for my Uber ID."

"Uber doesn't pay in rolled up bank notes."

"How do you know?"

"Because it's not a cash business, bro."

"Don't call me bro. We're not friends."

Mickey snorted out a bitter laugh. "Trust me, it's better than what I want to call you right now."

"Fuck you."

"No thanks. We're done with that."

Benito flinched. He leaned back against the closed front door, recoiling from the impact that felt worse than if Mickey had hit him. The nausea he'd brought home that morning reignited, and for a horrifying moment, he thought he might puke. *Don't look at him.* But it was like asking a river to stop flowing. Benito was as drawn to Mickey as he'd always been, and he couldn't look away.

Long seconds passed. Heavy moments cloaked in a dread Benito couldn't stomach. He was drowning under the weight of Mickey's stare. Suffocating. "You don't know me," he whispered.

Mickey's face softened. "I know, man. I'm trying to do the right thing here, for everyone. Not just your mum."

"Why?"

"Because it's my job. I want this resolved as much as you do. It's gone on way too long."

Benito choked on his own bitter laugh. "For you, maybe. I already told you I didn't know about it until today."

"For real?"

"For real. My mum poked your letter through the letterbox at me this morning."

"Did you read it?"

"I tried. Couldn't make most of it out."

Mickey winced. "That bad? I got my boss to read it before I brought it here."

Benito eyed Mickey's suddenly stricken expression. Watched it deepen and then pass, as if it had never been there at all. "My mum spilt oil and coffee all over it, like she thinks that deletes it from the matrix."

"Oh."

"What did you think I meant?"

"Nothing."

Liar. Benito let his gaze pass over Mickey again, lingering this time from his boots, to his jeans, to the navy-blue shirt he wore. And then his hands. Benito stared and pictured them as he'd last seen them, pressed against his own skin, rough and hot. Recalled Mickey's dirty moan as they'd kissed against his front door, and then his hazy smile when they'd parted ways two blood-heating orgasms later. Benito had fixated on it for days. Dreamt of it.

We're done with that.

Fuck.

Losing it to Rosetta's bullshit felt like a slow death.

"How involved are you with this?" Mickey said. The interjection felt sudden. Invasive. But it wasn't. It was a fair question.

Benito willed his shoulders to relax and his hands to uncurl from fists, but he couldn't make it happen. His body was a live wire of painful tension. And he still wanted to throw up. "Are you asking me if this is a one-time thing?"

"You showing up with an envelope of dirty cash? Yeah, I guess. And I'm trying to figure out if you're the person I need to discuss a payment plan with and your mum's ability to make the rent going forward."

"What if I'm not?"

Mickey breathed slowly through his nose. "Then I'm out of options. Your mum won't talk to me. I've been trying for months."

"And that's your job, right? At the housing association?"

"I'm a housing officer at DOSHA."

Benito forced himself to look at Mickey. "You didn't seem like one. In the club . . ."

"We can't talk about that here."

"Why not? You don't want anyone to know you—"

Mickey pushed off the railing, in Benito's face before either of them could blink. "*Stop.*"

"Why?"

"Because you don't get to do that. I don't care who knows shit about me, but you don't get to make this about that when all I'm trying to do is my fucking job. I didn't ask you to be here."

Benito lost himself in Mickey's hard gaze. Absorbed the angry tremors as he stared Benito down. They'd been this close before. More than once. But those moments had been fantasy come to life. Not the real world with its ugliness. "I didn't know," Benito whispered. "About any of it—the debt, my mum losing her job. And I didn't know about you, I fucking swear, man. I had no idea."

"I know you didn't," Mickey said. "That's not what I'm saying."

Benito knew that, but he couldn't shake the fear that everything that had brought them to this point was an elaborate conspiracy. *Karma's a bitch, right?* More than that, it was a certainty, and if life had taught Benito anything, it was that there was always further to fall.

"Hey." Mickey leaned in further, crowding Benito even more, his chest so close Benito imagined his heartbeat thudding against his ribs. "Stay with me."

A hysterical laugh bubbled in Benito's throat. "I didn't go anywhere."

Mickey tilted his head. "Sure about that? You look like you're about to puke.

Benito couldn't deny it. Barnfield always left him claustrophobic, but right now, the walls were closing in on him. He couldn't breathe. Couldn't think. Could only drown in Mickey's broad shoulders and hot glare and wonder what the fuck his life had become.

Mickey backed off.

Benito shook his head. *Don't go*. But he couldn't find the words. His brain was scorched earth, stripped bare of coherent thought.

"We're out of time," Mickey said quietly. "I can't get this cash paid in tonight or register the payment. The office is closed."

"What?"

"It's after five."

"But—"

Mickey held his hand up. "Don't panic. I can send an email to my boss—he'll pick it up and place a hold on the account. But I'll still need to negotiate down from two thousand and get his agreement on a payment plan."

"Can you do that?"

"I can try. You said your mum lost her job. We don't have that on record. Is she receiving UC?"

"UC?"

"Universal Credit. It replaced income support and housing benefit a while ago."

"I know what it is," Benito snapped, willing his brain to catch up.

"And?" Mickey spread his hands. "Come on, mate. I know this is shit, but right now, I'm all your family have, so work with me, yeah? Then hopefully you'll never see me again."

Benito slid down the wall. He rested his elbows on his bent knees.

Mickey crouched in front of him. "Talk to me."

"I don't know anything."

"Okay. What about your mum? Is there a medical condition that's making her act like this? A mental health issue?"

"Fuck. Agoraphobia, maybe? I don't *know*."

Mickey sighed.

Benito waited for him to stand and walk away, taking the money and *everything* else with him.

Mickey sat back, crossed his legs in front of him, and pulled out his phone. He swiped the screen and started typing, a harsh frown creasing his forehead.

Benito watched, transfixed by the frown line, itching to smooth it away. The impulse was strange, but he welcomed it, bathed in it as it gave him room to breathe.

His heart slowed and his hands stopped tingling. Sensation returned to his toes and he wondered if he'd been holding his breath from the moment he'd looked up to see Mickey on the stairs in front of him.

It felt that way.

Mickey swore, still scowling at his phone. His frown deepened, and his thumb taps grew louder.

Frustration seeped from him.

In spite of himself, Benito leaned forward. "What's the matter? Did your boss say no?"

Mickey shook his head. "I haven't got that far yet. This is a *me* problem, don't worry about it."

"What kind of problem?"

Mickey said nothing, still tapping. Then he closed his eyes and expelled an angry whoosh of air. "I'm not good at spontaneous composition. As in, I'm shit at writing. It takes me too long to get the words out in the right order, especially if I don't have much time to do it."

"You're dyslexic?"

"Yup. Like a motherfucker. Shit, sorry. I'm not supposed to swear at work."

Benito started to smile, then reality kicked him in the dick and he changed his mind. Mickey's work was Benito's clusterfuck of a life, and there was nothing funny about that. "Gianna's dyslexic. She writes all her numbers backwards."

Mickey grunted. "Sounds familiar. I'm okay with numbers, though. And reading. It's just when it comes to putting my own words into something legible that I lose the fucking plot—"

He stopped and shook his head. At the TMI or the swearing, Benito couldn't tell.

Mickey went back to his phone. He finished whatever he was doing and held it out to Benito. "I need you to check it before I send it. My boss knows me well enough to look past the bad grammar and weird spelling, but I need it to be clear so he can do what I need him to do."

"What makes you think I can write any better than you?"

"Most people can. Please? We need this to reach Isha before he checks out for the night. He usually responds to emails all weekend, but I can't rely on that."

Benito took the phone and scanned the email Mickey had hammered out. He was right about the weird spelling, and his text messages now made sense—as in, Benito understood why they sometimes made no sense at all. "Can I change stuff?"

"Show me?"

Benito scrambled to his knees and pointed at the screen. "This part would be clearer if it came before what you say right here." He dragged his fingertip from the middle of the email to the top. "And these words are the wrong way round."

Mickey nodded. "I can see that now. Can you change it for me?"

Benito made the edits and passed the phone back. Mickey frowned at it again, then hit Send.

"What happens next?" Benito asked.

"I'll wait for him to call me back," Mickey said. "In the meantime, we need a plan. I can't stress that enough, man. My bosses are good people and they like me, but they can't go in to bat for me if I don't give them anything to work with."

"Does that mean you're on our side?"

Mickey rolled his eyes halfway round the world and back. "Dude. I always was."

9

It was the longest day in the world. Mickey was shaking by the time he got home. Or perhaps he had been all along.

He shut his front door and leaned against it, closing his eyes. It was too easy to recall how Benito had pushed against him just days ago, smothering him with rough kisses and bruising hands. It was far harder to stay in those stolen moments and avoid the monumental mess his day had become.

I need a fucking beer. Mickey didn't move, though. His feet felt glued to the floor. *Shit, shit, shit.* How the hell had this happened? His mind flashed to the night he'd met Benito, to the moment he'd spotted him sitting alone at the bar in Freefall, and every microsecond they'd shared since, searching for clues—for *anything*—that could've led them here. But he found nothing. Benito had been Mickey's wildest wet dream come to life, and now he was the estranged son of Mickey's most difficult tenant, and almost certainly up to his neck in the kind of bullshit that still gave Mickey panic attacks.

You don't know that. He might not be a road boy.

But common sense said otherwise. Benito had offered no explanation for the pile of cash he'd showed up with or the extra phone stuffed in his pocket. A phone that three years ago, on another estate, in another city, could've been Mickey's. *Fuck*, he could almost smell his old life—the close city air, the permanent scent of dirty money on his fingers.

The white powder blocking his nose.

His fingers trembled. His jaw. Even his eyeballs felt unstable.

Mickey shook his head to clear it, but the voice in his head wouldn't stop. *Just one line. It'll calm you down. Come on. Even round here, you know where to get it.*

Fucking hell.

Mickey pushed off the door and meandered to the kitchen on heavy legs that didn't match the renewed riot going on in the rest of him. He opened the fridge and reached for a beer, then changed his mind and moved to the kettle instead. Alcohol wasn't on his list of vices, but using it as a crutch was a sure-fire way to put it there.

Fuck my life.

Mickey boiled the kettle and made tea. Then he retreated to the couch to try and make sense of the notes he'd made for Rosetta De Luca's payment plan.

It was easier than he'd feared, given that Benito had typed most of them, slouched down on the landing of Barnfield Court, his full bottom lip caught between his teeth. Mickey had left him the Universal Credit forms to fill out for his mother and advised him to get a letter from her GP, but Benito hadn't seemed hopeful about communicating with her any better than Mickey had recently.

Such a fucking mess.

And that was without considering the fact that Mickey had fucked her son six ways from Sunday in a sex club *and* upstairs on his bed. *Jesus fucking Christ.*

Mickey's hands *wouldn't* stop shaking. Cravings made his head spin, but he wanted more than a line of grainy coke. He wanted to go back to the world he'd woken up to—the one where his sex life and his *real* life were separate and the heat blooming in his groin was a safe place to be.

He wanted Benito.

He hated how they'd left things.

"I'm going to send all this to Isha in the morning. Hopefully by Monday, we'll have something in place the council will accept."

Benito was hard to read as Mickey reclaimed his phone and stood. He rose slowly, as if his spine was locked solid, and resumed his lean against the wall. "Is Isha the big boss you have to convince?"

"One of them. Dom's not so bad, but he's harder to get hold of at weekends. Isha is our best shot."

"And if it works, you never have to see me again, right?"

Mickey forced himself to meet Benito's dark gaze. "That's the plan. Once your mum's on track, I'm going to ask him to assign Barnfield to another HO."

"Why not before?"

Unwilling to admit that no other housing officer would be willing to spend their Friday evening camped on a grimy stairwell fudging through emails, Mickey said nothing.

As though he knew, Benito made a low noise, then silence cloaked them.

Mickey felt it like an incoming storm. Benito's dishevelled hair taunted him. He wanted to run his fingers through it and tug

Benito into the kind of hug that never truly ended, but he couldn't, for too many reasons to count. Aside from the obvious, mainly because it'd be weird as fuck. Their relationship was sexual. They weren't friends or even acquaintances. Just blokes who'd hooked up once upon a time in a world where no one had jobs or mothers or whatever else was going on in Benito's life right now.

As the thought completed, a phone buzzed. Not Mickey's, and not the first one Benito fished from his pocket.

Coldness settled over Mickey's heart, hesitant and fragile, but he clung to it with both hands, smothering the flickers of affection he'd felt for Benito since they'd met. After today, they were done. They couldn't see each other again.

They *couldn't*.

In any capacity.

Benito didn't reach for his other phone. He tucked the Universal Credit forms under his arm and leaned harder against the wall. "How do I make the payments for the plan you're setting up?"

"Your mum has a payment card. I can arrange for another one to be sent to you if she requests it, or you can do it online."

"The card is better."

Of course it was. With the payment card, Benito could take cash into any shop with pay-point facilities, no questions asked.

Mickey's gut churned, every instinct he had screaming at him to get as far from this case as possible so he wouldn't need to know where Benito's money was coming from. But his conscience and . . . something else had him nodding and making a note to order the payment card. "I'm leaving," he said.

Benito didn't blink. Or speak.

Mickey zeroed in on his lips, then his set, unshaven jaw and sharp cheekbones—anywhere but his quicksand gaze—but wher-

ever he looked, there were no answers to be found. He had to go.
"You need to lose my number."

Benito nodded. "I know."

"After this is sorted, I mean."

"Whatever, man."

"I'm not the fucking enemy here."

Benito laughed, no humour, just a brittle sound that scraped
Mickey's soul.

Nothing else.

Mickey had left after that. And now here he was, alone in his kitchen, rehashing every moment, all the while eyeing the microwave where he'd hidden Benito's cash until he could take it to the bank in the morning. *Genius.*

Tea in hand, Mickey flicked the TV on. Netflix filled the screen with the synopsis for *Top Boy*. The irony was fucking biblical, though Mickey couldn't put his finger on the specifics. How could he when he knew nothing *specific* about Benito except how to make him come and that his mother hadn't left her flat for six months?

Stop thinking about him.

Nope. Wasn't happening.

Mickey lay down on the couch and closed his eyes, digging deep for the tools he'd learned over the years to force his muscles to relax, joint by joint, nerve by nerve. At some point, he'd have to go to the gym and punish his body into submission, but not tonight. Leaving the house right now was a risk too heavy to bear. *Just breathe, man. If you can do that, you can do anything.*

Wise words Mickey had almost forgotten, but they still meant something.

Eventually, the itch in his veins died down to the low

simmer he could happily ignore. He drank his tea, then switched to water as he read through Isha's replies to his emails. Without Benito scowling over his shoulder, constructing an intelligent response felt impossible, so he took a chance and made a call.

Isha answered on the third ring, breathless.

"Sorry it's late," Mickey said. "Am I interrupting you?"

Isha laughed. "Rescuing me, more like. My daughter wants me to watch *The Next Step* with her."

"The what?"

"If you don't know, you lead a blessed life. What do you need, Mickey?"

"I just wanted to talk about the De Luca case, and I figured it would be quicker to do it over the phone than bombard you with emails all weekend."

"It's only bombarding me if I chose to look, and that's my decision."

"Yeah, but—"

"No buts. I'm here for you. Tell me what you need."

Mickey didn't know what he needed. Just that the only way out of the hole he'd dug with Benito was to secure his mother's account as quickly as possible. "I need the council to agree to a payment plan of three hundred pounds a month and to hold the arrears until the UC claim goes through."

"That could take weeks."

"I know."

Isha let a pause draw out between them, but it was contemplative, not combative. "We can sponsor any missed rent payments while we wait for UC," he said eventually. "It also sounds to me as if the mother could be entitled to a PIP allowance if her agoraphobia can be diagnosed."

Personal Independence Payment. Damn. In his Benito-fuelled daze, Mickey had forgotten that. "I don't know if she's seen a GP. Not likely if she won't leave the house."

"Can you find out? Maybe a GP can visit her at home?"

Fresh anxiety blanketed Mickey. He nodded, then remembered Isha couldn't see him. "I can talk to the son again. Maybe. I don't know."

"Do you have his contact details? I can—"

"I have them. It's okay. I'll call him."

"Sure? Because this case seems to be getting to you a bit. Is there anything else I should know?"

This was it—the window to break down and tell Isha everything. He was good and kind and understanding. He wasn't the kind of boss who'd throw Mickey under the bus, but the harder Mickey tried to form the words, the more his throat closed up.

He took a breath. "It's fine . . . it's just hard to know I'm making the right decisions when I can't get Mrs De Luca to talk to me."

"But her daughter trusted you enough to track you down, and her son showed up and bailed her out. If you hadn't persisted with her, none of that would've happened and her account would've gone back to the council months ago."

"I know, but . . ." Mickey sighed. "I just feel like I should've known sooner that she had a mental health issue. This whole mess could've been avoided if we'd helped her claim UC earlier."

"You can only know what tenants are prepared to share with you. We're a charitable trust, but we're not social work-ers. In fact, that's another call we need to make if you're worried about the daughter. How did she look to you?"

"Okay, actually," Mickey said absently, mind half on the Universal Credit forms he'd passed Benito. "I think there's a father out there somewhere who makes sporadic maintenance payments, and Benito—the son—gives them money too. I don't know how much or how regularly. We didn't get into it."

"What's he like? Does he work?"

"Uber driver."

"Full-time?"

Mickey pinched the bridge of his nose. "I don't know."

"Okay, well, talk to him again. See if he can help his mother get some assistance from her GP. If not, speaking to social services *is* an option—"

"No. I'm not doing that."

Silence. Then it was Isha's turn to sigh. "All right. I hear you. Talk to the son on Monday and get back to me when you can. In the meantime, I'll hold the account while we wait for UC. *But* . . . all of this hinges on the repayment plan. The council won't give us an inch if the arrears aren't being repaid."

"I think the son will pay the three hundred pounds a month if we can swing it."

"They're going to ask for more."

"They can't have more. She's been out of work for months when she should've been claiming UC. If they won't let it go, that's on me."

"On *us*. Let me deal with the council. Something tells me you'll get us in worse trouble if you speak to them right now."

He was more right than he probably knew. Mickey said his goodbyes and ended the call. Then he collapsed on the couch again, spent but too wired to shut down. *"Talk to the son on Monday . . ."*

As if Mickey could wait that long.

———

Mickey: *u hve a fob for powr Fitness*

Benito stared at the message. It was six in the morning, twelve hours since Mickey had walked out of Barnfield Court, and he'd just about resigned himself to never seeing him again, at least not in the capacity he wanted to.

He was also parked outside the gym with the key fob in question *literally in his hands.*

What the hell was life right now?

Benito: *Yeah. I do. Why?*

Mickey: *theres 1 in newport pagnell. meat me there?*

Benito: *Again . . . why?*

Mickey: *to talk*

Benito: *About?*

Mickey didn't answer straight away. Benito drummed his fingers on the steering wheel. His body was tired from the hour-long workout he'd just put in, but his brain had been full of Mickey even before the message had chimed in. Never once had he pictured *this* moment, though. *He wants to meet.*

It felt like a cruel trick.

Benito caved and sent another message.

Benito: *When?*

Mickey: *6 am 2morw*

Damn. Twenty-four hours. Could he wait that long? Benito honestly wasn't sure, but he sent his response all the same.

Benito: *I'll be there*

Mickey went offline. Benito wondered if he'd just got up, or if he was on his way to bed. Before yesterday, he'd pegged Mickey for a night owl, not a suit who worked for the social.

He wasn't wearing a suit, and the housing association has nothing to do with social services.

But still. The Mickey that Benito had concocted in his head had existed on the other side of the divide. On *Benito's* side. They'd met twice and had even fewer real conversations, but the common ground had felt so real Benito hadn't stopped to contemplate that it wasn't. That his interpretation of Mickey had been just that—another fucking fantasy, and this time, it hadn't come true.

Benito drove home via the supermarket and picked up a week's worth of groceries for Rosetta and Gianna. Rosetta's peasant-style cooking meant they didn't need much, but he still felt sick when he thought of all the things they'd managed without all this time. He bought extra chocolate for Gianna and the expensive espresso beans Rosetta liked; then he steered the car towards Barnfield Court and tried to accept the cloud of doom that settled over him.

I hate this place.

The exterior door had been vandalised overnight. The glass was smashed and the lock nowhere to be seen.

Benito stepped over the mess and jogged upstairs. Praying Rosetta was still asleep, he let himself into the flat with the key Gianna had given him the night before.

Silence greeted him. Benito set the shopping bags down in the hall and tiptoed to Gianna's room. Her door was open, and she was curled beneath the purple sheets he'd bought her a few months back, fast asleep with one hand on the orange cat and her cheek on her phone.

Under Sullivan's watchful gaze, Benito crept closer and plucked the phone free. He set it on the chest of drawers with the chocolate and backed up, shutting her door behind him.

"What are you doing here?" Rosetta stepped out of the shadows, a robe clutched tight around her, face pale, eyes wide, a kitchen knife in her hand. "I thought you were a burglar."

Benito rolled his eyes. "What would I be stealing? You don't have jack shit in this place."

"Your sister is here."

"Yeah, well. Anyone kidnapped her, they'd soon bring her back."

"I used to say that about you when you were little."

"I know. That's why I said it." Benito pointed to the bags by the front door. "I brought you some stuff. Text me if you need anything else."

"What did the man from the housing association say?"

"The man? Why are you pretending you don't know his name? He's been your contact at DOSHA for ages."

"I've forgotten it."

"It's Mickey."

"He doesn't look like a Mickey."

Benito shook his head. "Whatever. If you wanted to know, you'd have let Gianna open the door to me last night and tell you."

"*You're* not going to tell me?"

"There's nothing to tell. I'm sorting it. You need to fill out some forms. Gianna has them on her iPad, or you can do the paper ones I gave her last night."

Rosetta stepped forward. "Benito—"

"Don't. I need to sleep. I'm too tired to fight you today."

Benito drifted to the front door. For a moment, he imagined he heard Rosetta following him, but when he turned to say goodbye, she was gone.

10

Time crawled. Then it evaporated. Benito drove until dawn, counting the minutes. Then it was 5.30 in the morning and he was an hour away from where he needed to be.

Goddamnit.

He burned up the A5 as fast as he dared, keeping a sharp eye out for transport police and speed cameras the in-car sat nav didn't flag. The roads were deserted, but even with his foot to the floor, it still took forty-five minutes to reach the unfamiliar gym.

The bargain membership he'd bought a few months back gave him access to every premises in the branded chain. He swiped through the barriers with his fob and scanned the ground floor of the warehouse-style building. Cardio machines were crammed into the open space, a couple occupied by diehard runners and cyclists who couldn't face the damp gloom outside.

None were Mickey.

Benito found the stairs and jogged to the second-floor weight rooms. They were quiet, save a grunting bodybuilder on the leg press, and Benito's heart sank, eclipsing the nerves he'd carried all night. *I'm too late.* Then an instinct he couldn't pinpoint drew him to the back of the room. A lone figure sat on a weight bench, head down, a set of heavy dumbbells in front of him. He was dressed in sweats and a muscle tee that gifted Benito the outline of his strong shoulders, but his deep frown was hard to miss.

It was the same frown Benito had become acquainted with on the grimy landing outside Rosetta's flat, and he *hated* it.

Benito crossed the room, reaching the weight bench as Mickey happened to glance up. Their gazes locked and sank into each other, drawing Mickey to his feet as Benito took a final step.

They were almost nose to nose. "You're late," Mickey said, quieter than he usually spoke.

Benito winced. "Sorry. I was working all night. Last job took me too far in the wrong direction."

"Your Uber job?"

"My only job."

The lie tasted bitter, contrasting with the faint ray of dawn sunshine that broke through the grey drizzle outside. A prism lightened the room, casting warmth over Mickey's handsome face. His eyes sparkled, hard to read. Then he smiled—a soft rise of his full lips—and Benito's lungs expelled his caged breath. "I thought you'd left."

Mickey shook his head. "Even if you didn't show, I still need the workout. Keeps me calm, you know?"

"I know the theory. I've never seen you not calm, though. Except maybe when—"

Mickey placed his hand over Benito's mouth, sealing it shut. "Don't say it. That's not why we're here."

Benito waited, resisting the urge to lick Mickey's palm. Six thudding heartbeats passed between them, loaded and raw. It felt like a dream, the kind Benito had on the rare occasions he smoked weed. Dark, and yet so crammed with vivid colour he wasn't afraid.

Mickey let his hand fall.

Benito took in the dark smudges beneath his smoky blue eyes and the way his sandy hair stuck up in ten different directions. This wasn't the same man who'd sat on the landing with him twenty-four hours ago. Something had changed. For both of them, but most of all, for Mickey. "What's wrong?"

"Nothing."

Benito raised a brow. "Liar. You're fucking vibrating."

"Am I?"

Benito placed a tentative hand on Mickey's shoulder. Mickey didn't stop him. Benito slid his palm lower, to Mickey's chest, and pressed deeper. Beneath his touch, Mickey's muscles twitched and jumped with nervous energy that no workout was ever going to ease. "You feel like you banged six grams of coke before you came here."

Mickey laughed. It was sudden and harsh and lacked enough humour that Benito flinched.

"What?" he said. "Did I guess right, or are you so offended right now you want to deck me?"

"All of it."

"That makes no sense."

Mickey backed up, removing himself from Benito's touch. "I know. I'm sorry, man. Just didn't get much sleep last night."

"Because you were . . . ?"

Benito let the question hang, no judgement. How could there be? The hypocrisy would kill him.

Mickey sank down on the weight bench again.

Benito stared, then dropped to a crouch. His hands itched to find a home on Mickey's knees, but he kept them to himself. "You don't have to tell me," he said. "We can just workout and forget everything else."

Mickey regarded him through reddened eyes. "Everything?"

"Yeah. Sex clubs, family drama, and whatever's making you look like you wanna die right now."

Mickey laughed again, softer this time, and it reached his eyes. "*That's* dramatic. No one's gonna die."

"I might if I don't get some water and warm up. Where are you at with your circuit?"

"Back and shoulders. I did five miles on the bike while I was waiting for you."

"Wow. Okay. Give me ten minutes to catch up and I'll find you?"

Mickey nodded. "Sounds good."

Reluctantly, Benito left Mickey alone and retreated downstairs to buy water from the vending machine and churn out a couple of miles on the treadmill. Running indoors usually made him antsy, but with Mickey waiting for him upstairs, dying of boredom seemed a long way off.

What if he left already?

Benito climbed off the treadmill and wiped it down, gaze flitting between the stairs and the exit. Fear made his warmed-up heart thud louder, but . . . *no.* He'd had his back to both while he'd been running, but his senses still tingled with Mickey's presence.

He's still here. And, as it turned out, was exactly where Benito had left him, though he was bent over the bench now, doing dumbbell rows. "Thought you might've legged it," he said.

Benito claimed the spare dumbbell at Mickey's feet. "You're not that lucky."

Mickey made a sound that could've been a laugh, but it was hard to tell. Benito eyed him as he mirrored his pose and began working his lats. After a night spent behind the wheel, death-glaring any Saturday-night mofo who looked like they might throw up in his car, it felt good to move his body.

It felt even better to be with Mickey. Not talking. Not fucking. Not staring each other down. Just making a loop around the weight room, working the equipment in companionable silence.

Mickey was in amazing shape. And he looked good flushed and covered in a layer of fresh sweat. Better than good. Benito watched him own the pull-up bar and tried to forget how complicated their acquaintance had abruptly become.

"Stop staring." Mickey dropped to the floor. "You're gonna give me a complex."

"Unfounded. You've got nothing to be self-conscious about." Benito spoke without thought but didn't regret it. Life was weird right now. Straight-talking this shit was all he had.

Mickey reached for his water bottle and took a long, slow gulp while Benito took his turn on the bar. On a normal day, Benito could smash out twenty with ease, but watching Mickey's throat work was distracting. He caved after fifteen and joined Mickey on the floor.

They sat side by side for a moment, both spent and sweaty. Benito's pulse drummed in his ears, and he itched to put his hands on Mickey again for many reasons, but mostly to see if the shudder in his broad shoulders had gone.

"How are you doing?" Mickey asked suddenly. "I know everything's fucked up, but I should've asked you that."

"Why?"

"Because it's important."

Benito side-eyed Mickey, then wished he hadn't. Despite the hour they'd spent together, he wasn't prepared for Mickey's piercing gaze. "To who?"

"You. Me. Your sister."

"Why is it important to you?"

Mickey rolled his eyes. "If you don't want to talk, just say so. You don't have to deflect, bro."

"Bro. Fucking hell." Benito rose and searched their surroundings for the hooded sweatshirt he'd discarded. "I thought we *talked* about that?"

"Maybe I forgot. We talked about lots of stuff yesterday."

"It was Friday, but whatever." Benito found the sweatshirt and pulled it over his head before facing Mickey again.

While he'd had his face buried in cloth, Mickey had got up too. He was closer than Benito anticipated, and the urge to touch him flared again, hotly enough that Benito almost did it.

Mickey seemed to twitch too. Then he shook his head. "All right. I'll shut up."

"Don't."

Mickey's brows cinched. "Don't what?"

"Shut up. Stop talking to me. What*ever*. I'm just shit at answering questions like that cos no one ever asks me them —fuck." *Fuck.* Where had that come from? Benito couldn't recall a time he'd spoken those words aloud before or cared that they were true. *Man, I need to eat.*

Mickey touched Benito's arm, a light brush of his fingers. "What are you thinking?"

"That I'm hungry," Benito said absently. "I can't function without breakfast, even if I eat it and go straight to bed."

"What do you like eating?"

"Hmm?"

"For breakfast." Mickey reclaimed his hand. "There's a twenty-four-hour place by the motorway junction. You want to go there?"

"With you?"

Mickey shrugged. "Yeah. I mean, I'm hungry too."

Benito considered his options for less than a second, then scooped his water bottle, car keys, and phone from the floor. "Works for me."

Mickey nodded and led the way downstairs and out of the gym. His Focus was parked beside Benito's SUV. *How did I not see that?* Mickey clicked the lock and jerked his head to the main road. "You know the way?"

"If I didn't, I could figure it out," Benito said dryly. "I'm a taxi driver, mate."

"Yeah, yeah."

Mickey got in his car and started the engine.

Benito did the same and followed him out of the car park. He lost sight of the Focus at a busy roundabout, but he knew the road well enough to find his way to the motorway junction.

Somehow, he beat Mickey there. He parked outside the all-night greasy spoon and finished his water. His stomach rumbled hard enough to hurt, but he ignored it, waiting for Mickey.

The Focus appeared a few minutes later, and Benito wondered when his brain had started thinking of Mickey and his car as entwined elements. *You're losing it.*

Benito got out of his car. Mickey was already close enough that two strides brought them together. For a moment, they stared, caught in something unknown. Then Benito's stomach growled again, and Mickey laughed.

"Come on." He jerked his head at the caff. "Let's eat."

———

Benito hadn't been joking about needing breakfast to function. Mickey watched him inhale scrambled eggs and four rounds of toast like a starving man and witnessed every spark of life as it returned to him. His tense shoulders relaxed; his eyes brightened. Even his rare half-smile seemed more frequent.

Or maybe Mickey was imagining it. After a weekend spent pacing his tiny house, nothing would've shocked him. His body ached with beautiful fatigue from the punishing workout they'd shared at the gym, but his mind was still scratchily awake.

He picked at his own food, happy to lose himself in Benito. Under the table, their knees brushed, as if this was a date, not a bizarre sequence of events that made Mickey's brain itch and his conscience flicker with dark, ominous warnings he tried to ignore. *He's your tenant's son. He has two phones and piles of cash from who the fuck knows where. He's probably got fifty grams of coke stashed in his car—*

Mickey pushed his plate away and curled his hands into fists before hiding them under the table.

Benito drank orange juice from a plastic bottle, his gaze curious but easy. As if he spent time with twitching addicts all the time.

Maybe he did.

Maybe—

"How often do you work out?"

Benito's voice startled Mickey. He blinked. "Hmm?"

"How much do you work out?" Benito leaned forward. "I'm a lone wolf in the gym, but I liked working out with you. It was fun."

"Fun?"

"Yeah. I'm not much of a talker, but I guess I like company more than I realise sometimes."

"I'm shit company," Mickey said flatly.

"Not always."

"Just today?"

"Your words, mate. Don't make them fact."

Mickey sat back in his seat, then regretted it as the shift took him further away from Benito. "What do you think of me?"

"Right now? Or in general?"

"Both."

Benito narrowed his eyes, just a touch, and retrieved Mickey's plate from the other side of the table. "Unless there's a medical reason you're not eating, I'll talk if you eat your breakfast."

"What do you care if I eat my breakfast or not?"

"We went hard with the weights, and I don't see a protein shake in your hand, so you need to replenish if you're not going to fucking hurt yourself."

It still begged the question why Mickey's wellbeing was Benito's concern, but his rough glare was hard to ignore. And Mickey was *curious*. Benito didn't give much away, which left too much scope for Mickey's wild imagination. Hard facts were too precious to give up.

He picked up his fork and pointed it across the table. "Speak."

"Eat."

Mickey ate.

Benito watched him a moment, then leaned back in his seat, putting a respectable distance between them again. "I think you're nice."

Mickey snorted.

Benito spoke again before he could. "I wasn't finished."

"Go on."

"Okay . . . I think you're a nice guy, but you're nowhere near as respectable as my sister seems to think you are. And not because you like to get rough when the lights go out. It's more than that, and . . . I think it's something we have in common that you're trying to forget about."

"As in?"

"As in, you're from the same kind of ends as me. Different city, but the same fucking streets."

Mickey swallowed and slowly wiped his mouth. "What the fuck makes you think that?"

Benito shrugged. "You walk and talk like me, and when you stare like you are right now, I know you see straight through me. Why is that, Mickey? Are you a fed? Or are you a fucking road man?"

Dead air whistled in Mickey's ears. He scrambled to catch the threads of Benito's words. Two things stood out. One, that Benito was all but admitting he did more for his money than drive an Uber. Second, that he'd seen a glimpse of Mickey's present and somehow found his past. "I'm not a fed. You know what I am. I'm a housing officer. You've *seen* me at work."

"So?" Benito drained his juice bottle and dropped it on the table, a tic in his jaw muscles the only outward sign of stress. "That could be a front for moving product around the estates. I've seen coppers do worse."

"I'm not a fucking *fed*."

"You know the fact that it offends you so much gives you away, right?"

"Gives me away as what?" Mickey pushed his plate away a second time and leaned closer to Benito. "What do you think I am that I haven't shown you in plain sight?"

Benito started to speak. Then stopped and shook his head, uncertainty clouding his face, sudden and dark. "I don't know. I just—feel something with you that I recognise. It's weird."

"Maybe you're the weird one."

"Or maybe you've lived the same life."

"Lived isn't living." Mickey spoke without thinking.

Benito's gaze sparked again. He sucked in a breath that seemed to go nowhere, then released it in a shaky whoosh. "Why do I feel like I just busted open the trapdoor to hell?"

Mickey let out a strangled laugh. "That's the realest fucking thing you've said all day."

"It's eight in the morning."

"So? Feels like a write off to me."

"Pessimist?"

"Does it matter?"

"No. None of it does."

Mickey felt like he was living someone else's life. Who he'd been three days ago was a different man to the one so lost in Benito now. "Why did you say it then?"

"You asked."

"I didn't ask for that."

"What did you want then?"

"I—" The caff closed in on Mickey. Then retreated, like hot and cold water being poured over his head. It flayed him open, then left him bereft, icy wind blasting the cavernous space his *real* self had once been. "I wanted you to know I understood. That I wasn't standing in your mum's flat judging you."

"So you asked me to judge *you*. Dude, that makes no sense."

"Doesn't it?"

Benito shook his head. "I never felt judged by you. Or ashamed that my mum can't get herself together enough to take care of business. I wish you never saw it, but not because of that."

"Why then?"

"Because I liked what we were doing. I liked how you made me feel when we hooked up. It—I don't know—made me feel human."

"How do you feel now?"

"Like I've been on a bender for three days straight. When I saw you across the gym, it went away. Then I looked in your eyes and it was like a mirror. You feel what I feel, and I thought I needed to know why."

Mickey's head spun a bewilderment he'd never felt before. "You don't anymore?"

"No, man. I just need to know you're okay before I say goodbye to you."

Goodbye. It sounded so final. And perhaps it was. Whatever madness the world had been since Friday, it was finite. Benito had his life, and Mickey had his. They couldn't entwine. They *couldn't.*

But for reasons Mickey didn't understand, he couldn't lie to Benito either. "I'm not like you," he said, voice like gravel. "At least, I don't think I am. You seem stronger."

"Than you?" Benito laughed. "Wow, son. I'd love to know how you figure that."

Mickey shrugged and his tense muscles shrieked in protest. "You're doing something I had to stop because I'm fucking weak. I couldn't be around what I was doing without becoming what I was trying to exploit, and I'm still fighting that. I'll *always* be fighting that."

Benito frowned, piecing together Mickey's cryptic confession. Perhaps a different person would've found no logic in it, but Benito, whether he knew it or not, was a thinker. He took the scraps Mickey offered him and put them together. "Are you trying to tell me you're a fiend, and the wreckage I see in you right now is you fighting that battle over and over, like you have long before we fucking met?"

Relief swept over Mickey, fast and kind, even if the wasteland it left behind was cold and cruel. "Don't call me a fucking fiend. But, yeah. I'm an addict. Coke. It's been years, but it never goes away, and I can't look at someone like you without . . . Jesus fucking Christ, I can almost *smell* it on you."

"I don't use. Never have."

"Doesn't matter. You move it, and don't deny it. I *know* your life. It was mine before I fucked it up so bad I had to run a thousand miles to make it right." Mickey slammed his mouth shut and closed his eyes. *Fuck.* This was why he didn't have deep conversations. With *anyone.* Because he was *shit* at keeping himself locked up. The gates looked strong, but up close, they were rusted and weak.

He blew out a breath.

Opened his eyes.

Benito was still there, still leaning forward, gaze open, searching. Under the table, his hand found Mickey's knee. He laid his palm over it, warm and soothing. "Breathe," he whispered. "It's okay."

It wasn't okay, but Mickey obeyed anyway. After a minute, he dropped his elbows on the table. "I'm sorry. Maybe I got it all wrong and I'm just fucking paranoid. That's a thing I have too, or I used to, anyway. It's not so bad these days."

"What about the rest of it?"

"What do you mean?"

"How long have you been clean?"

"Three years."

"That's a long time."

"Doesn't feel that way." Mickey reached for his cold coffee. Glared at it and set it aside again. "Some days it's brand new, and I'm not as good at dealing with it as I need to be."

"I'm sorry."

"Why?"

"For putting you back there. I had no idea."

"I'm not wrong, am I?"

"About what?"

"All of it."

It was Benito's turn to shiver and close his eyes. Mickey gave him a minute, caught up counting his own pulse as it thumped in his brain. This wasn't how he'd imagined this morning to play out. He'd picked the gym to meet as neutral ground. Where they could be two blokes who liked to lift while having a simple conversation. But nothing about either one of them was fucking simple. *So let it go. Let* him *go.*

No chance. Mickey added it to the long list of things he was too weak to do.

Benito opened his eyes. Where they'd been clear since he'd demolished his breakfast, now they were strained. "I can't tell you anything."

"I know."

"You *don't.* It's not as easy as being what I am or what I do. It's all I know."

"I thought that too."

"What changed?"

"I couldn't be that person. I had to escape and evolve or I was going to die."

Benito let out a short, dark laugh. "Been there, done that."

"That how you got shanked?" Mickey pictured the scar on Benito's inked torso and shuddered again. It was a vicious mark on glorious skin. He couldn't imagine Benito without it, though he wanted to. Mickey had scars of his own, and he knew how deeply they hurt.

Benito rubbed his arms. "I got stabbed in a fight I started."

"Are you trying to tell me you deserved it?"

"Maybe. That's how it goes, though, isn't it? Where we come from. I had a tool in my hand. I'd have cut him if he hadn't cut me first."

Mickey shivered again. He'd pressed Benito for brutal honesty, but he wasn't ready to hear it. Or to picture Benito with a blade, ready to hurt someone as badly as they'd hurt him. "Where's your dad?" he asked, abruptly switching subjects. "His name was on your mum's tenancy for a while. Roberto De Luca, right?"

Benito's gaze turned to stone. He leaned back in his chair and threaded his arms across his chest. "He's not my dad."

Mickey frowned. "Who is he then?"

"Gianna's dad. He shacked up with my mum when I was eight."

"And you hate him?"

"What makes you say that?"

"Your face."

"You don't know my face."

I want to. Mickey took a sip of cold coffee. Regretted it but clung to the mug anyway to keep his shaky hands occupied. "I didn't know you and Gianna had different fathers."

"You're not going to ask what happened to mine?"

No. Because he's dead. Mickey could tell by the deep sadness glassing Benito's soulful eyes. And he regretted bringing it up more than anything he had in a long while.

Benito blinked hard and scrubbed a hand down his face. All of a sudden, he seemed more exhausted than Mickey. "Roberto's a nasty prick. He used to come around my mum's place to see Gianna, but he hasn't for a long time now. And he only sends money to stop the social taking it out of his wages. What's it called when they do that?"

"Attachment of earnings."

"Yeah. That. He does just enough to stop that happening, then fucks off again until next time."

"Nice guy."

Benito looked like he wanted to throw up. His usually warm skin turned an ashen shade of grey, and he reached in his pocket for his phone.

One of them, at least.

Silence reigned as he tapped the screen. Mickey absorbed his abrupt need for mental space but couldn't stop staring.

Benito sighed. "Stop."

"Stop what?"

"Dissecting my soul."

"What does that even mean?"

"You know what it means."

Mickey didn't. But the sense that he was missing something about Benito and Robert De Luca was so strong it overpowered even his scratchiest cravings. "What did he do to you?"

"Who?"

"Gianna's dad."

"What makes you think he did anything?"

"You just answered me with the same deflective question you did when I asked if you hated him. If it was nothing, you'd say so."

"Would I?"

"I don't know."

They'd hit a stalemate. Benito's gaze flickered to the exit. Mickey's breath caught in his throat, but Benito didn't leave. He let out another heavy sigh and slumped forward, dumping his forearms on the table. "I do hate him. And, trust me, the feeling's entirely mutual. He despised me from the moment he kicked me out of my mum's bed to sleep on a towel in the spare room."

"A towel?"

Benito shrugged like it was nothing. "It was temporary, but he wanted me out of my mum's bed so he could knock her up and get his feet under the table."

"How long did that take him?"

"Five years and three miscarriages."

Mickey winced. "Shit. I'm sorry."

"Why? It's history, man. That cunt is scared of *me* now, and I like it that way. Stops him hanging around too long."

"Did he hurt you worse than kicking you out of your bed?"

"It wasn't my bed, and I was too old to be sleeping with my mum anyway."

"That's not what I asked."

"I know it's not."

Mickey did some belated maths. If Gianna was twelve, that meant Benito was around twenty-five—the same age as Mickey. Did that mean anything?

Probably not. But the affinity between them seemed to grow with every second of heavy silence. They were different men from different streets, but perhaps Benito was right— something about them was the same. They *fit*.

"Would it make you feel better if I told you he kicked the shit out of me?"

Mickey blinked at Benito. "Better about what?"

Benito leaned further across the table. The warmth of his body radiated in the narrowed space between them, and Mickey felt it everywhere. His skin tingled and his nerves buzzed, aching to touch Benito, even if it was just to brush the backs of his fingers to his sharp cheekbone.

"You don't have to tell me," Mickey said. "It's none of my business."

More silence. Benito picked up a sugar packet and twirled it in his long fingers. Mickey's heart thumped louder than it had when they'd fucked. He was as sure of it as he was about anything right now.

With Benito so close, logical thought was impossible. Under the table, his leg sought out Benito of its own accord, melding their calves together. Mickey froze, waiting for Benito to pull back.

He didn't. Just closed his eyes for a brief moment in time that seemed to last forever and a day.

His gaze was unreadable when he opened them again. "He used to wait up for me."

"Roberto?"

"Yeah. I was a little shit and I stayed out till all hours, but most nights I'd come home and he'd still be up, fucking seething, you know? Like whatever bullshit had gone wrong in his day was my fault."

"How old were you?"

"Eleven, maybe? I can't remember. I started staying out all night to avoid him, and my mum liked it that way because she didn't want the hassle of us fighting."

"She knew you fought?"

"Yeah, but she figured we were as bad as each other."

"You were a child."

"I was tall. With a fucking mouth on me. Maybe I deserved it."

Rage like no other flared in Mickey's blood. He wanted to

tell Benito that no matter how hard he'd run his mouth, no kid deserved seven bells of shit kicked out of them by an adult who was supposed to keep them safe. But he didn't. He said nothing. Because whatever wisdom he wanted to spout to make *himself* feel better, Benito didn't need it. "He still sees Gianna?"

Benito nodded. "He's never laid a finger on her, though."

"That's something, I suppose."

"I wish he was dead," Benito retorted flatly.

Me too. The conversation dried up. Benito folded his arms and hid his face in them. He didn't seem particularly upset, but what did Mickey know? This was the fourth time they'd met. Benito could've been falling to bits inside and he'd have no idea.

Don't touch him.

The internal warning came too late. Mickey rubbed Benito's shoulder, then let his hand slide to his neck. He drew his thumb over smooth skin, forward and back, resisting the urge to tangle his fingers into Benito's soft, dark hair. "I wish things were different," he said. "I wish life was better for you, and for me, so we could fit together, but I can't be around you if you're still living the life I think you are, and . . . fuck, I've got nothing for you anyway. I'm a shit human."

A low sound rumbled out of Benito. He raised his head a fraction, showing Mickey his reddened eyes, gaze so fierce it was clear who'd taught Gianna to glare fire at anyone stupid enough to cross her. "You're not a shit human."

"You don't know me."

"Then fucking show me who you are. Don't act like I don't want to know."

"It doesn't matter. It can't happen. I already told you—"

Benito gripped Mickey's hand and pried it from his neck, lacing their fingers together. "You told me how you *think* I live my life. I told you I'm a taxi driver. One of us is wrong."

"Or lying."

"I have some fucking loose ends to tie up. Don't write me off."

"I have to. You're my tenant's son."

"And I'm a gangbanger. A dirty road man with deep pockets and a fucking piece in my waistband. Fuck you, man." Benito lurched to his feet, wrenching their hands apart.

His scowl was terrifying, but Mickey faced it down. *It's better this way*.

Benito gathered his things from the table. He looked as though he had more to say, but the silence was deafening.

He turned to leave.

Mickey caught his arm. "I'd never write you off. It's *me*, don't you get it? I'm gonna do everything I can to help your mum and your sister, but I can't see you again, not like this."

The heat drained from Benito's glare, leaving cold resignation in its place. He shrugged Mickey's hand from his arm and left.

11

Benito woke to the buzz of a phone. Groaning, he rolled over in bed and fumbled for it under his pillow, but it wasn't there. Or rather, it was, but it was the wrong phone. The one that had woken him up was on the floor by the clothes he'd abandoned last night.

He rolled out of bed and lunged for the phone, catching it seconds before it rang out. "What do you want?"

"There's another run. Ipswich this time."

"Ipswich?" Benito tensed, wide awake. "Why?"

"Why do you think? They don't want to risk Coventry again so soon after you slammed it last time."

"When?"

"Friday. I know the timings, but I'm not sure of the route."

"Text me from the road."

"I'm not gonna be there. Asa thinks I need to keep my head down in case what happened last time was personal."

Benito retrieved his other phone and brought up a map of the south-east. There were multiple ways to get from Ipswich to London, and worse—or better, depending on how he looked at it—all of them took him deep into territory he had no business getting tricky in. The Coventry gangs didn't scare him—and they didn't care if Asa lost product as long as they were paid. But the firm running Ipswich would cut his head off if they caught him on their turf.

So don't get caught. Leave it alone.

"You know he was talking about you the other day."

Benito snapped back to the present. "Who?"

"Asa. I think he misses you."

Benito gripped the phone tighter. An ominous creak sounded, and he made an effort to loosen his fingers, glad the caller couldn't see him. "How much is on the run?"

"Two. Can we meet soon? I want my cut."

"Soon." Benito calculated how much such a small haul would net him. It wasn't enough, but each run brought him closer to the magic figure he needed to buy his freedom and the life he needed to live for Gianna.

For himself.

Maybe . . .

He closed his eyes and pictured the pain in Mickey's eyes as he'd gazed at Benito and seen nothing but truth, even when Benito had lied to his face. Maybe if they'd met a few years later, things could've been—

"*Martell.*"

"What?"

"My money, man. I need to see some cash."

"Why?" Benito growled. "You know I'm good for it. You know too much for me to fuck you over."

"Not if you kill me."

Benito snorted. "What good would you be to me then?"

"I'm not the only one who'd help you. You only hit me up because I hate Asa for cheating on my sister."

"What do you want from this conversation?"

"I told you. A meet. I need my cash so I can get it somewhere safe. You know, in case something happens."

"Expecting trouble?"

"No. But you know Asa, man. He's shady as fuck."

"He's dumb as fuck. If he wasn't, you'd be dead already." Benito hung up, knowing his mole needed the money too much to back out anytime soon.

He dropped the phone on the carpet and flopped onto his bed, tired gaze fixed on the ceiling. If he had any hope of pulling off a raid at an unknown location against who the hell knew how many men, he needed more sleep, but his brain was a buzz of maps and worst-case scenarios. He needed a motor. And a weapon. He'd already dumped the pipe he'd used last time.

Leave it alone.

Benito pressed the heels of his hands to his eyes, hard enough to make his skull throb. *No.* He couldn't. As risky as the low-yield raid was, he needed every penny, and soon. Asa hadn't set a limit on his freedom bounty, but Benito knew the game well enough to know it was finite. Or at least a matter of time before the price went up.

I hate that motherfucker.

He didn't, though. *"Remember, Martell, I could've left you at the side of the road. Or with a bullet in you, like you did Dante."*

Benito leaned against the wall of the darkened underpass, blood seeping from the slash wound in his ribs. "I didn't shoot him."

"You did, though, didn't you? You went around him and made

deals with the Albanians to fuck him over. How long before you do the same to me?"

It wouldn't have been long. Asa had moved first. It was the only reason it was Benito on his knees instead of him.

It's the game, man. And if Benito wasn't gonna play, he had to *pay.*

Eventually, he fell asleep again, sprawled out sideways across the bed, legs hanging off the edge. Sometime later, he woke to a muscle spasm in his back and his phone buzzing under the pillow.

He moved stiffly to retrieve it and answered without opening his eyes or looking at the screen, swallowing a groan. "Yeah?"

"Morning."

Benito's eyes flew open, and another unintelligible sound escaped him.

Mickey laughed dryly. "Are you awake? I need to talk to you about your mum's repayment plan."

"I—uh. Fuck." Benito sat up, stretching out the kinks in his spine. "I'm awake."

"We can do this later if you don't have time right now."

"I have time." Another spasm of pain rocked Benito. He cringed. "Mother*fucker.*"

"Are you okay?" The concern in Mickey's rough, northern brogue was hard to miss.

And hard to take. Benito didn't want his concern. He wanted his kiss, his touch, all the shit he couldn't have. Mickey had made that clear yesterday. And Benito had accepted it.

Just.

Maybe.

Or perhaps he'd just smoked three joints before he'd gone to sleep last night and briefly forgotten how much it had hurt to walk away from Mickey.

It still hurt. Benito rubbed his chest, coughing. "I'm fine. I just woke up. Sorry."

"Don't apologise, mate. Just be okay."

"Why?"

Mickey sighed. "Because you deserve to be. Isn't that enough?"

No. "Why are you even on the phone to me right now?"

Silence. Then something unseen—and unheard—seemed to shift the air. Wherever Mickey was, he tapped on a keyboard, and when he spoke again, his deep voice was flat. "I spoke to the council. They've accepted an offer of three hundred a month on the arrears if the first payment on the account is made within twenty-four hours. A full rent payment is due at the end of the month, but DOSHA is going to sponsor it."

"Sponsor it? What does that mean?"

"They'll front it."

"Like, a loan?"

"No. They'll pay it as a one-off hardship benefit while your mum waits for her Universal Credit claim to go through. I helped your sister do the forms on her iPad this morning."

Another cough built in Benito's chest. He swallowed it down. "You saw Gianna?"

"I thought she'd be at school when I stopped by, but it's half term, right?"

Right. It was the only reason Benito was still in bed and not loitering by the bus stop with breakfast. "Was she okay?"

"Seemed to be. I didn't see your mum."

"You won't. She's agoraphobic, remember?"

"Is that her official diagnosis?"

"What do you think?" Benito snapped. "She hasn't left the flat in months. How the fuck is she going to get diagnosed with anything?"

"It would help her case if something like this happens again," Mickey said. "She could even get extra money if she can prove her condition is limiting her life."

"Yeah, well. She's not going to walk to the doctor's surgery anytime soon, so I guess that's a fucking pipe dream. Are we done here?"

"Unless there's anything else you need from me?"

"Like what?" Frustration rippled through Benito, driving him up from the bed and to the window, his free hand jammed in his hair. "Fuck. That's not what I meant."

"I know."

"Do you?"

"Yeah, Benito, I do. But it has to be this way. You know that. Just make the payments on your mum's account and stick to them, okay? And with clean money, man. Right now, it's all you can do."

Mickey ended the call without waiting for a response, and the quiet click rattled Benito's brain. He lay back on the bed, then changed his mind and sat up again. Hunger clawed at his belly. Dazed, he rose and sloped to the kitchen to dump oats in a bowl with milk. He nuked it in the microwave.

While he waited for his porridge to cook, he stood at the window, gazing out at the city he despised almost as much as London. The skyline was different, but the vibe was the same. Brutal. Grim. And for Benito, desperate. At least, it was getting that way.

I don't want to do it.

The thought was sudden and sharp-edged, and it took him a moment to pinpoint the context. Mickey's call had thrown him off kilter. He'd almost forgotten the one that had come before.

Ipswich. Benito pulled out his phone and studied the maps again. He highlighted the route he'd take if it were up to him, then the most obvious, then focused on the two that were left. One took the mule back country through roads similar to where Benito had hit it before. The other was a healthy mixture of urban and rural. *It's this one.* Benito knew it like he knew grass was green, and not just because the route passed two branches of KFC.

Benito wrote out the route, then deleted the searches and texts from the burner phone. The microwave had finished ten minutes ago. Benito retrieved his lukewarm breakfast and ate mechanically while his brain ran riot with plans for Friday's raid.

Location, vehicle, weapon.

Location, vehicle, weapon.

Location, vehicle, weapon.

He finished his breakfast and tapped his fingers on the countertop. Five days seemed a long time to wait, and his body thrummed with anticipation, wanting it over with.

The timings came through on the burner phone. He committed them to memory, then erased the message and regretted it instantly, as the moment it was gone, distraction set in like rot, sowing the self-doubt he'd spent his entire adult life fighting.

His painstaking plans jumbled and blurred. Benito shook his head to clear it, but in place of clarity came the plea he'd gone to sleep with a few short hours ago. *Leave it alone.* More than a warning, it was a clarion call from his soul, and the voice in his heart was *loud.*

But not loud enough.

I have to do this.

———

Benito was a patient man. It was what made him dangerous on the street, and sitting in another fake-named cash-bought car in a dark, disused farm entrance. So far, three ridiculous decoy vehicles had passed him, blacked-out windows, lowered suspensions, and spoilers like supermarket trolleys. They were trying to draw him out. Trouble was, they'd chosen cars Benito was familiar with as bait. Cars he'd noted and remembered five fucking years ago when Asa's thick-as-shit cousin had bought them and spent his days burning around the tower blocks scouting for weed and pussy.

People are fucking stupid.

Or maybe they didn't have memories as long as Benito's. After six hours in the unheated Corsa, he couldn't decide who was winning.

I'm fucking hungry.

Same shit, different day.

Another vehicle passed the dead-end lane. Benito sat up and peered over the steering wheel. It was a beat-up van playing rave music. Not even Asa's current muling crew would've been dumb-fuck enough to move product in that. Unless it was an audacious double bluff, in which case, he was inclined to let them have it, just for the fucking balls of it.

The van's tail lights faded. Benito finished his second Red Bull and crushed the can in the palm of his hand.

He tucked it into his jacket pocket and tugged the zip closed. A lorry rumbled past and then a couple more boy racers in Subarus. A heartbeat later, a nondescript people carrier slid by, quiet and five below the speed limit.

Instinct nipped at Benito's gut. He started the Corsa's engine and waited for the silver Zafira to disappear around the bend. Then he flicked the lights on half beam and eased out of his hiding place.

The Zafira hadn't got far, as if it had been waiting for him to follow. Tense, Benito pulled his black woollen hat lower and hung back, keeping a sharp eye out for other vehicles as he tracked the people carrier down the narrow country road, twisting and turning along a nonsensical route that made the hair at the nape of his neck stand on end.

Leave it alone. The instinct held more gravity now than ever, but Benito drove on, following the Zafira cross country for twenty miles in the wrong direction. Despite the strain in the air, the drive was uneventful enough for his mind to drift. His *crowded* mind. Even when he'd spent his days controlling the micro-kingdom he was now stalking through the back roads of nowheresville, he couldn't remember a time when he'd had more to think about. Rosetta. Gianna. Debts that weren't his own and yet still weighed so heavily on him he could barely breathe.

Mickey.

Benito's heart skipped a beat. They'd spoken on the phone three times since their brittle parting at the motorway caff, and each time, Mickey had been all business while Benito had gripped his phone so tight he was surprised the screen was still intact. They'd talked about Rosetta's payment plan, her mental health, and processing the Universal Credit application. Well, Mickey talked. Benito mainly listened while his heart thumped and his palms sweated. Seriously, the dude had a voice that set Benito on fire and eroded his brain to mush. It had taken him until the very end of the third call to tell Mickey he'd made the first payment on Rosetta's arrears.

"Let me guess, cash, right?"

Benito flinched at the edge in Mickey's deep voice. "No. I used my debit card like a good boy. Like you fucking told me to."

"You don't have to do what I say."

True, but Benito had known long before he'd met Mickey that paying Rosetta's bills with street money was a fool's game. If he hadn't, her and Gianna would have lived like queens. *Until you fucked everything up. And then what? She'd have been high and dry anyway.*

It wasn't a new realisation, but it sat grimly in Benito's heart all the same. The only way he could've prevented this from happening would've been to have lived a different life altogether. One where he'd stayed away from the street and worked harder to be a better man.

A better brother.

A better son.

A better anonymous face to come across in a sultry club.

But then, perhaps if Benito had lived a different life, he'd never have set foot in Freefall, and he wouldn't be spending his days now living for the moments Mickey's name lit up his phone screen.

Up ahead, the people carrier eased off the gas for a T-junction that branched onto a busier road. Benito slowed too, holding back until it was impossible to do so without giving himself away. He drew within three car lengths of the Zafira and held his breath, waiting for the doors to open and the four occupants to bear down on him. Or for them to simply drive on, taking him for an innocent driver who just happened to be heading the same way in the dead of night.

The Zafira stopped at the junction. Brake lights shut off and the passenger door opened.

Long legs breached the doorway. Benito reached for the metal cosh hidden beneath his seat. It was taped to stop it rolling under the pedals. He fumbled to free it, adrenaline burning his veins, his lungs, and roaring in his ears. This was it. He was going into battle for five-grand worth of coke on a fucking main road.

Or he was going to die. There were no other options.

The tall figure burst out of the Zafira. Dressed in black, with a mask over his face, Benito couldn't tell if it was someone he knew. And it didn't matter. Benito had to take him down, and the next man, and the next, if he stood any chance of survival.

The cosh dropped free. Benito snatched it and yanked the handbrake up on the Corsa. He reached for the door handle, but before his fingers closed around it, a blinding flash of light swept the area. Blue light. And then sirens, loud and obnoxious.

Unmarked police cars swarmed the junction and the road in front of Benito. A black BMW cut him off from the Zafira and his would-be assailant. Bodies poured from the police vehicles, shouting and holding up tasers, all pointed in the direction of the Zafira.

Shouted warnings filled the air, rattling Benito's bones.

For a heart-stopping moment, he was frozen, consumed by the sight of three more men stepping from the people carrier, hands in the air. Then it sunk in that no one had looked his way yet. The feds were focused on the Zafira. *It's like I'm not here.*

Stomach in his throat, Benito took his chance. He killed his lights, threw the Corsa into a three-point turn, and sped away, praying the feds had no helicopters covering their sting as he floored the accelerator.

With gritted teeth, he hit the country lane, the old Corsa shuddering in protest. The road seemed narrower than before, the bends tighter. He gritted his teeth as gravel sprayed behind him and worn tyres skidded, but the darkness held.

No one followed.

Benito felt sick. He breathed hard through his nose as the Corsa ate the miles up, taking him back to the abandoned dog food factory where he'd left his SUV.

He dumped the Corsa two miles away and hiked across fields to reach the derelict factory. A nearby storm drain gave a resting place for the cosh and his muddy clothes, and he dressed under the misty sky, cold biting into his skin.

Shivering, he slid into the SUV and activated the heated seats. He eased away from the factory site and drove to the main road. By the time he joined the slip road, the car was toasty warm, but the trembling didn't fade. Adrenaline turned to fear, an agitation he couldn't shake, and he pounded the steering wheel in frustration. "*Fuck!*"

His own voice startled him. He didn't shout much. Had never seen the point. But recent months had turned his world upside down, and as he glanced in the rear-view mirror and caught sight of his wild gaze, he didn't recognise himself.

Go home. Take a shower. Get some sleep. But the thought of being alone made him shake harder. *Don't puke. Don't puke.* Another thing he hadn't done since childhood that had somehow become his body's favourite coping mechanism.

Fuck my life.

Blindly, Benito drove on, lost in the battle to keep fucking breathing. The miles disappeared and the roads became more familiar, but he wasn't anywhere close to home.

Freefall appeared up ahead, and he drove into the car park with little conscious thought until he killed the engine.

Silence enveloped him, save his thumping heart. *The fuck are you doing?*

No answer was forthcoming, and he got out of his car, internally screaming at himself to *stop*. But he kept moving. Signed into the club and made his way to the locker room. He took a shower, then redressed in the clean clothes he'd thrown on outside the abandoned factory—dark jeans and a grey tee beneath a black bomber jacket that had cost more than his monthly car payments.

He was overdressed. Most of the men he passed on his way to the bar were in towels, or less, but Benito had never cared much for sitting around naked, waiting on a stranger. And he never hooked up *in* the bar.

I wonder if—

He ground his teeth, wiping all thoughts of Mickey before they could take hold. Whatever fucked-up setting his autopilot was stuck on, he already knew he wouldn't hook up. That he *couldn't*. Whatever he might've had with Mickey was a dead end, but Benito wasn't ready for another man's hands to touch his skin. Another man's kiss. Damn, he didn't know if he'd ever be ready for that.

Fuck, I just need a drink.

A quiet hour in a safe space.

Benito neared the bar. At 2.00 am it was quiet, only a lone figure at the opposite end, slumped over a glass while the bartender patted his shoulder. His *broad*, strong shoulder encased in a smart white shirt that clung to his leanly muscled frame.

Stop. You're fucking seeing things. He had to be.

There was no way he'd walked into a sex club in the middle of the night to find the one face he needed to forget.

12

Mickey felt him before he saw him. But like everything that day, it didn't seem real. The tingling on the back of his neck felt like a rash, and the flutter in his chest added a scratchy new layer to the anxiety he couldn't escape.

He reached for his rum.

Jaiden pulled the glass away. "Come on, mate. Let me call you a cab?"

He patted Mickey's shoulder. The touch made Mickey's skin crawl. He shrugged it off and laughed without humour. "You're not gonna try get me to fuck you this time?"

Jaiden scowled, scrunching up his pretty face. "Not when you're drunk enough to actually agree, no. It's only banter. I know you don't want it."

"How do you know that?"

"Because you've been face down in that glass for three hours. You didn't come here to score."

Score. Jaiden meant dick, but in the world Mickey was trying to forget, it meant something else. Something that would quiet the agitation crawling in his veins, if only for a moment. "If you want to help me, get me another drink."

Jaiden shook his head. "Nope. I'm cutting you off while you're still steady enough to make good decisions."

"You're a prick."

"And you're a nice bloke having a bad day. Don't let it ruin our beautiful friendship."

Mickey glared. "You don't know I'm a nice bloke. And we aren't fucking friends."

"Either way, I'm not serving you anymore." Jaiden snatched Mickey's glass away.

Irritated, Mickey lurched from his stool. Jaiden's pretty brown eyes widened in alarm, but warm hands steadied Mickey before he stumbled, guiding him into an embrace that felt like home. "Leave him. I got this."

It took Mickey a moment to realise the growled words weren't for him. And even longer for the voice that had uttered them to solidify.

Benito.

No. Mickey wasn't that lucky. And in any case, he couldn't recall a moment where Benito had ever *hugged* him, and this shit felt so familiar there was no way he hadn't experienced it a thousand times before.

That voice, though.

Mickey forced his head up, robbing his senses of the scent of clean cotton and *man.*

Benito stared back at him, his dark eyes wide and worried and his handsome face too perfect to be real. Mickey zeroed in on a tiny scar that bisected Benito's eyebrow. It clearly wasn't new, but it was to Mickey. *How have I not noticed it before?* Until this moment, he'd been sure he'd committed every inch of Benito's face to an indelible memory.

"Hey." Benito squeezed Mickey's shoulders. "Are you okay?"

"What?"

Benito repeated the question, but Mickey didn't know the answer. All he knew was his brain wouldn't work fast enough to engage Benito before he slipped away.

He shook his head.

Benito stepped back to take a better look at him.

Mickey grabbed him. "Don't go."

"I'm not." Benito shot a glance at the glass Jaiden was still clutching. "How many of those have you had?"

"Not enough."

"Enough for what?"

"Enough to watch you find a hook-up and walk out with him. So do me a favour and wait for me to leave first, yeah?"

Benito frowned. "I'm not going to do that."

"Which part?"

"Any of it."

"Why not? Dude, this is a sex club."

Benito's dark gaze flickered. "So *you* came here to hook up, right?"

Wrong. Mickey'd come to the club for something to do, but he'd known the second he'd stepped through the door— hell, before that—that he didn't want to play. *Just one drink*, he'd told himself, but silent promises were too easy to break. One drink had become four, and now he was too drunk to drive home. "I didn't hook up," he said. "I had a drink, and now I'm going home."

He didn't move.

Neither did Benito, his hands still on Mickey's shoulders while Mickey fisted the sleeve of his jacket. Tension blistered between them, a beautiful pain Mickey couldn't decipher. If Benito didn't want to join one of the snake pits of men scattered around the club, then why the fuck was he here?

Jaiden said something to Benito.

Benito growled a response that made Jaiden nod and stomp away, then he focused on Mickey again. "I didn't come here to hook up. I just needed some space, and unless I'm with you, this is the only place I know these days where I can fucking breathe. I don't care why you're here or if you banged ten dudes before I got here, will you let me take you home?"

Mickey's head swam, and not from the rum. "You want to take me home?"

"I'm not leaving you here."

"Why not? Dude, I'm a fucking mess."

Benito laughed a little and pulled Mickey closer. He pressed their foreheads together, his stare intense. "There is nowhere I want to be right now more than somewhere safe with you. You can come to my place if you want, I don't care."

"Kiss me first."

"What?"

Mickey moved slowly, giving Benito time to pull back.

Benito didn't.

Mickey gripped his chin and kissed him, soft and sweet, then harder as Benito made a sound low in his throat. Mickey groaned too, and the effects of the rum he'd drunk faded as the intoxication of kissing Benito took over. The club disappeared, save the throbbing beat of the sultry electronica. Oppressive heat became warmth that built and built until

Mickey was glad they were in a place where he didn't have to hide the growing bulge in his jeans.

He slid his hands down Benito's chest, palms curving around his cut muscles, tracing the jagged scar on his ribs through the dark shirt he wore.

Mickey resented that shirt, but as hard as he was for Benito right now, the heat blazing inside him was far more than the desire to lay him down and fuck him. *I want to kiss him all night.*

Maybe he could, if he let Benito take him home.

As though he'd heard Mickey's wandering thoughts, Benito drew back. He brought his hand to his lips and touched them. "Damn. I wasn't planning on jumping you."

"No? Why do you want to take me home then?"

"I already told you, man. I just wanna be with you for a while."

Mickey's heart was still thumping. Kissing Benito was better than any high. But his words made sense. They could fuck upstairs if they wanted to. There was no reason to leave if that was all they were. "I'm sorry I made you kiss me."

"You didn't make me do shit. Kissing you is a fucking trip. I love it."

Mickey leaned back against the bar. His gut—and other organs—was screaming at him to grab Benito and get the hell out of there, but he needed more truth before he was truly alone with Benito again. Or maybe he needed a moment to process the subtle shift leaving the club together for any reason other than sex would bring. *I want to fuck him, though.*

But that had always been true. Even in the stairwell outside Rosetta De Luca's flat, when Mickey's priorities had been professional, he'd still pictured Benito naked and pressed against the nearest available surface. *For a split second.*

Like that made it better.

"Look," Benito said when Mickey failed to speak. "We don't have to do shit, or we can do it all, I *don't care.* Just let me drive you home."

"I need my car," Mickey said absently.

"Not tonight, you don't. Or this morning. Whatever fucking time it is."

Mickey had no idea. He'd left his house after hours of pacing the kitchen, tugging at his hair, and opening and closing his message thread with Benito, all the while imagining himself tapping the local shithead for a gram bag. Actual time had ceased to matter. And *fuck* if he didn't still crave that dirty, tainted high. "I don't know why you want to be with me right now. I keep telling *you* no, then doing shit that pulls you back in. Why are you okay with that?"

Benito's gaze darkened. "Is this the part where you tell me you're a shit human again? Because I'm fucking done with that."

"Why, though? It's all true."

"So? What if none of it matters right now? What if it's just you and me for a while? It's all still gonna be there tomorrow."

"That's kind of my point, mate."

"Is it?"

Mickey shook his head. "Fucked if I know. I'm not as drunk as I need to be."

"For what?"

"To stop thinking. My brain hurts."

Benito's expression softened. He narrowed the distance

between them again and took Mickey's hand. "Trust me," he whispered. "Just for tonight . . . please?"

Something buried deep inside Mickey crumbled. He found Benito's other hand and tangled their fingers together. His lips ached to kiss him again, but he just nodded. "Let's go."

———

Fresh air sobered Mickey up. Perhaps he'd never been that drunk in the first place, Benito couldn't tell. All he knew was he couldn't stand the vibrating tension that made Mickey's hands shake and his eyes wild.

He drove them to Mickey's house in Northamptonshire, glad Mickey had shown little interest in a grand tour of Benito's Milton Keynes flat. It wasn't the worst place he'd ever lived, but he hated it anyway. Perhaps he'd have gone home with just about anyone to avoid it.

No, you wouldn't.

Only Mickey.

Two simple words that made Benito's head spin too hard for him to stop and make sense of what they were doing. Only Mickey's hand on his thigh kept him grounded as he drove, and he latched onto the warmth of his palm. Bathed in it, as if the rest of the world had ceased to exist.

It was almost too easy to forget how he'd spent his evening before he'd meandered into Freefall.

The night was fading when he pulled up outside Mickey's house. He parked on the kerb and switched the engine off. "You don't have to invite me in. I can come back later and give you a ride to your car."

Mickey snorted softly. "As if that's happening."

"Which part?"

"The part where I leave you in this car and go inside without you. We can worry about the rest tomorrow."

"It is tomorrow."

"Later, then."

"Works for me." Benito tried for a smile, but it hurt.

Mickey nodded and got out of the car. Benito followed suit and trailed him to his front door and inside.

He shut the door behind him, like he had the last time he'd been here. In fact, every time they'd been together until real life had caught up with them. But in the dreary early morning, Mickey didn't pounce. And neither did Benito. Instead, they stared at each other while a clock that looked too old to be anything Mickey had bought in the last century ticked like a metronome.

Benito took slow breaths, fighting for a handle on every want and need that spun through him.

I want to kiss him.

I want to hold him.

I need him to be okay.

The last one confused him most. They weren't friends or lovers. There was no tangible reason for the ache in Benito's chest as he took in Mickey's pale face and reddened eyes.

It hurt all the same.

"I'm going to take a shower," Mickey said eventually. "You want anything to drink?"

"Water?" Benito was hungry too. He'd been too keyed up before the ill-fated raid to eat, but he kept his growling stomach to himself and accepted the bottled water Mickey fetched from the kitchen.

"Come on." Mickey jerked his head at the stairs. "You can chill in my room. I won't be long."

It was the best offer Benito'd had in years. He followed Mickey upstairs and stretched out on his bed while Mickey stripped and tossed his clothes at a basket in the corner of the room.

Naked, he was almost more than Benito could bear, but he grabbed a towel from the airing cupboard on the landing and covered himself before the boner Benito had carried halfway home from the club came back. "Dude, get *in* the bed," he said. "You're not going anywhere for a while."

It didn't sound like a sexual proposition, so Benito left his underwear on and crawled under sheets that smelled of Mickey while Mickey disappeared into the bathroom. A TV hung on the wall opposite the bed. Benito found the remote and flicked it on, navigating through Netflix until he found reruns of *Shameless*.

He lay back and fought his heavy eyes as he watched Kev and Veronica fight and fuck—each other as much as the system—while everyone around them did pretty much the same. It was rough background noise that suited Benito's mood while he drowsed and tried not to hawk-eye the bathroom door.

Mickey took long showers, apparently. Benito envied his hot water tank. Then he took to cataloguing his surroundings. Distracted by other things, he hadn't taken much notice of Mickey's bedroom the last time he'd been in it, but it was a nice space. The old house had bay windows and high ceilings, and the original features were still intact. Mickey's weathered furniture suited the aesthetic. The Man City scarf pinned to the wall, not so much, but Benito didn't care about football.

"Still awake?"

Benito blinked as Mickey padded back into the room, hair damp and sticking up, skin sheened with moisture. "Think so."

"Sure about that? Pretty sure I could hear you snoring from the landing."

"Fuck off."

"You're in my bed, mate."

"At your invitation."

Mickey smiled a little and opened a drawer for under-wear. He pulled black briefs up his muscular legs, then slipped into bed. His gaze flickered to the TV, and another half-smile warmed his face. "I can't fall asleep to this. I dream of it and wake up thinking I'm somewhere else."

Benito shifted onto his side and eyed the football scarf again. "You're from Manchester?"

"Yeah."

"You ever go back there?"

"No. I can't."

"Old ghosts?"

"Nope. I brought them with me."

"Burned bridges then," Benito guessed. "Unless you didn't like the weather."

Mickey snorted. "You were right the first time, more or less. I can't go back there because I fucked up enough that people I care about would get hurt the second I showed my face. Don't tell me you don't know how that goes."

Benito said nothing. Couldn't, with his tongue wedged to the roof of his mouth and a cinderblock wedged in his throat.

He lay a cautious hand on Mickey's chest, absorbing the still muscles and the steady thump of his heart. *He's calm. Maybe he needs this . . . to talk.*

Maybe Benito needed to listen.

He rubbed Mickey's warm skin, ignoring the ache in his groin. "I know what it's like to get cornered by shit you can't control."

Mickey watched Benito's fingers trace patterns on his torso. "I could've controlled it—at least at the start, but I was weak, man, and it swallowed me whole."

"The coke?"

"Yeah. We were moving so much product I thought they wouldn't noticed if I lifted some for myself, but then one gram became five, then ten, and I couldn't keep up with the lies."

"You got caught?"

"I think so. Even now, I'm not sure, and that's the worst part. I'll take addiction over paranoia any day of the week."

Benito turned it over in his mind. Addiction wasn't a vice he owned, but he knew paranoia all too well. The shadows that danced too fast to catch. "What do you think happened?"

"I think I spent a week locked in my flat thinking someone was coming to murder me. The bloke I lived with found me boarding up the windows with a nail gun."

"How likely was it that someone was gonna whack you?"

Mickey shrugged. "Fifty-fifty. That's the game, right? Kill or be killed?"

"If you play it that way."

Mickey caught Benito's hand. For a moment, Benito feared it was to push him away, but Mickey laced their fingers together and held tight. "I thought he was trying to help me."

"Who? Your flatmate?"

"Yeah. But he called our boss. They took me to a field in the middle of fucking nowhere and told me to get the fuck out of the city and stay out, or they'd burn my whole family. I didn't question if they meant it or not. I'd seen shit, you know?"

Benito nodded, guilt and pain manifesting so tightly in his chest he couldn't breathe. Again. "What did you do?"

"What they said. I had fifty quid in clean money, so I bought a ticket heading south and got on a train. I woke up in hospital three days later. I'm not sure what happened in between."

"Did they help you? In the hospital?"

"They had to. I'd banged so much coke I'd had a fucking stroke, so I was in there a while."

"You had a stroke?"

"A tiny one. Couldn't close my eye properly for six months or use my left hand. It was some fucked-up shit."

Benito squeezed Mickey's hand. "You're okay now, though, right?"

"Yeah. I was lucky. Getting hooked on the gym helped. And I kept busy with night courses and stuff. It's harder now I have more free time."

"I meant the after-effects of the stroke, not your addiction."

"I know you did, but I don't care about the stroke. Recovering from that was easy because there was an end point. I'd reach milestones and move past them forever. Addiction isn't like that. Some days I wake up—if I ever fucking sleep—and I'm back where I started."

"When did you last use?"

"The day I left Manchester."

"When you got on the train?"

Mickey hummed and fixed Benito with a gaze that was somehow penetrating and yet so distant Benito wanted to cry. "It was three years ago, and I'm still a mess. You need to think about that when you're out there doing whatever you do with two phones and bundles of dirty cash."

"What about your family?" Benito deflected. "Did they come looking for you?"

Mickey laughed without humour. "No. I mean, I think my mum might've wanted to, but me and my dad were done a long time before I hit rock bottom. We clashed, you know? He wanted me to join the army like my cousins. I wanted to work in social care so the old people in the home across the street didn't sit in their horrible chairs all day and wait to die."

"You wanted to work in an old people's home?"

"Hell, yeah." Mickey laughed for real this time and his face lit up so much Benito *had* to touch it, just to check it was real. "Old folk are the best. They say the funniest shit."

"I don't know any. My grandparents died when I was a kid."

"What about your dad?"

"Same."

"How?"

Benito let his hand fall from Mickey's rough jaw. "Heart attack. He dropped dead on the factory floor where he worked."

"How old were you?"

"Eight."

Mickey whistled. "That's young for a kid to lose their father."

"Maybe, but at least I had one—a good one—for that long. Gianna's dad is a fucking wasteman."

"She wouldn't tell me about him when I asked. I thought he was dead too."

"She's not that lucky."

"She is, though, to have you. I have a big brother and he's never given two shits about me."

Benito scowled. "He's a fuckhead then."

Mickey's laughter filled the room again. "He's a data scientist for some huge conglomerate, but okay. We'll go with fuckhead."

Benito enjoyed Mickey's smile for as long as it was there. It helped with the rage building inside at the thought of anyone not seeing Mickey for the compassionate, kind man Benito needed in his life so badly.

"What about you?" Mickey said.

"What about me? Unless it's more dead dad stuff. I'm kind of done with that."

"Valid. I was going to ask what you wanted to be when you were a kid."

"Oh. Well. A footballer, obviously. It was all kids round my ends did until they either got good or went on the road."

Mickey's grin turned dry. "You weren't that good then?"

"I didn't want to be. Football's bullshit, man. I only played because there was nothing else to do. Hey, so, I have a question, if that's what we're doing right now."

"It wasn't, but okay, I'll bite."

I wish. "How did you find your way to Freefall? Have you always been into that shit?"

"Which part? Dudes? Or rough play?"

"Rough play. I know you had a girlfriend back home."

"You like both, don't you? You're bi?"

Benito shrugged. "I like a lot of things. I found my way to the club because it was a safe place where no one knew me. There could be women there and I'd enjoy it."

"Why not go to a mixed club then?"

"Dunno. Maybe I need something extreme when I'm in that mood."

"You think fucking men is extreme?"

"That's not what I meant."

"I know." Mickey's grin widened a touch. "I'm taking the piss. I hear what you're saying. I don't drive all that way for something I could pick up on Grindr."

"You're on Grindr?"

"No."

Benito didn't deserve the relief that washed through him. Mickey wasn't his boyfriend. He could fuck whoever he liked. They both could. But—

I don't want anyone else.

"Hey." Mickey waved his hand in front of Benito's face. "Where did you go?"

Benito blinked. "Nowhere."

Mickey stared, then seemed to let it go. "I know it sounds super heavy when I lay it out, but it saved me, really. I don't think I'd have ever stopped if I hadn't hit the bottom so hard."

Benito blew out a slow breath, digesting. "You don't know that."

"*Mate.*" Mickey closed his eyes. "I was off my nut for three years straight. You think I'm a wreck now? I was another level of carnage back then."

"I don't think you're a wreck."

Mickey cracked an eye open. "Then you're blind. I spent

the night tweaking out *alone* at a sex club because I couldn't handle being at home."

Alone. More relief flooded Benito. "So? You didn't use. And you weren't the only one. You think I came there to fuck someone? Nah, bruv."

The street slang made Mickey grin, then he cocked a brow. "You didn't go to hook up?"

"No. I just . . ." Benito released Mickey's hand, rolled onto his back, and stared at Mickey's bedroom ceiling. "I just needed to be somewhere else . . . somewhere I could just be a faceless dude who likes getting dick. I didn't need the actual, uh—"

"The actual dick?"

"Yeah." Benito smiled as the room grew ever lighter around them. "I guess so. Apparently the only *actual* dick I'm craving these days is yours."

Mickey shifted onto his side. "I can relate to that. In reverse, obviously."

"You didn't hook up at the club?"

"It didn't even cross my mind."

"For real?" Benito tore his gaze from the ceiling and lost himself instantly in Mickey's flinty greys. "You don't have to tell me either way. It's not my business."

"It's not my business if you've fucked anyone else recently either. I'm still glad you haven't, though, if I've got that right."

"You have. But why do you care who I fuck?"

Mickey brought his hand to Benito's face. He cupped his cheek and rubbed his thumb beneath Benito's scratchy eyes. "Because I'm a masochist. I know your life could undo me, but I can't give you up. Maybe you're my new addiction."

It was the easiest thing in the world to kiss Mickey. Benito stretched his neck and captured Mickey's mouth with his, slow and sweet, but laced with every fractured drop of hunger he carried for this complex motherfucker.

Daylight forgotten, they shifted until they were the sum total of their bare skin and entwined limbs and nothing else. But despite the rising heat, Mickey made no move to bypass Benito's underwear, and Benito kept his hands where he could see them. His body screamed to welcome Mickey inside, but his heart ached for something else. For comfort and safety.

For Mickey, more than himself.

Can I be that for him?

Benito had no idea.

13

Mickey woke to the unmistakable sensation of a hot mouth on his dick. *I'm dreaming. For fuck's sake, stay asleep and get to the punchline.*

He squeezed his eyes shut, giving in to the heat unfurling with every sweep of Benito's tongue on his hard length. Because it had to be Benito. Even in Mickey's dreams, there was no one else who made him feel this way—like he was careening at a hundred miles an hour towards an orgasm so intense it would probably kill him.

I could die like this. Take me. I'm ready.

As if he'd heard Mickey's pleasured delirium, Benito worked Mickey harder.

Faster.

Deeper.

His throat clung to Mickey's cock, a tight, wet passage that was almost as incredible as fucking him.

Almost.

Mickey groaned and thrust his hips, but strong hands held him down.

Benito's hands.

Shit. Am I dreaming about him while he's right fucking here? Mickey's eyes flew open. He blinked in the bright light of—fuck, whatever-hell time of day it was—half convinced he'd find himself alone. That Benito would be gone already, if he'd ever been there at all.

Then his gaze fell on the dark mop of hair halfway down the bed, moving up and down as he sucked Mickey dry.

Okay. Not a dream then.

Mickey's heart leapt, and in the split second it took to come to terms with this strange new world, Benito upped the ante. He tightened his grip on Mickey's thighs, fingers digging into taut muscle, and turned his molten stare on Mickey, pure fire from beneath his inky lashes.

Fuck fuck fuck. Mickey couldn't take it. His dick throbbed and pulsed, and a frantic moan tore from his chest. He'd never been blown like this before, by anyone, not just Benito. Mickey loved control too much. Until this moment, he'd honestly believed there was nothing hotter than fucking the mouth of a man on his knees.

But Benito had challenged his beliefs since they'd met. Toppled his resolve and trampled over it. Mickey had gone to sleep with grand plans to keep their friendship platonic—no more kissing. *Definitely* no more kissing. But he'd been a damn fool. Benito was the best high he'd ever had.

I can't give him up.

I—

Release barrelled into Mickey, eclipsing rational thought. More crazed sounds fell from him, and he came hard, shooting every drop into Benito's willing mouth, still fighting his hold on his legs.

"Fuck." Mickey shuddered, arching from the bed, jolting with each wave of pleasure until his body gave out. "*Fuck.*" He collapsed against the pillows, panting, sweat shining every inch of his skin. His heart pounded, and for the first time in days, for all the right reasons.

He gazed down at Benito, watching him pull off and wipe his mouth. In his head, he seized his shoulders and tugged him up the bed, but he couldn't move. "Come here."

Benito crawled up the bed on shaky arms. He pressed a soft kiss to Mickey's cheek, then dropped his head, shoulders heaving as if he were the one who'd just shot brain cells out of his dick. "Man, I didn't mean to do that. Pretty sure I started blowing you before I woke up."

Mickey rested a cautious hand on top of Benito's head. "I'm not complaining. I've woken up to worse things."

"Me too, but . . ."

"What?"

Benito finally looked up. His eyes were more guarded than Mickey could deal with. "It's not why I stayed."

"I know that."

"You do?"

"It's not why I asked you either, or we'd have fucked last night."

"This morning."

"That too."

Benito laughed. The tension knotting his shoulders faded, and he leant against Mickey, his weight gifting Mickey the comforting warmth he'd craved all along.

They lay together for a long moment before Mickey remembered he was the only one who'd had a mind-shaking orgasm. "You know I can blow you too, right? Don't be shy."

Benito snorted. "You might have to give me ten minutes. I shot my load just watching you."

"For real?"

"Real talk. You have no idea how hot you are."

Deflection bubbled so fast up Mickey's throat it *burned*, but Benito's stomach growled before he could speak, and concern overtook him. "Damn, you missed breakfast."

"We slept through it." Benito shrugged. "I'll get something later."

"Fuck off. I'll bring you something. Wait here."

Mickey detached himself from Benito's warm embrace and slid out of bed. His feet hit the bare floorboards and he ducked out of the bedroom before Benito could protest.

Naked, he padded downstairs and into the kitchen. As luck would have it, a basket of clean clothes was on the counter. For the sake of his neighbours, he found a pair of clean sweats and dragged them on. Then he opened the fridge and pondered the contents.

Living alone, he didn't cook much, especially in the morning, but the soul-deep urge to take care of Benito was impossible to ignore. And he had bacon, obviously. Because, well, bacon.

Mickey scrambled eggs and grilled the bacon. Then he toasted English muffins to go with and slathered them in butter.

He had no milk, but a vague memory of Gianna telling him everyone she knew drank black coffee let him worry about it less as he climbed the stairs.

Benito was exactly where he'd left him, sprawled out on his bed, poking at the phone Mickey knew to be the one Gianna called him on. *His legal phone.*

Stop it. Just ten more minutes . . . please?

Mickey ignored the phone and held out the plate and coffee mug. "Back in a sec."

He ran back for his own and returned to find Benito sitting up, grinning as if he'd won the fucking lottery. "Wow. This is the first breakfast I haven't paid someone to make me since I was about fourteen."

"Don't get too excited," Mickey cautioned. "At best, it won't kill you."

Benito looked as though he had more to say, but his appetite got the better of him, and wouldn't you know? Watching a fine dude eat a plate of food Mickey had cooked was the hottest thing ever.

After, Benito disappeared downstairs to clean up. That was pretty hot too, but with reality closing in, Mickey forced himself into the shower instead of following him and pressing him up against the kitchen sink.

When he was done, Benito took his turn and dressed in the clothes he'd worn to the club. "Gianna messaged me. She's locked herself out of her iPad. I gotta take her to the Apple store to get it fixed, but I can come back after and take you to your car?"

Mickey shook his head. "Nah. It's too far out of your way. I'll get a cab later."

"That's gonna rinse you."

"Serves me fucking right."

Benito mauled his bottom lip with his teeth. Mickey regarded him from the bed where he'd stretched out in denial that it was past lunchtime and he had a million things to do. "You know I'm just going to get my car, don't you? I'm not going in the club."

"Not my business if you do, mate."

"Yeah, but I meant what I said last night—this morning—whenever it was. I kind of lost track."

"You remember everything you said?"

"Of course I do. I was too drunk to *drive*, not function."

Benito leaned against the doorframe and thrust his hands in his pockets. His phone—singular—and his car keys were on the chest of drawers beside him. *Where's his other phone? Did he even have it last night?*

Now *that* Mickey couldn't remember, and not because of the rum he'd drunk before Jaiden had cut him off. Or the crazy-hot blow job he'd woken up to. But because apparently his brain had cherry picked the details of their latest encounter, and all Mickey clearly recalled was the relief in his soul when he'd looked up to see Benito *right fucking there.*

"What's the matter?"

"Hmm?" Mickey snapped his gaze back to reality. "What?"

Benito pushed off the door and came to the side of the bed.

Mickey sat up.

Benito crouched in front of him and frowned. "Are you okay? I mean, like, really? Last night was pretty heavy."

"It wasn't, actually. I'm years into this journey, and what happened last night was fucking tame. I do know better than to medicate cravings with booze, though, so I'm sorry about that."

"Don't apologise to me. I don't deserve it."

"Why not?"

Benito's gaze shuttered, then slid over Mickey's shoulder, staring past him at the window. "I don't know. I just don't."

The bubble they'd created overnight began to deflate.

Mickey eyed Benito's shower-damp hair and itched to comb his fingers through it, but the heartfelt yearning was ten minutes too late. "I've never asked you straight up," he said. "Maybe I didn't want the answer, but we can't hide from it forever."

Benito said nothing, and tension blanketed the room, settling deep in Mickey's bones.

He leaned forward and found Benito's hands, tangling their fingers together. "This might not make much sense to you, but I have to know what it is. Whatever you're into, I have to *know*, okay? If we're gonna keep seeing each other, I can't live with the fucking wondering. I can't—fuck. I just can't."

Benito sucked in a shaky breath and tore his stare from the window.

The apprehension in his gaze was killer. Mickey shivered, and every moment they'd shared till this point seemed to hang over a gaping cliff. "Tell me," he whispered. "Please."

Desperation flashed in Benito's dark eyes. He took another breath; then something seemed to shut him down. Iron gates went up, and whatever he'd been about to say died a fiery death. "There's nothing to tell," he said flatly. "I ran with a bad crew in London, but I don't do that shit anymore."

"Sure about that? Because—"

"Fucking hell." Benito rocked back on his heels. "Why won't you listen to me?"

"I am listening," Mickey said. "I'm just trying to tell you it's okay if there's more to it. I know I said I couldn't be around road life anymore, but maybe I overreacted. Or it's something I can work on. I just don't want any bullshit between us."

"It's not bullshit. How many times do I have to tell you I'm a broke taxi driver?"

Benito spoke low, but his words echoed in the quiet room all the same, and another shudder clutched the base of Mickey's spine.

He repressed it, swallowing down the roiling mass of doubt and fear that bloomed in his chest. "I'm sorry," he blurted. "I told you already I'm a paranoid freak, and it gets on top of me sometimes—"

Benito silenced him with a kiss, a fierce clash of lips that took Mickey back to the night they'd met. When they'd been strangers in an unfamiliar room, about to jump into the abyss.

No parachutes.

Freefall.

Some days Mickey was still falling. Others, he'd crash landed already and fucked everything up.

They broke apart, panting. Benito's gaze was bottomless.

Fierce.

He gripped Mickey's chin. "You're not a fucking freak. Don't ever say that shit around me again, or we're gonna have a problem. You feel me?"

A thousand rebuttals danced on Mickey's tongue, but he swallowed those too.

Just for this moment.

———

"I don't understand how you could forget the password when your password for everything is Sullivan."

Gianna glowered and strode ahead of Benito, her precious iPad tucked under her arm.

Suppressing a grin, Benito jogged to catch up and caught her shoulder. "Whoa, there. Don't run off. It's busy up here."

"So?" Gianna cast a baleful glance around the crowded shopping centre that smelled of bad burgers and stale coffee. "It's Milton Keynes, not Oxford Street. It's not like I couldn't walk to your flat if we got separated."

"How about we don't get separated in the first place and you stop being shitty with me because you fucked up?"

"Don't swear."

"Whatever," Benito retorted, but without the edge Gianna deserved. It was hard to be angry with her. He relied on her for the good emotions in life. "Don't be a brat then."

"I'm not. And you're wrong about the password thing. It's a pass*code*, for your information, so I can't use Sullivan."

"Yes, you can. Just use the numbers that correspond to the letters."

Gianna's sharp gaze flattened. "What?"

"You don't do that with your phone?"

"I use my thumb for my phone."

"And the number? You have to have one when you set it up."

"I can't remember it. Beni, you *know* I'm rubbish at numbers. Don't be a dickhead."

"Don't swear."

"But—"

"*Don't*. It'll get you in trouble eventually." Benito glanced ahead. The Apple store was twenty metres away, a queue snaking out of the doors. A sigh escaped him and he reconciled himself with the reality that this was going to take forever. "Listen, I'm going to get in the queue. Take my card and go buy some cookies from Millie's, okay? When you get back, I'll show you how to spell Sullivan's name with numbers."

Gianna wasn't convinced, but she took the card anyway and stomped to the cookie stand while Benito took their place in the line and kept a sharp eye on her and every face that seemed to look at her a second too long. In his pocket, his second phone buzzed like it had been doing ever since he'd retrieved it from his glovebox and turned it back on. He ignored it and tried to quell the sharp paranoia rising in his chest.

It's all in your head. You've let talking to Mickey feed your own fucking demons.

True story. And the parallels between Mickey's past and Benito's present made him sick to his stomach.

That and the barefaced lie he'd told Mickey. *"I don't do that shit anymore."* Fuck. If his night had gone better, there was every chance he'd have told that lie with the scent of packaged product still lacing his skin. With mud beneath his fingernails from burying the dirty cash with another fractured piece of his soul.

Your soul? Yeah, right. Until Mickey, you didn't give a fuck who got hurt in the game. Don't grow a conscience now.

"Beni?" Gianna was back. She handed him a white chocolate walnut cookie with a conciliatory half-smile. "I got your favourite."

"I don't have a favourite."

"I know, I know, you don't like sweet things, but you might like this one—it's got nuts in. They're healthy, right?"

Nothing about Benito's life was healthy right now. He took

the cookie and ruffled Gianna's curls. "Thanks, squirt. You ready to figure this passcode mystery out?"

"Is it hard?"

"No. Just different. Here, I'll show you on my phone."

"I don't want to."

"Why not?"

"Because I *don't*. Leave me alone."

Benito's patience wore thin. He shoved his phone into Gianna's hands. "If I left you alone, you'd be at home with Mum and a locked iPad. I haven't got time to do this shit every time you mess up, so pay attention, okay? Unless you want to factory reset every time."

He so rarely snapped that Gianna didn't protest as he forced her to watch him type in his passcode over and over, while he spelt out the corresponding word, then gave her the phone to practise on. But her silence was mutinous. And suffocating. The front of the Genius Bar line couldn't come fast enough.

The Apple employee called their number. Benito rooted his feet to the floor and propelled Gianna forward.

She grabbed his arm. "You're not coming?"

"Nope. Your device, your problem."

More discontent filled Gianna's dark gaze. She stuck her tongue out and stalked to the meeting pod, taking Benito's phone with him.

Sighing, he retreated to a set of white benches to wait for her to realise and bring it back.

She didn't. And after a while, he didn't miss it. How could he when the demon phone ruining his life was still angrily buzzing in his pocket? He'd ignored it all day, but alone in the crowded Apple store, it seemed louder than ever.

With one eye on Gianna, he retrieved the phone and cancelled the incoming call while he caught up on the dozen messages he'd missed. All were variants of the same thing.

call me

it's bad man

they think it's a rat

call me

we in trouble

i think they made me

Dread filled Benito's heart, hot and vicious. He rubbed his chest and then his lips as fear laced every sharp breath. If his contact had been made as a rat—even if it was to Benito and not the feds—Asa would take him out. And he'd do it *after* he'd made him talk. Benito knew how that shit went down. There was zero chance his man inside wouldn't give him up, especially as he'd yet to receive a penny for his trouble.

So put that right. Maybe he'll have enough to run.

The burner phone rang again. Glancing around, Benito answered. "Yeah?"

"Finally. I've been calling since last night."

"You shouldn't be calling at all considering what went down." Benito fought to keep his mind off Mickey—the only thing from last night that seemed to matter. "What the fuck was that?"

"I dunno, man. Someone tipped the feds."

"Sure about that? Or have they been watching this whole time?"

"I told you, I don't know. Asa thinks there's a rat."

"There is. It's you."

"Not that kind of rat."

"He won't see it that way."

"He can't find out. I'm a dead man walking if he does."

Benito said nothing. In another world, he'd have convinced himself the voice at the end of the phone was expendable. That his conscience could take it. But these days, he wasn't so sure. "He won't find out unless you're stupid. Lay low for a few weeks. Let some runs happen. Then I'll hit a big one before we walk away."

"That's your plan? To walk away?"

Benito cringed. *Fuck*. He'd said too much. And worse, forgotten his contact had been banking on something more dramatic. After all, he'd *seen* Benito do it before—seen him pull off a coup that had landed Dante Pope in prison and propelled Benito to the top until Asa had played his winning hand.

Like magic, Gianna emerged from the meeting pod, still clutching her iPad like it was solid gold, but a small smile in place of her scowl. Outside, the sun came out, bathing the glass walled store in warm light. It softened the stark warning that blasted through Benito's conscience, but he felt every jagged edge all the same. *Get out while you still can. Or she's dead anyway*.

"I have to walk away," he said. "But I'll see you right first, and I'll pay you double if you help me."

Fury crackled down the phone line. His contact blew out a hot breath. "You said Asa was finished. It's the only reason I risked my neck for you."

"He is finished. You think other crews are gonna do business with him with the feds on his back *and* his transport runs compromised? You don't need me. It's done."

"It's not done until he's dead."

"I never said I'd do that."

"You—"

"No," Benito snapped. "I made no promises. Remember who you are and who you're fucking talking to. I'll be in touch."

He killed the call as Gianna drew closer. He tried for a smile, but it hurt. Adrenaline pumped in his veins, and his heart thundered against his ribs. Deception boiled his blood, and unbidden, Mickey clouded his thoughts *again*.

Benito shivered. *You're a lying fucking liar, Martell.*

It was an accusation he'd faced many times, most of them justified, but never more so than as he'd driven away from Mickey's cosy house, the taste of his deceit still bitter on his tongue. It didn't matter that he'd done it to stop fresh panic clouding Mickey's beautiful face. That even now, he still felt the shuddering anxiety jumping beneath Mickey's warm skin. He'd *lied*, and there was no deliverance from that except telling the fucking truth.

I can't.

"What's wrong?"

Benito blinked. Gianna was practically on top of him. "What?"

"You're doing that thing again," she said. "You know, where you look like you're going to be sick and die."

"Nice. You know what? I'm gonna take you home to live with me. You're all the motivation I need in the morning."

Gianna rolled her eyes. "Don't be so sensitive. It's not my fault you're weird sometimes."

It really wasn't. Benito fought to calm himself enough to school his features. Fuck knew what Gianna was seeing in his face right now. And whatever it was, she didn't deserve it. "Sorry."

She nodded slowly, dark eyes narrowed in thought. "Why do you have two phones?"

"I told you why. Because . . ." But the lie died in his throat. He couldn't stomach it. "Because I have to work a job I don't like for a while."

"It's not for Uber?"

"No. It's something else."

"It's what Mum said, isn't it? It's the same thing you did in London when you got hurt."

The scar on Benito's ribs throbbed. He'd hidden it from Gianna for weeks. Then she'd taken the bus to Willen Lake to meet him and got caught in the rain. He'd given her his sweatshirt and she'd seen the gruesome wound.

She'd wept at the side of the lake, fresh rain merging with her hot tears. All the while Benito had remained a stagnant pit of nothing. Unfeeling. Cold.

He wasn't the same man now, though. *Now*, it seemed a day didn't pass when *everything* didn't hurt.

Benito dropped his head, and the truth bubbled out of him. "It's just for a little while, G, I promise."

"What is?"

"Every terrible thing you think of me. It's all true, but I'm trying to be a better man. You know that, right?"

Gianna had small hands, with long, slender fingers. She'd always wanted to play the piano, but no one in her life had ever got it together enough to make it happen. She brought her elegant fingers to Benito's unshaven jaw and compelled him with the sweetest force to look at her. "You are a better man, Beni. The *best*. I don't care what you do for a job."

"It's not a job. It's fucking criminal, but it's not forever. I'll be out soon, I promise."

"Then what?"

"Then I'll be a taxi driver for real. All day, every day, and you won't have to worry about me ever again."

"What about Mum?"

"What about her?"

"Will you still pay her arrears?"

Benito flinched. "Of course. I don't use dirty money for that."

"Then why are you doing it? It's not for me, is it? I don't want street money either."

You shouldn't even know what that is. But for once, Benito didn't blame himself. Gianna was old enough to know how things were. "You've never touched street money, I swear. It's not even about that anymore. There's just some shit I have to do before I can leave."

"How long?"

"A few weeks? A month maybe?"

"Then you'll stop?"

"Yes." Benito took Gianna's hand from his face and tucked it against his larger palm. "I don't want this life, G. For me or for you. You know that, right?"

Gianna nodded and burrowed into Benito's chest for a hug. He held her tight, using her familiar scent to tie himself down to the world, all the while chasing thoughts he couldn't quite catch. The endgame he'd promised Gianna, combined with the barefaced lie he'd told Mickey, was a mountain he wasn't fit to climb, and he was more out of his depth than ever. But as long as he held Gianna in his arms, he could breathe.

He felt like crying when she pulled away. "Mum's got a counsellor coming round on Monday."

"What? From where?"

"A charity in Wolverton. I think the housing association sent them."

"Was it Mickey—I mean, the housing officer?"

"I don't know. But they called Mum's phone and she answered, so that's something, right?"

"I guess." Guilt flamed in Benito's gut, and the lies he'd told suffocated him a little bit more. The whole time he'd been living a life that had hurt Mickey so badly, Mickey had done more for his family than anyone—including Benito—had in years. "She still has to let them in, though."

Gianna hissed through her teeth. "Don't be like that. I think she wants to be better this time. It's not all her fault."

"I never said it was."

"Why are you so hard on her then?"

Because she let your dad stamp on my head until I threw up. "I'm not hard on her, just realistic. She's been like this for years. It's going to take more than a phone call to fix it."

"You're mean."

"I'm not."

"You *are*." Gianna poked Benito in the side. "Can I have a milkshake?"

"From where?"

"Maccy D's. I'll pay you back."

"With what?"

"Erm . . . your phone? I still have it in my pocket." Gianna flashed a bright grin and took off like a rocket, darting out of the Apple store before Benito could stand.

Little shit. He rose and followed her, trailing her out of the store and into the throng of weekend shoppers. Her dark hair bobbed up and down as she ran, but knowing where she was headed, Benito didn't rush. He was too old to be charging through the shopping centre without attracting attention, and he wasn't in the mood to deal with overzealous rent-a-feds.

Fuck that noise.

He caught up with Gianna at McDonalds. Her smile was blinding, but Benito was distracted by the stare of a lone figure loitering outside Nando's. Hood up, head down, but his eyes seemed to track Benito's every move, his slow-moving gaze like pin pricks in Benito's skull. Just a couple at first; then they spread like wildfire and set every sense ablaze.

Growling, Benito speared the teenager with a glare, daring him to keep looking. The teenager slid his attention away, but another replaced him, then another, and another, until Benito couldn't keep up.

Calm your tits, man. You're paranoid. But it didn't feel like paranoia, it felt *real*, and for the hundredth time that day, Benito couldn't breathe.

"Beni?" Gianna's soft hand grazed Benito's fingers. "Do you want one too?"

"No," Benito said absently. Even without the fact that he couldn't stomach any more sugar without hitting the gym for an extra hour, it was a sad fact that after paying Rosetta's monthly arrears payment, two shitty milkshakes was probably pushing it.

He dropped a handful of change into Gianna's palm and waited outside, back to the wall, surveying the crowds. Hoodie kid was back, but so were a hundred other slingers. McDonalds was the place to be. Benito glared at the hoodie kid anyway, though. It suited his mood.

Gianna came back with a banana milkshake that smelt like hell.

Benito grimaced and backed away. "Don't spill that shit in my car."

"Don't swear. And don't drive next time. I could've met you here."

"You're not getting the bus to the city centre on your own." Another hooded figure breached Benito's peripheral. Taller this time and built like a man. Benito tracked him as he led Gianna back to the multi-storey where he'd left his car, trying not to flinch as the devil on his shoulder argued with itself.

Double back. See if he follows.

Idiot. He's going to Subway like every other dickhead who doesn't want nuggets.

What if he isn't, though? What if he jumps you in the stairwell and takes Gianna?

Taking a child in broad daylight was a stretch even for the monsters Benito created in his head, but he avoided the stairs anyway and bundled Gianna into the lift.

She eyed him over her milkshake. "You hate lifts."

"No, I don't."

"Uh, yeah you do. I haven't been in one with you since I was a toddler and it got stuck and you punched the security guard who let us out."

"That didn't happen."

"Yes, it did."

Benito made an impatient noise and willed the lift to hurry the fuck up to the uppermost parking floor. He couldn't clearly recall the incident Gianna was talking about. It had happened in the weeks after Roberto had given him a concussion, and months and months had gone by in a blur of headaches and shaky hands. His skull throbbed now just thinking about it.

The lift dinged at the top floor. The doors opened so slowly Benito wanted to kick through them, but he made himself wait, holding Gianna back until the lift had emptied out.

At the car, she leaned against the bonnet, grinning.

Benito scowled. "What?"

"I still have your phone."

"Keep it," Benito snapped tiredly. "The pass*code* is your name, if you can figure it out."

"Don't be a dick."

"Don't swear."

Gianna held up Benito's legitimate phone. The other felt like a brick in his pocket. "You got a bunch of messages," she said. "I didn't mean to read them, but they came up on the screen."

"My messages don't do that."

"They do if you got the new WhatsApp update and didn't reset all your notification settings."

Benito frowned, his brain mush. "How do you know all this stuff?"

"Everyone knows unless they live in a cave."

"Just give me my phone."

Gianna grinned wider.

"*Gianna.*"

"What? Am I not supposed to know Mickey thinks you're cute when you sleep?"

Burn. Benito froze, half relieved by the nonchalance in Gianna's teasing and half mortified that she'd caught a glimpse of his sex life. He'd never hidden his bisexuality from her, but at the same time, they'd never come close to discussing it either. And he'd certainly never imagined himself confessing to fucking his mother's housing officer.

Lie. Tell her it's a different Mickey. But no words came to him. Benito could only stare while Gianna laughed.

"He wants to see you again, by the way," she said. "On Monday. He has the day off."

Benito rounded the car like a bullet and snatched the phone.

Gianna giggled and sensibly slid into her seat and shut the car door.

Benito turned his back to the window, blocking her out, and opened the message thread he shared with Mickey. Three messages came after the one Gianna had paraphrased.

Mickey: *come out with me on monday? day off.*

Mickey: *fck. I spelt it all rigth*

Mickey: *2 soon oops mondy?*

Monday. Somehow Benito had convinced himself it would be weeks and weeks before he saw Mickey again. Perhaps there was a part of him that had believed he never would. That his lie would burst free before he found a chance to make it the truth.

Heart full, he closed his eyes and made himself the same promise he had Gianna.

Just a little while longer.

14

Mickey asked Benito to meet him at Bletchley Park. He thought about waiting in his car like a weirdo, but the sun drew him out to a bench outside the grand old house. He tapped at his phone, fudging his way through email drafts he'd check over later. Messages pinged through from the office and from Isha, but they were all signed off with the same instruction: *Don't action this until tomorrow. Enjoy your day off.*

It had been months since he'd taken a four-day week, and when he'd checked his phone after Benito had left the day before, Isha had finally rumbled him.

"Self-care days are mandatory. You have no home visits on Monday. Take the day, and I'll look at the rest of your schedule to make sure you're not pulling too many hours."

Mickey sighed. Isha was the best boss in the world, but he didn't understand that Mickey *needed* to be busy. Those hours and hours home alone with nothing and no one to occupy his time sent him crawling back to hell. *You're not alone, though. Benito is coming.*

If Benito came. He'd gone offline before he'd read Mickey's last message, and Mickey hadn't looked at WhatsApp since. Sometimes leaving things to chance reset his brain.

Others it sent him round the bend, but today was a good day. Spending eight hours in his bed with Benito simply sleeping and talking had left him feeling oddly zen, and he clung to the sensation like a drowning man.

Or like an addict obsessed with anything that made him feel good.

Because *fuck*, Benito made him feel amazing, even when he was asleep, stretched out beside Mickey with his lovely face half hidden by a pillow, his arm flung over Mickey's belly.

He's cute. A reach for a self-confessed ex-gangster, but it fit.

Ex-gangster? Mickey frowned at his phone and pushed the creeping suspicion away. He'd wasted enough time on paranoid thoughts lately. Right now, he wanted to walk in the sun with a hot dude and discover things about him that didn't make his dark eyes flash with pain. *I want to know the other stuff.* Because whatever Benito said about himself, he was still the kind of man who left groceries on the doorstep of the mother he could barely stand and brought his little sister breakfast every morning before school.

He's good. I know he is.

"Is that porn?"

Mickey jumped. Benito stood in front of him, bundled up in a North Face jacket and squinting into the winter sun. "You think I'd look at porn outside a museum?"

Benito shrugged. "I've never thought about you outside a museum."

"You don't think I'm the type?"

"To wank at a museum?"

A grin warmed Mickey from the inside out. "Yeah, that's exactly what I meant."

Benito smiled too and rubbed his hands together, blowing on them. "Wanker or not, it's fucking *cold*."

"Don't like the great outdoors?"

"I like it well enough. Just figured we'd be spending the day inside."

"I have you for the whole day?"

"If you like."

Mickey rose from the bench. "Works for me."

They set off at a slow amble, meandering past the clusters of buildings that housed various displays of the enigma codebreakers. Benito thrust his hands in his pockets and stared at the ground. "There's something I should probably tell you."

Cold dread threatened the easy warmth Benito's appearance had gifted Mickey. He shot Benito major side eye. "Is it bad?"

"Depends on your definition of bad."

Mickey smirked. "You know my definition of bad. It's good, right? Always fucking good."

Benito's lips twitched. He licked them, as if it helped simmer down whatever image Mickey had planted in his head. Then he shook his head. "I'm not talking about that."

"Then what?"

"This place." Benito raised his head and glanced around. "I came here on every school trip since it opened, so I've been here a hundred times."

Relief so acute Mickey could taste it spread through him.

He laughed. "That's it? I thought you were going to tell me you'd killed my cat."

"You have a cat?"

"Metaphorical cat."

"You don't have a cat? You can have my sister's. Fucking thing is a vandalistic shit bag."

"Vandalistic?" Mickey laughed again. "Okay, man. So, you don't like cats?"

"I don't like that cat," Benito corrected. "He fucks with me on purpose."

"Cute motherfucker, though."

"You know him?"

"If it's the same massive beast your mum had last year, then yeah, I think so. He sat on my laptop bag and wouldn't get off."

"That's the prick." Benito swivelled his own side-stare at Mickey. "I keep forgetting you've been around all this time and it's me that hasn't."

Mickey's humour settled into a soft smile. He didn't know what to say to that. Before Benito, despite a work ethic that left him little time for himself, he'd never had any trouble separating his job from his personal life. Now it felt so entwined he couldn't fathom what was the past, the present, or yet to come. *What are we doing?*

God, he had no idea.

Benito led the way around the park. Mickey followed, amused by his word-perfect descriptions of every exhibit.

"You really have been here a thousand times."

"Yup. I wouldn't lie about that."

What would you lie about?

Stop it.

They were by the actual enigma machine. Mickey gazed at it and pushed the noisy demon off his shoulder. "You know, I don't even like history that much. I just wanted to be somewhere I didn't want to jump on you the whole time. Just to see what it's like."

Benito crouched on the floor, reading a low displayed plaque as if it was the first time he'd ever seen it, not the thousandth. "And?"

"I still want to jump you, but I like the fact you're a closet nerd."

"I'm not in the closet," Benito retorted. "Everyone I've ever cared about knows this about me."

"That's not many people."

Benito sighed. "I guess not. You're on the list, though. In case you were wondering."

Mickey couldn't deny it. He grinned a little and offered Benito his hand to help him up.

Benito took it, and for the six seconds their hands were clasped, all felt right with the world.

Mickey missed the sensation when Benito let go. "We should eat soon," he said. "You want to go for a walk first?"

"Okay."

They left the exhibition buildings behind and began a slow walk around the park. Despite the sun, it really was cold, but Mickey's northern blood didn't mind. He turned his face into the wind and took deep, bracing breaths while Benito hid behind his coat. "We can go somewhere warmer if you want."

"Nah." Benito drifted closer, so their elbows bumped. "This is nice."

"You're not bored?"

"With you?"

"I meant in general, but okay."

Benito snorted out a laugh. "Trust me, mate. Nothing about you is boring, but even if it was, I think I'd still love it. I think I need boring in my life right now."

Mickey tried not to overanalyse Benito's words. He kept his gaze on the landscape around them and nodded. "I've felt that before. Don't go too far the other way, though. Too much quiet . . . it's as destructive as chaos."

Benito shot him another sideways glance. "Is that what's going on with you? Too much quiet?"

"Maybe. My bosses keep asking me to go to London and have dinner with them near the office or to their big houses in this posh village they live in, but I never go."

"Why not?"

Mickey frowned. "They're too happy, I suppose, with their boyfriends and husbands, and I just don't know what to do with it. Sometimes I think I only function properly when everything is a fucking struggle."

"You don't think it's because you don't know any different yet?"

"Yet?"

Benito fixed his dark stare on the horizon. "Is this so hard for you?"

"What?"

"Being here. Me and you."

Mickey thought about his answer for less than a second. "No. This is, like, utopia for me. Like we're in another world being regular people doing regular shit."

Benito shrugged. "Maybe we are."

———

Benito fought for breath, sweat beading his skin and running down his spine. He squeezed his eyes shut and bunched his screaming muscles. *Just one more.*

He wrestled the loaded bar bell and won, raising it from his chest, then dumping it back on the rack. Panting, he sat up, heart thumping, head swimming. It was his fourth set, and he already regretted it, but putting his body on blast was the best alternative he had to fixating on his growing obsession with Mickey.

Growing obsession? Like it wasn't sky high before?

Whatever. Benito moved to the leg press and inflicted the same punishment on his quads that he had on his upper body. Lactic acid screamed through his thighs, and he gritted his teeth, a quiet grunt escaping him. *Don't think about him.*

Fuck.

Benito wasn't sure he even knew how. Since Bletchley Park, they'd spent three more entire days together, wandering around, eating, talking. Mickey thought he was terrible at being ordinary, but despite the fact there was *nothing* ordinary about him, he was the best company Benito had ever had. He sucked up every mundane moment they shared like a sponge and bottled the feeling to soak in when they were apart, and he *missed* Mickey so much it hurt.

They hadn't fucked again, though. Or even kissed. Not even after the late-night dinner they'd shared at the weekend. Benito didn't know why. All he knew for certain was that Mickey had made no move to close the distance between them, and Benito hadn't either. *And* that the heat between them still raged as hot as ever, so *nothing* about the impasse made any fucking sense.

Impasse. You learn that word from the history channel?

Of course. Benito didn't even try to silence Mickey's voice in his head. He liked it. It stopped his treacherous self-esteem wondering if Mickey was burning off steam in Freefall rather than the gym, because the rational human he could be when he really tried *knew* he wasn't.

An hour later, Benito limped out of the gym and to his car with every intention of driving home for a nap. It was ten in the morning. He'd worked all night long, seen Gianna onto the bus, and hit the gym straight after. He was so tired he could barely focus, but hunger outweighed fatigue. Breakfast—and his last text from Mickey—seemed a long time ago.

Benito drove to Fenny Stratford and pulled up outside the Italian bakery Roberto's family had once owned before he'd run it into the ground. A new family fronted it now, and they weren't even Italian, but Benito didn't care. The chicken, mushroom, and mozzarella paninis were too good for principled food choices. He bought two and picked up some cannoli for Gianna. He hadn't planned on stopping by Rosetta's place but somehow found himself outside Barnfield Court ten minutes later.

Twat. You were only here three hours ago.

Story of his fucking life.

Leaving his precious sandwiches behind, he took the stairs two at a time and knocked on Rosetta's door as a courtesy before letting himself inside. "Mum? Where you at?"

Somewhere inside the flat, a door opened and closed. Assuming it was Rosetta locking herself away, Benito toed his trainers off and padded through the flat to the kitchen to put Gianna's dessert away.

"Beni?"

"Jesus *fuck*." Benito jumped and whirled around. Rosetta was behind him, still in her dressing gown. "Don't sneak up on me."

She offered him a wan smile. "I didn't. You're in *my* home. And don't swear."

Benito had forgotten that Rosetta had once been in on the running joke he shared with Gianna.

Sadness flared. He dampened it down and opened the fridge. "I brought Gianna cannoli from Pepe's. Is there anything else you need? I've got time for a supermarket run."

"We're fine. How about you?"

"What do you mean?"

"I mean, how are you, Benito? You look like you haven't slept for a week."

"What do you care?"

"That's not fair."

"Really? This again?"

Rosetta ventured further into the kitchen. She retrieved her favourite frying pan from the hook above the stove and the decanter of olive oil that was never out of reach. "I know I haven't been the best mother to you, but I'm allowed to care. You don't get to decide that for me."

"I'm not—fuck. You know what? Never mind. I'm leaving anyway."

Benito moved to step around her.

Rosetta caught his arm in her cold, bony hand. "Wait."

"Why?"

"Because you look hungry and I can help you with that."

"Help me?"

"Yes. I have plenty of food now. My Universal Credit payments came through and the housing officer helped me set up a budget plan."

"Mickey?"

"Yes." Rosetta slid him a glance he couldn't decipher. "You've met him. The northern boy with the nice eyes."

"If you say so." Benito felt faint. He gripped the peeling laminate counter behind him and leaned against it. "I should still go. I don't want to make you uncomfortable."

"You don't," Rosetta said shortly. "*I* do that all by myself. Did you know anxiety is ninety per cent worrying about worrying?"

"Um, no?" *Am I even awake right now?* "Who told you that? Doctor Google?"

"No. The counsellor that came round last week. We talked about you a lot."

"Why?"

"Because I told her I wanted you around more, but every time I think about asking you to come, I panic about being anxious when you're here."

Why are you telling me this? Benito leaned harder against the counter and watched Rosetta move around the kitchen, retrieving eggs from the windowsill and a loaf of Italian bread from the cupboard.

She poured olive oil into her pan and fried eggs with oregano and chilli flakes. Then she dunked the sliced bread in the pan and fried that too, like she had when he was little.

The world seemed to stick its feet in treacle. Time stopped, then retreated, and Benito was six years old again. Gianna didn't exist, and it was just him, Rosetta, and his dad eating breakfast on a Sunday morning—the only day of the week Victor Martell hadn't got up at the crack of dawn and left for work before Benito was awake.

Numb, Benito sat at the same battered kitchen table and stared at the same plate of food.

Rosetta nudged him. "Eat. I can't do much for you anymore, but I can do this."

Benito ate, clearing his plate slower than his growling stomach wanted to, while he watched Rosetta flit around her kitchen. She seemed different, somehow, though he couldn't say how. Christ, she wasn't even dressed, let alone close to functioning like anyone's mother, but for the first time in years, it felt like she was. "You'll be offering to do my washing next." In his head, he uttered the words flatly. Out loud, his tone was warm, surprising Rosetta as much as himself.

She brought him a mug of coffee. "I . . . I could do that for you, if you needed me to."

"I was joking, Mum. I don't need you to wash my clothes."

"Oh well. Okay. I'm just saying that I could. Maybe if you left them outside?"

Benito pushed his plate away, a familiar frown replacing any semblance of good humour. "I don't understand. If you don't want me to come in anymore, just say so. I only have a key to keep Gianna safe."

"It's not that. I *like* that you have a key now. It's—"

"*What*? You're not making any fucking sense."

He regretted snapping as soon as the words left his mouth, but Rosetta didn't flinch. She pulled out a chair, sat beside Benito, and folded her hands on the table. "It's easier for me if I don't know you're coming. Like today. I didn't have time to be afraid. It's the waiting, you see, that makes me that way."

Benito processed, turning the explanation over in his mind until it made some kind of sense. He thought of the big raid his contact in Asa's crew had turned him onto just a few hours ago. How the anticipation was killing him and he'd hit it *right now* if he could.

He thought of Mickey too, and the wild butterflies in his belly each time he drove to meet him. Sometimes he thought *that* might kill him, but it was the sweetest pain.

Focus. He looked at Rosetta again. "Thank you for telling me," he said slowly. "I've never thought about it like that. I can try and come by at less obvious times, if that helps."

Rosetta's hesitant smile turned wry. "My boy, you never do anything obvious. It's what makes you so formidable."

A bitter laugh escaped Benito before he could catch it. "That's a big word I don't deserve, but thanks."

He drained his coffee and stood, taking his plate to the sink and washing it on autopilot. Roberto had been the scuzziest human to live with, but he'd always been quick to punish Benito for not completing his chores fast enough. If Benito thought too hard, he could still feel the heel of Roberto's hand hitting his temple.

So don't think about it.

Mickey was the quickest remedy. Benito thought of the last time they'd been together, leaning against his car as Benito had walked to his own. It had been raining and windy, but Mickey didn't seem to feel the cold. He was solid warmth, in every fucking sense, and with damp hair? Man. Benito couldn't cope.

He turned from the sink to find Rosetta watching him. "What?"

"I was speaking," she said. "You didn't hear me. Is something on your mind?"

"What were you saying?"

"I was saying that I told the housing officer what I told you. He said he'll surprise me next time he comes. I like him, Beni. He's a nice boy.

"He's a grown man, Mum."

"Is he? I thought he was younger than you."

"He could be eight years younger than me and still be a man."

"Oh. Yes. I suppose he could be." Rosetta reached around Benito and took his plate from the rack.

She dried it and put it away.

Benito took it as his cue to leave. He snagged his keys from the table and drifted to the door, but his feet seemed to drag with every step.

Rosetta followed him into the hallway. For a moment, Benito thought—perhaps even feared—she might hug him.

She didn't.

15

"Why are you answering your mum's phone? Is everything okay?" Mickey swung his car into a space on an estate on the other side of Bletchley and checked he'd called the right number. He was used to Rosetta De Luca's phone ringing out or going straight to voicemail. It had been . . . fuck, he didn't even know how long it had been since an actual human had answered.

Gianna De Luca giggled. "You sound really freaked out."

"I'm just surprised. I was going to leave a message. Now, answer my question. Everything okay?"

"Yeah. Mum's in the bath. I think she would've answered if she'd heard the phone. She's doing much better at that."

"It went well with the counsellor then?"

"Uh-huh. She's trying really hard. She made my brother breakfast the other day."

Mickey searched his car for cigarettes. Over the past few weeks, the time he'd spent with Benito had been so healthy and wholesome his consumption had gone down, but in the middle of the longest Wednesday in the history of Wednesdays, he needed a fucking smoke.

The glovebox was empty, though, and a scrambled hand under the seats turned up nothing either.

Sighing, he focused on Gianna. On *Benito's* sister. Because wasn't that a lovely conflict of interest? "Breakfast? That's nice." *I know he likes breakfast.* "For you too, I guess?"

"I wasn't here. I was at school. But Beni said he's going to come and see Mum more when I'm not around. Surprise her so she doesn't get scared and lock him out."

"She asked me to do that too. No breakfast offer, though. Maybe I'm in the wrong job."

Gianna laughed like a tinkling bell. Mickey smiled too. Benito's little sister was wise beyond her years, and it felt good to hear her sound her age. "She has lemon cake in the fridge if you wanted to drop by today. I won't tell her you might come."

Mickey eyed the clock. Convincing an elderly tenant she didn't need to keep every newspaper she'd ever bought had already taken an hour longer than he had time for, and he had no real reason to visit Rosetta De Luca beyond a welfare check that wasn't strictly necessary now he'd spoken to Gianna, but . . .

She was Benito's mother. His family. Whatever he and Mickey were to each other, he wasn't going to miss an opportunity to make sure her and Gianna were safe and well.

"Okay," he said. "Don't tell her I'm coming because I might not make it, but if I get time, I'll swing by before I head home."

Gianna agreed and ended the call, leaving Mickey to stare

at his phone and wonder if Wednesday was trying to turn his entire world upside down.

He spent the rest of the day on the Netherfield estate, driving from house to house and dealing with everything from unpaid rent to fixing doors that had been kicked in by the police. Sometimes he screwed the doors back in himself and "forgot" to write a report. Not because he gave a shit about whoever was stashing coke and weed in their nan's loft, but because he wasn't about to evict a ninety-year-old from her home because her grandson was a scrote.

Is he a scrote, though? Or is he just a kid with no options?

Mickey drowned out whatever answer his brain conjured up with his drill. The crunching sound suited his mood, and the vibration of the drill masked any jitters in his hands, but it wasn't all bad. He'd be lying if he didn't admit the last few weeks had been easier with Benito around. They didn't do much, just walked around, shared cheap meals, and worked out at Mickey's gym. They hadn't fucked. Or even kissed. And despite a raging inferno in his bones every time Benito was close, Mickey was okay with that.

He wanted Benito more than ever, but somehow, the simple things had begun to matter more.

It was five o'clock when he left Netherfield. Traffic was murder. By the time Isha called, Mickey hadn't moved for twenty minutes.

Isha chuckled. "Sorry about that, but it's probably just as well. I just got out of a meeting with the council and the cladding firm that did Barnfield. They're coming in two weeks to install the fire breaks."

"The fire breaks they said we didn't need because there's nothing unsafe about that fucking cladding?"

"Yes, those ones," Isha said dryly. "Turns out they were full of shit, but that's no surprise. They wanted to wait until the summer to install the breaks, but Dom went postal on them and they, er, changed their minds."

"Too fucking right," Mickey grunted, grateful, as ever, that he worked for people who didn't flinch when he spoke his mind. "Are they doing the whole building or just our flats?"

"The whole building. Dom went off in front of the council bosses, so I'm pretty sure the entire city will be done by the end of the year."

"Nice one."

"Yes, I thought so. Are you okay to visit our residents before you go home tonight and let them know what's happening? We'll send letters, but I'd like them to hear it in person too, if that's possible, so we can reassure them we're doing everything we can to keep them safe."

"I can do that," Mickey said, his rueful grin all for himself. "As it happens, I'm not far away."

"I was hoping you'd say that. I'm sorry for adding extra hours onto your day. I'll make sure you get them back next week."

"Honestly, it's fine. I was heading that way anyhow."

Isha didn't ask why. He said goodbye and hung up, abandoning Mickey to his tapping fingers and his Libertines playlist. His heart and soul missed the dark drum and bass he'd grown up with, but he couldn't listen to those beats when he was alone. It scared him. So he settled for scratchy indie music and his own bad singing voice.

A *full hour* later, he pulled into Barnfield Court.

He had seven households to visit. Leaving the De Lucas till last, he started at the bottom, and made his way up the tower block, doubling back when the second tenant came home from work.

The final flat before Rosetta's was Mr Morris, a Gulf War veteran who was one of Mickey's favourite residents to visit. He was also a stubborn old git who insisted on doing everything himself, despite the fact his arthritic hands could barely hold a knife and fork.

"I can do it," Mickey said for the fourth time as he stood by the badly leaking kitchen tap. "You don't even have to wait for maintenance to come out. I can fix it right now."

"No need, son. No need." Mr Morris wrapped his stiff fingers around the spanner he'd been clutching when Mickey had arrived for his impromptu visit. "Now tell me about this building work. Was the council lying when they told us these blocks weren't wrapped in the same cladding as Grenfell Tower?"

That was the other thing about Mr Morris. He was sharp as a tack and missed *nothing*.

Mickey gave up his attempt to coax the tools from the older man's hands and claimed a seat at his kitchen table. "It's not the same cladding. DOSHA checked before they took these flats on, but there are some fire breaks missing from the interior cavities. If fire broke out, it would affect compartmentation, meaning—"

"It would spread too fast from flat to flat for residents to escape." Mr Morris shot Mickey a dead-eyed stare. "Especially if they obeyed the current instructions to stay inside and wait for the fire brigade."

"That's why I'm here," Mickey countered. "And why I remind you every couple of months to check the updated safety advice on a regular basis—why are you looking at me like that?"

Mr Morris shrugged. "I'm just thinking that's all well and good for everyone in this building that has you as their housing officer, but what about the rest? I don't know about you, but I can't remember the last time I saw anyone from the council on this estate."

In a warped kind of way, it was probably the nicest thing anyone had said to Mickey all week, but it planted a seed in his brain. One that sprouted green and voracious shoots that wrapped around his conscience and wouldn't let go. He sighed. "Are you suggesting that I knock on *every* door in this building tonight, and the one next door?"

Mr Morris turned back to his leaky tap. "I'm not suggesting anything. Just playing devil's advocate, son."

Bastard. Mickey's mind flitted to the ton of fire safety leaflets he still had in a box in the boot of his car and resigned himself to the extra hour he'd have to spend delivering them *and* explaining himself to whoever asked why he was spamming council properties with DOSHA material. *I hate my job*.

Sometimes he even believed it.

Ten minutes later found him in front of Rosetta De Luca's door. He knocked and braced himself for silence.

She opened up three seconds later, catching them both off guard.

"*Oh*. I wasn't expecting you today."

"Neither was I." Mickey stepped back, letting her know he didn't need to be invited in. "I'm just letting you know there's going to be some maintenance work going on later this month. Contractors are going to need access to your property.

Is that something you can handle, or do you need me to find you alternative accommodation for a couple of days?"

Rosetta blanched. "You want me to leave?"

"No. Not at all. But it's an option if you need it."

"How long will the work take?"

"Depends."

"On?"

Mickey measured his words. The last thing he wanted to do was make an already anxious tenant feel unsafe in her home. "It depends what they find that needs fixing, but the email I just read says each flat should take no more than a day." He thought back to the last conversation he'd had with Rosetta. "Would it be easier if I asked for yours to be done first? So you don't have to wait?"

Rosetta's lips twitched in a half-smile that reminded Mickey so much of Benito his bones *ached*. "You know, it always surprises me when people listen. I don't know why."

"Maybe because you don't believe anyone would want to make your life easier?"

"Maybe. The last person to do your job told Gianna he'd give her cat to the RSPCA when she was at school. She didn't sleep for a month after that."

Mickey grimaced. "He didn't work for DOSHA."

"I know, sweetheart. You look tired. Do you want something to eat?"

"Honestly, I'm fine. I have more people to see before I can go home. Do you want me to text you with the exact time and date for the work, or would you rather I didn't?"

"I don't want to know," Rosetta said. "Perhaps you could tell my son, though? Just in case?"

It was on the tip of Mickey's tongue to lie and say he

didn't have Benito's contact details, but something in Rosetta's dark, familiar gaze quieted him. He nodded and backed away until Benito's mother shut her front door.

Bemused, he jogged down the stairs, half a mind on the leaflets he still had to dig out of his car, the other entrenched in his favourite place: Benito.

Alone at night, in his bed, Mickey allowed himself to focus on the parts of Benito that made his blood run hot—his warm skin, cut muscles, and sinful lips. In the cold light of day—though the sun had set an hour ago—he tried to think of other things. Like the fact that Rosetta and Benito had apparently repaired their relationship enough for her to cook him breakfast. *I wonder—*

Mickey's foot hit the bottom step, and his distracted gaze solidified on the outside world. There wasn't much to the entrance of Barnfield Court—just a ramp and a railing that needed painting, but it was never quiet. Right now, it was bustling with folk coming home from work, and kids hanging out in menacing clusters because they had nowhere else to go.

By the ramp was a set of steps where residents who didn't want to smoke in their flats caught a few moments of peace. A lone figure sat there now with Mickey's favourite set of gym-honed shoulders.

Benito.

Mickey's heart skipped a beat. He jogged forward with little conscious thought, as drawn to Benito's cigarette as he was to the man himself.

He dropped down beside Benito and plucked the smoke from his fingers. "Cheers, man. You read my fucking mind."

Benito nodded, as if he'd heard Mickey coming *and* sensed his hours-long craving for nicotine. "I saw your car."

"And you waited for me?"

Benito shrugged. "I didn't know if I should, but somehow I couldn't leave before I saw you."

"You'd have seen me a lot quicker if you'd come inside. I was just talking to your mum."

"You just missed me then. I was there five minutes ago."

"Oh."

"Yeah. Oh. She likes me at the moment."

Mickey took a deep, soul-clearing drag on Benito's cigarette. "How do you feel about her?"

"Depends how much sleep I've had. Right now, I'm running on an eight-hour nap, and she made me the best sandwich I've ever had, so we're pretty tight."

"That's the way to your heart, eh? Feed you?"

"Like you didn't already know that."

Mickey said nothing. He couldn't deny he'd known for a long time now that presenting Benito with something to eat was a sure-fire way to put a smile on his face. But his heart?

Man. Mickey wasn't ready for that conversation. Or maybe he was, and he just didn't have a fucking clue where to start.

Benito nudged him. "What did you need to speak to her about? She hasn't missed a rent payment, has she?"

"Nope. She's all square. I needed to tell her about some maintenance work happening in a few weeks. Actually, she asked me to give you the date and time so she didn't freak out about it, so I'd have been calling you soon enough anyway."

"That's the only reason you were going to call me?"

Mickey grinned, letting his mind drift back to the scene

he'd conjured up in his dreams the previous night. Putting short-term brakes on their physical relationship had done wonders for his imagination and absolutely *nothing* to cool the current that thrummed between them. "As it goes, I was going to invite you for a sleepover."

Benito raised a brow. "A sleepover? With horror films and popcorn?"

"If you like. I've got the catering and accommodation covered, but feel free to take charge of the entertainment."

"You might be sorry you said that."

"Doubt it." Mickey finished Benito's cigarette, stubbed it out, and flicked it into a nearby bin with perfect aim. "You've never let me down yet."

"What about the chilli noodles I bought you that burnt your lips?"

"That entertained *you*, which is good enough for me."

"It shouldn't be. I want you to have fun too." Benito's gaze flashed with heat.

Mickey absorbed it as it travelled through him like wild-fire, setting light to the temporary gates they'd silently constructed over the last few weeks. "You know what I like," he said. "I trust you to bring your A game."

Benito nodded slowly, as if his mind was stoking the flames. "I can do that. When?"

"Tomorrow?"

"I can't. I have to work, and the next day too. I can do Friday?"

It pained Mickey to wait that long, but he tried not to let it show on his face. After all, a Friday encounter had the potential to last the whole weekend, but it still felt like a lifetime away. As if the world could change before then and snatch it away from them. "Friday is good," he said after a beat of tense silence. "You like pizza, right?"

Benito smiled a little. "You're not going to cook for me, Larwood?"

"Probably not. I have other plans."

"Thought I was in charge of the entertainment?"

"You are, but . . . not that much."

A full-on belly laugh escaped Benito. Mickey laughed too—a reflexive reaction that seemed to kick his heart free of whatever hill it had been stuck on until now. "I should go," he said. "I need to fetch something from my car, then visit the other block before I can go home."

"I have to leave too," Benito said. "Work."

Neither of them moved. Then Benito sighed. "Can I walk you to your car?"

"If you like."

They rose together and made the short walk to where Mickey had abandoned his car by the garages. He opened the boot and rummaged around while Benito hovered. "What are you looking for?"

"Fire safety leaflets. Mr Morris put the wind up me, so I'm going to stick them through every letterbox before I go."

"He's the one with the gun under his pillow, right?"

"What?"

"I'm messing with you." Benito held up his hands. "It's just when he first moved in, everyone said he'd shoot you if you tried to fuck with him, because he was a soldier."

"I don't know about that, but I get the feeling he could handle himself back in the day."

"This was twenty years ago. He was the biggest man I'd ever seen back then."

"He's still big," Mickey said. "But he's pushing seventy, so I reckon you could outrun him."

Benito snorted and dropped his gaze to the leaflets Mickey had rooted out. "Has this got anything to do with the maintenance you were talking about?"

Mickey shifted the stack of leaflets to the front of the boot and grabbed a handful. "Indirectly. DOSHA did a cladding inspection a while ago and turned up some missing fire breaks in the cavities. Not enough to make the building lethal—I hope, at least—but it's still fucking criminal."

"Cladding? You mean, like Grenfell?"

Mickey understood why Benito's mind went there. Anyone who'd seen that tower block burning would never forget it. "It's not the same cladding as Grenfell. Trust me, it was the first thing my bosses checked when we took these flats on. But the firebreaks are just as important, so we're having them installed at the end of the month."

"What if there's a fire before then?"

Mickey held up the leaflets. "I'm making sure everyone knows to get the fuck out."

Real worry creased Benito's handsome face. Mickey felt terrible. He stole a glance around, saw no one, then stepped into Benito's space. "Fuck, I'm sorry. I didn't mean to worry you. The building is safe; I wouldn't leave my tenants here if it wasn't."

"Bet the Grenfell housing officers thought that too. How do you know those corrupt fuckers aren't lying to you?"

Mickey didn't, and they both knew it. All Mickey could do was kiss the worry from Benito's lips.

Actually, there were plenty of other things he could've

done, but he kissed Benito anyway, trusting the shadows to hide them from the outside world.

Benito trusted them too, or perhaps he didn't care. For the split second their lips pressed together, he kissed Mickey back as though starved of oxygen and Mickey was his only source of air.

Then he was gone.

16

Mickey's goodbye kiss was seared on Benito's soul. Lips tingling, he melted into the night and returned to his own car. He'd left it outside the fried chicken shop, not giving a single fuck about the baby road boys and slingers gathered near it, but as he got closer, fresh paranoia licked at his veins. Cloaked in darkness, kissing Mickey by the garages had felt safe. Right, even. Fuck, nothing about kissing Mickey had ever felt wrong. But now they were apart again, the danger of it hit Benito square in the gut. *You're a fucking idiot. If Asa's got eyes on you, he's got eyes on Mickey too.*

Nauseous, Benito slid behind the wheel of his car. The lie he'd told Mickey crushed his chest, and the ache to put it right *burned. So put it right. Tell him the truth and walk away. Keep him safe.*

But if Asa already knew about Mickey, it would make no difference. The connection was out in the wild to stay. *Benito* had taught Asa that. And Dante, when he'd convinced the older Pope brother to go after the only man his little brother Luis had ever loved. *Karma's a bitch. You deserve this shit.*

Maybe.

But Mickey didn't.

Benito started the car and drove away from Barnfield in a daze, heading to the city centre for the first pick up of a long night on the road. He hit the dual carriageway and opened the windows, blasting the scent of cigarette smoke with fresh air so he wouldn't break his five-star streak on the Uber app.

He hit the city and collected his first fare, a couple who hopefully wouldn't screw on his backseat like another had last week, while Benito had driven on, silent and fuming in the front. He was a stoic taxi driver—discreet and non-verbal —but every man had his limits, and unsolicited p-in-the-v action in his car was one of Benito's, apparently.

The fare took him to Newport Pagnell and past Mickey's gym. Despite seeing him less than an hour ago, Benito's chest tightened with longing, a deep, deep yearning that merged with fear and anxiety until he choked on it.

Unsettled, he drove on, back to Milton Keynes and out east towards Bedford. It was a journey he made four times before the burner phone rang in the early hours of the morning.

Startled, though he couldn't say why, Benito pulled over and answered it. "What?"

"End game," his contact whispered. "Asa's made me, so I have to get away. I'm leaving tonight with every fucking penny I can find. Where's my cut from the last few months?"

Benito tensed, every nerve strained to breaking point. "Somewhere safe. Let me know when you land and I'll get it to you."

"I need it now."

"That can't happen. If you've been made, they'll be watching you. We can't meet until the heat dies down."

"We don't have to meet. Just leave it somewhere for me."

"*No.*"

Silence.

Then a snatched intake of breath. "You're not understanding me. If I can't get my money, I can't get away, which means I'll have to open my fucking mouth to protect myself."

"You think Asa won't whack you if you give me up?" Benito laughed without humour. "Damn, you're a fucking idiot."

"At least I'll know you're not sitting pretty with all my cash."

"You won't know anything. You'll be pig feed on his uncle's farm."

"He doesn't do that."

"Doesn't he?"

More silence. It was the worst game of chicken Benito had ever played. Whichever way it fell, he lost.

He stifled a sigh. "Look, I can't help you tonight, but if you tell me how I can finish this shit for good, I'll give you everything you're owed and more as soon as it's done."

"You can't finish it. Don't you get it? It's too big. He'll snuff you out like you're nothing."

"I am nothing," Benito snapped. "I just need—" *Fuck.* He pressed his fist to his mouth, swallowing a shout of frustration. "Okay," he tried again. "I'm hearing you. I'll get you what you need tonight, but you've gotta give me something in return. *Anything.*"

"I don't know anything. That's how I know they've made me. They shut me out."

"Who's they?"

"Asa and his boys—Nino and Tariq."

"Nino Moretti?"

"Yup."

Benito whistled softly. "I thought he was just a weed slinger."

"He was, then him and Asa got tight. Pretty sure he's the one fronting the next product run. Asa don't trust no one else."

Benito turned it over in his mind. He barely remembered Nino Moretti. Somehow, over the past few months, faces that had once been razor sharp had blurred to become almost meaningless. Only Mickey's face came to him with ease—his slate grey eyes, sandy hair, and his rough, sexy grin. Benito saw it in his dreams, awake, asleep, always.

"You still there?"

Benito nodded slowly. *Finish this.* "Tell me everything you can about Moretti, then we'll arrange the drop."

———

Cherry Bank Way. Three miles outside London, the sprawling industrial estate was a place Benito had spent more time than he cared to admit. He knew it like the back of his hand.

He also knew it was three miles too close to the city he was forbidden to enter without a parley with Asa Gerrard. *"Stay out of London . . ."* Benito shivered, and not from the cold, though the battered Ford Fiesta he was currently holed up in was the worst car he'd commandeered so far—damp and draughty. Even the gear stick was mouldy. But it ran, and it was nondescript enough that no one noticed it had been parked in the same space on the industrial estate for nine hours.

Nine *long* hours that felt like years.

Benito blew warm air onto his frozen fingers and flexed them, trying not to wish he was in the SUV he'd abandoned earlier that day. Heated seats. Windows that closed all the way to the top. A steering wheel that didn't seem perilously close to falling off.

Was it all for nothing?

Hours ago, Benito might've feared it was, but in the last ten minutes, things had changed. Across the darkened car park, a thrum of activity had sprung up around the loading bay of a faceless unit. A BMW backed up to the loading bay, boot open, wheels off, while men moved with a silent efficiency and rhythm Benito knew all too well.

They're loading up.

Better still, after twenty-four hours of stalking the locations his contact had named, Benito's target, Nino Moretti, was front and centre, getting his hands dirty like a man who knew he'd bear the consequences if shit went south. If he'd needed confirmation this was Asa's run, this was it. Benito wished he couldn't see Moretti's face, though. His strained shoulders. The tightness around his eyes. Damn. How many times had Benito been in his position? Worse, how many times had he dumped it on other people with no care to what happened to them beyond how it affected his own agenda?

Benito's heart skipped a beat, adrenaline and guilt sparking a slow tattoo in his chest he'd been dreading all day. *You're growing a conscience.*

He'd said those words to Asa once.

Asa had laughed, and yet . . . he'd still set Luis Pope free.
Maybe—

Benito killed the thought before it took hold.

Focus.

His gaze flickered to the clock. Nine on a night he'd planned to while away driving for Uber and sending Mickey thirsty texts, and now he was going to spend it tailing the BMW who the fuck knew where, praying the piece-of-shit car he'd bought could keep up until it was time to strike.

Benito counted heads. Four in total. Too many to fight on his own, but he was banking on one of them staying behind to clean house in the unit. *I can take three.* It was a risk, but with a haul the size Benito was witnessing on the move, if he won, it was over . . . *if* he could shift the product, bank the money, and somehow convince Asa to accept his own cash as payment for Benito's freedom.

You're insane. It wasn't the first time the thought had crossed Benito's mind, but he was starting to care less. If he lost tonight, he was finished, but staying tied to Asa for the rest of his life, caught in a lie he couldn't escape, he was dead anyway.

The crew loading the BMW finished up. They fixed the wheels back on and resealed the boot. Then, as Benito had predicted, three of them got in the car while the last remained behind.

Nino Moretti climbed behind the wheel. Benito eyed him, wondering why he'd never crossed his radar in a meaningful way before. Had he been a foot soldier all along? A cog in Asa's hidden machine that had taken Benito down? Or was he a grunt? A kid who'd come up too fast and was now way out of his depth.

The last option suited Benito better. He waited for the BMW to cruise out of the unit and leave the car park. The metal door descended, shielding the remaining crew member and concealing Benito's escape.

He started the Fiesta. It spluttered to life and he cringed. *Fuck, I'll be lucky to make it out of the city.* As if being behind enemy lines wasn't risky enough.

Nerves wound tight, he nursed the Fiesta out of the car park and into the labyrinth of the industrial estate. There were five different ways to get to the main road. The most obvious was the second longest. The shortest involved a series of twists and turns Benito figured a new guy on the crew perhaps wouldn't know.

He took the short route, and sure enough, up ahead, the BMW emerged from the longer one at the right moment for Benito to slide into the slip road behind a lorry he'd allowed to pass. The slip road merged into a dual carriageway. So close to the city, even this late, the road was busy. Traffic zipped past, and it took all Benito's concentration to keep the BMW in sight as he kept a safe distance.

The miles disappeared as he trailed the BMW away from the city and back in the direction from which he'd come. It was a cold night. Frigid wind whistled through the busted window and blasted the side of his face until it ached. But the pain kept him sharp. Running on a few snatched hours of sleep, he was starting to feel the strain of being so tightly wound, and he needed this shit to go down fast and without a hitch.

He'd already earmarked a location to run the beamer off the road. He just had to get there.

They hit the A5 and flew north. Benito eyed the junction

that would've taken him to Mickey's house, and his stomach clenched. *Tomorrow.* But what if he didn't make it? What if tonight was where it ended and he never saw Mickey again?

Gianna. Benito's heart lurched. What would happen to her? All this time he'd fought to keep her safe, but if he didn't come home, who the fuck would fight for her then?

This is only just occurring to you?

Of course it wasn't, but as the B road where he'd make his move drew ever closer, fear like he'd never felt before set in.

Doubt.

Guilt.

Or maybe it was reality and he'd been too dumb-fuck stupid to face it before.

Heart pounding, he fumbled for his phone—the legitimate one he'd turned off when he'd abandoned his SUV. He switched it on and waited a lifetime for it to power up. Then he scrolled through his recent contacts and placed a call on speakerphone without stopping to think about what he was doing.

Mickey answered on the third ring. "Hey."

"Hey." Benito snatched a shaky breath. "You okay?"

At Mickey's end, a door closed and then rustling, as if he had crawled onto his bed. "Yup. Just got out the shower. Are you driving?"

"Yeah."

"Bored?"

I wish. "Maybe," Benito hedged. "I, uh, kind of just wanted to hear your voice. Is that weird?"

"Weird for you, maybe. You don't seem the type to be so fucking cute."

In spite of the tension straining Benito's nerves, he rolled his eyes and let the customary warmth Mickey always brought him fill his chest. "I'm not cute."

"You're not," Mickey agreed. "You're too hot for that. What time are you clocking off?"

"When it's done," Benito replied without thinking.

Mickey chuckled. "Sounds ominous. I don't know how Uber works, to be honest. I'm a control freak, so I drive myself everywhere."

"I've noticed, apart from that one time you didn't. What would you have done if I hadn't been there? You wouldn't have—"

"Driven drunk? No way. I'd have swallowed the cab fare or gone home with Jaiden."

"The barman?"

"Yeah. We were almost friends once."

"You fucked him?"

"Is it gonna bother you if I say yes?"

Benito changed lanes, keeping a sharp eye on the BMW as the exits ticked by. *Three more.* "It shouldn't. I've fucked other people."

"But?"

"How do you know there's a but?"

"I don't. I'm guessing."

"Good guess."

"How so?"

Benito spoke without thought. *Again.* "I want you all to myself."

"You have me all to yourself." Mickey sounded surprised. "You think I'm fucking other people?"

"No."

"I'm not. I haven't even thought about it. I thought we covered this at the club that night."

Maybe they had. Sometimes, with Mickey, Benito couldn't clearly discern what they'd said aloud from what had happened in his dreams. "I'm sorry."

"What for?"

"For calling you up for chats that make no sense."

"Chats, bruv." Mickey mimicked Benito's southeast accent and matched his street talk. "Seriously, though. Don't be sorry. Life's fucking complicated. Just let it happen."

"That's a pretty zen philosophy."

"For me, or in general?"

"For you. You're a control freak, according to your own gospel."

Mickey laughed for real this time. "Yeah, well. I'm full of shit. You'll learn this if you stick around."

"I don't want to go anywhere."

"Then don't."

The air turned serious again. There were so many things Benito needed to say, but his throat closed up.

I wish I was with you.

Will you take care of my sister if it turns out that I can't?

I love you.

Benito's hands shook. He tightened them on the steering wheel.

"I should go," Mickey said when he didn't speak. "You shouldn't be on the phone when you're driving."

"You're on speaker."

"Yeah, but still. Focus on the road. Let me know when you get home?"

It was a new thing, the early morning texts Benito sent if

they didn't meet at the gym. Mickey always replied within seconds, and Benito was darkly addicted to the thrill in his soul when the simple *good morning* hit his screen. "Of course," he said. "And I'll see you after? Tomorrow, I mean?"

"For real. I'm counting on it, man. Have a good night."

"You too."

Mickey ended the call. Silence hit Benito like a brick wall. Then white noise filled his head, laced with searing panic. He thumped his chest as if he could subdue his racing heart with brute force, but nothing changed. And up ahead, the BMW began to slow, taking an exit Benito had discounted enough to leave the SUV close by. *What the hell?*

He flicked his indicator and followed the beamer off the main road. The exit led to a couple of dead-end villages and another faceless industrial estate. Benito's car was hidden on abandoned farmland nearby. The BMW drove *right past* it, and real fear gripped Benito's heart. Had he been made before the journey had even begun?

The Fiesta chugged past the turning that concealed the SUV. Benito reached for the scaffold pipe stashed beneath the passenger seat. His fingers closed around cold metal, and the familiar sensation soothed his nerves. *You can fight your way out of anything as long as no cunt brought a gun.*

He couldn't bank on it, though. Asa's crew, Benito's crew, Dante Pope's crew—it didn't matter, they'd never carried guns, but shit had changed in recent years. Hell, the last time Benito had seen Dante Pope he'd had a bullet in his foot. A bullet that had been there by Benito's design.

Karma. It's coming for you, bitch.

The BMW began to slow. Benito matched its pace, keeping his distance, then pulled into an unlit lay-by behind a lorry that had parked up for the night. Sliding the pole up his sleeve, he exited the car and ducked into the shadows, crouching, breath caged. His pulse clattered against his ribs as he hawk-eyed where the BMW had stopped. The occupants got out, scanning their surroundings, then disappeared into another faceless unit.

Benito let his breath go, momentarily dropping his guard as he tried to figure out what the hell they were doing. *Another load?* It seemed unlikely, unless Asa truly had moved into the Escobar leagues in Benito's absence.

If he had, it made what Benito planned to do all the more dangerous. The bigger the load, the more powerful the buyer, *and* a higher chance the feds had eyes on the entire operation. Especially as Asa had already lost a crew to a sting in recent months.

Fuck. Once again, doubt and fear warred with the desperate desire to just finish this shit already. If Asa was moving a mother load and Benito could lift it unscathed, shift it on, and make his escape, he was *done*. Forever. As long as Asa kept his word and didn't connect Benito's sudden wealth with his own misfortune. *Timing is everything.*

The thought of sitting on a hundred grand for a month made Benito shudder, but he'd lived through worse endgames. *I have to do this.*

Activity ahead brought his attention back to the present. The men from the BMW emerged from the unit, laughing, and . . . eating huge slices of pizza.

Benito blinked hard, afraid the long hours without sleep and plenty of stress were getting to him. Then he saw the sign hanging over the door: Martinis Wholesalers. Dear fucking god. This crew of idiots had stopped to cadge the leftovers from the Italian incarnation of Costco.

Shaking his head, Benito slipped back to the Fiesta, listening hard as car doors slammed behind him, and the modified engine of the BMW purred to life.

He jammed the key into the ignition and turned it.

Nothing happened.

Not even a sputter.

He tried again and again until the engine gave a gurgle that let him know it was flooded. "Fuck!" Benito slammed his fist against the wheel, cold forgotten as sweat beaded his brow. Then he scrambled out of the Fiesta and his feet hit tarmac before he could stop to make sense of what he was doing.

He sprinted away, racing back to the concealed spot where his SUV lay waiting. His *legitimate* car that, in its current state, would trace back to him the moment anyone took note of it on any CCTV or traffic cameras. *Idiot, idiot, idiot.* But he couldn't stop. Adrenaline consumed him, merging with the frantic need to finish the game. To find deliverance from a life that consumed his entire adulthood.

Benito ran and ran until he reached the SUV and threw the boot open, rummaging until he found the magnetic fake plates he'd kept for emergencies.

He slapped them on and hurled himself behind the wheel.

Gunning the engine, he peeled out of the hidden lay-by, only easing off when he spotted the lights of the BMW up ahead.

The BMW rejoined the A5 heading north. Benito followed, pipe still tucked up his sleeve, keeping a respectable distance until he took a chance and exited the main road a junction before the BMW.

If I don't catch them, that's it. I'm done. I can't do this anymore.

He would catch them, though. Leaving life to fate wasn't his bag, but trouble laced the air, Benito could taste it. One way or another, someone was going home broke.

Benito motored along the back roads until he found the unlit and unmonitored country lane where he'd planned his attack. The SUV was a bigger vehicle to hide, but its matte black paint became one with the shadows.

He killed the lights, leaving the engine running, and folded the mirrors against the car, relying on the dark night to give away the approach of another vehicle. He slouched in his seat, watching, until the glare of headlights broke the blackness.

The BMW passed at the speed limit, then slowed to hug the bend. Benito took his chance. He flashed his lights on full beam and stamped on the accelerator, hurtling out of the shadows into the path of the BMW, but where others before had frozen in shock, Nino Moretti was ready for him.

He drove at Benito head on, then swerved at the last second, foot to the floor, the BMW's powerful engine eating up the road at a speed that would've left the Fiesta in the dust.

But the SUV could handle it, and as loud as Benito's gut screamed at him that a fucking car chase was the most boneheaded mistake he could make right now, he couldn't stop.

He spun around, tyres squealing, and tore after the beamer, quickly gaining ground. Flat out, the BMW was a faster car, but it wasn't built for tight bends and poorly surfaced country lanes.

It swung off the B road and pelted down a narrower track that cut across farmland, sliding through icy mud patches that Benito's car mowed through with ease. Up ahead, derelict outbuildings loomed in the shadows, and debris from broken-down farm vehicles littered the roadside, signalling that they were on private land now.

Though there were no signs of occupation, the prospect of witnesses eased Benito's foot from the gas—an instinctive reaction that gave Nino Moretti the split second he needed to burn away, widening the gap between them.

Benito floored the accelerator again, but a straight stretch of road had given the BMW the advantage. It roared away, leaving Benito in its wake, then killed its lights, concealing Moretti's escape.

"Fuck fuck *fuck!*" Benito pounded the steering wheel and yelled his frustration, his shout ringing out over the growl of the engine. He dimmed his own lights but kept them on half beam as his foot eased from the accelerator, wary of the scattered obstacles still cluttering the road.

His speed returned to normal, and the sweat cooled on his skin, leaving him shivering despite the warmth from the heated seat beneath him. Teeth chattering, he wiped his brow and cranked the heaters, blasting himself with hot air as he fought to calm himself down.

"Shit!" He thumped the steering wheel again, then leaned over it, assessing his surroundings properly. The BMW was long gone, but he was still on private land with a scaffold pole tucked up his sleeve. *Jesus fucking Christ.* Perspective returned to him, carried by a harsh wave of self-loathing. He slowed to a crawl and opened the window. After a laser glance around, he launched the pipe into a nearby ditch.

The dull thud of metal on damp grass punctured the quiet. Benito flinched and let out a slow breath. He shut the window and sped up towards what he hoped was an exit onto public roads and not a driveway to a fucking house.

Please. I need this. He gripped the wheel tighter and prayed to Rosetta's god. Unbidden, flashbacks of the last time he'd attended mass bombarded him. Gianna's chubby toddler hand welded in his. Roberto's knuckles as he'd dusted Benito's skull for shits and giggles. Benito cursed and shook his head, forcing the memories away, clinging only to the vow that if he found the road, he'd drive and drive and drive until he was a better man than Roberto.

Somehow, his prayers were answered. His reward came in the form of a busted gate. He drove over it and around a pile of hay bales. Up ahead, a sign for a town he recognised reflected back at him from across a paved road, and relief flooded him, leaving him dizzy.

He pulled onto the B road, keeping a sharp eye out for blue lights or an ambush, but in the murky gloom of the unlit road, all he saw were the upended wheels of the smoking BMW and the wild eyes of the driver still trapped inside.

17

———

In the darkest depths of Benito's brain, he had two options: stop and empty the contents of the BMW into his own car, or drive on by—go home, take a shower, and forget tonight ever happened.

He slowed to a stop without making a conscious decision between the two and parked twenty feet away from the stricken beamer. *Take the stash and run. If you go now, you can move it on and be home and dry by the morning.*

The road was deserted. Benito covered his face and jogged to the BMW. He crouched to peer inside. Nino Moretti had fallen unconscious, blood dripping down his face, and his passengers were gone. They'd left their man behind to either die or get nicked when the feds finally showed up at the scene of the accident.

It wouldn't be long. The road was quiet, but it wouldn't stay that way forever. A good Samaritan, the police, whatever. Time was ticking by.

Help him. Pull him out. Take him somewhere safe. But the

better man Benito wanted to be was drowned out by the selfish bastard who craved to be free.

He stood and forced the boot of the car open with his foot. Upside down, the flooring had come loose, revealing the block of taped parcels. Eight in total, a *huge* haul. Too much for Benito to carry in one trip.

Ears trained for approaching vehicles, he dashed back and forth, hurling the parcels into the passenger seat of the SUV. One split, spraying him with cocaine. He tasted it on his lips, *burning*, and his heart cried out for Mickey.

The boot emptied out. Benito jammed it shut and crouched again to consider the wheel arches. He didn't have the time or the tools to get inside them properly, but if he reached—

A groan from inside the car stilled him, clawing at his gut.

Benito reclaimed his outstretched hand and squatted lower.

Nino Moretti stared back at him. His lips twitched to form words, but Benito stood before he could speak and backed away from the car, until he stumbled to a stop.

Go. Now. Run.

His feet stayed rooted to the floor.

"*Fuck!*" It was the thousandth curse to escape him that night, but his voice stayed low this time, strangled and hoarse. The demon on his shoulder was louder. *Get the hell out of here. You have a car full of product. If the feds catch you, you're going down for twenty fucking years. Don't get made for this arsehole. He wouldn't do it for you.*

Benito wrenched his feet from the gravelly road and rounded the car. He doubled down and took a closer look at

Moretti. He was bleeding and hanging by his seatbelt, but he was awake. "How bad are you hurt?"

Moretti blinked. "I—I don't know."

"Could you run if I get you out?"

"Run where?"

"Anywhere. I can't get all the product out, so the feds are gonna sweep the whole area when they get here."

Moretti swallowed hard. "They'll bring dogs. Doesn't matter if I run, they'll catch me anyway."

His point was valid. Benito cursed again and considered his options as his window for escape narrowed with every passing second.

Go. Now. Run.

The demon reached full volume, but as its words hit home, a new voice rose, calling its way from the ashes of Benito's conscience.

Be a better man.

Benito jolted into action. The driver's door was jammed shut. He smashed the passenger window and crawled through it to release Moretti's seatbelt. "Brace yourself. You're gonna drop."

He pressed the button. Moretti landed in a heap on the upturned ceiling of the car, his shoulders taking the impact.

Fuck. Benito cringed, praying he had no neck or spine injuries they'd just made worse, and snatched Moretti's smashed phone from the wreckage.

Blood roaring, he backed out of the car and helped Moretti do the same. Then he looped an arm beneath his shoulders and ran for the SUV.

He threw Moretti in the back and slid into the driver's

seat. "Don't try and jump me," he warned. "Or I'll fucking kill you."

Moretti said nothing. He lay flat and closed his eyes, and Benito wondered if he'd die anyway, leaving him with a shit ton of product *and* a dead body to shift. But his imagination wouldn't play that game for long. As though it refused to see an ending where Benito's attempts at redemption ended in failure.

He gunned the SUV engine and drove away from the beamer, forcing himself to keep a bland pace that wouldn't make them memorable to any passing car. The main road was three miles away. Benito cut across country, weaving along dirt tracks and lanes until he came to the quietest unmonitored junction.

Moretti perked up as they joined the A5 heading south. "Where are you taking me?"

"Where do you want to go?"

"Anywhere. Just drop me off at the services."

"Nah. Too risky with you covered in claret. And you need a hospital."

"Right, because that's not risky." Moretti hissed through his teeth, cringing in pain.

Benito glowered at him in the mirror, already regretting not leaving him behind, but as he glared, it dawned on him how young Moretti was. Benito remembered him as a kid slinging weed because that's what he'd been when he'd last seen him. Whatever had changed, the passage of time remained the same. Even if Moretti was an adult, he was barely out of his teens. "How old are you?"

"The fuck do you care?"

"I don't. Just don't want to get pulled with a busted-up kid in my car."

"I'm twenty-two, you cunt," Moretti muttered, heavy eyes closing.

Benito snorted. "Okay, mate."

The miles disappeared, taking them closer to London than Benito ever wanted to be. He left the main road near Watford and cruised through the backstreets until he came to a meet point he knew Asa's crew would find as soon as they knew where to look.

He got out of the car and opened the back door, rousing Moretti. "Get out."

"Where are we?"

"I'll tell you when you get the fuck out of my car."

Moretti came upright and slid shakily from the SUV.

Benito guided him to the roadside and sat him down, passing him his ruined phone. "It's dead. Give me a number and I'll let someone know you're here."

"Who are you?"

Benito was flummoxed he hadn't already been made. He shook his head. "That doesn't matter. Just give me a number, unless you want to stay here forever."

It wouldn't be forever. If Moretti couldn't walk, at some point, he'd be found, but it was *cold*, and despite his bravado, the youngster was in shock, shaking and pale. There was every chance he'd fucking freeze, and he knew it.

Moretti parroted a phone number. Benito typed it into his burner phone and sent a message with their vague location. Moretti watched him, eyes beginning to droop again. "I feel sick, man."

"You might have a concussion."

"Lucky me."

"You'll be fine. Just get your boys to keep an eye on you when they pick you up."

"Man, you're a regular Florence Nightingale, huh?"

"If you say so." Benito zipped Moretti's jacket higher, then backed up, keeping his gaze on him until he reached his car. The fake plates seemed to mock him. Benito ducked behind the wheel and drove away, still watching Moretti as he slumped forward and buried his face in his knees. *He'll be fine.*

But what if he wasn't? What if he died at the side of the road and all Benito's fucked-up conscience had done was stop him getting medical help that could've kept him alive?

There were no right answers, save going back in time and living a different life. A better one, where driving a taxi all night was enough.

With a heavy heart, Benito placed a call on the burner phone, set a meet, and turned east to empty his life of the product dusted all over his car. He drove for two hours until he reached Felixstowe and his contact was waiting. "This is the last load," he said flatly. "Supply ran dry."

His contact nodded and handed over the envelope of cash.

Benito trudged back to his car and buried it under the backseat. He was so fucking tired, but he had a thousand things to do before he could sleep. Drive home. Bury the money. Clean the car. But as he drove away, fatigue hit him hard. His eyes felt like sandpaper, and a headache throbbed in his skull.

He opened the window. A sea breeze blasted the side of his face and ruffled his hair. It smelt good, of clean air and life. He hit the cliff-side road, listened to the waves pound the rocks, and imagined what it would feel like to drive through the barriers and tumble down to join them. Would it hurt?

For long moments, Benito wasn't sure he cared. Then he pictured Gianna and her face when she learned he'd died in a pit of wrecked metal and saltwater for no good reason other than he couldn't make right the mess he'd made.

He pictured Mickey too. *He wants you. You have a sleepover date tomorrow.* A crazed laugh burst from Benito's tight lungs. *A fucking sleepover? How old are you?*

Like it mattered.

In the dark, he drove on through the night until he came to a safe place to clean out his car with the handheld vacuum cleaner he kept in the boot. In the darkness, he imagined the cocaine seeping into his skin, fizzing in his bloodstream, and crackling into his weighted heart. It made him think of Mickey, and urgency spread through him like wildfire. *I need to get home.* Because the sooner he was home and asleep in his bed, the sooner it would be time to wake up and be with Mickey.

Benito cleaned his car in record time, then hit the road again to bury the cash in the woods. The extra made up for the withdrawal he'd made to pay off his informant for good. It was over . . . right?

The burner phone in his pocket felt like a rock. Halfway back to the SUV for what felt like the thousandth time that night, he pulled it out and glared at it, gripping it hard, willing it to self-combust in his hand so he didn't have to make the decision to destroy it.

Or choose wrong and keep it, so the wheel kept turning and he never got off.

Stamp on it. But for reasons he couldn't explain, he could only stare, until it buzzed in his hand and scared the ever-loving shit out of him.

An unknown number lit up the screen—one Benito hadn't seen before. He froze, heart in his throat, caught in headlights that somehow left him still trapped in the dark. Every instinct he had *knew* nothing good was at the end of that call, but ignoring it felt like a summit he couldn't reach.

Something buried deep inside compelled him to answer. "Yeah?"

The line crackled. Then a sigh. "Martell?"

"What?"

"It's Asa."

"What do you want?"

"To talk."

"What about?"

"You know what."

"Do I?"

Another sigh. It was Asa's callsign—to be gently frustrated with someone he wanted to kill with his bare hands. Benito had seen it so many times he didn't need to close his eyes to picture Asa. In the shadows of the forest, he was right there with him.

"Look," Asa said. "Whatever you think I'm going to say, you're wrong."

Benito turned his gaze to the sky. The stars were beginning to fade. It seemed morbidly poetic. "You have no idea what I think."

"I can guess. And I could be wrong. Whatever. It doesn't matter anymore."

"No?"

"No. I don't care about business. This is personal."

"What is?"

"What you did tonight. For Nino."

Nino. Benito's frozen joints began to thaw. Asa didn't use first names. For as long as Benito had known him, he'd addressed every fucker from the top to the bottom by their surname. Martell. Pope. Moretti. The only exception had been *Luis* Pope, and that had been because once upon a time, they'd—

Fuck. Benito sank to a crouch, his free hand flying to his head as a belated lightbulb illuminated his tired brain. *Seriously*? No. He had to be wrong. Asa's torch for Luis Pope had been plain to see for *years* to anyone who'd cared enough to look, and it had been a weak spot Benito had exploited time and time again to keep Asa down.

And Asa knew it. There was no logical reason for him to expose himself again, unless . . .

This is it. He doesn't care about business. Only his soft fucking heart.

Benito fell forward to his knees, sinking into the damp earth. Hope and cynicism warred hot and fast in his gut. He couldn't bear it. "What do you want from me?"

"Can we meet?"

"Why?"

"Because I want my money back. What happens after that is up to you."

Asa rattled off a time and place—a public place—for them to meet after the weekend. He hung up without waiting for Benito's reply, leaving Benito to stagger to his feet and continue back to his car.

Benito drove home on autopilot, thoughts whirling so fast he couldn't keep up. His bones vibrated with a heady mix of elation, fear, and exhaustion. It imprisoned him in his own mind. He craved release. In the past, he might've gone to the club, but he could only think of Mickey.

He parked his car outside his flat and dug his legitimate phone from the glove box, the burner left in pieces in a storm drain. His shaking fingers flew over the screen.

Benito: *Home. Can't wait to see you.*

A reply pinged back seconds later.

Mickey: *conting the fking hrs.*

18

Mickey watched from his bedroom window as the matte black SUV pulled up outside. It was already dark, concealing Benito from view, but even without hawk-eyeing the car like a stalker, Mickey reckoned he'd have known the moment he arrived.

Everything was different when Benito was close—light, and yet somehow addictively darker.

Benito opened his car door. Mickey took his cue and jogged downstairs to meet him, opening the front door before he could knock.

He caught Benito with his hand raised, long fingers curled into a fist.

Benito blinked. "Don't want your neighbours to see me?"

"You think I give a shit what my neighbours think?"

"You did that one time I came here to—"

"Yeah, yeah." Mickey grabbed Benito's wrist and yanked him inside. As ever, they fell naturally against the door as it swung shut. Mickey crowded Benito against it, leaning in, their faces inches apart, a whisper away from the rough kiss he'd been dreaming of for days. "I don't care what my neigh-bours think," he said lowly, in case there was any confusion.

Benito smirked. "You should."

"Why?"

"Because I'm done with the cute game we've been playing for weeks now. I—fuck, I needed it, but I *want* you, and I don't know how much longer I can wait to have you again."

"Have me?"

"Figure of speech. You know what I mean."

Mickey let a slow grin warm his face. "Well, we have all night, so maybe you can show me what you mean."

"Now?"

"If you like. Or later. Or both. You are staying, right?"

"If you want me to."

"I do." *So fucking much*. The first, last, and only time Benito had slept in Mickey's bed was hazy, but the blurred memories of Benito in his arms for hours and hours and hours were enthralling enough that Mickey knew he wanted it again.

And again.

And again.

As much as he wanted Benito naked and writhing beneath him.

Benito pushed off the door, squaring up to Mickey like he had the first time they'd been alone together in the by-the-hour room above Freefall, but the aggression Mickey had craved from him then wasn't there, and Mickey didn't miss it. The release he desired now was primal in a different way.

Sweeter.

Deeper.

He released his death grip on Benito's wrist and slid his

arms around his waist. Their bodies fit together with perfect alchemy, but it had nothing on the magic of Benito's lips brushing his, lightly at first, but then with enough force to rock Mickey backwards.

A low sound escaped him, or maybe it was Benito's broken moan. Together, like this, he couldn't tell. All he knew for certain was that the few weeks they'd spent without moments like these had done nothing to calm the inferno that blazed between them.

Kissing Benito was everything. It stole Mickey's breath and his ability to think about anything except the next sweep of his tongue in Benito's sinful mouth. Only the fact that he'd barely let Benito through the door made him pull back. "Come on," he said. "I bought food from the posh supermarket and put it in the oven."

"You cooked?"

"Not even close, but keep thinking I did if it makes you smile like that." Mickey spun around and padded barefoot to the kitchen.

Benito was a heartbeat behind him. Somewhere along the way he'd abandoned his Yeezys and the dark jacket he'd arrived with. He stepped up to Mickey with socked feet, forearms bare. "I don't care what you did. It smells amazing."

"You wanna eat now?"

"Whatever. I'm easy."

Mickey snorted. Nothing about Benito—even this—was easy. He turned the oven off, leaving the fancy pizza inside, and opened the fridge. He hadn't drunk much since the night he'd made a twitchy, emotional arse of himself at the club, but drinking with Benito felt safe. *He knows you. He'll catch you if you fall.*

Maybe. But the feeling was tangible enough that Mickey latched onto it.

He handed Benito a beer.

Benito opened his mouth, but his phone cut him off. "Shit. Sorry."

He fished a black iPhone Mickey had seen before from his pocket and answered it. "What's up, G?"

Gianna. Mickey relaxed and stepped away to give Benito space, all the while taking the time to soak him up while his attention was diverted by his spiky little sister. Benito was wearing dark grey track pants and a plain white T-shirt. His hair was longer than when they'd met and had started to curl like Gianna's. His jaw remained unshaven, but there was a neatness to it that was deliberate and about as groomed as either one of them ever got.

Benito seemed to sense Mickey's gaze taking him apart. He smirked as he listened to whatever Gianna had to say and licked his lips, dark eyes smouldering.

Casually edible, and yet . . .

Mickey blinked first, suppressing a shiver. He was used to wanting Benito by now, but there was something about him tonight—a current that simmered below the surface of his dirty gaze and contradictory sweet smile. Some of the tension he usually carried had faded too, giving way to a wildness that lit Mickey on fire.

Benito ended his call and set his phone on the kitchen counter. "Gianna keeps locking herself out of her iPad. She gets herself in a mess with words and numbers, then loses her shit and chucks it across the room."

"Valid. If she's anything like me, her brain gets overloaded and makes everything seem worse than it is."

"Do you think— Never mind." Benito clamped his lips shut.

Mickey hoisted himself onto the counter and drank his beer, giving Benito a chance to change his mind.

He didn't.

Curiosity won out. "What were you going to say?"

"I was going to ask you if you could talk to Gianna about shit like that next time you happen to see her, but that's weird, right? You're not a social worker."

"No," Mickey agreed. "But I'd do it if the opportunity ever came up. I don't think it will, though. I'm handing Barnfield to another HO soon."

"When?"

Mickey shrugged. "When the fire safety updates are done. It doesn't feel right to abandon ship before then."

"Is that what you're doing? Abandoning the residents there?"

Mickey widened his legs, waiting until Benito took the hint and stepped between them. "Not exactly. It's just . . . I don't know, fucked up, I guess, that fate made everything so complicated."

"It doesn't have to be complicated." Benito knocked his head on Mickey's shoulder. "We could stop seeing each other. Then you wouldn't have to change your job."

"I'd still be going to see your mum knowing I'd fucked her son in a sex club, though. It's been inappropriate since we met, so don't put it on yourself, okay? Even if we'd never seen each other again after that night, I'd have done this as soon as I found out you were connected to one of my residents."

"What if you'd never found out, though? Then you'd still be helping all those people."

"Yeah, well, now they'll get someone else who can advocate for them without needing seventy-five grammar and punctuation apps to check up on them."

Benito leaned back and shot Mickey a dry glare. "Don't talk shit about yourself."

"Make me stop."

"How?"

"Put something in my mouth."

Benito's gaze darkened. "That escalated."

"I'm not sorry."

"I don't want you to be." Benito ghosted his hands up Mickey's thighs until he came to the waistband of the soft sweatpants Mickey wore. No shirt. Benito skimmed the bare skin of Mickey's abdomen. "I've been thinking about you since forever."

"Forever?"

"Yeah." Benito didn't elaborate—he found better things to do with his mouth.

He kissed Mickey's neck, then sank his teeth in, sucking hard enough to send pain-laced pleasure jolting through Mickey's entire body.

It was going to leave a mark, but Mickey didn't stop him. Couldn't. It felt too good. He found bare skin of his own to play with, and his hands roamed beneath Benito's T-shirt, tracing his lean muscles, and then the raised scar on his ribs.

Benito shivered, tensing, as though bracing himself for Mickey to ask him *again* how he got it.

Mickey didn't. He wanted to know, but tonight the past was going to stay where it belonged. The present was this. It was them, alone with each other in Mickey's kitchen with nothing between them but heat and too many clothes.

He gripped Benito's T-shirt and pulled it over his head. Benito's chest was a vision of smooth skin, dark ink, and that damn fucking scar. Mickey placed his palm over it. Benito closed his eyes, and something shifted between them—something permanent, that even if they never saw each other again, would never, ever change.

You got it bad, brother. And for once, the realisation didn't scare Mickey. His worst fears seemed suddenly stupid. They'd come this far and the world hadn't ended. No one had died. *Not even me.*

He claimed Benito's mouth in a fierce kiss, and slid off the countertop, impacting Benito's body with a thud.

Benito didn't waver, and it felt symbolic. As if nothing Mickey threw at him could topple him over. He kissed Mickey back, and the bulge in his track pants grew harder, pressing against Mickey's aching cock.

I want him. But everything they needed to fuck was upstairs, and Mickey couldn't wait that long.

He spun them around, pinning Benito against the counter, then dropped to his knees, taking Benito's track pants and underwear with him.

Benito's cock sprang free, rigid and waiting. Mickey took a breath and sucked him down, opening his throat to swallow Benito whole.

"Jesus *fuck*." Benito staggered, then gasped as Mickey began to work him, taking him deep and slow, sharp and fast, mixing it up until Benito was struggling to stay upright.

Dismantling him was hot as fuck. Mickey dragged it out, bringing him to the edge over and over, enjoying the desperation that built in Benito with every cruel swipe of his tongue.

Benito gripped Mickey's face with sweat-damp hands. "You fucker," he grit out. "I can't—*shit*—"

Without warning, he came hard, shooting down Mickey's throat with a tortured groan, blunt nails digging into Mickey's scalp.

When it was over, he slumped against the counter, breathing laboured like he'd run a marathon. He glowered down at Mickey. "Was that fun for you?"

Mickey laughed. "Yup. And I'm going to have loads more *fun*, so eat all your dinner. You're gonna need your strength."

———

They messed around all night with lube and poppers, fingers and tongues, drinking beer in between and eating the pizzas Mickey had left in the oven while a film neither of them watched played in the background.

It was late when Mickey finally let himself coax Benito towards the bedroom.

They didn't make it. Mickey fucked him on the stairs, driving into him from behind, sheathed with a condom snatched from his secret stash in a kitchen drawer, lost in the entrancing tension of Benito's strong body as he held steady beneath him. *He's so fucking beautiful.*

After, they stumbled to bed. Mickey fell asleep with Benito sprawled on his chest, but when he woke a few hours later, they'd shifted. Benito was behind him, curved around his body, hand resting on Mickey's hip.

Mickey reached back and laced their fingers together. Benito sighed and ground his hips forward. The movement was fractional but fitted his cock so perfectly against Mickey's body that they both moaned.

Benito laughed sleepily and braced himself to move away. "Sorry—"

"Shh." Mickey held him in place. "I like it."

"Yeah?"

"Yeah. Not with everyone, but definitely with you."

Benito circled his hips again, a little harder this time, his body waking up and aligning with wherever his head was at. His length hardened, adding pressure and friction to his movements.

Amazing pressure and friction.

Mickey inhaled a shaky breath and went with it, cutting himself free from the last remaining ties to earth. He arched his neck, giving Benito access to his throat, and pressed back against Benito's dick, inviting him, without words, to do whatever he wanted.

Benito groaned. "You're fucking killing me."

"Don't die, bro."

"I don't want to. I want—I want to fuck you. Is that okay? Or have I read this wrong?"

"You haven't read it wrong."

Benito shuddered and nuzzled Mickey's neck. The gesture was sweet and intimate, and hotter than hell. Mickey's pulse banged against his eardrums, chaotic and loud.

"I want it," he blurted, in case he hadn't been clear.

Benito disappeared for a moment, rolling away to fumble in Mickey's drawers. He came back with lube, a condom, and poppers.

He pressed the cold metal bottle into Mickey's hand. "If you need them."

There was no doubt in Mickey's mind that he would. He wasn't a natural bottom, and it had been . . . fuck, he didn't even know, since he'd last taken a dick inside him, and Benito was *big*.

Thick.

Hard.

Fucking hell.

Benito rubbed Mickey's forearm. Mickey had missed him returning to the space behind him and moulding their bodies together again. "We don't have to, you know. I love what we already do. I fucking need that shit in my life."

Mickey hummed. "I need it too, but I've been dreaming about being with you like this. I want it—I want you."

Benito's eyes shone brightly in the darkness. Sometimes they didn't get round to these moments, life seemed to move too fast, but as Benito stared and Mickey gazed back, the world was as perfect as it had ever been.

They kissed, then Benito moved behind him, aligning himself with Mickey's body again, slick with lube and sheathed in a condom. He trailed fingers over Mickey's hole.

Mickey pushed them away. "I want *you*."

"Are you sure?"

"Yeah." Mickey exhaled a trembling breath and unscrewed the lid of the poppers bottle.

Benito replaced his fingers with his cock and pressed, slow and steady, against the resistance Mickey's body threw up in his path.

Tense pain spread through Mickey. He grimaced and brought the poppers to his nose, inhaling deeply, chasing the tingling rush that would help him *relax* and let Benito in.

It hit him in a slow wave. Warmth and fear fought for

dominance, and warmth won. Discomfort ebbed away, beaten back by Mickey's pounding heart.

He let go, and Benito rode the wave, sliding into him until he was buried deep.

Long seconds passed.

Mickey trembled, grounding himself in the twin sensation of Benito splitting him open with his massive cock and tenderly stroking his face.

He was still clutching the metal bottle. Benito pried it from his hand and screwed the cap back on. "All right?"

Mickey nodded. "I'm good."

"You're better than good. You're fucking everything." Benito rubbed Mickey's hip in warning, then slowly thrust his own, hitting every spot that made Mickey's nerves sing.

"Fuck." Mickey raised his leg, taking Benito deeper, and the shifted angle sent white lights pinging through his vision. Sweet madness descended. He flailed a hand back and found purchase at the nape of Benito's neck, anchoring himself to the solid warmth of him, then gave himself up to the ride.

Benito fucked him steadily, whispering dirty things in Mickey's ear, but as the heat rose, his words fell away, replaced by harsh gasps and growled curses.

His ruined sounds sent Mickey soaring. He jacked himself, almost afraid of the pleasure building inside him, but unable to turn away from it. "*Benito.*"

"Do it." Benito tightened his death grip on Mickey's shoulder. "Fuck, I need to feel you come."

Mickey groaned and clenched Benito tighter with one hand, the other a blur as it flew over his cock. He shook. Fresh sweat coated his skin, and his body clamped down on Benito of its own accord, lost to the beat of his surging cock.

Rhythmic.

Hypnotic.

Orgasm flared inside Mickey, unfurling from a part of him perhaps no one else had ever reached. It hit hard and deep. He yelled out, digging his fingers into Benito's neck, and his dick erupted, coating his fist with wet warmth.

Behind him, Benito's breath grew ragged. He stilled, burying his face in Mickey's neck. Then he jerked, and a rough moan rumbled out of him. "*Fuck.*"

Mickey fought for breath, reeling from every swelling pulse of Benito's dick inside him. Beautiful tension seized every part of him, every nerve, muscle, and bone, and he couldn't see how he'd ever move again.

For long moments, Benito didn't move either. Then he sighed and unhooked Mickey's arm from around his neck. "I'll be right back."

He slipped out of Mickey and left the bed. True to his word, he was back a few seconds later with a flannel.

They cleaned up, then sprawled out, staring at the ceiling, still flushed and breathing hard.

"I don't usually fuck people," Benito said into the darkness.

"Coulda fooled me," Mickey retorted with a smirk. "You didn't seem out of practice."

Benito snorted softly. "Six years."

Mickey rolled over and propped himself up on his elbow. "For real?"

"Yeah. I had a girlfriend too. I haven't fucked anyone like that since her."

Mickey took a second to process. Had they talked about

this before? Nonsensically, he couldn't remember—he remembered *every moment* he'd spent with Benito, right?

Or maybe he didn't. Maybe obsession was a state of mind, not a reality. "Did you love her?"

Benito nodded. "I think so."

"What happened?"

"She was clever, with prospects and dreams, and I was a road boy. I left her so she'd go to uni and be someone instead of drowning in my bullshit."

"How long were you together?"

"Years. Can't remember how many."

"Did she know you were bi?"

"Yeah." Benito shifted to face Mickey. "I know it was different for you and your missus, but I couldn't be with someone that long and them not know who I was. Road life is . . . fuck, you know what it's like, but the crew I ran with was different to most."

"How so?"

Benito shrugged. "There were some top boys who used to roll together. Everyone knew it and no one cared. They were too fucking fierce, you know? Like, if you'd tried to queer bash Luis Pope, you'd have fucking died before anyone else did."

Luis Pope. Mickey didn't know the name and he didn't want to. And despite a deep-rooted itch to learn every inch of Benito, inside and out, he didn't want to think about the past, not tonight. "I'm glad you had someone you could be yourself with. She taught you well, in case you're wondering. You blew my fucking mind so bad I'm going to need ten cigarettes to calm myself down."

Benito laughed. "I left mine in the car because I thought you were trying to quit."

"That's cute. I didn't buy any because I thought *you* were trying to quit."

"You want me to get them?"

Benito had his face pillowed on his bicep, eyes lidded and heavy, the perfect picture of sated relaxation. Mickey considered him leaving the bed, even for a moment, and shook his head. "Nah. I'll go. You want a drink?"

"Water?"

"Where are your car keys?"

Benito pointed at the floor. "Wherever you tossed my clothes, fam. You sure you don't want me to go?"

"I *want* you to stay right there."

Benito nodded and pulled Mickey down for a goodbye kiss.

Mickey slipped out of bed and padded downstairs, naked. On the way, he scooped up items of clothing and deposited them on the kitchen counter. Most were Benito's—Mickey hadn't been wearing much when he'd arrived. Track pants, T-shirt, socks. Underwear he'd found on the stairs.

Benito's keys were in his jacket pocket. Mickey searched out his own clothes and threw them on. Then he tramped out in the looming dawn to Benito's SUV.

He clicked the locks and opened the driver door, scanning the spotless car interior for any sign of the Mayfair Lights Benito usually smoked but came up blank. He stretched over the seats and opened the glove box. *Empty. Damn it. Why didn't you, I don't know, ask him where they were?*

No sensible answer was forthcoming. Mickey checked both doors, then peered under the passenger seat.

White dust greeted him.

Glittery, chalky white dust. Mangled gaffer tape.

An elastic band.

Mickey froze. Bile rose in his throat, and he jerked upright so fast he smacked his head on the console behind him.

Seeing stars, he shook his head to clear it. *Fucking idiot. It's probably protein powder. Or flour he bought for his mum. Or make-up for Gianna.*

A hundred other possibilities crowded Mickey's brain. Each one, however outlandish, made more sense than a burst brick of coke because Benito wasn't moving that shit anymore. Mickey knew it because Benito had fucking *told* him so.

It's not coke. Wind your neck in, son.

Mickey took a deep breath and shut the passenger door, forcing himself to open the back door instead. He crouched, unseeing, dread still hot and shaky in his chest. It took a moment to focus.

To see the dull red streak on the black leather.

Nausea returned, and he hated himself a little bit more.

No.

Stop.

But the longer Mickey stared at the stain, the stronger it solidified as the only thing guaranteed to accompany any fucker who moved the kind of substance staining the carpet beneath the passenger seat.

Pain.

Heartache.

Blood.

In the end, it led nowhere else.

Mickey reached out to touch the mark.

Retracted his hand at the last moment and stood, moving on autopilot to the boot of the car.

He yanked it open. It appeared empty, but Mickey knew better. He yanked the loose floor of the boot free, revealing the space where older cars stored spare tyres.

A baseball bat lay beside an unused road safety kit.

A weapon, unless Benito had a passion for American sports that Mickey had yet to discover.

The thought made him laugh, but there was no humour in the strangled sound that left his throat. He picked up the bat, balanced it on the end of his finger like a child as his world turned slowly to stone.

"What are you doing?"

Mickey didn't blink. He let the bat fall and turned around.

Benito was behind him, dressed in track pants and socks, no shirt, expression twisted with a lethal mix of fear and cautious amusement, as if he believed his own bullshit.

Head spinning, Mickey latched onto the fear. He *knew* that fear. He'd seen it in the mirror a thousand fucking times. "The fuck you think I'm doing?"

"Getting smokes," Benito snapped. "Not searching my car like a fucking fed."

Mickey slammed the boot shut and then the back door he'd left open. Numbness threatened the dismantling grief building in his gut, but he pushed it away. He'd spent too long not feeling. However much this hurt, he couldn't hide from it. Not anymore. He wouldn't survive.

Fight. He stepped up to Benito and put his fist to Benito's chest, shoving him back. "I wasn't searching your car until I found a snowfall of fucking blow under your seat. Guess you missed it when you last cleaned up, and the blood stain in the back. What happened? Nosebleed? Or did you fuck someone up with the bat in your boot?"

"Mate—"

"Fuck off!" Mickey shouted. "I'm not your mate. I never was."

Benito raised his hands, spreading them peacefully, though his street-fuelled instinct to fight back was clear to see. "You don't understand."

Mickey laughed. "That's what you're going with? That I don't understand what a car that moves product looks like? Wow. Go fuck yourself."

"That's not what I meant."

"I don't care what you meant. You're full of shit."

"I'm not."

"Yeah. You are."

Mickey moved to step around Benito.

Benito grabbed him, his strong hand clamping around Mickey's forearm. "Wait."

"Get off me."

"Or what?" Aggression sparked in Benito. His gaze narrowed and he stared Mickey down, blocking his path to the open front door. "You gonna fight me until you slow the fuck down long enough to listen?"

Mickey wrenched Benito's hand from his arm and pushed him again, harder than before, but this time, Benito didn't stumble. He stood his ground, fists clenched, fierce.

"I don't need to listen," Mickey growled. "I know what I saw. I could fucking taste it in the air. Do you know what that shit does to me?"

Benito's face fell, contorting with pain. It was brief, but enough to show Mickey that he'd scraped the truth.

The devil inside him spun around and ran to Benito's front seat. Crawled into the footwell and clawed at the dust until there was enough for a hit. A sweet punch of pleasure that would last long enough for him to find his way to a dealer and score. But the stronger man he'd learned to be knew it wouldn't play out that way. No pleasure, only *hurt*, masked by a racing pulse and synthetic energy that made him sick to his stomach.

"Mickey."

"Stop saying my name."

Benito reached for Mickey again.

Mickey evaded and stumbled to the house with heavy legs. The rest of Benito's clothes were still on the counter, his shoes by the door. Mickey snatched them up and threw them out of the house.

They landed at Benito's feet.

Benito flinched. "You don't understand."

"*You* don't understand. If you did, you'd never have brought that shit to my house."

"I didn't think you'd go in my car—fuck, I thought I got it all—" Benito brought his hands to his head. "Fuck, *fuck.*" Desperation filled his wild eyes. He tugged so hard on his hair Mickey *felt* it. "Please. I know I've fucked up, but you have to let me explain. It's not what you think."

Mickey clung to the front door as if it could anchor him to the world where ten minutes ago they'd been screwing like lovers. *Real* lovers, because there was no doubt in Mickey's heart that he loved Benito. If he didn't, it wouldn't hurt so much.

You can't love him. He's a liar. And he'll break you.

Mickey couldn't afford to be broken again. He let himself sink into Benito's deep brown gaze.

Then he shut the fucking door, and the dull thud felt like the gates of hell slamming shut.

He sank to his knees, tears burning, a sob caught in his chest, pressing his hands over his ears to block out Benito as he gathered his clothes from the ground and trudged to his car.

Lost to white noise and his shattering heart, he didn't hear him drive away, but as his fucking soul crumbled, he knew the moment Benito was gone.

No. Mickey fell forward, his head hitting the door. A scream of devastation tore through him, drowned out only by the cynicism falling for Benito had eased.

It was loud now. Bitter. Spewing out four words that stomped out the glowing embers of the last few months.

You gullible fucking idiot.

19

———

Benito's head swayed with the movement of the train. Forward and back. Up and down. With his eyes open, it made him feel sick. If he closed them and shut the world out, he wanted to die though, so motion sickness it was.

Besides, he had a hundred grand in his bag. Only a moron would take his eyes off it.

No, only a moron would've got on the train in the first place when they have a perfectly good car at home.

But if Benito had proven anything over the last few weeks, months, *years*, it was that he was indeed a fucking imbecile. How else could he explain his life up until this moment?

He leaned his head against the train window, focusing on the cool glass against his skin as grief lanced his chest. The slam of Mickey's front door echoed in his head. His furious, agonised scream as Benito had unfrozen his feet from the doorstep and walked away. *So much pain.* And Benito wasn't naive enough to believe Mickey's distress had been all about him, even if it had been all his fault. Lies were one thing. Betrayal something else

—something bigger—but the worst of Mickey's anger had been directed at himself, and Benito could never forgive himself for that. For dragging Mickey back to a place where he believed he was anything less than the fucking *hero* he was to Benito. That he'd done it within ten minutes of being inside him, slow-screwing them both to oblivion, all the while losing himself to the reality that he was *in love* with this dude?

Yeah. It was too much.

Money be damned, Benito let his eyes fall closed, but as his luck seemed to be going lately, as he did, the train jolted to a stop at Bushey station. He jerked forward and smashed his face into the seat in front of him. The impact was glancing, but it hurt his already aching bones. He hadn't slept much since Saturday. Hadn't eaten. Instead he'd paced his flat and played chicken with his phone, counting the hours until his meet with Asa had come around and he could finish what he'd started.

Probably.

Maybe.

He still wasn't sure what he was walking into, and he cared less than he had when he'd agreed to the meet. *Kill me. I don't give a fuck anymore.* Gianna flashed into his mind, but he pushed her away. She was better off without him.

The train rumbled through the stops until Euston. Benito drifted through the ticket barriers and made himself walk past the sniffer dogs checking commuters for explosives. *Arrest me. Take it. Take it all.*

No one did. For once in his life, he was invisible.

Asa wanted to meet in central London, a world away from the grotty tower blocks Benito had briefly ruled over, but

Benito was four hours early, and he got on the tube in the opposite direction.

Half an hour later, he found himself staring at a tatty sign from across the street—*Toni's Cafe*—as tired and somehow welcoming as it had always been, the same condensation in the windows.

The same moody Italian grilling bacon and scowling at customers.

Benito almost smiled, but he didn't have it in him, and despite the nostalgia, he didn't go in.

Never had. Instead, he waited on a bench opposite the door, knowing it wouldn't be long before he was seen.

"What the fuck are you doing here?"

Benito looked up. Paolo Cilberto stood in front of him, fire in his dark eyes, rage in his clenched fists. Benito tried not to smile. He'd always admired this about Paolo, the way he wore every emotion on his sleeve and didn't give a single fuck who saw. He was brave beyond anything Benito could even dream of.

Like Mickey.

Like the man Paolo loved enough to abandon his work and charge across the road to fight to the death for.

"I need to see Luis," Benito said.

Paolo's glower burned hotter. "Fuck off."

"Easy. It's not business. It's personal."

"You don't have anything personal with him. You're a piece-of-shit road man and you promised you'd leave him alone. What's *wrong* with you people?"

"Everything," Benito quipped before he caught himself. "That's why I need to see Luis. I need his advice."

"I have some for you. Go die somewhere else."

Benito pursed his lips. If Paolo hadn't meant every syllable with enough venom to kill them both, it might've been funny. But it wasn't funny. Not even close. Paolo had good reason to protect Luis, especially from Benito.

I deserve his hate. "I'm all right with dying just here, thanks," Benito said. "I just need to see Luis before I expire. Please? I'll be quick."

"Go fuck your—"

"Paolo." Luis Pope appeared like a god. Before Mickey, Benito had considered him beautiful, with his too-long hair and soulful eyes. His mean mug that disguised the heart of a man who just wanted to live. Now, two days after Benito had fucked up enough that he'd probably never see Mickey again, Luis just looked irritated.

He stepped in front of Paolo and faced Benito down. "You're supposed to be dead," he said flatly.

"Am I?"

"What do you want?"

"Advice. I don't want any trouble, honest."

"Advice," Luis repeated slowly. "The fuck could I know that you don't? You're the brains of the game, aren't you?"

"Was. I haven't been around for a while. I'm dead, remember?"

"And yet, here you are."

Benito said nothing. Just stayed still, praying Luis would see past the hate and violence that had coloured their interactions up until now.

Luis turned away and said something to Paolo.

Paolo growled and stormed away.

Benito didn't watch him go. He fixed his gaze on the

ground and drifted until Luis gripped his elbow and tugged him to his feet.

"Come on."

"Come on where?"

Luis steered Benito across the road. "I'm not doing this on the street. You want to talk to me, you do it where I need to be."

That turned out to be inside the cafe. Luis pointed to a corner table. "I'll be there in a minute."

Still clutching his cash-stuffed bag, Benito took a seat in the corner, facing the cafe, gaze instinctively trained on the door, but it wasn't long before his attention shifted to the heated exchange happening over the grill.

Even from behind, Paolo's temper was popping. He moved bacon and sausages around with vicious, stabbing movements while Luis murmured in his ear, his hand splayed at the base of Paolo's spine.

Benito tracked Luis's hand as it began to move in slow, soothing circles, then as it travelled up Paolo's back and cupped the back of his head. They kissed, warm and sweet, and what was left of Benito's heart splintered. He'd known Luis had loved Paolo since before Luis had likely known it himself. It had made him vulnerable, and through Dante, Benito had exploited that vulnerability, leaving Luis at breaking point.

You don't deserve his help.

Benito shoved his chair back and stood, aiming for the door.

Luis intercepted him before he took a step. "Sit down. We don't have to talk if you've changed your mind. Just eat something, okay? It'll keep Paolo happy."

Nothing about those words made sense. Benito let Luis ease him back into his seat, then shook his head. "I'm not hungry."

"You look it."

"Do I?"

"Yeah. I mean, you're bigger than I remember, though, but maybe that's because Asa isn't standing beside you. I've only ever seen you together."

"You've seen Asa without me."

Luis's gaze flickered. "Not for a long time."

Of course it had been a long time. Asa and Luis had hooked up *before* Luis had served a six-year stretch inside. When he'd got out, he'd fought with all he had to stay away from the life that had brought Benito to his knees at his feet. "I'm sorry."

"What for?"

Benito shrugged. "Everything?"

"Be specific, man. I don't even like you, let alone got time for this bullshit."

"Asa wants a hundred grand to let me go."

Luis's brows shot up. Then he whistled. "That's a lot of Ps. To be honest, I thought you were already gone. You've been dark a long time."

"I wasn't dark, just somewhere else. He wanted me out of the ends, so I left. Went back to my girls cos he said he'd kill them if I stayed here."

"Girls? Your missus?"

"Nah. My mum and my sister."

A frown marred Luis's handsome face. "I thought you didn't have any family."

Benito laughed without humour. "I said that to protect

them. But it wasn't enough in the end. He found them anyway."

Luis was silent a moment. Benito could tell he was weighing it all against everything he knew Benito had inflicted on other people and trying to decide if he gave a shit about Benito's pain.

Benito wouldn't have blamed him if he didn't. He'd done more to hurt Luis than Luis would probably ever know. "You know it was me, don't you?"

"What was?"

"Dante. It wasn't his idea to creep on your boy's family. It was mine. I saw how close you were getting, and I knew he was your weak spot."

Confusion coloured the haunted haze descending on Luis's face. His gaze darted between Benito and Paolo banging plates on the counter. "But why? Asa said you never wanted me back on the road when I got out."

"I didn't. But fucking with you kept your brother distracted and I needed that."

"So you could fuck him over?"

"Yes."

"Then Asa fucked *you* over?"

"Something like that."

"It's everything like that," Luis snapped. "That's why you're here. Because it didn't work out for you, and now you want a chance you've never given to anyone else."

"I gave it to you."

"*Asa* gave it to me."

"We both did. I knew you were his weak spot too. I could've exploited that. I didn't."

"Why not?"

Benito let out a slow breath. It took everything he had not to slump on the table. "I wanted you to be happy. Seeing you with him—" Benito nodded at Paolo. "It was nice. It made me think—never mind. Maybe I'm just a nice bloke. Ever think of that?"

"No. You're a cold bastard, Martell. Always have been."

Benito laughed. Couldn't help it. "You're confusing me with Asa. He's the king, not me."

"But you wanted to be."

"I did." Benito couldn't deny it. "But I was sick, man . . . in the head. I've been away from it long enough to see that. Now, I want—"

"What?" Luis demanded. "What do you want from me?"

"I want to know how it feels."

"How what feels?"

"To be normal. To love someone and have them love you back and not spend your entire life looking over your shoulder."

"I still look over my shoulder," Luis said. "I looked today and there you were. It never goes away, so if you're looking for deliverance, you're not gonna find it."

"I know that. I just want my family to be safe. For my—to be trusted, you know? I don't care what happens to me."

Luis hit Benito with another suffocating silence. His gaze drilled holes in Benito's soul, and Benito couldn't stand it. His soul was Mickey's. And Gianna's. Rosetta's, maybe.

Not Luis Pope's.

"Why now?" Luis asked suddenly. "Did something happen?"

"Do you really want to know?"

Luis held his stare a moment longer, then shook his head.

"Nah, I guess not. Unless you killed someone. I'm not about that life. I can't be. I got too much to lose."

"I see that." Benito glanced at Paolo again.

Luis's gaze turned murderous. "Don't think I wouldn't. If anyone looks at him."

"I didn't mean it that way. Just that I know you love him. And I'm jealous."

"Of Paolo?"

"Of both of you. I had . . . something, and I fucked it up. Even if I can get off the road, I can't get it back."

"You know that for sure?"

"Yeah. If I've killed anything, bro, it's that."

Understanding warmed Luis's features. His hands twitched, as though he wanted to reach out and . . . whatever. Benito had no idea.

But Luis kept his hands to himself. He stood and returned to Paolo. Another fiery discussion ensued, then Luis came back. "Come on," he said. "I'll come with you."

"Where?"

"Wherever you're taking that grenade you're hiding under the table."

———

Luis escorted Benito to the underground. They rode ten stops west until they got to Hammersmith.

Benito followed Luis out of the station. "I'm supposed to meet him in Angel at ten."

"You're going to be early then," Luis said.

"Why are you doing this?"

"Doing what?"

"Marching me somewhere. You trying to get me whacked, Pope?"

Luis crossed the road. Then he stopped outside an ale pub that was already serving coffee and artisan cakes—a world away from the greasy spoon Luis had made his home with Paolo. "I'm taking you to see him on his turf—his real turf—so you can see what's important to him."

"I know what's important to him."

"No, you don't."

"How do you know?"

Luis tilted his head sideways. "You *are* bigger. It's not in my head."

"I hit the gym a lot," Benito said warily. "I guess going straight is like prison. You gotta fill your time with something."

"Find something better. Something that makes you feel alive, man. Even if it's just loving someone more than you've ever loved anyone."

Benito shook his head. "I already told you. I fucked that up. Now I just have to take care of my girls."

"You ever think of telling Asa that straight?"

"We've never got that far."

"Yet." Luis jerked his head at the ale pub. "Let's try."

Before Benito could respond, he ducked into the pub and nodded to the woman behind the counter. "Is he in?"

"Upstairs," she said. "Not sure if he's up."

Luis turned to Benito. "He'll be up. He can't sleep past dawn."

"I guess you'd know."

Luis snorted and kept walking.

Benito followed him into the back of the pub and to a

flight of stairs. At the top, they came to a door secured by a combination lock.

Luis knocked.

Benito steeled himself.

Asa answered the door a split second later, dressed in workout clothes, with a toddler on his hip.

His expression was stoic. Only a twitch in his jaw gave him away.

He glanced between Luis and Benito. "What are you doing here? Both of you, I mean. Together."

Luis smiled at the toddler, leaning on the doorframe like he visited every day.

Perhaps he did.

"I'm mediating," Luis said. "And I don't have time to traipse to Angel for your bullshit, so . . ."

Asa shrugged. "Whatever."

He stepped aside, waving them in.

Benito trailed Luis inside, wondering if he'd fallen asleep on the train and never woken up.

Asa led them to a living space with deep-seated couches and a huge TV. He left the room with the toddler and returned alone. "My sister's kid," he said to Benito. "I'm only allowed to spend time with her here, away from the road, so if you want to talk business, you gotta meet me in Angel later."

Benito propped his elbows on his knees, keeping them still. Being unnerved by Asa was new to him. How had he forgotten how potent Asa could be when he had the upper hand? "You said it was personal, but I was happy to wait. Luis brought me here."

"Pope's emotional," Asa said. "Being happy makes you that way, apparently."

"You're not happy, Asa?"

"Not yet. I have a better shot at it since you saved Nino."

Benito nodded. "I thought so."

"Of course you did. That's your thing, isn't it? Is that why you pulled him out? To get to me?"

"I didn't know you cared about him until you called. If you hadn't, we wouldn't be here."

"No? Not even now you have the Ps I asked you for?"

"How do you know that?"

Luis abruptly stood. "I don't need to know this shit. If you two aren't going to kill each other, I'm out."

"We're good," Asa said before Benito could speak. "Just ironing out some details."

Luis gave Asa a long look. "Don't be a cunt."

"Can't now, can I?" Asa retorted. "You've showed him my arse."

"I showed him you're human. And so is he, man. He's out the other side. Let him be."

Asa nodded.

Luis left without looking at Benito again, and Benito wondered if that was it. If Luis had bullshitted him all the way here, and now Asa was going to finish the job.

He waited for fear to grip him.

It didn't come. He took his bag from his shoulder and held it out. "You're right. I have it."

Asa laughed and reached for the tea mug on the coffee table. "I know I'm right. I knew it before I made you. There isn't anyone else on the road persuasive enough to turn my muscle into rats."

Persuasive. Benito let the bag drop as he took the word and tried to apply it to the mess his life was in. Another involuntary laugh spilled out of him. "So . . . you're telling me you know I'm gonna give *your* money back to you and ask you to set me free?"

"Yup," Asa said easily. "I should be more lairy about it than I feel."

"What's stopping you being lairy about it?"

"A few things. Nino for one. The fucking cheek of it for another. You're an audacious motherfucker, Martell."

"That amuses you?"

"It has to. Or we're back where we started."

"That would suit you, though, wouldn't it? To have a reason to stomp me out for good?"

"Not really. Getting rid of you is hassle I don't need, or I'd have done it in the first place."

"You kept me on a fucking noose," Benito snapped. "It would've been easier if you'd killed me."

"Easier for you. What about that kid in the block? Your sister? You think her life would be better without you?"

"What do you care?"

"I don't. But I'm not a monster. And I'd been watching them long enough to know she'd be fucked if I left her with just your ma to take care of her."

Being so exposed should've left Benito reeling. And furious with himself more than ever. *He'd* taught Asa to look deeper when he was trying to get under someone's skin. If he'd taken that and turned it on Benito . . . well, fuck. Wasn't that something?

"I need to know," Benito said. "Are you gonna kill me now? You know what I did. The disrespect. The money. The product. I'd kill me if I wore your crown."

"You want my crown, Martell?"

"No."

"What *do* you want?"

Benito let his mind race, flipping through every dream he'd ever had. Every heart he'd ever loved. Every soul he'd take to his grave, even if he never saw them again. "I want to live," he said, so quietly he barely heard himself. "I want to take care of my family and be a better man."

Asa nodded. "You should give me that money then. So we can talk about that with a clean slate."

"Are you fucking with me?"

Asa drained his tea mug and leaned forwards. "As tempting as it is, no. I'm not. I want what you want, man. And if I'm good to you, maybe somewhere down the line someone will be good to me."

The relief Benito was counting on never came. Not even when Asa had given his word that Benito and his family would be safe forever unless Benito broke the terms of their agreement.

"Stay out of London. Stay legitimate. Don't talk to anyone from the road. You're dead to anyone you ever knew from this life."

Only Luis Pope was left off the list, but Benito couldn't see that line of communication ever opening up. As perspective returned with every mile he got away from the city, he was beginning to realise that maybe Luis's actions had been for Asa's benefit, not Benito's. A message . . . that if an arsehole like Benito could go straight, anyone could.

Even Asa. Benito couldn't fathom why Luis cared, but perhaps he was a better man than the rest of them combined.

On the train home, Benito let his mind wander to the tail end of the conversation he'd had with Asa before he'd handed the money over and walked away for good.

Asa leaned back on the couch, the picture of relaxation. "I'm not sorry about shanking you. I hope you know that."

Despite his thundering heart, Benito rolled his eyes. "I saw the joy in your face, you sick fuck."

"I'm not a sick fuck. But you were. Admit it—you needed that pain. You'd been untouchable for too long."

"Jealous, Asa?"

"Fuck you, Martell. Oh, wait . . . I already did."

It had taken a moment for Benito to catch up. For the loose threads of the last few days to separate into their appropriate sections. And then it had clicked.

Benito uttered the name of his contact.

Asa's expression turned predatory. "He flipped six months ago. I've been riding you ever since, waiting for you to fuck up." Then the malice in his smile faded. "I didn't think it would be like this, though. I thought I really would have to kill you."

"Is that what you wanted?"

"No, fam. Or I'd have done it years ago."

Benito came back to the present with a shudder. Until Asa's blade had pierced his skin, he'd never thought about either one of them killing the other. For long months after, he'd thought of little else. It should've unnerved him that Asa had been a lifetime ahead of him the whole time, but it wasn't that making him shiver—it was the realisation that he was glad they'd both lived to laugh about it.

The train ambled into Milton Keynes Central. Benito stumbled off and walked home. His bed called to him. *Sleep.* For as long as the sandpaper in his brain would allow. But first, a deeper need propelled him to his car, and he drove to Bletchley on autopilot.

He parked in the same spot the police had moved him on from months ago. Turned the car off and waited, letting the cold of the frosty winter day seep into him. He didn't sleep, but as he rotated his attention between Rosetta's flat and the bus stop, strains of consciousness abandoned him.

Time slipped away.

School's end came and went.

Benito thought he'd spot Gianna the moment she got off the bus, but she surprised him with a sharp knock on his window.

Startled, he sat up and opened the door.

She was on the phone. He waited without trying to pretend he wasn't listening.

"I'll tell him," Gianna said. "Yeah. I know. I thought he was dead."

Her word choice shook any remnants of sleep from Benito. He snatched the phone from her, but the screen was blank. Whoever she'd been talking to was already gone. "Who was that?"

"It was Mum, you freak. She said you've been out here for hours and she's worried you're cold. She tried calling you, but your phone is off."

Benito fished his phone from his pocket. Sure enough, it was dead. "I haven't been here that long."

Gianna scowled. "You're a bad liar. Mum says you're to come inside right now."

"Oh yeah? She said that, did she?"

"Yes. And she means it, so don't sulk like a man-child."

"Man-child? Where did you get that from?"

"*Pretty Little Liars.*"

"What's that?"

"It's on Netflix. I can watch it on my iPad now Mum can afford broadband."

"Excellent," Benito said dryly. "Glad you're using it for productive shit."

"Don't swear. And come inside . . . please?"

Benito was too tired to resist Gianna. He let her steal his keys, lock his car, and tug him into the Barnfield Court tower block. Inside, she took his dead phone and plugged it into her iPad charger. "Now you can relax, can't he, Mum?"

Rosetta was watching from the kitchen doorway. She smiled a little and nodded. "Of course he can. Beni, come and sit down. We'll take care of you."

Benito eyed them both with suspicion. "I don't need taking care of. Is there something in the water round here?"

"Only spaghetti," Gianna said. "Mum made carbonara. Your favourite."

"Yeah, when I was twelve. Like you."

"You still act twelve," Gianna retorted. "Just sit down."

Benito sat on the sofa. It was the same one that he had slept on many times after Gianna's dad had thrown his bed out. Soft and worn, it cocooned him like an old friend. He tipped his head back and watched Rosetta move around the kitchen, only half listening to Gianna as she told him how well Rosetta had done with the tradesmen who'd visited to complete the maintenance work.

"They were nice," Gianna said. "Sullivan tried to escape, but Mickey brought him back for Mum."

"Mickey? He was here?"

"This morning," Rosetta called from the kitchen. "He came to make sure they got the work done in a day so we didn't have to move out."

"And did they?"

"I think so. I hid in the bathroom." Rosetta came back to

the doorway. "Mickey said he'd call me this afternoon if they needed to come back, and I haven't heard from him."

Neither had Benito, and the gaping hole he'd left behind was a vortex of pain. Now things with Asa were settled, it was all Benito could think about. *He* was all he could think about. His sandy hair. His scent. His laugh.

His low groan when Benito had eased inside him.

Bitter heat flared in Benito's chest. He focused on Rosetta, all the while drowning in the pressure behind his eyes. "That's good," he said absently.

Rosetta gave him a strange frown. As if his reply had come ten minutes too late.

She disappeared back into the kitchen.

Gianna plopped down beside Benito, dumping her cat on his chest in the process.

The orange beast stared at Benito, owlish and aloof. Benito stared back, as was their current relationship.

"Don't be nice to him," Gianna said. "He's been bad all weekend."

"Does that apply to everyone, or just cats?"

"Just him. What's wrong?"

"Nothing's wrong."

"Yes, it is. You never let Sullivan sit on you."

"Maybe I've changed."

"Have you?" Gianna turned to face him. "Did something happen with Mickey?"

Benito blinked. "Mickey?"

"Mum said he was in a funny mood too."

"That's not what I said." Rosetta came back with bowls of steaming pasta. Gianna took one.

Benito waved his away.

Rosetta set it on the coffee table. "I didn't say Mickey was in a funny mood. Just that he wasn't himself. Then I wondered if it was me. I haven't seen him in person for a while."

Benito said nothing.

Gianna ate spaghetti while they all gawped at him, even the cat.

He shifted on the couch, dislodging Sullivan. "Stop staring at me."

Rosetta took a seat in the armchair closest to the TV. She wasn't eating either, but her gaze was steady. Kind, almost. "Did something happen between you two?"

"Who?"

"Mickey. I thought you liked each other."

"What made you think that?"

"I saw you," she said. "Out of the window. I thought maybe..."

"What? That he had the power to evict you from your home and I was chatting him up so he wouldn't?"

"I thought you might be seeing each other."

"Are you?" Gianna asked. "Because he's really nice. If you were going to have a boyfriend, I'd pick him for you."

Benito's head suddenly felt so heavy he could hardly hold it up. He slow-blinked again, denial blooming on his tongue, but when he opened his mouth, nothing came out.

He shut it again.

Rosetta nodded to herself.

Gianna went back to her dinner, leaving Benito to reel in peace. He'd never told them he was bisexual, and he'd only ever brought one person home—a girl who Gianna had idolised and Rosetta had ignored. Had they known all this time? Or had the show he'd apparently put on for Rosetta in recent days, weeks—however long it had been—been her first clue?

What about Gianna?

Did it even matter?

"Benito," Rosetta said. "Are you sure you won't eat something?"

"What?"

"Your dinner. It's getting cold."

Benito shook his head. "I fucked it up."

"It's fine. I was cooking anyway."

"Not that. With Mickey."

Gianna stopped eating and wrapped her small hand around Benito's forearm. "What did you do?"

"I lied to him about what I was doing for money. He found out before I got away from it."

"Got away?" Rosetta folded her hands in her lap. "What does that mean?"

"It means I'm just a taxi driver now, so it really is going to take me until the end of time to pay your arrears off."

"But you'll be safe?" she said. "No more fighting? Or bad men in London?"

"No more. It's done."

Gianna set her half-empty bowl on the coffee table next to Benito's untouched dinner. "Can't you tell Mickey that?"

It struck Benito that she had gone with that rather than the concrete revelation that her brother was a criminal.

Maybe she'd known that all along too.

"Beni?"

"Hmm?"

"Can't you talk to Mickey?" Gianna repeated. "Tell him

you're sorry, but it's okay now? And you're not going to do that stuff anymore?"

Benito shook his head. "It's too late. What I did . . . it really hurt him. More than I can explain. And I knew it would before it happened, and I did it anyway. We can't come back from that, G."

"You can try."

"*No*. It's over, okay? Just let it go."

Gianna looked as though she might cry. She left the room. Rosetta took the pasta plates to the kitchen, and for a few minutes, Benito was alone. He shivered, cold again for no reason.

The cat took advantage of his distraction and reclaimed his belly, settling in for a good dig about.

Benito tried to anchor himself to the tiny pinpricks against his skin but found himself drifting, spinning until Gianna came back with a bar of Dairy Milk.

"For your broken heart," she said.

Benito shook his head at her grave expression. "You're trippin', girl."

"You're sad, Beni. Why won't you admit it?"

Benito had nothing. He set the chocolate on the arm of the sofa as Rosetta returned to the room and turned the TV up. No one spoke. *EastEnders* came on. Benito stared at it, unseeing and unhearing until somehow, in a place that hadn't been his home for more years than he could remember, he fell asleep.

He dreamed of looming shadows and dark country roads.

Of running through fields and choking on the thick mud slowing him down.

He woke coughing, eyes streaming, head pounding, and

his vision blurred. A piercing shriek rattled his brain, forcing him awake when all he wanted to do was close his eyes and sleep forever.

Yeah. Fuck it. Sleep.

Benito sank back into the couch, down and down and down, the ancient cushions sucking him in. It should've been a pleasant journey to the bottom, but it felt like freefall, and not the good kind. Also, the persistent shriek wouldn't quit, and a tapping sensation on his cheek had joined the party.

Groaning, Benito forced his eyes open again. Round, green irises awaited him, inches from his own. It took Benito a long, sluggish moment to place them as Sullivan's and that the batting on his cheek was the cat's paw insistently punching him in the face.

"Fuck off." Benito hooked his hands beneath the cat. Lifted him to fling him off, but nothing happened. His arms didn't move the way he asked them to, and the cat stayed put, yowling.

Benito blinked hard, fighting the scratching burn that filled his eyes, his throat, his chest. He couldn't see. He couldn't breathe. He was nothing but the obnoxious screech of the smoke alarm he'd screwed to the ceiling after the third time Gianna's dad had passed out drunk with a lit cigarette in his hand.

Smoke alarm.

Somewhere in the thick sludge Benito's mind had become, the words meant something. His heart beat louder.

Thump. Thump. Thump.

The cat hit him again, and finally it clicked.

Fire.

Fuck.

Fire!

Benito rolled from the couch, dislodging the cat, and landed on his knees. He hooked the cat under one arm and scrambled forward, barrelling into Gianna's room. "Get up. There's a fire. We need to get out."

Gianna stirred.

Benito shook her, and she bolted upright. "Get up. Hold the cat and wait here. I'll get Mum."

He left Gianna, shutting the door behind him and staggered into the hallway. "Mum! *Mum!* Wake up. We have to leave."

Rosetta heard him and opened her bedroom door, already fastening her robe around her waist. She coughed into her hand. "Gianna!"

"I got her." Benito ducked into the bathroom and grabbed two towels. He soaked them and passed one to Rosetta. "Hold this over your mouth and keep your hands on me, okay? Follow me. I don't know where the fire is, so we'll have to go slow."

"It's not in here?" Rosetta shouted over the smoke alarm.

"No. It's out there somewhere."

"Shouldn't we stay here?"

Images of Grenfell Tower ambushed Benito. He gripped Rosetta's arms and shook her. "*No.* There's cladding on this building. We need to get out."

Rosetta nodded and hooked her fingers into Benito's belt loops.

He dashed back to Gianna's room and wrapped the damp towel around her face. "Hold on to me," he ordered.

Fear filled her young eyes. Suddenly she was six years old again and waiting on Benito to make everything okay.

He gripped her chin. "Don't let go. Not for anything."

There was no time for anything else. He pulled Gianna in front of him and guided her to the front door with Rosetta behind him.

He opened it slowly, bracing for whatever was on the other side.

Carnage greeted them.

Heavy smoke.

Stumbling bodies.

The orange glow of flames somewhere below them.

Panic seized Benito's heart. The flat was already too smoke-filled for them to survive long, but to get out, they had to pass through thicker smoke and heat. What if it overcame them? What if they passed out before they reached the bottom?

Just go. Get them out. Keep moving till you get there.

It was all they had.

Benito urged Gianna forward and they inched down the stairs, step by step, over and around anyone who got in their way. People shouted. Hands reached for them. Benito shoved them aside, not caring who they left behind until Gianna and Rosetta were safe.

The smoke was densest on the third floor. Heat enveloped them, and flames crackled at the windows, creeping up the building, sparking the flammable cladding as it went. A loud bang busted the glass.

Gianna jumped and the cat escaped her clutch, disappearing into the murky gloom. "Sullivan!" she wailed. "Sullivan! No no no! Beni, he's gone. We have to find him."

"No. We have to keep going."

Benito forced her on, taking her sharp elbows and fists as

she flailed against him, hardening his soul to her heartbreak. She loved that cat so fucking much, but he loved her more.

Rosetta still clinging to his back, he pushed on, herding them to the ground floor, and fought his way to the exit.

Fresh air hit them, and they staggered into the night, coughing.

Gianna kicked and screamed, tossing her damp towel aside. "Sullivan! Sullivan! We have to go back for him."

Benito dragged her away from the building to the chicken shop where a crowd had begun to form. Good Samaritans eased Rosetta away from him, guiding her to safety while he fought with Gianna. "Stop. You can't go back, okay? He's a clever cat. He'll find his own way. He's probably already out here."

"He's not, he's not. I saw him. He ran up the corridor."

"Which corridor?"

"By the fire. I saw him, Beni. He went past the blue doors."

Benito turned back to the tower block. Fierce flames were creeping up one side, enveloping the cladding. It wouldn't be long before the entire building was acting like a chimney, drawing the blaze to the sky.

Now or never. Benito marched Gianna to the pavement and sat her down. "Wait here. Don't move unless a firefighter or a fed tells you to, you hear me?"

"But—"

"Promise me, G, or I'm not going back for him."

Gianna nodded and hugged her knees to her chest, tears streaming down her soot-stained face.

Benito backed away from her, then turned against the tide of people flowing from the block and ran back inside.

The smoke was thicker than ever. He wrapped his arm around his face, wishing he'd thought to grab Gianna's wet towel, and dropped low, crawling up the stairs towards the heat of the flames, sweeping his hand for any sign of Sullivan. *That damn fucking cat.*

On the third floor, his legs gave out. He slumped against the wall, coughing. Away from Gianna and his mum, the urge to sleep forever returned.

Just for a minute.

Seconds and minutes past with the slowing thump of his heartbeat. Half his brain knew he was dying, the other screamed at him to keep moving. He listened to neither and felt nothing. Floating. Or maybe he was sinking, it was hard to tell.

And I don't care. I don't—

A soft thud battered his legs. Then claws. For the second time in five terrifying minutes, Benito opened his eyes to a wily orange feline scaling his body.

Sullivan. You little bastard.

For a moment, they stared at each other, man and heroic, and yet awkward as fuck, beast. Then the survivor in Benito's soul kicked in too. He grabbed the cat and lurched to his feet, coming upright as another body emerged on the landing.

They collided hard, sending both of them sprawling.

Benito cursed, squeezing his hands around the cat. He couldn't lose him now.

Somehow, he kept Sullivan tucked against his body. He found his footing again and turned to face a weathered-looking man he'd seen around.

A tall man with *strong* hands.

He gripped Benito's wrist. "Come on, son. Down we go."

They found their way to the first floor, picking up stragglers on the way. Benito hooked his arm around the little old lady from number seven, hiding her face with his free arm.

The final set of stairs was three feet ahead. Benito hauled them forward, chest burning, but as he reached the banister, it fell away, and the staircase collapsed, obliterating their only way out.

Mickey drove like a madman, speeding through the night as fast as the icy roads would allow, white knuckling the steering wheel as he shouted at Isha. "How did this happen the same goddamn day we start installing fire breaks? Is this a fucking joke?"

"I don't know how it started," Isha said urgently. "Just that the whole block has gone up. I'm half an hour away. Where are you?"

"Ten minutes out. I can fucking see it from the road."

"How bad is it?"

"Bad. If that cladding catches like it did at Grenfell, it's going to be a massacre."

Isha swore, as caught up in the moment as Mickey. He'd founded DOSHA with Dom to protect lower income households from unsafe housing, but contained by bureaucracy and red tape, it took *years* to facilitate real change, and this was the result: tower blocks that could kill hundreds of people at once if the right kind of fire took hold. Elderly folk. Kids. Whole families.

Benito's family if they hadn't got out in time.

Mickey ended the call with Isha and jabbed at the screen on the dashboard, keeping a sharp eye on the road. He called Rosetta. Her phone was off.

He called Gianna.

No answer.

"*Fuck.*" Mickey pounded the steering wheel as the orange glow on the horizon grew bigger. *Call him. He needs to be here.* But coward that Mickey was, he didn't have the balls to call Benito and tell him his mother's home was burning and he had no idea if his family was safe.

Just get there.

Six minutes later, Mickey was as close to Barnfield Court as the emergency cordon would allow him to be. He threw his car up the kerb and leapt out.

He raced to the nearest police officer controlling the crowd. "I need to get past. This is my building."

The officer shook his head. "We're not letting anyone through. If you're worried about relatives, you need to give your name to the incident command and wait over there."

"I'm not a resident. I'm from the housing association that manages some of the properties. I have a list of every household, blueprints of the building, and documentation for the ongoing maintenance work."

Mickey flashed his DOSHA ID and the folder of paperwork he'd had the foresight to grab when he'd charged out of his house.

The officer let him through.

Mickey dashed across the road, smoke from the fire already burning his eyes. Firefighters swarmed the area at the foot of the tower, shepherding coughing residents across the precinct to the fried chicken shop. Mickey scanned every face, searching out those he knew, ticking them off in his brain.

Mrs Foggarty
The Howlets
The Aslams
Mr Grecco

For a heart-stopping moment, that was it, then he *finally* found the fear-filled gaze of Rosetta De Luca.

Gianna was at her feet, curled into an upright foetal position on the pavement, pale and tear-streaked. Mickey longed to go to her and scoop her up while he called Benito to come and be with his family, but he couldn't. Before he could stop pretending Benito and his family weren't everything to him, he had to locate Mr Morris and track down the lead fire fighter.

The white hat of the lead firefighter was by the engine closest to the building. Mickey ran to him and handed over the household list he'd gathered for the maintenance work. "I only manage the housing association properties, but this is a full list. Did you get everyone out? I can't see one of my residents. Mr Morris. Third floor."

"Morris. Yup. We're looking for him. The third floor caught the worst of it. We're also missing the son of the lady in the De Luca flat at the top. He went back in for the cat."

Dread gripped Mickey's heart. "Benito? But—but he doesn't live here."

"Visiting, apparently. Stayed the night on the couch. We're looking for him, but there's a structural weakness in the stairs. Access is—"

A loud crash from inside the building cut the firefighter off.

He swore and abandoned Mickey to intercept the fire crews exiting the tower.

Mickey watched him go, then tipped his head to gaze up at the tower block as fresh flames shot from the third-floor windows, completing a loop of the building and cutting off the upper storeys.

The dread in Mickey's heart grew jagged edges. Sharp fear choked him. If Benito was anywhere above the third floor, it was over. He wasn't getting out.

"Mickey!"

Mickey turned on autopilot.

Gianna ran towards him, arms outstretched. She threw herself against him as he reached for her, and he lifted her as if she was years younger than twelve. "It's my fault, it's my fault," she wailed. "I made him go back for Sullivan."

Mickey carried her away from the building and back to Rosetta. "You need to stay over here. It's not safe that close, okay?"

Gianna nodded, still clinging to him.

Rosetta gripped Mickey's shoulder. "Beni went back in. It happened too fast; I couldn't stop him."

"He wouldn't have listened to you," Mickey said numbly. "Just wait here. Please. Wherever he is, all he'd want is for you both to be safe."

He peeled Gianna from his front and forced her into Rosetta's arms. A firefighter stepped between them, throwing up a new barrier, leaving Mickey on one side and Benito's family on the other. Another crash sounded from the building, but he couldn't look.

He couldn't watch Benito die.

I can't fucking breathe.

Mickey turned away from Rosetta and Gianna and moved mechanically along the line of shellshocked residents pressed against the barrier, doing his job. He checked in with the DOSHA households, double checking against his mental list, but with every step, the pain in his chest grew. *How is this happening?* He pinched himself hard, praying it would wake him. But nothing changed. The nightmare remained. His worlds had collided in the very worst way. The only man he'd ever fallen for was trapped in a burning building, and Mickey would probably have to tell his twelve-year-old sister that he wasn't coming back.

Mr Morris was still MIA too. Mickey had his son's number in his phone, but he couldn't bring himself to make that call either. How did you tell someone their loved one was dead?

"Mickey!" Gianna's shriek pierced the air again.

Mickey spun back to her. "Gianna—"

She cut him off, pointing wildly behind him. "Look! Someone came out!"

Mickey turned slowly, bracing himself for the worst, and at first it seemed nothing had changed. Thirty firefighters stood between him and the door. He couldn't see a thing. And he didn't want to. *I fucking love him too much to see his fucking body.*

The realisation, though it wasn't new, hit Mickey like a sledgehammer. He forced himself forward on ten-ton legs. He shouldered his way closer to the door. Behind him, Gianna screamed his name over and over, and then Benito's too, and the desolation in her broken voice cut Mickey in two. *She can't lose him.* She wouldn't survive it, and neither would Mickey.

Grief had already laid roots in his gut. They bloomed with every step he took, gnarled branches that wrapped around every fibre in his body, weighing him down more than addiction ever had and ever would. But just when he thought he might drown and this pain would swallow him whole for good, the crowd of firefighters parted, revealing a cluster of soot-smeared survivors.

An old lady was carried straight into an ambulance. Mr Morris limped of his own volition to a waiting paramedic, and behind him stood a policeman, grim faced and clutching a giant orange cat.

22

———

The world stopped turning. There were no blue lights and smoke. There was no towering inferno.

Just a limping old man and a cat with no owner.

No. A scream built in Mickey's throat. *I have to find him.* He started forward. Stopped again as his legs wobbled, threatening to give out. The pain in his chest ramped up, eroding every scrap of muscle and bone in his body, and for a devastating moment, he thought he might puke.

Then more movement caught his tear-blurred eyes. The policeman turned, handing the cat to someone else. To someone tall, with dark hair, strong shoulders, and once-spotless white trainers that were now covered in soot and grime.

Benito.

Relief swayed Mickey on his feet. His hand flew to his chest, as if he could push the *terror* of thinking Benito was dead back where it had come from and keep it locked up forever.

He stared at Benito, and Benito stared right back.

Then reality set in. Emergency workers rushed Benito, taking the cat and leading him away, and Mickey went back to work.

Isha arrived. "Tell me what you need."

Distracted, Mickey watched a paramedic hold an oxygen mask over Benito's face and check his blood pressure. "What?"

"Where are we at?" Isha barked. "Everyone's out, right? No serious injuries?"

"I don't know." Mickey pointed to where Benito and Mr Morris were being checked over. "They were the last out, with an old girl from one of the council properties. She's in the ambulance."

"How did she look?"

"I—fuck, I don't know. I didn't take it in."

Isha clapped Mickey's shoulder. "You're here. That's what matters. Right, we need to get our residents housed for the night, then work on helping the council tenants if no one shows up for them until the morning."

Mickey nodded, still eyeing Benito. Bar the filth staining his skin, he looked all right, but he'd been inside a long time. *So much smoke. What about his lungs? What about—*

"Mickey. Are you with me?"

Mickey reeled himself in and focused on Isha. "I'm here."

"Good. Let's get to work and get these people somewhere warm."

They split the list in half. Rosetta was on Isha's list, and Mickey didn't argue. He glued his phone to his ear and moved mountains to get his residents housed overnight in nearby hotels while he worked on alternative accommodation moving forward.

He checked back on Benito approximately every six seconds but somehow still missed the paramedic packing up and walking away, leaving Benito alone in the chaos of the night.

Benito rubbed his chest and glanced at the sky, handsome face twisted in an expression Mickey didn't recognise. He *ached* to comfort him, but Gianna was there before Mickey could take another breath, gripping a cat box and hugging her brother so fiercely Mickey almost smiled. Then his gaze fell on Rosetta. Isha was with her, his face patient as she waved her arms in distress.

Fuck. Mickey wrapped up his phone call and hurried to her side. "What's the matter?"

"I don't want to go to a hotel," she said. "I just—I can't. All those people, and—"

"You don't have to, Mum." Benito appeared in Mickey's peripheral, a shadow at first, then real flesh and bone. "Come home with me—"

"Shouldn't you be on oxygen or something?" Mickey broke in.

"He refused." Gianna slipped her small hand into Benito's. "Can we really stay with you, Beni?"

Benito ignored Mickey and gave Gianna a smile so sweet Mickey wanted to weep. "Of course."

"Are you sure that's feasible?" Isha scanned his list. "We'll work around the clock to secure new accommodation for you, but it could be a few days. A week, maybe."

"It's fine—" Benito coughed and reached around Isha for Rosetta. "They can stay with me as long as it takes."

Isha nodded. "Okay. Take them home then. Did anyone's

phone make it out of the building? We'll need a way for Mickey to contact you in the morning."

"I have mine," Benito said. "Mickey has my number."

Mickey opened his mouth to confirm it, but Benito was already walking away, towing Rosetta, Gianna, and the cat to his car.

He drove away without looking at Mickey.

And took Mickey's heart with him.

Isha watched them go, then turned his shrewd gaze to Mickey. "Well, that was interesting."

"Hmm?"

Isha's jaw ticked with faint amusement. "The vibe between you two. Something you want to tell me?"

"About what?"

"About why this household had you so torn up. And why you're so desperate to walk away from this block. Is there something between you and the son?"

"No."

"Sure about that? Because you were eyeballing each other pretty hard."

"He never looked at me."

"Not when you were looking at him, maybe, but trust me, he was looking, and I *know* that look."

"You don't know anything," Mickey snapped. "Just leave it, okay? It doesn't matter anymore."

Isha nodded, unfazed by Mickey's lack of control. "If you say so, but if there's something you need to talk about, know that I'll listen. Or call Dom if you don't want to talk to me. What's gone down tonight is huge and it's going to take months to unpick, but you matter, Mickey, to both of us."

Mickey believed him, but he didn't have the headspace to

unravel the mess between him and Benito. Not yet. Right now, all that mattered was that Benito was still breathing. The gut-wrenching moments he might not have been would stay with Mickey forever, but as long as Benito was okay, he could live with that.

He worked through the night with Isha, transporting residents to hotels and gathering supplies to keep them going while their flats were inaccessible. It was close to dawn when he pointed his car in the direction of home.

With the smoking tower block behind him, he drove north, the radio keeping him company. News reports came in thick and fast. After a while, Mickey switched to a DAB station. Mellow drum and bass filtered into the car. It reminded him of dirty nights with Benito, and yearning consumed him. He tapped the dashboard and brought up Benito's number, but his phone rang before he could place the call.

Benito.

Warmth filled his chest. He answered so fast he gave his thumb whiplash. "Hey."

"Mickey?" Gianna's panicked voice filled the car and stopped his heart. "Mickey, please, you have to come quick. Something's wrong with Benito."

23

Mickey had never been to Benito's flat. All he knew about it was that it existed, and there was no time for him to digest that the city-centre apartment was exactly as he'd pictured it.

For the second time that night, he flung his car up a kerb and abandoned it.

He sprinted across the road to the new-build block opposite the shopping centre. The exterior door was open. Mickey shouldered through it and charged upstairs to Benito's flat.

Gianna met him at the door, clutching a phone. "He's in the bathroom. We can't get him up and he can't breathe."

Mickey pushed past her and followed the sound of a hacking cough to the bathroom.

Benito was on the floor, hunched over his knees, shirtless and coughing. Rosetta was close by, rubbing his back.

She moved back when she saw Mickey. "He's been really sick," she said. "It's only just stopped."

Mickey dropped down beside Benito and took over rubbing his back, flinching as Benito's bare skin touched his palm. "Why's he so cold? How long has he been like this?"

"Since we got back. I thought it was just from the smoke; then he passed out."

"How long ago was that?"

"Twenty minutes, maybe? I called III. They think it's a delayed reaction to the smoke he inhaled. They're sending paramedics to check on him, but it could be awhile before they get here."

"Did he hit his head when he passed out?"

"No. He was already on the floor."

Benito's coughing fit died down as Rosetta finished speaking. Mickey gripped his shoulders and eased him upright, taking in his grey skin and unseeing gaze as he tried to remember the last first aid training he'd taken. Most of the course had centred around dealing with elderly tenants prone to falling, and as Benito shivered in his arms, he realised he was totally out of his depth.

Get him in the recovery position. As the thought crossed his mind, Benito began to come round. His face contorted with pain and he brought his hands to his head. "Fuck. My head, man—" He broke off with an agonised groan.

Mickey manoeuvred him into his lap and cupped his face. He rubbed his thumbs over Benito's cheekbones. *Why does he look thinner? It's only been a couple of days.* "Paramedics are coming to help you, okay? They'll make it stop."

Benito gazed up at him, his eyes bloodshot and wild and still so unfocused Mickey couldn't be sure he was fully conscious. "I need you."

"I know. I'm here. Everything's okay."

"It's not. I—"

"Shh. You're okay."

Benito's eyes rolled shut. He curled into Mickey's chest, tremors still wracking his body. "I can't."

"You can. You're okay, I promise." Mickey held Benito tight and kissed his temple. He stroked his face and whispered anything he could think of until paramedics appeared in the doorway sometime later.

They helped Mickey lean Benito against the wall, then Mickey got out of their way.

He found Gianna crying in the kitchen while Rosetta hovered in the hallway, torn between her children.

Mickey lifted Gianna onto the countertop and gave her a quick hug. "You want something to drink? I bet your brother keeps hot chocolate around here somewhere for you."

"He does." Gianna hiccupped. "It's in the cupboard over the microwave with the marshmallows."

Mickey opened a cupboard that was otherwise empty save a jar of Galaxy hot chocolate and a bag of mini marshmallows. The sight of it warmed and broke his heart in equal measure, and everything hurt as he tried to make sense of how he felt for Benito. *I love him.*

It was the truest story ever told, but—

But nothing. He's dying on his bathroom floor. Everything else is fucking noise.

Mickey filled the kettle and set it to boil. He gave Gianna another hug, then left her to check on Benito.

A paramedic emerged from the bathroom and beckoned Mickey and Rosetta into the living room. "He's had some oxygen and he's doing much better. Sometimes the effects of smoke inhalation can take a while to manifest, but his vital signs are strong so he's probably going to be okay."

"Are you sure?" Rosetta twisted her hands in knots. "He wasn't right even before the fire. He fell asleep on the sofa and he never does that, even when he's been driving all night."

"His blood sugar is low," the paramedic said. "Did he eat this evening? He said something about pizza when I asked him, but he wasn't making much sense."

Rosetta shook her head. "He was in his car all day waiting for Gianna to come home from school, and he didn't eat the dinner I made him." She glanced at Mickey. "He was upset."

The paramedic nodded slowly. "Well, whatever's happened today, it's a lot, so seeing as he's refusing hospital treatment, the best thing you can do is keep him warm and safe. Maybe a light meal, if he can eat? And plenty of fluids. Keep an eye on him and call us back if you're the slightest bit worried."

Worried didn't even come close. Mickey drifted to the doorway where he could see Benito's legs. They were no longer shaking, and if he strained his ears, he could hear the low rumble of Benito's voice. "Are you sure he doesn't need more oxygen? He was struggling to breathe."

"Some of that might've been shock," the paramedic said. "It's been quite a night for him. I was at the fire scene and I saw him carry that old lady out."

"Benito carried her out?" Mickey said faintly.

The paramedic nodded. "And the cat who seems happy enough now, eh?" He tickled the big ginger cat's ears, earning a chirruping purr in response.

Rosetta asked more questions.

He answered them while Mickey gave in to the pull in his chest dragging him back to Benito.

Mickey reached the bathroom as the other paramedic was packing up and rising to her feet.

Benito remained on the floor, leaning against the wall, head tipped back, eyes closed.

"Is he okay?" Mickey asked the paramedic.

She smiled. "I think so. You can call us back any time if you're concerned about anything. But for now, something to eat and then some rest is probably the best thing for him."

Mickey nodded, absorbing the repeated instructions.

The paramedic patted his arm and left the bathroom.

Mickey crouched beside Benito and took his hand. "You still with us?"

Benito cracked a heavy eye, colour already returning to his face. "Think so. What are you—fuck, how are you even here? Am I trippin'?"

Mickey squeezed Benito's fingers hard enough that it had to hurt. "Gianna called me. I came running."

"Why?"

"Because I fucking love you, that's why. I—" Mickey snatched a shaky breath. "As stupid as it sounds after everything I've said before, there's nothing I wouldn't do for you— you damn fucking *motherfucker*. I—"

Mickey pressed the fist of his free hand to his lips, willing the words to stop spilling out. He stared at where his fingers wrapped so tightly around Benito's, picturing Benito cold and grey.

Picturing him dead, lips and nose blackened by soot. "I love you," he said again, almost to himself. "I don't know what that means right now, but we can talk about it later, okay?"

Benito took a shallow breath, but the older paramedic appeared before he could speak.

"We're leaving," she said. "Are you staying here for the next few hours?"

"Of course he is." Gianna slipped under the paramedic's arm and into the bathroom. "He's my brother's boyfriend."

A beat of silence blanketed the room.

Mickey cocked a brow at Benito.

Benito shook his head. "I got nothing, man. I fucking can't."

He closed his eyes. Mickey made room for Gianna, then claimed his place on the floor. "I'm staying. We all are."

The paramedic nodded and left. Rosetta locked the front door and came to the bathroom door. "Gianna, it's time for bed now."

Gianna pressed herself tighter to Benito's side. "But it's morning already."

"Exactly. You need to get some sleep."

"No."

"Yes." Benito opened his eyes. "Go and get in my bed. I changed the sheets yesterday, so they don't smell of boys."

"I'm not getting in your bed, Beni. You are."

"I'm fine right here, G."

"Fuck off."

"Don't swear," Benito said.

"*Gianna*," Rosetta snapped at the same time.

Mickey laughed. "Wow. Okay. You have a couch, right? And I can go and find an airbed from somewhere. No one needs to be telling each other to fuck off right now."

Gianna sat up and folded her slender arms. "I'm not getting in Benito's bed."

"Neither am I," Rosetta said. "We'll be fine on the couch, so no one needs to go anywhere that isn't in this flat. Gianna, come *on*. The longer you take, the longer your brother will stay on the bathroom floor."

Rosetta held out her hand. After a gentle push from Benito, Gianna took it and allowed herself to be towed from the bathroom.

The living room door shut a moment later, gifting Mickey a split second of peace before reality consumed him. Before he looked at Benito again and saw him broken on the floor.

"Hey." Benito's hand twitched weakly in Mickey's. "You don't have to be here."

Mickey tore his gaze from the empty hallway and lost himself in Benito's tired brown eyes. "I do, actually, because I'd rather die than be anywhere else."

"I don't deserve that. I hurt you."

"I know." Mickey couldn't deny it. "But we're more than what we do. At least, I hope so, or I'm not worth shit."

Benito snorted. "You're worth everything. I love you too . . . You know that, right?"

"You don't need to say that."

"It's true."

Mickey stood and filled the glass by Benito's sink with water. He crouched down again and held it to Benito's mouth so he could drink. "Can I ask you something?"

Benito nodded, licking his dry lips.

"Have you eaten anything since the shitty pizza I fed you on Saturday?"

"What?"

"Your blood sugar was really low. And Rosetta said you didn't eat dinner."

"Oh. Fuck. I don't know. Maybe not . . . it's been hectic, man. I—" Benito stopped and shook his head. "You probably don't want to know."

"I do. But maybe later? You need to get off this floor before you put down roots."

Mickey helped Benito stand and guided him to the bedroom. His bed was perfectly made with fresh white sheets, like no one ever slept in it, but wherever Benito usually laid his head, he had little choice now. He was so dizzy he could hardly stand.

He sat on the edge of the bed and buried his face in his hands.

Mickey gave him a moment, then helped him into bed.

Benito shivered, still cold.

Mickey rubbed his arms, then turned to leave the room and raid the kitchen.

Benito clutched his hand. "Don't go. Please—I—"

His breath caught.

"Hey, hey." Mickey turned back and pulled Benito into a fierce embrace. "I'm not going anywhere."

Benito made a low, broken sound.

Mickey rubbed his back and held him tighter. "Shh. Just breathe, man. I'm right here."

24

Benito felt like death for *hours*. Shivers, cold sweats, coughing up a lung every ten minutes. And his head hurt more than he ever thought possible. It pounded and throbbed, and the only relief he could find was buried in Mickey's bare chest, soaking up his scent and his warmth.

Drowning in him.

Clinging to him.

It was embarrassing as fuck, but he couldn't bring himself to care. All that mattered was that his girls were safe and he was holding onto the fantasy that Mickey had said he loved him. Because that's what it was—a fantasy. A dream. And he didn't want to wake up, so he held onto the pain in his head, kept it close, so he could stay with Mickey a little while longer.

Eventually, though, his body fought back. The painkillers kicked in, and he fell into a deep, *deep* sleep. When he woke up, he was alone, and it made more sense than any dream he'd ever had.

Still dizzy, Benito sat up and rubbed his sore chest. He heard voices somewhere in the flat.

Gianna.

Rosetta.

He swung his legs out of bed. His feet hit the floor and he staggered upright, head swimming, blood pounding in his ears. *Damn.* He took a step towards the door and swayed, bracing himself on the wall. *Fuck. Why do I still feel like I'm dying?*

"You should be in bed."

Benito's eyes snapped open. Gianna was watching him from the doorway. "I'm fine," he said. "What time is it?"

"Nine o'clock."

Benito frowned at the window. "But it's still light."

"In the morning, Beni."

"What?"

Gianna laughed and disappeared.

Rosetta replaced her. She brandished a mug at him. Coffee, dark and strong. "Are you all right? You've been asleep since yesterday."

"Yesterday?" Benito felt high. "When yesterday?"

"I don't know. I wasn't with you. You don't remember?"

Benito remembered plenty, but nothing he wanted to rehash with Rosetta. He took the coffee and stared at it. His dry throat cried out for the scalding liquid, but the anxiety churning in his gut made him wary, as if his heart already teetered on a knife edge. "Sorry I haven't been with it. Are you okay?"

Rosetta ventured into the room. She took Benito's arm and guided him back to the bed. "We're fine. Mickey's gone to the flat to see if he can get some of our things. He thinks he'll have another place for us by the end of the day."

"Mickey?"

"Yes. He's been taking care of all of us. He's a nice boy. You should hold on to him."

Benito took a sip of coffee. Choked on it and set it aside. He wrapped an arm around himself and coughed into his elbow. It went on and on, and without Mickey rubbing his back to distract him, it burned like a bitch. Or maybe it was Rosetta playing along with his imagination that hurt. "I don't get to hold on to him. I fucked it all up, remember?"

"You think that matters to him now? Benito, I saw his face when you were so sick yesterday. He cares for you."

"He's always cared for me. It's not enough if I'm a fucking wasteman."

"Don't say things like that. A wasteman doesn't do the things you have."

Benito snorted. "You don't know what I've done."

"I know enough. You're a good son and a good man. Mickey knows it—he must do, or he wouldn't be here."

"He's not here."

"He had to work. He's coming back. I gave him a key."

"What key?"

"The only key." Rosetta smiled a little. "At least, the only one I could find, and I didn't want to poke around your things too much."

"Since when? You were all up in my shit when I was a kid."

"You're not a child anymore, Benito. Lord help me, neither is Gianna. She's a good, strong girl, and it's all because of you."

Benito rubbed his chest again, bemused. "Did you bang your head since I last saw you?"

Rosetta's smile vanished. "I've been working hard to be grateful for things instead of afraid of them. It's distracting me from the fact I'm trapped in your flat until I have to go somewhere new. But it's all true. I'm proud of my kids."

"Be proud of Gianna."

"I'm proud of *both* of you."

Benito lost the will to argue. He forced himself up again and shuffled to the bathroom. It felt like returning to the scene of a crime. He gazed at the floor, flashes of the worst moments ambushing him as he stumbled to the shower. Puking his guts up. Falling. Gianna screaming. The relentless headache and the burn in his lungs so fierce he'd thought he was dying until Mickey had saved him. His hands had been so warm Benito had nearly cried. Perhaps he had. *Why can't I think clearly?*

He got his answer later that day. A nurse from the hospital called and explained the symptoms of smoke inhalation to him.

"It doesn't always happen right away," she said. "Sometimes it can be a few hours before the body reacts. The doctor would like you to come for a chest X-ray as soon as possible. Could you come tomorrow?"

"Tomorrow? Fuck, I have to work."

"No, you don't."

Benito glanced up as the new voice came from the bedroom doorway. Mickey glared back at him, slate gaze as flinty as Benito had ever seen.

"You're not fucking working," he growled. "Wherever you need to go, I'll take you."

"Um . . . okay." Benito took the appointment the nurse was offering and ended the call. He eyed Mickey, taking in his untucked shirt, messy hair, and tired face. Gorgeous as he was, he didn't look much better than Benito felt. "Long day?"

Mickey grunted and disappeared.

Panic seized Benito's chest, but Mickey was back before it manifested. He had a pizza box in one hand, a giant bottle of water in the other. "Rosetta said you've been eating like a bird, and I know you like pizza, right?"

Benito rubbed his temple. "Why is my mother discussing my eating habits with you? Has she had a fucking lobotomy?"

"Since you nearly died in a tower-block inferno? Probably." Mickey shut the bedroom door and came closer. "She's taking a nap. I think I freaked her out with the good news."

"What good news?"

"We found her a new flat, and most of her belongings—and Gianna's—survived. It was smoky as hell up there, but the flames didn't get past the breaks."

Benito let out a low whistle. "The breaks installed the same day a gigantic fire started?"

"Yup. The cladding still went up like a rocket, but the new breaks were spread out enough that it didn't turn into Grenfell mark two."

Benito shuddered. "It was all I could think of when I saw what was happening."

"Me too."

"I don't remember you being there . . . I mean, I know you were. I can *feel* it. But when it gets in my head, I can't see your face."

Mickey set the pizza box on the bedside table and sat

down. He nudged Benito's hand away from his aching head and replaced it with his own.

His fingers were magic, light and soothing and yet somehow as intense as the rest of him.

Benito sighed. "Tell me you're real?"

"I'm real." Mickey held Benito against him. "We should talk, though. If you're up to it."

"I'm fine."

"You're a liar."

Mickey spoke without edge, but his word choice cut deep. Benito forced himself to pull back from his embrace and stood, his legs stronger than they had been in days. "You must really hate me right now."

"It would be easier if I did." Mickey watched Benito pace to the window. His hands twitched, and he folded his arms across his chest. "But I meant what I said the night of the fire . . . if you can remember."

Benito rested his forehead on the cool glass and gazed at the twinkly lights of the shopping district across the street. "I think I do. Then I'm worried I don't, and I'm remembering what I wish you'd said."

"Maybe the details don't matter. At least until you tell me why you had blow dust under your car seat. Because I can feel whatever fucking way I want to about you, but none of it matters if you're on the road, Benito. I can't be near that shit, and that's not going to change."

"I know. That's why—*fuck*." Benito banged his head on the window. "I'm so fucking sorry."

"Don't be sorry, man. Your life was your life before you met me."

"I lied to you."

"Fix it then. Tell me the truth."

Nausea rattled Benito's bones. He closed his eyes, willing it away and praying he wouldn't faint. When the rush faded, he turned away from the window.

Mickey was still on the bed. He'd closed his eyes too, as if he couldn't bear to look at Benito, and Benito *ached* to go to him.

But he couldn't. Not yet. "I lied about being off the street because I was scared of losing you. I knew it was wrong, but I thought I had time to make it right. That it would be the truth before you ever found out."

Mickey opened his eyes. "That you'd be out before I found out that you weren't?"

"Yeah. I had a plan."

"But you'd have lied to me forever, though, right? Whatever happened?"

"Maybe. I don't know." Benito took a breath. "I might've told you later on, but maybe I'm a shittier human than you ever were."

Mickey snorted. "Don't underestimate what a nasty cunt I was. It's why I have no fucking right to sit here and judge you. It's just . . . hard. I wish I didn't understand. Then I could walk away."

"Is that what you want? To walk away?"

"No. I didn't mean that."

Benito shivered. It seemed to be all he did these days. Shiver and shake. Puke his sins into the ground while yearning for something better. "A year ago, I lost a fight to be the top boy of my crew. I got shanked and chased out. They threatened my family. Said if I didn't stay out of London, they'd hurt Gianna."

"The scar on your ribs?"

"Yeah."

Mickey whistled. "Nasty."

"It was a big knife. I deserved it, though. Kind of. Maybe not like that, but it needed to happen."

"Why?"

Benito shrugged. "I was a bad man, and I was blind to it. I didn't care who I hurt. I just wanted to win."

"What happened next?"

"I came home—came here, I mean. I got this place and watched over my mum and Gianna, and that should've been it, but I couldn't let it go. I was seething, man. Fucking fuming, you know? It was all I could think about."

Mickey stood. Benito thought he might come to him, but he didn't. He drifted to the opposite wall and leant against it, gesturing for Benito to keep talking.

"I couldn't let it go," Benito repeated. "I had a contact I'd left behind. Someone who hated Asa more than I did."

"Your boss?"

"My wingman . . . at least he was until he stuck a blade in me. He was king after me. Still is, actually."

"And you hate him?"

"For a long time, but I respect him now."

"What changed?"

"Everything. I told you. I had a plan. I used my contact to track the product Asa was moving, and I robbed him blind. Took kilos and kilos from him and sold it on. Buried all the money in the woods."

Mickey frowned, digesting. "How did you rob him?"

"I hit the muling runs. Fought every fucker he sent to protect the load until I got what I wanted. Then I'd drive it on to the coast and flog it cheap to the crews out there. It was a win-win for everyone except Asa."

"Unless you got caught."

"Yeah. About that." Benito shook his head. "This shit is wild."

"Can't be worse than getting fried in a fire."

"It was close."

Mickey pushed off the wall. He crossed the room and joined Benito at the window. "When did this go down?"

"Friday. I had one more run to hit before I had enough."

"Enough what?"

"Enough Ps to pay my bounty. When Asa shanked me, he offered me a price to get out for good. A hundred grand and I'd be free. Gianna would be safe and I'd never have to worry about him again."

"Wow." Mickey slow-blinked. "That's a lot. My crew never moved that kind of money. I reckon the price on my head would be a couple of grand."

"We played a good game. Asa still does."

"But not you?"

Benito sighed. "I did the run on Friday, but it went tits up. My contact told me he'd been made, and Asa switched the crew who were moving the product. They were ready for me."

"You got caught?"

"Not exactly."

"Then how was it? Exactly?"

"They crashed their car and left their driver behind."

"Dead?"

"No. Bleeding. I got him out and left him somewhere Asa would find him. Then I took the product and sold it, but it was too late. Asa already knew it was me. He'd known it all along."

Mickey turned his gaze to the window. He stared with bottomless eyes at the same view Benito had for the last twelve months. "This is some heavy shit. Are you telling me you've been shafting your boss this whole time and he knew about it?"

"Yup."

"How are you still breathing right now?"

"Nino," Benito said.

"What?"

"The driver. He was closer to Asa than I thought, and Asa was all kinds of grateful I didn't leave him to die or get picked up by the feds. He took his money back from me and let me go."

"For good?"

Benito nodded. "Yeah. It's hard to believe, but it's true. I'm out for real this time."

Mickey said nothing. He kept his gaze on the shopping centre while his brain worked to dissect the convoluted tale Benito had told him. Perhaps it helped that he understood road life enough to fill in the blanks.

Or maybe it didn't. Maybe he understood it so well he hated Benito more than ever.

"What happened to the money?" Mickey said suddenly. "The stuff you buried in the woods?"

"I told you . . . I gave it back to him."

"Your bounty money?"

"Yup."

"So if you hadn't been caught, you were going to pay him with his own money?"

"Yup."

"You're a cold motherfucker."

Benito shook his head. "Nah. I thought I was, but it wasn't worth it. I thought I was dying the other night, after the fire, but the truth is, I've been dying for years. If Asa hadn't got ahead of me and finished the game, I think I would've driven my car into the sea."

"I wish that didn't make sense to me, but it does." Mickey's hand hovered over Benito's forearm. He curled it into a fist, then flexed it again before he finally made contact with Benito's tingling skin. "And this all happened on Friday?"

"The raid happened on Friday. That's why my car had dust and blood in it. I thought I got it all before I came to you, but I was so fucking tired I must've missed it. I didn't see Asa until Monday, though, and by then I didn't give a shit. I'd already lost you."

"You did give a shit, about Gianna and your mum, even if you didn't care about yourself."

"Right." Benito was done. He had nothing left. He gripped the windowsill, white knuckling it, holding himself up.

Mickey read him and slipped an arm under his shoulders. He walked Benito to the bed and sat him down, then crouched, his hands warm on Benito's knees. "This is a mess," he said bluntly. "I can't see a way out."

"What do you mean?"

"I mean, it's so fucking complicated, I can't see how you could ever have made it work. You could've told me the truth and nothing would be different."

"Maybe we wouldn't have got this far. You'd have walked away weeks ago and—" Benito couldn't say it. He couldn't give voice to the possibility that he'd never have felt about Mickey the way he did right now.

He hung his head. "I'm so fucking sorry."

"Don't." Mickey squeezed Benito's thighs. "Don't be acting like I'm something better than you. I didn't leave the road by saving some fuckboy's life. The old me would've left him to die."

"No, you wouldn't."

"I wouldn't *now*. And neither would you. You *didn't*. And that's why I fucking love you."

"You do?"

"Yeah, Benito. I do. And I know you love me too because you told me so."

Benito leaned forward, spent, but so drawn to Mickey he couldn't contemplate doing anything else. "I thought I'd dreamed that. But I meant it. I don't know how I got to this place, but I love you, so fucking much."

There was so much more they needed to say, but Benito had run out of spoons. Perhaps they both had.

Mickey coaxed him into bed and fed him pizza and water. Then he let Benito doze for a while before he shook him awake sometime later. "There's something else."

"What?" Benito started to sit up, but Mickey eased him back down.

"Relax. It's not bad." He held up his phone. "The money bloke at the housing association called while I was waiting for the pizza. They've cleared your mum's debt with the council."

"Cleared? What does that mean?"

"It's paid. Gone. As in, it doesn't exist anymore, so you don't have to drive yourself into an early grave to pay for it."

A rush Benito couldn't explain swept over him. "The payment plan?"

Mickey grinned. "What payment plan?"

"Fuck." Benito sank back on the pillows. "That's crazy. Did you ask them to do that?"

Mickey loomed over Benito. At some point, he'd shed his shirt, and his chest was the best pillow in the world. "I would have if I thought it was something they'd do, but . . . no. My bosses made the decision and actioned it without talking to me about it—and that's kind of a thing now, as far as your mum's concerned. They know about us—or they suspect it, at least—so they assigned Rosetta to someone else."

"Oh."

"Yeah. Oh. But it's for the best. If we're going to be together, your mum doesn't need me up in her shit all the time. It's not fair."

"She likes you."

"Does she?"

"Yeah." Benito laid his palm over Mickey's heart, grounding himself in the steady beat. "I told her I fucked it all up, though, so she's probably not holding out much hope of you sticking around."

"I can fix that."

Benito let Mickey's softened gaze seep into him. "You really want this? With me? I'm out of the game, but I'm still a fucking loser."

"Shh." Mickey pressed a hand over Benito's mouth. "I don't want to hear that shit. I'm here because I want to be. If you turn out to be a prick after all, that's on me."

Benito licked Mickey's palm.

Mickey's eyes flashed. "Don't do that either. Unless you're

suddenly recovered enough for me to fuck you into this mattress."

Benito's heart sped up, and for the first time in what felt like a year, it felt *good*. He pulled Mickey's hand from his mouth.

Mickey didn't fight him, even as Benito tugged him down and down and down until their faces were inches apart.

Benito pressed their foreheads together. "I think I'd die right now if you fucked me, but . . . will you stay with me? Tonight, I mean, to sleep . . . in my bed with me?"

Mickey stole a quick, blood-warming kiss from Benito's lips before he answered with a smile. "Motherfucker, I couldn't leave you if I tried."

Benito's chest X-ray was clear. The hospital gave him an inhaler to use every day for a month and discharged him.

After the appointment, Mickey drove him straight to Rosetta's new flat and left him there while he visited other residents who needed his help.

It was dark when he picked him up. Benito was exhausted. Mickey took him back to his house in Northampton and left him dozing on the couch while he got ragey with his laptop and made breakfast for dinner.

Dom Ramos called as Mickey was dumping the dishes in the sink.

Benito waved him away. "Go on, I got it."

"Leave them," Mickey said. "Rest."

"I'm fine."

Mickey rolled his eyes but left Benito alone with the Fairy liquid and retreated outside. He lit a cigarette and blew smoke into the cold sky as he answered the phone. "Hey."

"Evening," Dom said. "I'm just checking in. It's been a crazy few days, hasn't it?"

"Something like that. It's coming together now, though. I took the last household to their new place this afternoon. I can help the council with the rest tomorrow if you can spare me."

"We can spare you, but I'd rather you took a couple of days off. There's nothing more to be done that can't wait or be done by someone else."

"Someone else?"

"Yeah. Me. Isha. Whoever. You've been a hundred miles an hour ever since the fire. You need some time."

"I'm okay."

"You deserve better than okay."

Mickey took another deep drag of smoke into his lungs. "Did Isha tell you he busted me sleeping with a tenant's son?"

Dom chuckled quietly. "He told me he thought you were in a relationship with someone and you'd done everything you could to make it fall right. Does that count?"

"It's one way of looking at it."

"It's the truth, Mickey."

"How do you know?"

"Because you're good people, and there's nothing you won't do for the tenants in your care. If you're trying to convince me you took advantage of the situation to sleep with someone, you're going to have to try harder."

"I didn't do that. I met him before I knew his mum was a resident."

"You don't have to explain that to me. Life happens, mate. You did everything right."

Mickey stubbed his smoke out. "No one's ever said that to me before."

"Maybe it hasn't been true before now, but it is this time round. You identified a conflict of interest and fixed it. There's nothing else you could've done."

"You don't think I should've told you straight away?"

"What I think isn't important. Your private life is your own and not even remotely why I called you."

"Why did you call me?"

"Apart from everything I've already said, I thought you'd want to know the preliminary report is in from the fire investigation, and it looks like we're dealing with a fluke electrical fault."

"A fault? Where?"

"Somewhere in the lift mechanisms. They're not sure where yet. Only thing we're sure of is that the fire breaks did their job, and if we hadn't installed them, people would've died."

Mickey felt sick, and the pull to return to Benito was so strong he could hardly breathe.

Dom seemed to know it. He rang off after extracting a promise from Mickey that he'd take a few days for self-care, and Mickey went back inside.

Benito was nowhere to be seen.

Mickey followed the sound of running water upstairs and into the bathroom.

Benito was beneath the hot spray, leaning against the wall, head tipped back, eyes closed.

Mickey brushed his teeth, then stripped his clothes, dumping them on top of Benito's folded pile.

He stepped into the shower and right into Benito's personal space.

Benito opened his eyes. "Hey there."

"Hey." Mickey pushed wet hair off Benito's face. "I was worried you'd gone to sleep in here."

"That's why you got in?"

Mickey answered him with a kiss, slow and deep, the first they'd shared since the night of the fire. Benito's lips felt like home, and he lost himself for as long as he dared before he pulled back.

He kept his hands on Benito's face. "I got in because I needed to be close to you. Is that okay?"

Benito flexed his hips, digging his hard length against Mickey's. "Is that a real question?"

Mickey laughed and kissed Benito again. They didn't need words. Despite the heaviness of the last few days, the air between them was featherlight. He let his hands roam Benito's body, exploring his heated skin as if it was the first time, until it occurred to him that the first time he'd had Benito naked had been nothing like this. That night, he'd consumed all Benito had offered with a violence that seemed out of place as Benito trembled now from his gentle touch. One day he'd want to get rough and dirty with Benito again. Soon, even. But right now, he needed something else far more.

He turned the shower off and tugged Benito to the bedroom.

Still dripping wet, they fell onto the bed, and Benito let it happen, sprawling on his back, letting Mickey take what he wanted. And *fuck*, Mickey wanted him. He kissed Benito until they ran out of breath, then he moved down his body, worshipping every inch of skin in his path. He sucked Benito's cock, sliding him whole down his throat.

Benito cried out and cursed, body tense with need.

But Mickey didn't let him come. He took him to the edge, then drew back and reached for the drawer in the bedside table.

He waved condoms and lube at Benito. "You okay with this?"

Benito nodded. "I want it."

Mickey dropped down for a kiss and pressed lubed fingers inside Benito, opening him up so slowly he thought he'd combust before they got round to fucking. Or die a fiery death watching Benito shudder beneath him, his chest flushed, skin shiny with sweat as his hot palms roamed Mickey's back, his kiss desperate, moans ragged.

Hands shaking, Mickey rolled a condom on and bent Benito's legs to his chest. He eased inside, swallowing Benito's sharp groan with another kiss. Then he pulled back to watch it happen. They'd never fucked like this—face to face, so caught up in each other there was nothing else in the world.

Mickey fucked Benito gently, gripping his face with one hand, his strong thigh with the other. His body curled around Benito like they were two halves of the same man. They fit together in a heated mess of limbs and skin. An alchemy Mickey had never found before with anyone, not even Benito.

A slow crescendo took hold, building in volume. Benito shook his head from side to side, eyes wild. "So fucking good. I can't. Fuck."

Mickey fucked him a tiny bit harder, lifting his hips and driving deep inside him, carving out the pleasure.

Benito's groans grew louder and rose in pitch. He clung to Mickey's shoulders, digging his fingers in, and his eyes widened. "Shit. Fuck. That feels amazing. I've never—*fuck*."

He came, shattering in Mickey's arms as wet warmth

splashed between them, smearing messily as Mickey pumped his hips a little faster, chasing his own release.

And he didn't have to run far. It was there, on the precipice, and it came crashing down, blinding Mickey with the impact, barrelling into him like a runaway train. A deep groan escaped him. He buried himself inside Benito and stayed there, emptying his body, his soul, his heart—whatever. Benito could have it all. He'd come too close to losing him for anything less.

He didn't realise he was crying until Benito wiped the tears from his cheeks. "Shit, I'm sorry."

"Don't be." Benito held his face and kissed him. "Just be okay. I love you."

"I am okay, honest. I love you."

Mickey composed himself, got up, and dealt with the condom. Benito didn't move, save to drop his arm over his eyes, chest heaving. Heart full, Mickey lay down again and nudged Benito until he looked at him. "Did I hurt you?"

Benito shook his head. "Not even close. I just—fuck. I've never had sex like that. It's blown my mind."

"Mine too. What was left of it, at least."

"Fuck off. You're the cleverest person I know."

"Get better friends then."

Benito snorted, apparently too wiped out to argue. And cold too, despite the sweat still beading his skin. Mickey had noticed that since the fire, how Benito couldn't seem to get warm.

He retrieved the rumpled sheets from the floor and tugged them up the bed. He covered them both, then coaxed Benito into his arms. Then he relayed what Dom had told him on the phone about the electrical fault and the fire.

Benito breathed through his nose, blinking hard.

Mickey stroked his face. "What is it?"

"Nothing."

Mickey waited.

Benito sighed. "I was scared it might've been Asa. That he'd lied to me about letting me go and tried to kill me and the girls as revenge."

"That's a big thing to be scared of without telling anyone."

"And stupid. Asa's a dick, but he's not a mass murderer."

"Good to know."

Benito snorted, but his shudders remained, wracking his strong body as if he'd never find peace.

Mickey held him closer. "You're safe here. You know that, don't you? From everything, not just gang wars and fires."

Benito's shivers didn't ease, but he smiled. "I know. I'm sorry I haven't been that for you this whole time. It kills me that I've made your head a bad place to be."

"I do that all by myself, mate. And you know what?"

"What?"

Mickey tightened his embrace around Benito's trembling shoulders. "Caring about you gave me a safe place . . . from my own fucking head. You made mistakes, but so did I, lots of them, long before I met you. I never should've put that pressure on you in the first place. Maybe if I hadn't, you could've talked to me before you went all fucking gangster rogue by your damn self."

"None of this is your fault—"

"Shh." Mickey laid a finger against Benito's lips. "We think what we think and we're probably both wrong. It doesn't matter anymore. I've got you, okay? It's over."

Benito nodded, then he fell asleep. His arms were a vice around Mickey's waist, and he held on tight all night long.

EPILOGUE

Nine months later

The water in the lake was the lowest Benito had ever seen it. The long, hot summer had dried it out, and the shallower end had been exposed as rough concrete banks.

"Man-made lakes are weird."

Benito tore his gaze from the shimmering water. Mickey was, as ever, three strides ahead of him, leading him around the lake for their early evening run. Somewhere behind them, Gianna was sulking over a can of Rubicon, pissed off at being dragged away from her iPad screen. "You don't have them up north?"

"Maybe. Just never sought them out."

"Well, you don't like mud either, bro, so if you want a paved running track, it's here or the sports centre."

"I never said I didn't like it, *bro*, just that it was weird. I like you, don't I?"

Mickey didn't wait for an answer. He took off faster, leaving Benito behind, and that was how it usually went.

Mickey was quicker over the ground, light on his feet, elegant and smooth despite his irrepressible energy. Benito was the patient one, happy to plug away until he got where he wanted to be—which, these days, was wherever Mickey was, as it had been since they'd met.

The loop around the lake was three miles. They ran it twice before Mickey got bored and whisked Gianna into the pub for the milkshake he'd promised her if she came out with them.

Benito watched them go, heart straining with an emotion too complex to be only love. Mickey and Gianna had a friendship that didn't include him, and he knew why: because Mickey had been there for her in moments Benito hadn't. He'd kept a roof over her head, coaxed her mother out of an agoraphobic black hole, and scooped her brother off the bathroom floor.

"You did those things too. You're the best brother she could ever have, and she loves you more than anything in the fucking world." But it didn't seem to matter how many times Mickey said shit like that, Benito still had trouble believing it. He'd never been the best at anything, and he had the scar to prove it. A scar that still buzzed and throbbed when his thoughts got away from him.

So don't let them. You're stronger than that.

His phone rang as the voice in his head said its piece, an unknown number, but he was less scared of them than he used to be.

He answered with actual words instead of a grunt. "Hello?"

"Martell? That you?"

Benito's heart froze. He shot to his feet, searching rapidly for Gianna and Mickey.

He found them still waiting in line at the bar, but the panic in his chest remained. "Who wants to know?"

"Easy, mate. It's Luis."

"Pope?"

"Yeah, that's the one. Sorry, I didn't mean to freak you out."

"How did you get this number?"

"Asa. I asked him for it a few days ago."

"Why?"

"Because I need to tell you something."

"If it's business related, don't bother. I don't give a fuck."

Luis laughed. "You think I do? Remember who you're talking to."

Benito relaxed a little, but it was fractional. He'd gone to Luis for help all those months ago out of sheer desperation, not because they'd ever been anything remotely close to being friends. "I remember. What do you need to tell me?"

"It's about my brother. He's getting out. I don't know when, but it could be as soon as a couple of months."

"What? But he's got years left on his sentence."

"Yeah, well, time flies, doesn't it? And he's coming up to halfway through. Either that, or he's conned a governor into doing him a solid. You know how he be."

Benito did, all too well. If there was anyone who could manipulate their way out of prison early, it was Dante Pope. He sank down heavily on a nearby bench, stretching his tired legs out in front of him. "Why are you telling me this? You think he wants to start beef with me?"

Luis sighed. "Honestly? I don't know. He writes me letters

sometimes, but I burn them, so I have no clue where his head's at."

"So you tapped Asa for this number . . . just to warn me?"

"Does that surprise you?"

Benito tracked Mickey and Gianna as they moved to the front of the queue at the bar. Gianna had stuck four paper-wrapped straws in Mickey's back pocket. He was pretending not to notice, all the while sprinkling sugar in her hair. "I don't know. I'm still getting used to being around good people."

"You're doing okay then?"

"What do you care?"

"I don't. Paolo does, though. If you're still a massive cunt, he'll say I stepped backwards for no good reason."

"Maybe you did."

"Nah. You're too clever for that shit. And you play the long game. If you want it enough, you'll get there."

"I already did. I'm happy, man. Life is good. I could do without your brother rocking up to fight me."

Luis was silent a moment. Benito wondered if he'd gone. Then rustling crackled the line, and Luis spoke again. "I saw him once, a couple of years ago. He sent me a visiting order and I let it reel me in. Even if he hadn't changed, I thought it might give me closure, you know? That it would remind me how fucking evil he was, and I could walk away for good and never think about him again."

Mickey handed Gianna a milkshake the size of her head, then he turned and found Benito watching from the bench. A grin warmed his handsome face, but it was guarded, as if he knew Benito had one foot in the past.

Benito forced his attention back to Luis Pope. "What happened?"

"He was different. Not so much that I can tell you he won't come after you when he gets out, but enough that I think he might listen if someone asked him not to."

"And that someone can't be you, right?"

Luis snorted. "What do you think?"

Benito had no idea what he thought. He'd always known this day would come—that Dante Pope would get out eventually—but he'd never imagined he'd be having a deep and meaningful about it with his brother. "I think you're a dude for giving me the heads-up, and I can't ask you to do more than that. I gotta ask why, though. The fuck do you care if your brother puts me in the ground?"

"Not caring is the worst thing in the world. If you didn't already know that, you'd still be on the road."

Luis hung up without saying goodbye. Benito stared at the blank screen he left behind, then slowly pocketed his phone.

He looked up to find Mickey and Gianna in front of him. Gianna was engrossed in her milkshake.

Mickey's expression was blank—too blank for Benito's soul to cope with.

He stood, inserting himself into Mickey's bubble without giving a single shit who saw them. "Luis Pope just called me. His brother is getting out."

Mickey frowned, clearly tracking back to every conversation they'd ever had to put names to Benito's tales from the road. "The one you stitched up?"

Benito's gaze flickered to Gianna, but she'd wandered off

to take pictures of a duck. "That's the one. I'm thinking he probably wants me dead."

"Is that what his brother said?"

"He said he didn't know."

"How would you find out?"

"By asking, I guess."

Mickey's frown deepened. "Won't that put you on his radar? He might have moved on."

"Dude, he got shot because of me, on top of bare time in prison. Unless he became a fucking monk inside, there's no way he's moved on from that shit."

"You don't know that."

"And you don't know Dante Pope."

"Neither do you."

Benito exhaled a long breath through his nose. "I can't do this with him. He doesn't think like the rest of us, and he's relentless. If he wants to hurt me, he won't stop until he has."

Mickey gripped Benito's shoulders, forcing him to meet his gaze. "You used to be like that too. We both did. But people change."

"No, they don't."

"They *do*. Or we wouldn't be here, either of us."

Benito took Mickey's hands and squeezed them. "You're nothing like Dante Pope."

"How do you know? I've been alive twenty-five years and you've only known me for eighteen months. You have no idea what I'd be capable of if I was living his life."

Benito shook his head. He got Mickey's point, but Dante Pope was a unique creature. Clever. Unpredictable. He had his weak points, though—his ego and chronic inability to be alone. *Maybe—*

No. Benito shook his head again, more violently this time. "I can't fight him. Or even think about it. I can't be that person anymore."

Mickey nodded. "So what are you going to do?"

"I'm going to ask him to give me what I gave his brother. I'm going to ask him to set me free."

———

Benito wrote Dante Pope a letter. Mickey never read it, but he was there the day the reply landed on the doormat from Manchester Prison, because it was Mickey's doormat, in Mickey's house, where Benito had lived since he'd given up his city-centre flat.

Mickey held up the note from Dante Pope and read it aloud.

> *Martell,*
>
> *Life moves on. I hope yours is as good as I want mine to be.*
> *Be well,*
> *D*

"Is he being sincere or bluffing like a motherfucker?"

"Honestly?" Benito came up behind Mickey and kissed his neck. "With him, it's hard to tell, but I've never heard him say shit like that before, so maybe it's real."

"You believe that, don't you?"

Benito shrugged. "I want to, and I can't live my life looking over my shoulder. Sometimes you have to see the best in people until they show you otherwise."

"He never showed you the worst of him?"

"As much as he saw the worst of me, but maybe seeing his brother go straight changed him as much as it did the rest of us."

Mickey matched Benito's words to what he knew of the crew he'd run with on the road. Young men fighting for a crown no one seemed to want. It was a fucking mess, and even thinking about it made him twitch. Or, at least, think about twitching. Cravings were easier to manage when Benito was around. Some days, addiction never crossed Mickey's mind.

The days it did, he went to a meeting in a village hall six miles away. Benito came with him and ate all the biscuits while they listened to other people talk. Every Thursday, he did the same at the anxiety support group he took Rosetta to, and he *still* had no idea he was Mickey's fucking hero.

Mickey let the note fall to the kitchen counter and spun around, quickly caging Benito in his arms. "You want to go out tonight?"

"Out where?"

"To the club, maybe? I'll drive so you can drink."

A flush heated Benito's neck. "I'm going to need a fucking drink if you still want to do that thing we talked about."

Mickey laughed. "Fucking in the club instead of getting a room? I was taking the piss, mate, but hey, I'm game if you are."

Benito rolled his eyes and ducked out of Mickey's embrace. He wandered off to take a shower. Mickey considered the conversation closed. They'd been to the club together a few times—it was a safe space they were both familiar with. They drank rum and got handsy, then alternated between stumbling upstairs to revisit where it had all begun or going home to love each other all night long in the bed they'd shared since Mickey had brought Benito home for good.

The idea of fucking *in* the club was a new one, for Benito, at least. Mickey had been thinking about it from day one.

Was still thinking about it when Benito came back downstairs dressed in dark jeans and a white shirt that made him look like expensive sin. "Stop looking at me like that," he said. "Or we'll be fucking on the couch instead."

Mickey laughed and retreated to take his own shower.

Half an hour later, they were speeding away from reality in Benito's car—a different SUV now; he'd sent the old one back and leased a new one to drive his Uber clients around in. He'd never said he'd done it to save Mickey from wondering if there was still coke under the passenger seat, but Mickey knew he had. *Fuck, I love him.*

And perhaps more importantly, he knew Benito loved him too.

————

The club was dark and sultry. Mickey and Benito propped up the bar, Benito drinking lime-spiked rum while Mickey nursed a bottle of water. They stood close together, legs touching, Benito's arm around Mickey's shoulder while they talked about anything and nothing.

When the time for talk was over, they kissed, bodies moving with the throbbing pulse of the music, blood heating with every slow sweep of their lips.

Mickey was on fire for Benito. They hadn't fucked in a couple of days, and he wondered if it had been subconsciously deliberate, so they'd find that magical place right here, where nothing and no one could keep them apart.

He pulled back from Benito's kiss and found his dark gaze. "We can go home if you want?"

Benito shook his head. "I want you now."

"Sure?"

"You don't believe me?" Benito ground his hips against Mickey's. His dick was rock solid in his jeans, and Mickey's eyes rolled.

"I believe you," he said. "Just giving you a way out."

"I don't need one from you. Never from you. You're my fucking world."

Mickey smiled. Benito was a walking contradiction. Some days he didn't talk. Others he had so much to say, Mickey couldn't keep up.

Then there were days like today when he said all he needed to in three concise sentences. *I love him.*

Mickey kissed Benito again, then led him away from the bar to a quiet corner of the play area. It wasn't exactly front and centre, but it was exposed enough that anyone who wanted to watch would see them.

Benito took a seat on the chaise. He kept his gaze on Mickey and beckoned him closer. "You're wearing too many clothes."

"Fix it."

Benito untucked Mickey's shirt and popped the buttons. It seemed to find its own way to the floor, and Mickey laughed as Benito scooped it up and draped it somewhere safer. "You're such a neat freak."

"Until I get messy with you."

"I like messy."

"I know. I live with you."

Mickey's heart skipped a beat. "Sometimes I can't believe that's a real thing."

"Me either. The mess you make is biblical."

"Liar."

"Not anymore." Benito tapped his chest. "I'm truth bombs all day long."

"And all night long?"

"Come here and find out."

Mickey pushed Benito onto the chaise and made short work of stripping his clothes, then he rose and shed the rest of his too.

They fell to the floor, and this time, Benito didn't pick them up. He took Mickey in his mouth instead, sucking him with his full lips and sinful tongue, until Mickey was panting out his name and begging him to stop. "If you want to fuck, you gotta stop. *Fuck*, you're killing me."

Benito pulled back. He shot an unreadable glance over Mickey's shoulder and scooted away to lie down, propped up on his elbows. "I don't want you to die."

"No?"

"No. Never."

"What are you going to do about that?"

Benito licked his lips. "I don't know. Maybe I have stage fright."

Mickey considered him. Years on the road had left Benito hard to read at the best of times, but shyness wasn't in his usual armoury, especially when it came to sex. Benito was a lover who knew what he wanted and how to take it.

Or give it up, which was most often his mood. *What does he want right now?*

No.

That was the wrong question.

What did Benito *need*?

Mickey covered Benito with his body, kissing him everywhere he could reach: his lips, his neck, his exposed chest. Around them, he sensed watchful eyes, but with Benito so close, they were easy to ignore.

Everything was.

Mickey made a cradle for himself between Benito's legs. A lube bottle was within easy reach, and they didn't need anything else. They'd tested negative a few months back and ditched the condoms for good. So far, Mickey had been inside Benito bare more times than he could count, but never yet—

It clicked. What Benito needed in this moment more than anything else. The unforgettable. Something that *mattered*. He stole another searing kiss from Benito's lips, then drew back.

Benito widened his legs, brow already furrowed with a tension that hadn't been there before.

Mickey shook his head and grinned, nudging them back where they'd come from. "Relax," he whispered. "I got this."

Benito took a shuddery breath, watching as Mickey slicked lube on his cock. "You don't have to—"

Mickey cut him off with a slow, impaling slide, sinking down on Benito's dick without the thought and preparation he usually put into taking a man's cock. *Benito's* cock, because it had been *years* since he'd let anyone else fuck him.

The sensation made his eyes water. He fell forward onto Benito's chest. Benito held him tight, his arms a solid cage of love and affection.

He pushed Mickey's damp hair back from his face. "I'm not ready to be bareback inside you. I'm wrecked already."

"That's probably a good thing."

"Why's that?"

"Because having you inside me like this is going to make me come in ten seconds flat."

Benito laughed, his dark gaze dancing. He'd let his inky scruff thicken in recent weeks, and the bearded look was good on him. It made his face timeless, but when he laughed, it showed Mickey the boy he'd once been. "We'd better make this a good ten seconds then," he said.

He bent his legs, supporting Mickey's body, and dragged him down to ravage his mouth. Humour faded, replaced by a desire so fierce Mickey forgot about the club and the eyes on them.

Perhaps Benito did too. He let Mickey screw him senseless. Slow. Deep. As if every grind of his hips was a declaration of how hard they loved each other.

Because love *was* hard.

But it was worth it.

Everything about Benito was worth it.

Mickey brought them to the brink, then Benito took over. He rolled Mickey onto his back and fucked him like they were the only two souls left on earth until they came together with low cries no one else would hear.

After, they lay panting, foreheads pressed together.

"How do you feel?" Mickey whispered.

Benito smiled. "I feel free."

———

Can't wait for the next instalment? **Preorder Salvation TODAY.**

———

Missing Benito and Mickey already? Sign up for my newsletter HERE for a bonus scene. (Will be sent to existing subscribers on release day)

———

Not ready to let go of Benito and Mickey? Or looking for sneak peeks at future books in the series? Alternative POVs, outtakes, and missing moments from **all** Garrett's books can be found on her **Patreon** site. Misfits, Slide, Strays...the works. Because you know what? Garrett wasn't ready to let her boys go either.

Pledges start from as little as $2, and all content is available at the lowest tier.

ABOUT THE AUTHOR

Bonus Material available for all books on Garrett's Patreon account. Includes short stories from Misfits, Slide, Strays, What Remains, Dream, and much more. Sign up here: https://www.patreon.com/garrettleigh

Facebook Fan Group, Garrett's Den... https://www.facebook.com/groups/garre...

Garrett Leigh is an award-winning British writer, cover artist, and book designer. Her debut novel, Slide, won Best Bisexual Debut at the 2014 Rainbow Book Awards, and her polyamorous novel, Misfits was a finalist in the 2016 LAMBDA awards, and was again a finalist in 2017 with Rented Heart.

In 2017, she won the EPIC award in contemporary romance with her military novel, Between Ghosts, and the contemporary romance category in the Bisexual Book Awards with her novel What Remains.

When not writing, Garrett can generally be found procrastinating on Twitter, cooking up a storm, or sitting on her behind doing as little as possible, all the while shouting at her menagerie of children and animals and attempting to tame her unruly and wonderful FOX.

Garrett is also an award winning cover artist, taking the silver medal at the Benjamin Franklin Book Awards in 2016. She designs for various publishing houses and independent authors at blackjazzdesign.com, and co-owns the specialist stock site moonstockphotography.com

Connect with Garrett
www.garrettleigh.com